Praise for *New York Times* bestselling author Heather Graham

"[Heather] Graham has the uncanny ability to bring her books to life, using exceptionally vivid details to add depth to all the people and places."
—*RT Book Reviews*

"You may never know in advance what harrowing situations Graham will place her characters in, but… rest assured that the end result will be satisfying."
—*Suspense Magazine* on *Let the Dead Sleep*

"Heather Graham knows what readers want."
—*Publishers Weekly*

Praise for *USA TODAY* bestselling author Tara Taylor Quinn

"[Tara Taylor Quinn's] talent for skillfully weaving in both description and dialogue makes reading her novels effortless."
—*RT Book Reviews*

"Quinn writes touching stories about real people that transcend plot type or genre."
—*All About Romance*

New York Times and *USA TODAY* bestselling author **Heather Graham** has written more than a hundred novels, many of which have been featured by the Doubleday Book Club and the Literary Guild. An avid scuba diver, ballroom dancer and mother of five, she still enjoys her South Florida home, but loves to travel, as well, from locations such as Cairo, Egypt, to the Florida Keys. Reading, however, is the pastime she still loves best, and she is a member of many writing groups. She's a winner of the Romance Writers of America's Lifetime Achievement Award and the Thriller Writers' Silver Bullet. She is an active member of International Thriller Writers and Mystery Writers of America, and also the founder of The Slush Pile Players, an author band and theatrical group. Heather annually hosts the Writers for New Orleans conference to benefit both the city, which is near and dear to her heart, and various other causes, and she hosts a ball each year at the RT Booklover's Convention to benefit pediatric AIDS foundations.

For more information, check out her website, TheOriginalHeatherGraham.com. You can also find Heather on Facebook.

The author of more than seventy original novels, published in twenty languages, **Tara Taylor Quinn** is a *USA TODAY* bestselling author with over seven million copies sold. She is known for delivering deeply emotional and psychologically astute novels of suspense and romance. Tara is a recipient of the Readers' Choice Award, a four-time finalist for the RWA RITA® Award, and a finalist for the Reviewer's Choice Award and the Booksellers' Best Award. She has had multiple #1 bestseller rankings on Amazon. Tara is the past president of Romance Writers of America and served eight years on that board of directors. She has appeared on national and local TV across the country, including CBS' *Sunday Morning*, and is a frequent guest speaker. In her spare time Tara likes to travel and enjoys crafting and in-line skating. She is a supporter of the National Domestic Violence Hotline. If you or someone you know might be a victim of domestic violence in the United States, please contact 1-800-799-7233.

New York Times Bestselling Author

HEATHER GRAHAM

SUSPICIOUS

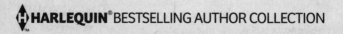HARLEQUIN® BESTSELLING AUTHOR COLLECTION

ISBN-13: 978-0-373-01022-6

Suspicious
Copyright © 2015 by Harlequin Books S.A.

The publisher acknowledges the copyright holders of the individual works as follows:

Suspicious
Copyright © 2005 by Heather Graham Pozzessere

The Sheriff of Shelter Valley
Copyright © 2015 by Tara Taylor Quinn
Originally published as:
The Sheriff of Shelter Valley
Copyright © 2002 by Tara Lee Reames

Recycling programs
for this product may
not exist in your area.

Printed in U.S.A.

CONTENTS

Also by HEATHER GRAHAM

And look for the next books
in the Krewe of Hunters series,
The Silenced and *The Forgotten*, available soon!

SUSPICIOUS

Heather Graham

To the Miccosukkee tribe of Florida

PROLOGUE

THE EYES STARED across the water.

They were soulless eyes, the eyes of a cold-blooded predator, an animal equipped throughout millions of years of existence to hunt and kill.

Just visible over the water's surface, the eyes appeared as innately evil as a pair of black pits in hell.

The prehistoric monster watched. It waited.

From the center seat of his beat-to-shit motorboat, Billy Ray Hare lifted his beer can to the creature. He squinted as he tried to make out the size of the beast, an estimation at best, since the bulk of the body was hidden by the water. Big boy, he thought. Didn't see too many of the really big boys down here anymore. He'd even read some article about the Everglades alligators being kind of thin and scrawny these days, since they were surviving on insects and small prey. But every once in a while now, he'd still see a big beast sunning along the banks of the canals in the deep swamp.

He heard a slithering sound from the canal bank and turned. A smaller gator, maybe five feet long, was moving. Despite the ugly and awkward appearance of the creature, it was swift, fluid and graceful. Uncannily fast. The smaller crocodilian eased down the damp embankment and into the water. Billy watched. He knew the canals, and he knew gators, and he knew that the long-legged, hapless crane fishing for shiners near the shore was a goner.

"Hey, birdie, birdie," Billy Ray crooned. "Ain't you seen the sun? It's dinnertime, baby, dinnertime."

The gator slid into the water, only its eyes visible as the body swiftly disappeared.

A split second later, the beast burst from the water with a spray of power and gaping jaws. The bird let out a screech; its white wings frantically, pathetically, beat the water. But the huge jaws were clamped. The gator slung its head back and forth, shaking its prey near death, then slid back into the water to issue the coup de grâce, drowning its victim.

"It's a damned dog-eat-dog world, ain't it?" Billy murmured dryly aloud. He finished his beer, groped for another, and realized that he'd finished the last of his twelve-pack. Swearing, he noticed that the big gator across the canal hadn't moved. Black reptilian eyes, evil as Satan's own, continued to survey him. He threw his beer can in the direction of the creature. "Eat that, ugly whoreson!" he croaked, and began to laugh. Then he sobered, looking around, thinking for a minute that Jesse Crane might be behind him, ready to haul him in for desecrating his precious muck hole. But Billy Ray was alone in the swamp. Alone with the bugs and birds and reptiles, with no more beer and no fish biting. "Bang-bang, you're dead! I'm hungry, and it's dinnertime. Damned environmentalists." Once upon a time, he could have shot the gator. Now the damn things were protected. You had to wait for gator season to kill the suckers, and then you had to play by all kinds of rules. You could only kill the wretched things according to certain regulations. Too bad. Once upon a time, a big gator like that could have meant some big money....

Big money. What the heck.

They made big money out at that gator farm. Old Harry and his scientist fellow, Dr. Michael, the stinking Australian who thought he was Crocodile Dundee, and Jack Pine, the Seminole, and hell, that whole lot. They made money on alligators. Damn Jesse and his reeking white man's law. Now he was the frigging tribal police.

Billy Ray shook his head. The hell with Jesse Crane and his whole bleeding-heart crowd. What did Jesse know? Tall and dark and too damned good-looking, and all powerful, one foot in the swamp, the other foot firmly planted in the white world. College education, plenty of money now—his late *wife's* money, at that. The hell with him, the hell with all the environmentalists, the hell with the whites all the way. They'd been the ones who screwed up the swamp to begin with. While the whole country was running around screaming about rights—equal pay for women, real justice for blacks, food stamps for refugees—Jesse Crane didn't see that the Indians—the *Native Americans*—were still rotting in the swamps. Jesse had a habit of just leaning back, shrugging, and staring at him with those cool green— white-blooded—eyes of his and saying that no white man was making old Billy Ray be a mean, dirty alcoholic who liked to beat up on his wife. Jesse wanted him in jail. But Ginny, bless her fat, ugly butt, Ginny wouldn't file charges against him. Ginny knew where a wife's place was supposed to be.

Alcoholic, hell. He wasn't no alcoholic. God, he wanted another beer. Screw Jesse Crane.

"And screw you," he said aloud, staring at the gator.

Those black eyes hadn't moved; the creature was still staring at him like some prehistoric sentinel. Maybe it was already dead. He squinted, staring hard. Tough now to see, because it was growing late. Dinnertime.

Sunset. It was almost night. He didn't know what he wanted more, something to eat or another beer. He had neither. No fish, and he'd used up his government money.

The sky was orange and red, the beautiful shades that came right before the sun pitched into the horizon. But now the dying orb was creating a beautiful but eerie mantle of color on the water, the trees that draped their branches over it, and the seemingly endless "river of grass" that made up the Everglades. With sunset, everything took on a different hue; white birds were cast in pink and gold, and even the killer heat took a brief holiday. Jesse would sit out here like a lump on a log himself, just thinking that the place—with its thick carpet of mosquitoes and frequent smell of rot—was only a small step from heaven. Their land. Hell, he had news for Jesse. They hadn't been the first Indians—Native Americans—here. The first ones who'd been here had been wiped out far worse than animals ever had. But Jesse seemed to think that being half Indian made him Lord Protector of the realm or something.

Billy smiled. Screw Jesse. It gave him great pleasure just to think nasty thoughts about the man.

A crane called overhead, swooped and soared low, making a sudden catch in the shimmering water, flying away with a fish dangling from its beak. Smart bird—caught his fish, flew away, didn't wait around to become bait himself. In fact, it was a darned great scene, Billy thought sourly. Right out of *National Geographic*. It was all just one rosy-hued, beautiful picture. The damn crane had captured his dinner, the five-foot gator had captured *his* dinner, and all Billy Ray had caught himself was a deeper burn and a beer headache.

And that other gator. The big one. Big enough to gulp up the five-footer. Hell, it was big enough, maybe, to be well over ten feet long. Maybe it was way more than that, even. Son of a bitch, he didn't know. He couldn't tell its size; it was just one big mother, that was all. It was still staring at him. Eyes like glittering onyx as the sun set. Not looking, not moving. The creature didn't seem to blink.

Maybe the big ole gator staring at him was dead. Maybe he could haul the monster in, skin and eat it before any of the sappy-eyed ecologists got wind of the situation.

Ginny always knew what to do with gator meat. She'd "gourmeted" it long before fashionable restaurants had started putting it on their menus. Hell, with that gator, they could eat for weeks....

"Hey, there, you butt-ugly thing!" Billy Ray called. He stood up; the boat rocked. Better sit down. The beer had gotten to him more than he'd realized. He picked up an oar and started slowly toward the big gator. It still didn't move. He lifted his oar from the water. Damn, but he was one asshole himself, he realized. Gator had to be alive, the way it was just sitting there in the water, eyes above the surface.

Watching him.

Watching him, just like the smaller gator had watched the crane.

"Oh, no, you big ugly asshole!" Billy Ray called out. "Don't you get any ideas. It's *my* dinnertime."

As if duly challenged, the gator suddenly began to move. Billy Ray saw more of its length. More and more…ten feet, twelve, fifteen…hell more, maybe…it was the biggest damned gator he'd seen in his whole life. Maybe it was a stray croc—no, he knew a croc, and he knew a gator. This fellow had a broad snout and clearly separated nostrils, it was just one big mother…cruising. Cruising smoothly toward him, massive body just gliding through the water. Coming fast, fast, faster…

He frowned, shaking his head, realizing he really was in something of a beer fog. Gators didn't come after boats and ram them. They might swim along and take a bite at a hand trailing in the water, but he'd only seen a gator make a run at a boat once, and that was a mother protecting her nest, and she only charged the boat, she didn't ram it.

This one was just warning him away. Hell, where was his gun? He had his shotgun in the boat somewhere.…

Unable to tear his eyes from the creature's menacing black orbs, he groped in the boat for his shotgun. His hand gripped the weapon; the creature was still coming. He half stood again, taking aim.

He fired.

He hit the sucker; he knew he hit it.

But the gator kept coming with a sudden ferocious speed.

The animal rammed the boat.

Billy Ray pitched over.

Sunset.

The water had grown dark. He couldn't see a damned thing. He began to kick madly, aiming for the bank. He swam. He had hit the gator with a shotgun. Surely he had pierced the creature's tough hide; it had just taken the stupid monster a long time to die. He'd been an idiot. His rifle was at the bottom of the muck now; his boat was wrecked, and the water was cool and sobering.

Sober...yeah, dammit, all of a sudden he was just too damned sober.

He twisted around and was just in time to see the monster. Like the others of its kind, it stalked him smoothly. Gracefully. He saw the eyes again, briefly. Cold, brutal, merciless, the eyes of a hell-spawned predator. He saw the head, the long jaws. Biggest damn head he'd ever seen. Couldn't be real.

The eyes slipped beneath the surface.

Billy Ray started to scream. He felt more sober than he had ever felt in his life. Felt everything perfectly clearly.

Felt the movement in the water, the rush beneath him...

He screamed and screamed and screamed. Until the giant jaws snapped shut on him. He felt the excruciating, piercing pain. Then he ceased to scream as the razor-sharp teeth pierced his rib cage, lungs and windpipe.

The creature began to toss its massive head, literally shaking its prey into more easily digestible pieces.

The giant gator sank beneath the surface.

And more of Billy Ray's bones began to crunch....

Billy Ray had been right all along.

It was dinnertime.

CHAPTER ONE

AT FIRST IT seemed that the sound of the siren wasn't even penetrating the driver's mind.

Either that, or the Lexus intended to race him all the way across the lower portion of the state to the city of Naples, Jesse Crane thought irritably.

It was natural to speed out here—it felt like one of the world's longest, strangest drives, with mile after mile of grass and muck and canal, interspersed by a gas station or tackle shop here or there, the airboat rides, and the Miccosukee camps.

But after you passed the casino, heading west, traces of civilization became few and far between. Despite that, the road was a treacherous one. Impatient drivers trying to pass had caused many a traffic fatality.

He overlooked it when someone seemed competent and was going a rational number of miles over the limit.

But this Lexus...

At last the driver seemed to become aware that he was trailing, the siren blazing. The Lexus pulled over on the embankment.

As Jesse pulled his cruiser off on the shoulder, he saw a blond head dipping—the occupant was obviously searching for the registration. *Or a gun?* There were plenty of toughs who made it out to this section of the world, because there was enough godforsaken space out here for all manner of things to go on. He trod carefully. He was a man who always trod carefully.

As he approached the car, the window came down and a blond head appeared. He was startled, faltering for a fraction of a second.

The woman was stunning. Not just attractive. Stunning. She had the kind of golden beauty that was almost spellbinding. Blond hair that caught the daylight. Delicate features. Huge eyes that reflected a multitude of colors: green, brown, rimmed with gray. Sweeping lashes. Full lips, colored in shell-pink gloss. Perfect for her light complexion and hair.

"Was I speeding?" She sounded as if he were merely a distraction in her important life.

Yeah, the kind of beauty that was almost *spellbinding. But there was also something about her that was irritating as hell!*

The soft sound of a splash drew his attention. Her head jerked around, and she shuddered as they both looked toward the canal. A small alligator had left its sunning spot on the high mud and slipped into the water.

Then she turned back to him and gave him her full attention. She studied him for a moment. "Is this...a joke?"

"No, ma'am. No joke," he said curtly. "License and registration, please."

"Was I speeding?" she asked again, and her seriousness was well done, especially after her earlier remark.

"Speeding? Oh, yeah," he said. "License and registration, please."

"Surely I wasn't going that fast," she said. She was staring at him, not distracted anymore, and frowning. "Are you really a cop?" she demanded suddenly.

"Yes."

She twisted around. "That's not a Metro-Dade car."

"No, I'm not Metro-Dade."

"Then—"

"Miccosukee. Indian police," he said curtly.

"Indian police?" she said, and looked back to him. His temper rose. He felt as if he might as well have said *play* police, or *pretend* police.

"This is my jurisdiction," he said curtly. "One more time. License and registration."

She gritted her teeth, staring at him, antagonism replacing the curiosity in her eyes. Then, every movement irate, she dug into the glove compartment. "Registration," she snapped, handing him the document.

"And license," he said politely.

"Yes, of course. I need to get it."

"Do you know how fast you were going?"

"Um…not that far over the speed limit, surely?"

"Way over," he told her. "See that sign? It says fifty-five. You were topping that by thirty miles an hour."

"I'm sorry," she said. "It didn't feel like I was going that fast."

She dug in her handbag, which was tightly packed and jumbled, in contrast to the businesslike appearance of the pale blue jacket she wore over a tailored shirt. He began writing the ticket. She produced her license. He kept writing. Her fingers, long, elegant, curled tightly around the steering wheel. "I don't know what's waiting for you in Naples, Miss Fortier, but it's not worth dying for. And if you're not worried about killing yourself, try to remember that you could kill someone else. Slow down on this road."

"I still don't believe I was going that fast," she murmured.

"Trust me, you were," he assured her curtly. He didn't know why she was getting beneath his skin to such a degree. She was passing through. Lots of people tried to speed their way through, east to west, west to east, completely careless of their surroundings, immune to the fact that the populations of Seminoles and Miccosukees in the area might be small, but they existed.

And their lives were as important as any others.

"Fine, then," she murmured, as if barely aware of him, just anxious to be on her way.

"Hey!" He demanded her attention.

She blinked, staring at him. She definitely seemed distracted. And yet, when she stared at him, it was with a strange interest. As if she wanted to listen but somehow couldn't.

"Slow down," he repeated softly and firmly.

She nodded curtly and reached out, accepting her license and registration back, along with the ticket he had written.

Then she shook her head slightly, trying to control her temper. "Thanks," she muttered.

"I'm a real cop, and it's a real ticket, Ms. Fortier."

"Yes, thank you. I'll pay it, with real money," she said sweetly.

He forced a grim smile in return. *Spoiled little rich girl, heading from the playgrounds of Miami Beach to the playgrounds of the western coast of the state.*

He tipped his hat, grateful that she couldn't know what he was thinking. His sunglasses were darkly tinted, well able to hide his thoughts. "Good day, Miss Fortier."

He turned to leave.

"Jerk!" he heard her mutter.

He stiffened, straightened, turned back.

"Pardon? Did you say something?" he asked politely.

She forced a smile. "I said good day to you, too, Officer."

"That's what I thought you said," he told her, turning to go. "Bitch," he murmured beneath his breath.

Or, at least, he thought he'd murmured beneath his breath.

"What did you say?" she demanded sharply.

He turned back. "I said we should both have a lovely day. One big old wonderful, lovely day. Take care, Ms. Fortier."

He proceeded back to his car.

The Lexus slid back onto the road.

He followed it for a good twenty miles. And she knew it. She drove the speed limit.

Not a mile under.

Not a mile over.

The dash phone buzzed softly. He hit the answer button. "Hey, Chief. What's up? Some good ol' boy beating up on his wife again?" He spoke evenly, hoping that was all it was. Too often, out here, it was something else. Something that seldom had to do with his people, his work. The Everglades was a beautiful place for those who loved nature, but pure temptation for those who chose to commit certain crimes.

Over the distance, Emmy sighed. "Nope, just a call from Lars. He wants you to have lunch with him at the new fish place just east of the casino next Friday."

"Tell him sure," Jesse said. "See you soon. Time for me to call it a day."

Clayton Harrison's place was just up ahead. The driveway wasn't easily discernible from the trail, but Jesse knew right where it was. He took a sharp left, turned around and headed back.

He was certain that, as he did so, the Lexus once again picked up speed.

LORENA FORTIER SET down her pen, sighed, stood and stretched. She left her desk and walked to the door that led out to the hallway in the staff quarters of Harry's Alligator Farm and Museum. She hesitated, looked both ways, then walked down the shadowy hallway. Dim night-lights showed the signs on the various doors she passed.

Her second full day on the job. And her second day of living a deception. She thought about Naples and Marco Island. If only one of those lovely beach communities had been her destination.

She felt herself bristling again as she remembered being stopped the day before by the Miccosukee officer. She had been speeding, and she should have slowed down. It was just that her mind had been racing, and her foot had apparently gone along with it.

And the man who had stopped her...

She felt an odd little tremor shoot through her. He'd just been so startling, and then even a little frightening. For the good or bad, she couldn't remember anyone who had made such an impression on her in a long time. His appearance had been so striking, not at all what she expected from a police officer.

She had apparently made an impression on him, as well. *Rich bitch, no care for anything local...*

She gave herself a shake. Forget it! Move on. Concentrate on the matter at hand!

Large letters on the third door down read Dr. Michael Preston, Research.

She hesitated, then tried the knob. The door, as she had expected, was locked. She slipped her hand into the pocket of her lab coat, curling her fingers around the small lock pick she carried. She was about to work the door open when she heard voices coming from the far end of the hallway.

"So how are the tours going, Michael?" It was her new boss, Harry Rogers, speaking. He was a huge man, with a smile as wide as his belly.

Dr. Michael Preston replied with forced enthusiasm. "Great!"

"I know that you're a researcher, Michael, but part of my dream here is to educate people about reptiles."

"I don't mind the tours. I think I'm pretty good at conveying what we're doing."

Okay, so what did she do now? Lorena wondered. She was new at this whole secret-investigation thing. Should she run back down the hall and into her own office? Or should she bluff it out, walk on down the hall to meet the two of them and ask some kind of lame question?

Running would be insane. They might see her. She would have to bluff.

"Harry, Dr. Preston!" she called, smiling and starting toward them.

"You're the boss, but she calls you 'Harry,' while I'm 'Dr. Preston,'" Michael said to Harry with a groan.

"She knows she can trust me," Harry said, grinning. "She's the new girl on the block—she can't tell yet if you're a dangerously handsome devil, or simply an innocent charmer, a true bookworm."

Lorena laughed softly. "Which is it, Dr. Preston? Are you a devil in disguise? Or a man who is totally trustworthy?" she asked. He was a striking man, not bookish in appearance in the least, considering his reputation as a dedicated researcher, completely passionate about his work. The man was actually the epitome of "tall, dark and handsome," with a wicked grin that could easily seduce a woman into trusting him.

She didn't like the sound of her own laugh, or her question. She tended to be forthright; she wasn't a flirt or a tease, and acting like a coquette felt ridiculous.

But, as she was learning, Dr. Preston was aware of his looks, and more than willing to make use of his natural charm.

He turned it on her now, smiling in her direction, even though he directed his questions to their boss. "What about the lovely Ms. Fortier? Our mystery woman, a glorious golden-haired beauty suddenly landing in this small oasis in the middle of a swamp. Can she be totally trustworthy?" he asked Harry. "Or has she come to seduce our secrets out of us?"

"Well, whatever secrets I have aren't too fascinating, son," Harry said apologetically.

"And I'm afraid my mystery life is rather dull, as well," Lorena said sweetly.

"Were you looking for me?" Harry asked.

"Um…yes. You told me that you had a small gym for the employees. I thought I would take a look at it. If you could just direct me…"

"The gym is just past the holding pens. Be careful in the dark. The pens are walled, but you don't want to go getting curious, try to bend over the walls and fall in, you know. My gators are well fed, but they're wild animals, after all. And even though I've got security out there, the guards patrol, and with gators, help can never come fast enough."

"I know to be careful, Harry. Thanks." She flashed them both a smile and turned away, feeling frustrated. Did Preston sleep in his lab?

She returned to her room and changed into bike shorts and a tank top. When she left her room again, she could still hear Harry and Michael talking. They were in Preston's lab.

Maybe the gym wasn't such a bad idea, after all.

She left the staff area and started across the huge compound. There were hundreds of gators here, in various stages of growth. Then there was the special pen with Old Elijah. He was huge, a good fifteen feet. He was never part of any show; he was just there for visitors to look at. Next to him were Pat and Darien, both of them adolescents, five feet in length, the gators that were wrestled for the amusement of the crowds.

Jack Pine, a tall, well-muscled Seminole, was standing by the pens with Hugh Humphrey, a wiry blond handler from Australia. Hugh had experience with Outback crocs, and Harry valued having him. When she walked over, the two men were talking quietly with a tall, white-haired man and a veritable giant.

The white-haired man said goodbye, starting away before Lorena got close enough to be introduced to him.

The big man followed. He seemed to grunt, kind of like the alligators, but she assumed that was his way of saying goodbye.

"Ms. Fortier!" Hugh called to her, seeing her as he turned away from the pair who were leaving.

"Hi there!" she called back as she crossed over to the western arc of the building complex. "Who was that?" she asked.

"Who was who?" Hugh asked.

"The men who just left. Do they work here?"

"No, no. They do work for Harry now and then, but they're totally independent. The old guy is Dr. Thiessen, a local vet, and the Neanderthal is the doc's assistant, John Smith. I should have had Doc stay to meet you, but I didn't see you, and he's always busy. He just checks in with us now and then. Doc Thiessen is a hero among the local kids—he's the only guy out there who can really treat a sick turtle or a ball python. You'll meet him soon enough, I wager. He's something. Also knows cattle, gators—and dogs and cats."

"Ah," she murmured. "The big guy is kind of…big."

"Creepy, is that what you mean?" Hugh asked with a laugh.

"No, just…big."

"And dumb. But he's a good worker. Thiessen needs someone like that. He works with some big animals."

"That's certainly understandable. You guys work with some big animals, too," she reminded them.

Hugh offered a grin. "But we're fit and muscled—perfect specimens of manhood. You're supposed to notice that."

She laughed. "You're both in great shape."

"Thanks," Jack Pine offered. "You're welcome to go on about us if you want, but…how are you enjoying the work so far?"

"So far, things have been quite easy. I know you need

a nurse on staff, but I haven't even had to deal with a skinned knee yet."

"But you like the place all right?" Hugh asked.

"Yes, just fine."

"A lot of women would find it incredibly weird," Jack told her, inclining his head in a way that made her feel special. Like Preston, he was an intriguing man. Unlike Preston, there didn't seem to be anything cerebral about the attraction. His hair was dark and slick, his eyes nearly as black as his hair; he was bronzed and built—just as he had said. She had liked him instantly— but warily, as well.

He had proudly shown her when they'd met that he'd lost the pinkie finger on his left hand to a gator when he'd learned to wrestle the big reptiles as a boy growing up at Big Cypress Reservation. He seemed to be fearless.

"I like animals," she said.

"These guys are hardly cute and cuddly," Hugh remarked. As if they'd heard him, a number of the alligators set up a racket. They made the strangest noise, as if they were pigs grunting. The cacophony was eerie. She shivered, then thought about the animal's deadly jaws.

She thought about her reasons for being here. Whether she liked the guys who worked here or not, she had to remember to be wary.

She shivered again, suddenly uneasy about being with either man around the prehistoric predators.

Come to think of it, she thought, *she didn't want to be here at all, not at all.*

But she had to be. It was that simple. She had to be.

"You both seem to like gators a lot," she said.

Hugh shrugged. "Well, I made a good living off

crocs, so I figure I can make a good living off their cousins, too."

"Like 'em? Hell, no. Respect 'em? Hell, yes," Jack said with a shrug. "But if you're going to work with them, you need to know them. And I can definitely say I know them. I was born and bred in the swamp, so I knew about gators long before I knew about lions, tigers and bears." He grinned and shrugged. "But you, young lady, need to remember a few things that will be important if you ever get in trouble down here. Never get closer than fifteen feet to one of these suckers. And if he's hissing, back away slowly and get the hell away."

"And if you can't get away, make sure you get your weight on its back and push down hard on the nose. It's the top jaw that exerts the pressure. The lower jaw is pretty much worthless," Hugh said.

"I don't intend to get that close to any of them," she assured the men. "You're right—alligators definitely aren't cuddly, but so far, I like this place a lot. I seem to be working with great people," she said, forcing herself to sound nonchalant. They were giving her friendly warnings, nothing more. Despite the grunts from the creatures, which seemed more eerie and foreboding by the moment, she couldn't scream and run away.

"Why, shucks, thanks, ma'am," Hugh teased.

"Thank you both, and good night. See you guys in the morning."

She walked away. She could have sworn she heard the man whisper in her wake. Her skin crawled as she wondered what they were saying.

She entered the gym feeling winded, gasping for breath, though she hadn't walked far at all. She didn't want to work out; she wanted to lock herself into her room. Still, in case she was being followed or watched, she had to act normal. She'd come here to work out, so that was what she would do. She walked to a stationary bike, crawled on and pedaled away.

Fifteen minutes was enough for the night.

She exited the employee gym, more tired from feeling nervous than from her workout. She opened the door a crack, then paused, looking out.

There was a man in the compound. He was standing between two of the alligator pens, hands on hips. At first he was very still, nothing but a dark silhouette in the moonlight. He was tall, broad-shouldered, yet lithe-looking, somehow exuding energy, even in his stillness. He stood in plain view; then he walked around one of the pens, and she noticed that he moved with a sure, fluid stride that was both graceful and, somehow, menacing. Dangerous.

And oddly familiar.

It was her mind tonight, she thought. Everyone she saw seemed furtive, dangerous.

He might just be the security guard. There were several of them, she knew. And, she had been assured, their backgrounds had been checked out by the same careful procedures that casinos used.

No. This man wasn't a security guard. Somehow she knew it.

As he moved and her eyes became more accustomed to the shadows, she could see him more clearly.

He was in black jeans and a black T-shirt. The short sleeves were rolled, and in the moonlight, she could see the bulge of his arm muscles beneath the rolled cotton. His hair was on the long side, sleek, touching his shoulders. Very dark.

The cop! It was the jerk who had given her the ticket!

He turned toward the gym suddenly, as if he knew he was being watched. He couldn't, of course. The light was out. He had no way to know the door was open even a crack.

She continued to study him from her safe distance, trying to determine just what made him so imposing and unique.

His features were compelling. Hardened, fascinating. He was a combination of Native, white and God knew what else. His skin was bronzed, his cheekbones broad, his chin square, like that of a man who knew where he was going—and where he had been. His nose was slightly crooked, as if it might have been broken at some time. She couldn't make out the color of his eyes against the darkness of his hair and the bronze of his flesh. He couldn't possibly see her; still, she felt as if he was staring right through her. She almost stepped back, feeling as if she had been physically touched, as if a rush of smoke and fire had swept through her.

"Jesse," a soft feminine voice said from behind her.

She gasped, then spun around. Sally Dickerson, the head cashier and bookkeeper, was standing behind her. In her early thirties, she was an attractive redhead. Harry said she had a temper, a way with men, and one heck of a way with numbers that had dollar signs attached to them.

"Sorry, you startled me," Lorena said.

Sally glanced at her, and she realized the woman hadn't even heard her gasp. Her attention had been on the man in the moonlight.

"No, *I'm* sorry—I came in the back way, and I didn't

realize you hadn't heard me." She was still staring at the man and didn't offer anything more.

"Jesse?" Lorena pressed lightly.

Sally's eyes flicked her way, and the woman smiled broadly. "Yeah, Jesse. He's a cop. A local cop. On the Miccosukee force. He hasn't been back long."

"Oh, I realize that he's a cop," Lorena murmured, wondering if Sally could hear the slight note of bitterness in her tone. "But…he's back from where?"

"Oh…the city. He's something, huh?"

Lorena turned back to study the man in question. Sally didn't need an answer.

Yes, something. He seemed to be both pure grace and pure menace. Powerful, smooth. Sensual, she thought, with some embarrassment. In a thousand years, she never would have admitted that she understood exactly what Sally meant.

No, no, no, no. He was definitely a man with an attitude, and that attitude definitely contained an element of disdain for her. She shook her head slightly, mentally emitting an oath. It now seemed likely that she would meet him again.

Apparently, he hung out around here. And that made him…suspicious.

Cops had been known to be dirty, dirtier even than other men. Sometimes they needed money. Sometimes even good men went bad, seeing how the rich could buy good lawyers and get away with all kinds of things. They had more chance to abuse power, to sneak around, to bribe…

To threaten.

To kill?

"Interesting. We have security guards. Why is he here?" Lorena asked, looking at Sally once again.

"He checks in now and then, makes sure everything is running smoothly."

"Why did he come back?" she asked.

"Oh," Sally said slowly, "his wife was murdered. He was devastated."

"How horrible."

"I know. Damn, I have a busy night ahead of me... but still...Jesse. Excuse me, will you, honey? I want to talk to the man."

"Sure...friends help when you're devastated," Lorena said pleasantly.

Sally shot her a quick glance. "Honey, I said he was devastated, not dead. Take another look at the man, will you?" She opened the door fully and exited the gym. With a sway of her hips, she approached him, calling his name. He turned to her, arching a brow, acknowledging her presence. Sally went straight to him, placing her hands on his chest. She said something softly. He lowered his head, grinning, and the two turned to walk toward the staff quarters.

When they were gone, Lorena left the gym and hurried back across the compound. The alligators began to grunt in a wild, staccato song.

She let herself into her own room, closed and locked the door. She was breathing too heavily once again.

Maybe she was the wrong woman for this job.

No, there was no maybe about it, but that didn't matter. She had to become the right woman, and she would.

She showered, slipped into a nightgown, and assured herself once again that her door was securely locked. Even then, she also checked once more on the small

Smith & Wesson she carried. It was loaded, safety on, but close at hand in the top drawer of the nightstand next to the bed. She took one last look at it before she lay down to sleep.

Despite that, she dreamed.

She didn't want to have nightmares; she didn't want to toss and turn. She dreamed far too often of horrible things. She knew that dreams were often extensions of the day's worries, and she *was* constantly worried.

But that night, she didn't dream horrible things. She dreamed about him. The cop. The world was all foggy, and people were screaming all around her, but he was walking toward her, and she was waiting, heedless of whatever danger might be threatening her because he was watching her, coming for her....

She awoke, drenched with sweat, shaking.

She was definitely the wrong woman for this job. She was losing her mind.

No, she had to toughen up. What the hell was wrong with her? She had to be here.

Had to.

Because she, of all people, had to know the truth.

EAST OF THE deep swamp, Maria Hernandez plucked the last of her wash from the clothesline. The darkness had come; night dampness had set it. She pressed her clean sheets to her nose, deciding that they still smelled of the sunshine, even if she had cleaned up dinner late and gotten the clothes down even later. Sometimes it seemed that darkness came slowly. Sometimes it descended like a curtain, swift and complete.

But tonight...

Tonight was different.

There were lights. Strange lights appearing erratically down by the canal.

"Hector! Come see!" she called to her husband. He'd been picking all day. He picked their own crops, then rented his labor out like a migrant worker. This was the land of opportunity; and indeed, she had her nice little house, even if it was on the verge of the swamps, but one had to work very hard for opportunity.

"Maria, let me be!" Hector shouted back to her.

"But you must see."

"What is it?"

"Lights."

Hector appeared at the back of the house, a beer in his hand. He was a good man. One beer. Just one beer when he came in at night. He loved his children. They had grown quickly in this land of opportunity, and they had their own homes now. He was a hardworking and very good man. He had provided them with a dream.

But now he was tired.

"Lights?" He had spoken in English. Now he swore in Spanish, waving a hand in the air. "Maria, it's a plane. It's boys out in an airboat. It's poachers. What do I care? Come inside."

But the lights were so strange that Maria found herself walking toward them. The farther she got from the house, the stranger it seemed that there should be lights. What would children be doing out here? Or poachers? Yes, she was on the edge of the swamp, land just grasped from it, but...

Then she heard the noises.

Strange noises...

There was a big lump on the earth. She walked toward it, then paused. Instinctively, she knew she should go back. There were stories about things that needed to be watched out for—things that came from the swamp. Snakes…bad snakes. And there were reports of alligators snatching foolish dogs from the banks of the canal.

She started to back away from the lump on the ground, but then, just as she had instinctively felt that she was facing danger, she suddenly knew that the lump was a dead thing. She kept walking to it.

Clouds drifted against the dark sky, freeing the moon for a brief moment.

It was an alligator, but a dead one.

She didn't know much about alligators. Oh, yes, she lived out here; she had driven along the Trail, seen them basking in the sun. They came in close—the canals were theirs, really, this close to the Glades. But she didn't do foolish things. She didn't try to feed them, heaven forbid! She knew enough to stay away, and little else. But this one was dead, harmless, so she moved closer. And closer.

Because this one seemed very strange.

It had been big, very big. It lay on its back, and it looked almost as if it had been stuffed, and as if all the stuffing had been pulled out of it. There was a strange hole in the center of its chest, as if a fire had burned a perfect circle in the center of the white underbelly. Toes were missing. The jaw gaped open in death.

The lights started flickering again. Maria lifted a hand to her eyes so that they would not blind her.

Her heart quickened.

UFOs! Aliens, spacemen. She was proud of her English; she read all the papers in line at the grocery store. They came down to study earth creatures; they abducted men and women.

She'd seen lights before. Strange lights, late at night. In fact, she'd told her daughter, Julie, about them not so long ago, laughing at her own silliness, because of course Maria had never believed in aliens until now, and Hector scoffed at such silliness. But the lights...

And the alligator...

If they were UFOs, then her initial instinct to run had been right. She had to get back to the house and ask Hector to call the police. Maybe the tall Indian policeman was close by and could help them quickly, far more quickly than the white policemen from the city would make it.

She started to back away. At first it had seemed that the lights were coming from the sky. But now...

They were coming from the brush. From the foliage where the swampland that had not been reclaimed started, just feet from where her lawn began.

Suddenly she was very afraid. She looked at the alligator. A hole in its underbelly. Toes cut off. Eyes...

Eyes cut out.

She turned and started to run.

"Hector!"

A single bullet killed her. A rifle shot straight through her back, tearing through the anterior region of her heart.

Hector heard his wife's scream. He came running out.

The shot that killed him was square between his eyes. He dropped dead still wondering why his wife had called him.

CHAPTER TWO

IT HAD ALREADY been one hell of a bad morning.

It had started out with Ginny Hare calling first thing, before it had even begun to be light outside. Jesse was an early riser, but hell, Ginny's hysterical voice before coffee was not a good way to start off the morning.

Billy Ray hadn't come home.

He'd tried to calm Ginny. Lots of times Billy Ray would crash out wherever he'd been and find his way home the next morning.

This was different—Ginny was insistent. He'd gone out fishing with a twelve-pack of beer. And he hadn't come in the morning, the afternoon or the night, and now it was morning again and Billy Ray still wasn't back.

Jesse had tried to soothe her.

"Ginny, I'll get out there looking for him, but you quit worrying. A twelve-pack of beer, Ginny, think about it."

"But, Jesse, he's stayed out two nights!"

"Ginny, I'll look for him, I promise. But he probably got himself as drunk as a skunk and he's sleeping it off somewhere—or, he woke up and knew he'd be in major trouble, and he's trying to figure out how to come home."

When he'd hung up, he'd wondered about the power

of love. Billy Ray Hare was the worst loser he'd ever
met—white, Native, Hispanic or black. He hit Ginny
all the time, though he denied it, as Ginny did herself.
He was her man, and in Ginny's eyes, whatever he did,
he was hers, and she was going to stand up for him.

Jesse knew that Billy Ray hated him. That was all
right. He had no use whatsoever for Billy Ray. Billy
Ray liked to call him "white boy," which was all right,
because yes, his father had been white. But his mother
could trace her lineage back to Billy, Old King Mican-
opy, back before the start of the Seminole Wars, back
before the government had even recognized the Miccosukee as an independent tribe, speaking a different
language from the Seminoles with whom they had in-
termarried and fought throughout the years. Billy Ray
never understood that Jesse was proud of being Native
American—and furious when men like Billy Ray fell
into stereotypes and became lazy-ass alcoholics.

So Billy Ray was useless. But despite the fact that
she loved Billy Ray, there was something very special
about Ginny. And for her, Jesse would spend half his
day in the sweltering heat of summer looking for her
no-good husband.

But he hadn't had a chance to look for Billy Ray yet.

Before he'd gotten out of the house, he'd gotten the
call about Hector and Maria Hernandez.

Their property was on the county line, so the Metro
Police were already on the scene. The homicide detective in charge of the case was Lars Garcia, a man with
whom Jesse had gone to college up at the University of
Florida. His Cuban refugee father had married a Dan-
ish model, thus his ink-dark hair, slim, athletic build
and bright powder-blue eyes. The media liked to make

it sound as if the Indian—or Native American cops—
were half-wits who were given only a small measure of
authority and who hated their ever-present big brothers,
the Metro cops. Jesse resented the media for that, because it simply wasn't true. The Metro-Dade force had
suffered through some rough years, with rogue cops and
accusations of corruption and drug abuse. But they'd
cleaned house, and they weren't out to make fools of
the Miccosukee policing their own.

Besides which, he'd been a Metro homicide cop himself before making the decision to join the Miccosukee
police force.

He felt lucky wherever he got to work with Lars
when a body was discovered. Unfortunately, that wasn't
a rare happening.

A swamp was a good place to dump a body. There
had been the bizarre—body pieces dredged up in suit-
cases—and there had been the historical: bodies discovered that had lain in the muck and mud for more
than a century. Man's inhumanity to man was not a
new thing. Sad as it might be, he was accustomed to
the cruel and vicious.

Homicides happened.

But the unfairness of homicide happening to good
people never ceased to upset him.

Jesse had known Hector and Maria. Known and liked
them. They were as homespun as cotton jeans, without guile or cunning. She always wanted to bring him
in and feed him; Hector always wanted him to taste a
fresh strawberry or tomato. They had loved their small
home, loved their land more. It was theirs. He'd never
seen two people appreciate the simple things in life with
such pure and humble gratitude and pleasure.

Uniformed cops were cordoning off the crime scene as he arrived; Lars had been talking with the fingerprint expert but excused himself and walked over to Jesse as soon as he saw him. "Terrible thing, huh? It's technically outside your jurisdiction, but the killers must have come from somewhere. Maybe they were hiding in the swamp, maybe..." His voice trailed off.

"The bodies?" Jesse said.

"You don't have to see them."

"Yeah, I do."

Hector's body was covered when they walked to it; Lars hunkered down and pulled back the blanket. Hector looked oddly at peace. His eyes were closed; he just lay there—normal-looking except for the bullet hole in his forehead. Nothing had been done to the body; the killer probably hadn't even come near him.

"Tracks?" Jesse asked.

Lars shook his head. "None so far. The lawn is all grassy...then there's foliage, and the canal. No tracks yet."

Jimmy Page from the medical examiner's office was still bending over Maria when they reached her. She lay facedown, her head twisted. Her eyes were still open.

She had seen something terrible.

There was a hole through her back.

"Hi, Jesse," Jimmy said, making notes. "I'm sorry as hell, I heard you knew them."

"Yeah. Nice couple. Really good people. Have the children been notified?"

"The son is in the navy, on active duty—they're trying to reach him. The daughter will be here this afternoon."

He winced. Julie was going to come home alone to

see her murdered parents. He would have to make a point of being available later.

"Know when she's coming in?"

"American Airlines, two-thirty flight from LaGuardia. Want to meet her with me?" Lars asked.

"Yeah."

"Thanks. I wasn't looking forward to talking to her on my own."

"Have you got anything, Jimmy?" Jesse asked. "I mean…" He looked down into Maria's eyes, thinking he would remember the way she looked for a very long time to come. "This is no drug hit. These people were as clean as they came."

Jimmy shook his head. "Jesse…I've got to admit, about all we're going to know is the caliber of bullet that hit them, maybe the weapon that fired it, an approximate time of death and maybe a trajectory. They were shot," he said, sounding angry. "As to why they were shot…Jesus, you're right. Who can tell?"

"Mind if I take a look around?" Jesse asked Lars.

"Be my guest. We think the killers must have been to the southwest, from the way Maria fell. She was running. Hector was coming to help her."

Jesse nodded, surveying the expanse of lawn. The neat yard the couple had tended so lovingly reached a point where it became long, thick grasses. Back in the grass, the water table began to rise and mangroves grew. Beyond that lay the canal.

He walked carefully to where the thick grass began to grow, studying the lawn. Although his relations with the Metro police were good, he wondered if any of the beat cops were cracking jokes about an Indian being better at finding footprints than they were.

Hell. He was going to look for them, anyway. He was going to look for anything.

He turned, calling back to Lars, "I think an airboat came through here. See the flattening?"

"Yeah."

"And…" Jesse began, then trailed off. He walked a little further, seeing something in the grass. He moved closer. Bent over. Frowned.

"What is it?" Lars asked.

"Got a glove and an evidence bag?"

"Yeah."

Lars came over to him, slipping his hand into a glove. Jesse pointed to the grass. Lars reached for what appeared to be a branch.

"That?" he inquired. "Jesse, it's just a tree limb."

"No, it isn't."

"Then, what the hell…?"

"It's a gator arm," Jesse said. "From one damn big gator."

"A gator arm? What the hell do I want with a gator arm?"

"I don't know, but where's the rest of the body?"

"It looks like it was sliced off."

"I think the rest of the body was moved, and then this arm tore off."

"But…" Lars began.

"But why? And just where the hell is the rest of the body?"

Lars shook his head. "Maybe…"

"Maybe a dead gator and the murder have nothing to do with each other," Jesse said. "And maybe they do."

"Well, they shouldn't have anything to do with each other," Lars said. "Hell. I can't believe that someone out alligator-poaching would murder two people in cold blood just because he was seen. I mean, it's not as if we execute people for killing gators out of season without a license."

"No, it's not," Jesse agreed. He looked at Lars and shrugged. "But what else is there? Like Jimmy said, there are bullets, there's a time of death...but where the hell is a motive? You're not going to get prints, no fluids for DNA...that's all you've got—an alligator arm."

"I've got nothing," Lars said hollowly.

"Maybe. Maybe not. Send the gator limb to Dr. Thiessen. See what you can get, if anything."

"Of course we'll get it to the vet," Lars said impatiently. "Because you're right. I haven't got anything else. And I'm damned sorry that I may have to tell a young woman who loved her parents that I can't begin to explain why they're dead, except that maybe her mother saw an alligator poacher in the backyard!"

"Lars, you tell me. What else is there?" Jesse said. "This kind of killing looks like an execution, as if it were connected to drugs. But it wasn't. I'd bet my life on that. I'm telling you, Lars, I knew these people. They were bone clean."

"They must have seen something, then. They must have known something, but...you're sure? I mean, sometimes we think we know people, but they're living double lives."

"No. I knew them, Lars."

"All right. Maybe the daughter can help us."

"I doubt it. But I'll go with you. I'll talk to her with you. But, Lars, after today...you'll keep me informed on this one all the way, right?"

"Yes."

"No matter what goes on in Homicide?"

"Yes!"

"Swear it?"

Lars looked at him, arching a brow. "We're already blood brothers," he reminded him with a rueful grimace.

Jesse stared at him, shaking his head. Yeah. Forever ago, when they had been young and going to college.

Strangely, or so it seemed now, their college mascot had been an alligator.

They had both pledged the same fraternity. It had been during that period that they'd been out drinking together and Lars had gotten into the blood brother thing, having seen one too many John Wayne movies, Jesse decided.

"Yeah, blood brothers," Jesse returned, surprised that he could almost smile, even if that smile was grim.

"Jesse, the only thing—"

"I won't go off half cocked to shoot to kill if I find out who did it. I'm a cop. I'll bring them in."

Lars watched him for a moment. Jesse locked his jaw, staring back at his friend. Maybe Lars had the right to doubt him. When Connie had died...

Fate had kept him from killing the man who had murdered her. But there had been no question in his mind that, given the chance, he might well have committed murder himself in turn, so great had been his rage.

"I'm telling you, I'll be a by-the-book lawman." He shook his head, sobering. "They didn't deserve this, Lars."

"I swear, I will keep you up on what's happening. I'll have to—the killer or killers probably came from the swamp and maybe ran back that way. We'll have lots of our guys in your territory."

"I'll brief my men, as well."

"Get a warning out to them right away."

"Will do."

"You want to take this piece of gator over to Doc Thiessen?" Lars asked him. "You're more familiar with the damn things than I am." He didn't add, Jesse noticed, that he was probably also far more convinced than Lars was that the alligator remains might have something to do with the case.

They started back toward the house. Jesse found himself pausing by Maria's body. The forensic photographers were still at work. He looked into her eyes. In Metro Homicide, he'd seen a lot. A bullet was a fairly quick, clean way to die. He'd seen mutilations that had turned even his strong stomach.

But this...

He'd seen her face alight and beautiful when she'd smiled.

"Jesse, quit looking at her," Lars said.

"Yeah. Well, I'll inform the office, then get out there looking for Billy Ray Hare."

"Billy Ray? You don't think—"

"That Billy Ray killed these two? Not on your life. Billy Ray may be a drunk, and he may not be a prime husband, but he keeps to himself and wouldn't step outside the area he's accustomed to. And he'd also be too damned drunk to make it this far by that time of night. I've got work to do, and so do you. I'll meet you at two so we can get to the airport. Where?"

"The restaurant at the turnpike entrance."

"I'll be there," Jesse said.

When he left, his first stop was the vet's. Dr. Thorne Thiessen was a rare man, pleased to live deep in the Everglades, and fascinated more by birds and reptiles than the more cuddly creatures customarily kept as pets. He was such an expert with snakes that people traveled down from Palm Beach County, a good hour or so away, to bring him their pythons and boas, king snakes, rat snakes and more.

He was in his early fifties, both blond and bronzed, almost as weathered as some of the creatures he tended with such keen interest. He was just finishing with a little boy and his turtle when Jesse arrived, bearing the alligator limb.

He looked at Jesse with surprise. "People usually call on me with living creatures, you know."

"Yeah, but Metro-Dade and I both think you can help on this one. You *are* the reptile expert. You can make some preliminary findings, then pass some samples upstate. Hopefully, someone will figure something out."

Thiessen had been smiling; now he frowned. "What have you got?"

"What do you think?"

"I think it's a piece of an alligator."

"Great."

"No, no, I can do tissue and blood samples, do a profile…and get samples upstate, just like you suggested, but why?"

Jesse explained. Thiessen stared at him for long moments. "And you found this at the scene?"

"Yes."

"Jesse…"

Jesse sighed. "They weren't into drugs."

"Still, they might have witnessed an exchange in the Everglades, or, hell, God forbid, another murder."

"They might have. But this is what we've got for now."

Thiessen shrugged. "Big sucker," he said.

"Yep," Jesse agreed.

"I'll do what I can," Thiessen promised.

Jesse thanked him. In the waiting room, he looked for Jim Hidalgo, who worked for the vet, but then he remembered that Jim worked nights.

The man at the desk was a big guy, John Smith. He was so big, in fact, that he was almost apelike. Jesse didn't remember when he hadn't been with the vet.

Good man to have on, Jesse thought. Big enough to cope with any animal out there.

At least, almost any animal out there.

He grunted to Jesse in a combination of hello and goodbye.

Come to think of it, a grunt was the only conversation Jesse had ever shared with the man.

He waved and went out.

"LOOK INTO THE eyes of death! Stare into the burning pits of monster hell. See what it would have been like to face the hunger and rage of a carnivore older than the mighty *Tyrannosaurus rex!* Ah, but, believe it or not, once upon a Triassic age, this was an even more ferocious and terrifying creature, in fact, one that made minced meat of the mighty dinosaurs themselves." Michael Preston paused for effect as he talked to the small, wriggling creature he held in his right hand.

The week-old hatchling let out a strange little squeaking sound, its jaws opening, then snapping shut. The eyes were yellow with central stripes of black. It was small, almost cute in a weird sort of way, but the mouth shut with a pressure that was chilling, despite its size.

The hatchling began squealing and wriggling again.

"Loudmouth," Michael said, shrugging. He liked the fact that the American alligator made noise. Noise was good. Noise was warning. "But you *are* being awfully dramatic here," he told the hatchling. "Okay, so I'm a little dramatic myself. Because I *hate* tour groups," he grumbled.

Even as he slipped the hatchling back into its tank, the door to his lab opened and Lorena entered.

"Watch out—the monsters are coming," she warned.

Michael arched a brow. "Monsters," she whispered, emphasizing the warning. Then she turned, a beautiful smile plastered on her face as she allowed room for the tour group to enter. Ten in all, a full tour: two young couples, perhaps on their way to register for college, maybe on honeymoon. They looked like ecology-minded types, surveying the wonder of the Everglades. There was an attractive, elderly woman, probably a widow, seeing the Sunshine State now that old Harvey or whoever had finally bitten the dust. Then there was a harried-looking couple with three boys who looked to be about twelve. The woman had once been pretty. The man had a good smile and looked like a decent father. The boys seemed to be the monsters. They walked right up to his lab table, barged against it, then leaned on it, peering into his tanks and petri dishes.

"Uh, uh, uh—back now," Michael said, frowning at Lorena as if she might have forgotten to warn her group that the tour was hands-off. She shrugged innocently and grinned back with a combination of mischief and amusement. No doubt the boys had been a handful since they'd started their tour. Actually, Lorena wasn't responsible for leading tours. She was a trouper, though. She seemed to like to be in the middle of things; when there were no injuries or sniffles to attend to, her work was probably boring. And it wasn't as if there were a dozen malls or movie theaters in the area to keep her busy.

"Back, boys," he repeated. "Even hatchlings can be dangerous."

"Those little things? What can they do?" demanded the biggest boy as he stuck his hand into the tank with the week-old hatchlings.

Michael grabbed his hand with a no-nonsense grip that seemed to surprise the boy.

"They can bite," Michael said firmly.

"Mark Henson, stand back and behave, now," the boy's obviously stressed mother said, stepping forward to set a hand on Mark's shoulders. "We're guests here. The doctor has asked you—"

"He ain't no doctor—are you?" the boy demanded.

The woman shot Michael an apologetic look. "I'm so sorry. Mark is my son Ben's cousin, and I don't think he gets out very often."

"It's all right," Michael said. He was lying. Mark was a brat. "Mark seems to be very curious. Yes, Mark, I *am* a doctor. I have a doctorate in marine science. Salt- and freshwater reptiles are my specialty. I also studied biochemistry, animal behavior and psychology, so trust me, hatchlings can give you a nasty bite. Especially these hatchlings."

"Why *those* hatchlings?" Mark demanded immediately.

Because we breed them especially to chew up nasty little rugrats like you! he was tempted to say. But Lorena was already answering for him.

"Because they're tough little critters, survivors," Lorena said flatly. "Ladies and gentlemen, Dr. Preston is in charge of our selective-breeding department. He knows a tremendous amount about crocodilians, past and present. He'll tell you all about his work now—for those interested in hearing," she finished with just the slightest edge of warning in her voice for the boys. They stared at her as she spoke, surveying her intently. No wonder she was glad to let the group heckle *him* now. Lorena was an exceptionally attractive woman with lush hair, brilliant eyes, and a build that not even a lab coat could hide.

The two older boys were at that age when they were just going into adolescence, a state when squeaky sopranos erupted every ten minutes, and sexual fantasies began. And they were obviously having a few of those over Lorena. She made a face at Michael, surprised him by slipping quickly from his lab. Well, she didn't have to be here, he told himself. It wasn't her job. But she'd seemed fascinated by everything here ever since she'd arrived.

Even him.

Not that he minded.

Except that…

She was bright. And really beautiful. So what was she doing out here?

She was good with people, he would definitely give her that. The complete opposite of the way he felt. He hated having to deal with people.

He gave the boys a sudden, ever-so-slightly malicious smile. "Well, gentlemen, let me introduce you more fully to these hatchlings. Alligators, as you might have heard already, date back to prehistoric times. They didn't descend from the dinosaurs. They were actually cousins to them. They shared common ancestors known as thecodonts. And way back in the late Cretaceous period, there was a creature called Deinosuchus—a distant relative of these guys—with a head that was six feet in length. Imagine that fellow opening his jaws on you. True crocodilians have been around for about two million years. They're fantastic survivors. They have no natural enemies—"

"That's not true!" Mark announced. "I saw a program on alligators and crocs. An anaconda can eat an alligator, I saw it. You could see the shape of the alligator in the snake. Man, it was cool—"

"We don't have anacondas in the Everglades," Michael said, gritting his teeth hard before he could continue. "Birds, snakes and small mammals eat alligator eggs, and it's easy for hatchlings to be picked off, but once it's reached a certain size, an alligator really only has one enemy here. And that's...?"

He let the question trail off, arching a brow toward Mark. He looked like a jock. Probably played football or basketball, at the very least. He liked to talk, but he didn't seem to have the answer to this one.

"Man," said one of the boys. He was thinner than his companion, with enormous dark eyes and long hair that fell over his forehead. Nice-looking kid. Shy, maybe, more of a bookish type than Mark. "Man is the only enemy of a grown alligator in the Everglades."

"That's right," Michael said, an honest smile curving

his lips. He could tell that this kid had a real interest in learning. "You're Ben?" Michael asked.

The boy nodded. He pulled the third kid up beside him. "This is my other cousin, Josh."

"Josh, Ben and Mark."

"Do we get to see the alligators eat a deer or something?" Mark asked.

"Sorry, you don't get to see them eat any living creatures here, kid. The juveniles and adults out in the pools and pens are fed chicken."

"They're so cool," Ben said, his brown eyes wide on Michael.

Michael nodded. "Yep, they're incredible. Alligators were near extinction here when I was young, but then they became protected. The alligator has made one of the most incredible comebacks in the world, mainly because of farms like this, but also in the wild. They look ugly, and they certainly can be fearsome creatures, but they have their place in the scheme of life, as well, keeping down the populations of other animals, often weeding out the sick and injured because they're easy prey."

"I think they're horrible creatures," Ben's mother said with a shudder.

"Some people hate spiders—but spiders keep down insect populations. And lots of people hate snakes, but snakes are largely responsible for controlling rodent populations," Michael said.

"What's that mean?" Mark asked.

"It means we'd be overrun by rats if it weren't for snakes," Ben answered, then flushed, staring at Michael.

"That's exactly what it means," Michael said.

"What do you do here, Dr. Preston?" the third kid, cousin Josh, asked.

"That's easy. He's a baby doctor for the alligators," Mark insisted.

"I study the growth patterns of alligators," Michael said. "We raise alligators here, but this is far from a petting zoo. We farm alligators just like some people farm beef cattle. We bring tourists in—and other scientists, by the way, to learn from the work we do here—but the owners are in this for the same reason other farmers work with animals. For the money. Alligators are valuable for their skins, and, more and more, for their meat."

"Tastes like chicken," Mark said.

"That's what some people say," Michael agreed, bristling inside at the boy's know-it-all attitude. "They're a good food source. The meat is nutritious, and little of the animal goes to waste. We're always working on methods to make the skin more resilient, the meat tastier and even more nutritious. By selective breeding and using the scientific method, we can create skins that improve upon what nature made nearly perfect to begin with."

"Perfect?" Ben's mother said with a shudder. Her husband slipped an arm around her.

"They make great boots," he said cheerfully.

"Belts, purses and other stuff, too," Ben supplied.

"You'll see more of that as your tour progresses," Michael said. "I'll tell you a bit more about what goes on in here, then you can watch them eat, Mark, and at the end, guess what?"

"We can all buy boots, belts and purses made out of alligator skin?" one of the young women inquired with a pleasant smile.

"That's right," Michael agreed.

"And we really get to see them chomp on chickens?" Mark demanded, as if that were the only possible reason for coming on the tour.

"Yeah, you can see them chomp on chickens," Michael agreed. He pointed at Ben. "Come back here, Ben, and you can help me." Michael looked up at the adults in the crowd. He never brought a kid back behind his workstation, but for some reason, it seemed important to let Ben lord it over Mark. He was sure that life usually went the other way around. "One of the most incredible things we're able to do in working with crocodilians is studying the growth of the embryo in the egg. Ben, lift that tray, so they can see what I mean."

"Wow!" Mark gasped, stepping forward again. Even he was impressed.

"It's possible to crack and remove the top of the alligators' eggs to study the growth of the embryos without killing them. It's also possible to cause changes and mutations in the growing embryos by introducing different drugs, genetic materials or even stimuli such as heat or cold. Here…in this egg, you'll see a naturally occurring mutation. This creature cannot survive even if it does reach the stage of hatching. You see, it's missing a lower jaw. Can you imagine an alligator incapable of using its jaws? Everywhere in nature, there are mishaps and imperfections. Over here, in this egg, you have an albino alligator. They have tremendous difficulty surviving because—"

"Because they sunburn!" Mark interrupted, laughing as if he'd made a joke.

"Actually, that's true. They have trouble coping with the intense sun that their relatives need to survive. They also lack the element of surprise in their attacks—they're easily seen in greenish or muddy waters where their relatives are camouflaged by their surroundings."

"He's a goner," Mark said.

"Well, not here," Michael told him. "He'll hatch and grow, and he'll have a nice home at the farm, and we'll feed him and take care of him—you know why?"

"Why?"

"Because he's unusual, and our visitors will like looking at him, that's why," Michael said, pleased with himself because he seemed to be growing a little more tolerant of Mark.

"So that's what you do—you try to make white alligators?" Mark asked.

Michael shook his head. "Selective breeding…well, it's what makes collies furry or Siamese cats Siamese. We find the alligators with the best skins and we breed them, and then we breed their offspring until we create a line of animals with incredibly hardy skins that make the very best boots and bags and purses. We also find the alligators that give the most meat with the most nutritional value—"

"Because it's a farm, and it's out to make money," Ben's mother said, and she shuddered again. "Thank God!"

"She thinks you should kill them all," Ben's father said.

Michael shrugged. "Like I said—"

"They should all be killed," the attractive older woman said, speaking out at last. She had keen blue eyes, and she stared at Michael, somehow giving him the creeps. "They eat people."

"They *do* eat people, right?" Mark demanded with a morbid determination.

"There have been instances, yes."

"A friend of mine was eaten!" the elderly woman said, and she kept staring at Michael, as if it was all his fault.

"Anytime man cohabits with nature, there can be a certain danger," he said gently. He looked at the others. "It's dangerous to feed alligators. The alligators are repopulating Florida, and they do get into residential canals, especially during mating season. I know of one incident in particular when a woman was feeding the alligators…and, well, to the alligator, there is no distinction between food and a hand offering food."

"And children," the woman said, growing shrill. "Children! It's happened. It's horrible, and they should all be destroyed. Little children, just walking by lakes, looking at flowers—these monsters need to be killed! All of them! How can you people do this, how can you!" Her voice had risen; she was shouting.

There was a buzzer beneath his workstation; all Michael had to do was hit it and the security people would come. Sign of the times. But Michael didn't touch the button; the older woman had stunned him by suddenly going so ballistic, and he just stared at her.

She pointed a finger at him. "Tell them. Tell them the truth. Tell them about the attacks."

"Yes, there have been attacks, and of course that's horrible. But we need to live sensibly with nature. In Africa, along the river, the Nile crocodiles are far more ferocious, but they're a part of the environment. We can't just eliminate animal populations because the animals are predators. We're predators ourselves, ma'am."

She shook her finger at him, and her voice grew more strident. "They're going to eat you. They're going to eat you all. Rise up and tear you to pieces, rip you to shreds—that's how they do it, you know, little boy!" she said, suddenly gripping Mark by the shoulders. She stared at him with her wild eyes. "They clamp down on your body, and they shake you, and they break you and rip you, and your bones crunch and your veins burst. Your blood streams into the water, and you're dying already while they drown you."

"Oh, my God, please!" Ben's mother cried, trying to pull Mark from the woman's grip.

"Hey now!" Michael said, and he came around his station, setting an arm around the woman's shoulders to hold her while Ben's mother, pale as a shadow, pulled Mark to her.

"You!" the elderly woman said, turning on him again. "You! They'll eat *you*. You made them, and they'll eat you. They'll tear you to bits, and your own mother won't be able to find enough bloody pieces to bury you!"

"Now, really, I didn't invent alligators, ma'am—"

"You'll die!" she screeched.

He reached for her again, aware that he had to take control of the situation before it became a monumental disaster. He could see her going completely insane and destroying his lab. Then the cops would be called in, and soon reporters would be crawling everywhere, and then...

"Please, now—" he began.

The door suddenly opened. Security hadn't come; Lorena had, presumably drawn by the noise. She stared reproachfully at Michael.

"What happened?"

"That lady is telling Dr. Preston that the alligators should eat him!" Mark said excitedly.

"We have a problem," Michael agreed. "I think I should call Security—" he began.

"No, no, we're all right." Lorena—who, he had been told, had a degree in psychology and another in public relations, as well as being an RN—assessed the situation quickly and took charge. "Mrs. Manning, right? Come along and tell me about it. We'll get you something cold to drink. It can be so hot here, even with the air-conditioning on the heat can get to you and—"

"Young woman, I am not suffering from the heat!" the elderly woman proclaimed. But her shoulders sank, and she suddenly seemed to deflate. "I'm sorry, I'm sorry. I'm not a lunatic, I don't usually behave this way.... I shouldn't have come. Yes, young woman, you may get me something cold to drink."

Lorena led her quickly toward the door, but once there, the woman stopped and turned back, staring at Michael. She pointed at him again. "I hope they don't eat you, young man," she said. Then she smiled, but it wasn't a pleasant expression, and despite himself, he felt the strangest chill snake along his spine.

Then she was gone, as Lorena whisked her out the door.

Michael, with the nine remaining members of the tour group, was dead silent as seconds ticked by.

He suddenly felt a small hand slipping into his. He looked down. Ben was staring up at him. "Don't worry. She was just crazy. She probably had a friend who got eaten, and she probably misses her. I'm sure you're not going to get eaten, Dr. Preston."

Michael smiled; the chill dissipated.

"All right, everyone. I have a question for you. What animal is most dangerous to Americans?"

There was silence for a moment, then Mark cried out, "I know, I know! Bees!"

"Bees are up there in the top ten, but they're not in the number-one slot."

"I know what it is." A young man, one of the two who looked like a newlywed, was speaking for the first time. He held his wife tightly against him, and seemed pale himself, probably shaken by the older woman's display. "The deer."

"The deer?" Ben protested.

"That's right," Michael said.

"The deer? You mean like Bambi?" Josh asked.

"More Americans are killed each year due to accidents involving deer than are killed by any rattler, spider, shark or reptile out there. So we have to remember to always be careful in any animal's environment," Michael said.

His door opened again; Peggy Martin, one of the guides, stepped in. "Well, ladies and gentlemen, it's time to move on to the pens, or straight into either the gift or coffee shop, if you'd rather," she said cheerfully.

"Mark, you get to see the gators eat chickens," Josh said.

Mark looked at Ben's parents. "I'm really hungry. Maybe we could just get a hamburger. Please?" he said politely.

"Sure, sure," Ben's father said. He looked at Michael. "Thank you for the information, Dr. Preston."

"Yeah, it was great," one of the pretty young women Michael had pegged as a newlywed agreed.

"Thanks," Michael said. "Thanks very much, you were, er, a great group."

He leaned back against his workstation, strangely exhausted. The old woman had given him the creeps. He kept a false smile plastered to his face as the group filed out, the boys in the rear.

Mark was the last. Before he exited, he turned back, looking uneasy.

"Dr. Preston?"

"Yes?"

The boy seemed about to say something, but then he shook his head. "Thanks. You were all right."

Michael nodded.

"Come back sometime," he told Mark, wondering if he meant it or not.

"Yeah."

The door closed behind Mark.

The hatchlings began to squeak.

CHAPTER THREE

IN THE GIFT SHOP, Josh began to play with a two-foot-long plastic alligator. "I've got five dollars," he told Ben. "Think this looks real?"

"Yeah, it's cool," Ben told him.

Mark walked up to the pair in the corner of the shop. He still looked a little pale—they had all been kind of spooked, the old lady had been *really, really* creepy, scarier than the alligators—but he was kind of swaggering again, which Ben was sure meant that Mark was all right.

"That don't look real, Josh. Not compared to this!"

Reaching into the pocket of his baggy, oversize jeans, he pulled out one of the hatchlings. The little creature's mouth was opened wide. Tiny teeth were already chillingly visible.

"Mark! You stole one of the hatchlings—" Josh began.

"Shh," Mark protested.

"Oh, man, you've got to give that back," Ben said.

"No way," Mark said. "Look at him!"

The jaw opened, snapped.

Mark shoved the hatchling toward Josh, who jumped back. "Don't do that, Mark."

"He's going to eat you all up," Mark said, laughing as he started to stuff the creature back into his pocket.

But suddenly he cried out, his hand still in his pocket.

"Oh, shut up," Ben commanded. His cousin was big stuff around school; he had looked up to Mark, and he'd wanted to be like him. But Ben had never been on an outing like this with Mark before. Mark was always on, like maybe there were always girls watching or something. Now the way people were staring was just embarrassing. "Come on, Mark, stop it. People are looking—"

Mark jerked his hand from his pocket. "Get it off! Get it off!" he screamed. The hatchling had his forefinger in its mouth. To Ben's amazement, there was a trail of blood dripping down his cousin's finger.

Instinctively, he reached for the hatchling. But Mark started screaming again. "No, no, don't pull. You'll tear my whole finger off!"

People were beginning to stare. Ben pushed Mark toward a rear door. It read No Admittance: Staff Only, but Ben ignored that; the way the buildings were set up, he could tell that the door led back into the hallway where the labs were housed.

"What are we doing? Where are we going?" Mark cried frantically. "Oh, my God, it hurts! He's eating me!"

"Shut up, shut up, we're taking him back!" Ben said. He moved Mark faster and faster down the hall, pushing back into Dr. Preston's lab without knocking at the door.

Dr. Preston was there, thankfully, standing almost where they had left him. He started when they entered, standing taller in his lab coat. He wasn't very old for a doctor; he was tall and nice-looking, with sandy hair and green eyes, and if Mark hadn't been such a jerk— and if the old lady hadn't freaked out—he might have spent more time with them and told them a lot more neat stuff.

"What the—" Dr. Preston began.

"Mark took one of the babies, but it bit him and we can't get it off and we're real sorry, honest to God, we're real sorry, but can you help—"

Preston helped. Right away, he knew where to pinch the hatchling so that it let go rather than ripping. He dropped the hatchling back into a tank. By then there were tears in Mark's eyes, ready to spill down his face.

"Come over here," Preston said to Mark, taking him back behind his workstation, washing the wound at a sterile-looking sink, then covering it with some slimy cream. "We'll have to take you to the nurse and tell your folks—"

"No, please, no!" Mark protested. "I'm here with Ben's parents. If my parents ever found out I—that I tried to steal from this place, they'd..."

Preston stared at Mark, then at Ben, and then at Josh, who had followed them, silent and so white that his freckles stood out on his face.

"Mark, you were bitten—"

"It's a tiny hole. Look, you can barely see it."

"Yes, but—"

"I've had a tetanus shot, honest."

"Mark, there's always a rare chance that reptiles can carry disease—"

"Not alligator-farm reptiles!" Mark said. "Please, please, please don't say anything. You don't know my dad."

Preston hesitated.

"Please," Mark whispered. "Please."

Ben held his breath. Preston was staring at Mark, studying his face.

The door behind them quietly opened and closed. Ben jumped, turning around. It was their first guide, the really pretty lady with the dark hair and bright blue eyes.

She didn't say anything, just leaned against the door, watching the situation. Dr. Preston looked at her. He lifted Mark's fingers. "They were trying to leave with a souvenir."

"Ah…" she murmured to the boys. "What were you going to do? Drop him in your hotel swimming pool?" She turned to Dr. Preston. "I need to look at that, and then we need to file a report."

Mark went pale.

"I was thinking about letting him go. I think he already paid enough of a price," Dr. Preston said.

Ben was surprised to see that the beautiful nurse was the one who seemed to think they needed the authorities. She was staring at Dr. Preston. "We really shouldn't take the chance. Just in case there are consequences, an infection…"

Dr. Preston stared back at her. "This is one of the cleanest labs you're ever going to find." He sounded indignant.

The nurse, however, wasn't backing down. "I don't know…."

"Please," Mark begged.

"Hey, I'd never let anything happen to a kid," Dr. Preston swore. "Though this one…all right. Call in the authorities."

"No, please," Mark begged.

The woman stared at Dr. Preston for a moment longer.

Then she looked at the boys. They were staring at her with downright prayers glittering in their eyes.

She nodded, a smile twitching at her lips; then she walked over to look at Mark's finger. Her glance at Michael assured him that it was a minor injury. "We have some antibacterial medicine to put on that."

Preston stared at Mark. "You know, Ms. Fortier has a point. This is against my better judgment. I could lose my job. I could be sued. Who knows, maybe I could go to jail. Lorena, could I go to jail for this?"

"I don't know, but there's a cop outside. Jesse Crane." She made a tsking sound. "I've heard that he feels passionately about people messing with things like this. The Everglades, well, this place is his passion. So I've heard."

"I'll never say a word, never, even if my finger drops off—even if my whole hand explodes!" Mark swore.

Lorena pulled a tube of cream from her pocket and dabbed some of the contents on the injured finger.

She took a bandage from another pocket and covered the bite. When she was finished, though, she was in a real hurry. "I've got to get back to the office. I just came by to make sure everyone was okay. That poor woman is still…well, in bad shape."

"This is just a tiny bite," Mark said apologetically. He gulped. "Thank you, Nurse," he murmured.

She took off. Preston watched her go.

Ben was surprised and pleased to see that Dr. Preston was actually smiling when he said, "Mark, you take this as a lesson. And if your hand swells up, don't keep it a secret. Tell the doctor you stuck your hand in the tank and got bitten by a hatchling, and then you have them call me right away, got it?"

"Yes, sir," Mark swore.

He turned, flying for the door. Ben ran after him. At the door, Mark stopped. Ben crashed into him. Josh, always close, crashed into Ben.

Mark didn't notice the pileup. He was staring back at Dr. Preston. "Thanks, Doc. Honest. I'll make it up to you one day."

Preston nodded at him.

"Okay. I'll hold you to your word."

The boys hurried back out to the gift shop. Ben plowed right into his mother.

"There you are! Thank God. If you're buying anything, do it now. I can't wait to leave this place. Honestly, Howard," she said to his father, "couldn't we have taken them on an overnighter to Disney World? I can't believe we're going from here to an airboat ride and a night in one of those open-air chickee things!"

"It will be fine, dear," Ben's father said. He winked at Ben.

"I knew I should have gone with Sally and the Girl Scouts," she said.

Ben flashed a quick smile to Mark. Mark smiled back. It was going to be all right.

No one was in trouble. The alligator farm wasn't going to call the police or Mark's parents; Ben's folks weren't even any the wiser.

The day was saved.

The airboat ride was next.

JESSE HAD PULLED into the parking lot at the alligator farm already tired. He hadn't found Billy Ray. Where the hell the man had crawled off to, he didn't know. He would need lots more time to comb the swamp to find Billy Ray.

Just what he needed to be doing when two friends had been shot down in their own yard for no apparent reason.

And now this.

A call because a woman had gone into a fit while visiting the alligator farm.

Lots of tourists, he noticed. That was good. Along the Tamiami Trail, a lot of the Miccosukee Indians depended on the tourist trade for a living. Along Alligator Alley, stretching from Broward westward across the state in a slightly more northerly route, a lot of the state's Seminole families depended on the tourist trade, as well. The big alligator farms pulled people in, and then they stayed and paid good tourist dollars for airboat rides, canoe treks along the endless canals at sunset, and even camping in traditional chickees. The locals made money, which was good, because they needed it.

Of course, the biggest earner in the area was the casino. Still, there were a lot of other good ways to make a living from tourists. Either way, it was money honestly earned, and to Jesse, the setting alone was worth the price of admission. The Everglades was a unique environment, and though civilization was steadily encroaching on the rare, semitropical wilderness, it was still just that: a wilderness. Deep in the "river of grass," a man could be so entirely alone with God and nature that civilization itself might not exist. There were miles and miles, acres and acres, where no one had as yet managed to lay a single cable or wire; there were places where even cell phones were no use. There were dangerous snakes and at times the insects were thick in the air. But it was also a place of peace unlike anything else he'd ever experienced. Every once in a while he thought of himself as a rare individual indeed—a man finally at peace with himself, satisfied with his job, and certain, most of the time, that he was the best man for it.

At least, he usually felt at peace with himself and as if he could make a difference in his work.

Today...

Today the world didn't make sense. That a couple as fine and hardworking as Maria and her husband could meet such a fate...hell, what good were the police then? Even if they solved the crime, his friends were still dead.

But thanks to his work, he wasn't powerless. He would find the killers and see justice done. That was his job, and it was one worth doing.

He wasn't making a fortune or knocking the world dead, but he didn't need money. He needed solitude, and the opportunity to be alone when he chose. And he needed to feel that he had some control over his own life and destiny, and this job certainly gave him that. Sometimes, he was very much alone, but that was a choice he had made, consciously or perhaps subconsciously, when he had lost Connie.

"Jesse!"

Harry Rogers, major stockholder and acting president and supervisor of Harry's Alligator Farm and Museum, hurried toward Jesse, who got out of his car. Harry was a big man, six foot two by what sometimes appeared to be six foot two of girth. He'd been born in a Deep South section of northern Florida, and he was proud of being a "Cracker," even if he'd gone on to acquire a degree in business administration from none other than such a prestigious Yankee institution as Harvard.

"Thank God!" Harry exclaimed, clapping him on the back. "We got a lady went berserk in the middle of Michael's speech, started screaming that he was going to get eaten up, and going on and on about how dangerous the gators were. I didn't want the Metro cops coming in here with their sirens blazing and all…and God knows, we don't need the community up in arms about the gators any worse than they already are, but…"

"Where is she?"

"My office, and is she a loose cannon or what? I'm telling you, she's downright scary. I've got Lorena, the new nurse, with her. We made her some tea, Lorena's talking to her, but she's still going off every few minutes or so."

Harry stopped talking and looked at Jesse closely. "Hey, what's the matter? You look grim."

"I am. An old Cuban couple in that new development east of here was murdered."

"How?"

"Shot."

"That your jurisdiction?" Harry asked, scratching his head.

"No, but they were friends."

"I'm sorry. Real sorry. Were they into drugs?"

That was the usual question, especially in a shooting. "No, it had nothing to do with drugs."

"You sure?" Harry asked skeptically.

Jesse gritted his teeth. "Yes, I'm sure."

"Well, if I can help…but at the moment, you've got to be a cop here for me, since this is your jurisdiction."

"All right. I'll see what I can do, but if this lady has really lost her mind, we may need some professionals out here, and we may have to call in the county boys."

"I hate the county boys."

"Hell, I like to settle our own problems, too, Harry. You know that."

"Sure do," Harry said. "'Course, you're the only man among us I've seen put those boys down."

"There are good county cops, Harry. We're a small community out here."

"We're an Indian community," Harry said dryly.

"Doesn't matter. We're small. You have to have the big boys around when you need real help. Hopefully, we don't need it now. Do you know where this woman is from? Has she said?"

Harry shook his head. "Every time we ask her, she goes on about her friend who was eaten. She's got to live near a lake somewhere, but that could be half the state. Don't that just beat all? The old broad has a friend eaten by a gator—so she comes to visit a gator farm. Folks are weird as hell, huh?"

"Folks are weird," Jesse agreed without elaborating. The whole thing was weird, he thought. The woman here had a friend who'd been eaten by an alligator.

A piece of an alligator had been found where two innocent people had been murdered.

He followed Harry in through a side entrance to the administrative buildings and down a long hallway.

The place might be an alligator farm out in the swamp, but Harry knew how to furnish an office. It was at the end of a long hallway. A single door opened onto a room with a massive oak desk surrounded by the best in leather sofas and chairs. To the rear were more seats, a large-screen TV, and state-of-the-art speakers for his elaborate sound system. Harry loved the Everglades; he even loved reptiles. He was part Creek, not Seminole or Miccosukee, but he'd worked his way up from cotton picking at the age of three to millionaire businessman, and he liked his creature comforts. His office might have been on Park Avenue.

Jesse could hear the woman as he followed Harry in. She was speaking in a shrill voice, talking about how nothing had been found of "Matty" other than a hand with a little flesh left on the fingers. Jesse glanced at Harry, then walked over to the woman, who was standing in a corner, flattened against the wall. Her hair was silver, her eyes a soft powder blue. She was trim and very attractive, except that now the flesh around her eyes was puffy from crying, and she gazed around with a hunted, trapped look of panic on her face.

In front of her, trying to calm her, was a young woman in a nurse's standard white uniform. Jesse couldn't see her face because a fall of sleek, honey-colored hair hid her features, but before she turned, he knew that he'd already met her.

And she was certainly the last person he'd expected to see at Harry's.

A woman who looked like that and drove a car like that, pedal to the metal...

To get *here?*

She stared back at him for a fleeting moment, instantly hostile—or defensive?

"You're going to get eaten!" the woman was shrieking, pointing at the nurse. "You've got to get out of here. Don't help these people breed monsters. They'll kill you, too. Crush you, drown you... Oh my God, a hand, a hand was all that was left…some flesh, just bits and pieces of flesh…."

"Hey, now, ma'am," Jesse said, stepping forward, trying to remember what he had learned in Psychology 101. "It's going to be all right, honest. Calm down. The alligators here are being raised as food. They're no danger to anyone on the outside—"

"They'll get loose!" the woman protested. But she had given Jesse her attention. He had kept his voice low, deep and calm—Psychology 101—and his firm tone seemed to be working with her. He stepped closer to her, reaching out a hand.

"They're not going to get loose. No one's going to let them get loose." He smiled. "Besides, Harry here is a charter member of the National Rifle Association. He and his staff wouldn't hesitate to shoot any gator that moved in the wrong direction. He's not out to save the gators, ma'am, he's out to make money off them."

She took his hand, staring into his eyes.

Next to him, Jesse heard a deep sigh of relief. He glanced at the woman standing by him, Harry's new nurse. Despite himself, he felt a little electric tremor.

Nature, simple biology, kicking in.

She was probably one of the most beautiful women he had ever seen.

Harry had a habit of finding pretty girls. Strange that a fat old man who owned an alligator farm could convince any young woman to come work in the middle of a swamp. Not that Harry was a lecher; he was as faithful as could be to Mathilda, his equally round and cheerful wife of thirty-odd years. But he did like attractive young people, and he had managed to fill the place with them, so this new nurse shouldn't have been too much of a surprise. Still, Jesse felt himself pause, as he hadn't in a very long time, staring at her.

Maybe it was just the day he'd had so far.

She looked back at him gravely, studying him with the same intensity as he had studied her. Then she looked down, biting her lower lip, embarrassed. In a moment she looked up again, straightening her shoulders and inclining her head, an acknowledgment that he had defused an uncomfortable situation. Her eyes were a dark-rimmed light hazel, startling against the classical, pure cream perfection of her face. Her hair was like a halo of crowning glory; she looked almost fragile in her blond beauty, yet he sensed that there was a lot of substance to her, as well.

He felt the warmth of the older woman's hand and, with a start, looked back to the gray-haired visitor—his current objective. He gave himself a little shake, surprised that Harry's new nurse had so impressed him, and continued to talk to the older woman. "It's okay. We're going to get you home. Except you're going to have to give us a bit of a hand to do that," he continued. "I'm Jesse Crane, a police officer out here. I'd like—"

"Oh!" the woman cried. "So now you're going to arrest me for telling the truth about these monsters and the horrible people purposely breeding them."

"No, ma'am, I just want to get you home and make sure you're going to be all right."

"Oh, like hell. You're just trying to shut me up!"

Jesse smiled at her. He couldn't help it. She was a tough old broad. She might be going over the edge, but she was going with passion and style.

"What's your name?"

"Theresa Manning."

"How do you do, Mrs. Manning? You're free to call the newspapers, or buy a banner ad and have a plane drag it through the sky. We guarantee freedom of speech in this country. But you're hot and miserable, and if you lost a friend to an alligator, this is not a good place for you to be. Let me take you home."

Theresa Manning hesitated, then sighed deeply.

"Where is your home?" he prodded.

"The Redlands."

"All right." He glanced at his watch. It was important to him that he meet Lars to go to the airport and pick up Julie Hernandez. "Let's go. Let me take you home now."

She nodded, looking at him. But as she rose, she suddenly gripped the nurse's hand.

"You, too. Please."

"But, Mrs. Manning—" the nurse protested.

"Please," Theresa Manning insisted.

"Go with her," Harry said softly to the nurse.

"Harry, I won't be able to bring her back for a while," Jesse said.

"Oh, please," Theresa Manning said, starting to grow hysterical again.

"Lorena, just go with him. When you get back, you get back!" Harry said impatiently.

Lorena's startling eyes fixed on Jesse's, and she said, "All right. If Mrs. Manning wants me with her, I'll be with her, and whatever you have to do, Officer, I'll wait until you're able to get me back. Shall we go?"

Jesse lifted his hands in surrender. He almost smiled. Maybe she felt this was her way of getting back at him for what had happened yesterday.

Fine. If she wanted to wind up involved in a murder

investigation and not get back until the wee hours of the morning, so be it.

"Yeah. Sure. Let's go," he said flatly. "Mrs. Manning?" He smiled, taking the older woman's arm. She actually smiled back.

He let Lorena follow behind as he escorted Theresa Manning from the office to his car.

Damn, this was one hell of a day.

CHAPTER FOUR

LORENA SAT IN the back of the car, while Theresa Manning sat in the front with Jesse Crane.

She felt somewhat useless being there, but the woman had been insistent. And though Lorena felt a twinge of guilt, aware that she had been eager to come not so much to help out—which she certainly was willing to do—but because she wanted the time with Jesse Crane.

As Sally had pointed out, the man was something special. But that wasn't why she was interested in him.

Despite the heavy traffic, he drove smoothly and adeptly. They left the Trail and headed south. He kept up a casual stream of conversation with Mrs. Manning, pointing out birds, asking about her home and family. By the time they neared her neighborhood, she seemed relaxed, even apologetic. Jesse told her not to be sorry, then suggested that she not take any more tours in the Everglades for a while.

At her house, she asked them in. Jesse very respectfully declined, but he gave her a card, telling her to call him if she needed him.

When they got back in the car, Lorena told him, "That was impressive."

He shrugged. "The woman isn't a maniac, just really upset. And maybe feeling that kind of rage we all do when something horrible has happened and we're powerless to change it." He glanced at his watch, then at her. "Sorry, I have to get to the airport, and it's not going to be pleasant."

"I told you…whatever you need to do…do it. I'll hang in the background," Lorena said.

He nodded, and after a few minutes she realized that he was heading for the turnpike. He glanced over at her, a curious smile tugging at his lips. "What brought you to our neck of the woods?" he asked her.

She shrugged, looking out the window. Then she looked at him sharply. "Well, I thought you'd already figured that out. I was racing out to one of the resorts. A spa. To be pampered."

"I'm sure you'll find time to slip out and hit some of the prime places," he said dryly.

"Really?" she murmured.

He couldn't resist a taunting smile. "You do your own hair and nails?" he asked.

"As a matter of fact, I do," she told him.

He shook his head. "You don't look the type," he said.

"You have to look a type to work out here?"

"You'll burn like a tomato in a matter of minutes," he warned her.

"They do make sunscreen," she returned.

"So…I repeat, what are you doing out here?"

"The job at Harry's," she said simply.

"There are nursing jobs all over the state. And most of them not in the Everglades."

She gazed over at him, surprised to realize that she was telling the truth when she said, "I like it out here."

"You're fond of mosquitoes the size of hippos and reptiles that grunt through the night?"

"I think the sunsets out here are some of the most beautiful I've ever seen. As to the alligators…well, they're just part of the environment, really. The birds are glorious. And the pay's exceptional."

"I see. Well, it's still a lonely existence."

It was her turn to smile. "Okay, so it may take an hour to get anywhere, but…it's a straight shot east to Miami and a straight shot west to Naples. Not so bad."

"I guess not. But in bad weather, you can be stuck out here and feel as if you're living in the Twilight Zone."

"You came back out here to work," she said softly.

There was silence for a minute. "This is home for me," he said.

"It's not so far off from home for me," she said.

"It's pretty far."

She glanced at him sharply.

"Jacksonville. I took your license, remember? And now that I know you were flying like a bat out of hell to reach Harry's, I'm more stunned than ever."

"I was starting a new job," she said defensively. "And however far it might be, I *am* from this state." Great. Now he was curious. What if *he* decided to investigate *her*?

She noticed that they had left the turnpike and were following the signs for the airport. He glanced at her again. "I'm meeting with a Metro-Dade detective. We're meeting a detective named Lars Garcia and picking up an old friend of mine." He hesitated just slightly. "That's why I didn't want you along. It's not going to be pleasant. Julie's parents were murdered last night."

"Oh, my God! I'm so sorry."

"I warned you."

"What happened?"

"They were shot," he said flatly.

She decided not to ask any questions for the next few minutes. He'd obviously been deeply affected by the murders.

They parked at the airport. Jesse knew where he was going and walked quickly. Lorena followed him. Outside the North Terminal, he walked over to a man in a plain suit, a man with light brown hair and green eyes, but dark brows and lashes. Even before she was introduced, Lorena knew that this was Lars Garcia.

She felt the keen assessment he gave her. Part of his job, she imagined. Summing people up quickly.

"So you're working out at Harry's?" he murmured.

She didn't have time to answer.

"There she is," Jesse said softly, spotting his old friend, Julie.

"I'll go," Lars Garcia offered.

But Jesse shook his head.

He left Lars and Lorena, and walked toward the dark-haired, exotic-looking Latin beauty who was coming their way. She was wearing glasses, apparently to hide the redness in her eyes, which was apparent when she saw Jesse and took them off. Then she dropped the overnight bag she'd been carrying and went into his arms, sobbing.

Lorena looked down, feeling like an intruder. "It's all right," Lars Garcia said softly.

She looked up at him.

"They're just good friends."

Lorena felt her cheeks flush hotly. "No, no, don't get the wrong impression. I'm just here…by accident, really. I barely know Officer Crane."

Lars Garcia continued to assess her as Jesse, an arm

around Julie, led her to where Lorena and Lars stood waiting.

"Julie, this is Detective Lars Garcia. He's in charge of the case," Jesse said. "And this is…Lorena. Lars, Lorena, Julie Hernandez."

Julie offered Lorena a teary, distraught but somehow still warm smile.

"Julie, I'm so sorry," Lorena murmured, feeling totally inadequate and wrenched by the girl's pain. She could all too easily remember the feelings of agony, frustration and fury, and always the question of why?

And after that, the *who?*

And now?

And now the gut-deep fury and determination that the truth would be known.

"Thank you." Julie looked at her for a long moment, as if sensing Lorena's sincerity. Then she turned to Garcia. "Whoever did this…why? My parents never hurt a soul in their entire lives."

"We're going to find out why," Lars vowed softly. "We need your help, though. We need anything you can give us."

Julie visibly toughened then, summoning her anger and determination from deep within, her inner reserves rising over the natural agony she was feeling. "I was just telling Jesse…I have no idea. They had no enemies. But I promise you, I'll help you in any way I can."

"Are you up to coming to the station with me now?" Lars asked. "It can wait, if you'd rather."

"No. No, I'll go now," Julie said, and swallowed. She looked at Jesse. "Jesse…?"

"Call me when you're done."

She nodded, trying to smile.

Lars took Julie's arm and cast a grateful glance over her dark head at Jesse.

The two walked off.

"I'm so sorry," Lorena said. She had never met the couple, but the sense of loss had seemed to envelop her. Impossible to see Julie and not feel it. She felt horrible, like an intruder, again. "I…wish there were something I could say, do."

Jesse nodded, then said only, "I can get you back now."

The silence, growing awkward between them, lasted as they left the airport, taking the expressway to the Trail, then heading straight down the road that stretched the width of the southern tip of the peninsula.

They passed homes and developments, and then the casino. After that, houses and businesses became few and far between.

She was startled when Jesse suddenly said, "Can you give me another half hour?" He turned and looked at her with those startling eyes of his. She wondered if he had decided he didn't feel quite so much contempt for her, or if he was merely so distracted he'd barely even been aware till then that she was there with him.

"I…of course. Of course. Harry said it was no problem," she murmured.

They pulled off onto something she wasn't sure she would have categorized as a road. As they proceeded along a winding trail, she realized that they were on farmland.

A minute later, she saw the crime tape. Jesse Crane pulled off the road.

"Excuse me. Stay here—I'll be just a minute," he said.

He exited the car, leaving her in the passenger's seat. Lorena hesitated for the briefest fraction of a second, then followed him.

She wasn't about to stay.

Jesse wasn't in the area enclosed by the tape. He was standing just outside of it, talking to a uniformed officer and a man in street clothes who had an ease in being there that suggested he was also a cop.

As she walked up, she could hear the man in street clothes talking. "Yeah, Doc Thiessen has the gator arm…the leg, whatever, that you discovered. I really don't see how it's going to help us. The Hernandezes were killed by bullets, not wildlife run amok!" He saw Lorena approaching before Jesse did, and he watched her, curiously and appreciatively, as she walked up to the scene.

Jesse turned to look at her with annoyance, a serious frown furrowing his brow.

"I told you to wait in the car," he said coldly.

"Hello, ma'am," the young uniformed officer said.

"Yes, hello," the man in plainclothes said. "How do you do? I'm Abe Hershall."

"Officer Gene Valley, ma'am," the uniform said.

"How do you do?" She shook hands with the tall, slender, dark-eyed man who was obviously a detective, and the uniformed officer. Jesse stood by silently, waiting, not apologizing for his rudeness, and certainly not offering any information about her.

"I'm working at Harry's," she said herself.

"The new nurse," Gene Valley said. "Well, welcome to the area."

"Thanks," she said softly.

"Working for old Harry, huh?" Abe Hershall said, shaking his head ruefully. "Well, good for Harry."

"This is a crime scene," Jesse reminded them all. "Ms. Fortier, now that you've met everyone, I believe it's time for me to get you back."

Taking Lorena by an elbow, he steered her forcefully back to the car.

"I can walk on my own," she said.

"I told you to stay in the car."

"It's a million degrees in there." She looked him in the eye. "Who was that?" she asked. "Abe...is he Lars's partner?"

"Yes."

He forced her determinedly back into the car. The door slammed. She gritted her teeth.

"You found a piece of a gator out there?" she asked when he was in the driver's seat.

"This is the Everglades. There are lots of alligators, and naturally, some die." He put the car in gear and started driving, his eyes straight ahead.

"But you found a *piece* of one."

Jesse slammed on the brakes, turned and stared at her, angry. Whether with her, or with himself, she wasn't sure. "Look, we found a piece of an alligator, yes. And I'd appreciate it if you would just shut up about it. I'm trying to keep that bit of information out of the press. You see, I'd really like to know if there's a connection between that and a murder. Damn! This is all my fault. I shouldn't have brought you out here, and I sure as hell shouldn't have counted on you staying in the car just because *I told you to!*"

Lorena looked straight ahead. "I have no intention of leaking any information," she said.

He stared at her. "Really? And should I ask for that as a guarantee, written in stone? After all, I don't know anything about you."

She grated her teeth. "Do I look like someone who would shoot an innocent couple?"

"No. But you don't look like someone who'd be working at Harry's, either," he said sharply.

She let out an explosion of exasperation. "I don't suppose you'd believe I actually like it out here?"

"Right. Nothing like being a nurse at an alligator farm," he murmured.

"Maybe it's just an easy gig," she said.

He didn't reply. Her heart sank. She had a feeling that he was going to know everything there was to know about her within the next forty-eight hours.

Maybe she should just tell him.

Maybe not. He obviously thought of her as some kind of fragile cream puff. Maybe a rich brat playing games. She shouldn't have brought her own car, she thought, hindsight bringing sudden brilliance.

If he found out anything about what she was doing, he might well find a way to get her out of Harry's—fast. Even that evening.

Could he do such a thing? Was he good friends with Harry—or whoever was involved?

She kept silent.

A few minutes later, they drove back into the complex that comprised Harry's Alligator Farm and Museum.

"Thanks," Lorena murmured, getting ready to hop out of the car as quickly as possible.

He caught her hand lightly. She held still, not meeting his eyes, but careful not to make any attempt to jerk free. She realized that he frightened her. Not because she thought he would hurt her, but because he aroused something in her, something emotional. She found herself waiting to tell him everything, wanting just to be with him.

"Be careful," he warned softly.

"Of...?" she murmured.

"Well, an elderly couple was just shot," he said impatiently.

"I'll be all right," she said. Then she pulled free. There was something far too unnerving about his touch. She didn't like the fact that though she barely knew him, she respected him already. Admired him. Even *liked* him. "Thanks."

"I'll be seeing you," he said pleasantly.

"Of course," she said, and then, at last, she managed to flee.

THERE WASN'T MUCH daylight left, but since Ginny had called in to the station several times saying that Billy Ray hadn't yet come home, Jesse decided it was time to check out his fishing spots.

Billy Ray was lazy, a creature of habit, and Jesse wasn't surprised when he found the man's beat-up old boat at his first stop in the vast grounds off the Trail.

The boat had been floating in the middle of the canal—already suspicious—and there was no sign of Billy Ray.

Jesse began walking along the embankment. At first he let his mind wander, mentally reminding himself that he had a record of Lorena Fortier's driver's license, enough to find out something about the woman. Frankly, he admitted to himself, he was worried about her. He could hardly say that he knew her from their two encounters, but there was something about her eyes, about the very real compassion she had shown the elderly woman, that made him feel she was—despite his original assessment—a decent human being.

There was something about her that made him feel a lot more, as well. Now that he'd gotten closer to her, it was far more than the simple fact that she was stunning, though that was good for a swift, hot rise of the libido. She was quick to show empathy, and in the right way. She seemed to sense pain and use her warmth to heal it. Her energy was electric.

Sensual.

He swore out loud, reminding himself that he was here trying to determine what had happened to Billy Ray Hare.

Still…

She had roused not just his senses, but thoughts that he had kept at bay for a long time. There was nothing casual about her. She evoked real interest—and very real desire. But, he realized, not the kind that could be easily sated, then forgotten.

What was it about her?

Her eyes? Her behavior? Or the way she looked? Like a blond goddess, tempting in the extreme.

He mentally shook his head, reminding himself again that this wasn't the time to discover that there was life not just in his limbs, but in his soul. Two good people had been murdered, and Billy Ray was missing. This definitely wasn't the time to be feeling a stab of desire just because a woman had walked into his neck of the woods.

Still, even as he concentrated his attention on the wet

ground, the endless saw grass and the canal, he felt a strange sense of tension regarding *her*.

She was involved. Somehow, she was involved.

Just as that thought came to his mind, he found Billy Ray.

What was left of him.

SALLY FINISHED UP with the day's entrance receipts, locked her strongbox and papers in the safe, and smoothed back her hair. Quite a day. All the commotion.

So much going on. Admittedly, most of the time so little went on here. That was why she had to make things happen. With that in mind, she started humming.

She was done for the day.

She walked determinedly down the hallway. News, any little bit of it, spread like wildfire around here. She loved to be the first to know any little tidbit.

She headed across the center of the complex.

"Hey, Sally!"

She smiled at the man leaning against one of the support poles.

"Hey, yourself," she said softly. Teasingly. It got boring out here, after all.

"Got anything for me?" he asked softly, since there were still both tourists and co-workers around.

She walked up to him, smiled, placed a hand lightly on his chest. "Maybe," she murmured seductively.

"Maybe?"

"Well, it depends."

"On what?"

"On what *you've* got for *me,*" she whispered.

She let her hand linger for a moment. A promise, just like her whisper. Then she walked away.

She could be warm; she could give.

But she fully intended to receive in return. After all, there was pleasure.

And then there was business.

THE GATES HAD CLOSED; the last of the tourists were flooding out as Lorena returned. She headed straight for her room, a quick shower and a change of clothes.

Though she wasn't accustomed to choosing her wardrobe for the purpose of seduction, she did so that night. A soft, pale blue halter dress seemed the right thing—cool enough for the summer heat, a garment that molded over the human form. She brushed her hair until it shone, then played with different ways to part it. She found a few of the effects amusing, but decided to go back to a simple side part and a sleek look. A touch of makeup, and she was off.

She found Dr. Michael Preston in the company cafeteria. The kitchen was centrally located between the employee dining area/lounge and the massive buffet area where visitors were welcome. During the day, a head chef worked with two assistants and three buffet hostesses. By night, only the offerings of the day and two cafeteria workers remained.

Alligator—sautéed, fried and even barbecued—was always on the menu. Lorena had dined on it in the past, but tonight she didn't want it, not in any form.

As she'd expected, she saw Michael Preston—who hadn't ordered gator, either—sitting with the keepers, the blond Australian, Hugh Humphrey, and the tall, striking Seminole, Jack Pine.

The three men rose as she approached. Jack whistled softly. "Wow! And welcome. Are you joining us?"

"If you don't mind."

"Are you kidding?" Hugh demanded pleasantly.

"You're definitely a breath of beautiful fresh air around this place," Jack assured her.

"Please," Michael Preston said, pulling out a chair.

She smiled, thanked him and sat down.

"I heard we had a bit of a freak-out today, and that you went with Jesse to take the woman home," Jack said. "Bizarre, huh?"

"Her friend was…eaten," Lorena said softly. "Why she was out here after that, I don't know."

Michael made an impatient sound. "Do you know what happens most of the time when gators kill? Some idiot thinks you can feed them like you feed the ducks at a pond." He shook his head. "First we destroy their natural habitat. Every year, development spreads farther west, into the Everglades. Naturally there are waterways. Then people wonder what the alligators are doing in their canals."

"Well, trust me," Jack said ruefully, his tone light and teasing, "you're not going to stop progress."

Hugh looked at Lorena seriously. "You're not afraid of being eaten, are you?"

She shook her head. "Trust me, I have no intention of feeding the gators. I'll leave that to you guys."

"Man is not the alligator's natural prey," Michael said. "Go out to Shark Valley. You can walk those trails, and, trust me, there are hundreds of gators around, but they don't bother anyone."

"It really is unusual, and there's always a reason, when a human is attacked," Jack explained. "Most of the time Hugh and I get called because a gator has strayed into a heavily populated area. We catch it and bring it back out to the wilds. The end."

"Do you ever keep the ones you 'rescue'?" Lorena asked.

"No. We breed our own alligators here," Michael said. "Harry's been here a long time now. He started up with a small place when they were still really endangered, so a couple were captured. But now all our gators are farm raised, because they do make good eating. And their hides make spectacular leather. Farms like this one are an important part of the state's economy. They're much more than just tourist attractions."

Lorena smiled. "They really are fascinating creatures," she told Michael. "I'm absolutely intrigued by your work."

"Cool," Jack said, folding his arms over his chest and leaning back. "We get a nurse who not only patches up our scrapes, she's into the entire operation. I hear that you don't mind working with the tour groups, either."

She shrugged. "I'd die of boredom here if I weren't interested."

"Hey, did you want something to eat?" Jack asked her.

She turned slightly to see that one of the remaining kitchen workers was standing by her side.

"Mary, have you met Lorena yet?" Jack continued, speaking to the heavyset woman at his side.

Mary shook her head, then pointed across the room to where Harry was sitting, engaged in conversation with Sally.

"The boss said to check on you," Mary said, looking at Lorena. "Usually people come up to the buffet. So are you hungry? You'd better eat now. We break down in half an hour, then there's nothing except the vending machines until morning—unless you want to drive for an hour to find something open." She shrugged. "You go into Miami, you got some places open twenty-four hours a day. But you want to drive back here in the middle of the night?" Mary shuddered. She'd been looking grim, but then she smiled. "You want some alligator?"

"Um, actually, no, thank you," Lorena said. "Is there another choice?"

"There's always chicken," Michael offered, grinning at last.

"How about a salad?" Lorena asked. She wasn't a vegetarian; she just didn't think that at the moment she wanted meat of any sort. Especially crocodilian.

"Caesar?" Mary suggested.

"Lovely."

"Of course, we do offer the caesar with a choice of chicken, sirloin or alligator," Mary said.

"A plain caesar would be perfect," Lorena said.

Mary shrugged, as if a plain caesar was probably the least appetizing thing in the world. "Something to drink?"

Lorena ordered iced tea and thanked Mary, assuring her that she would know to go to the buffet herself from then on.

When Mary was gone, Jack Pine nudged Lorena, his dark eyes dancing with amusement. "She's all right, really. Just a bit grim."

"She doesn't like alligators at all," Michael said.

"Why does she work out here?" Lorena asked.

"Harry pays well," Michael said. He leaned forward suddenly. "The guys and I were going to head to the casino for a few hours. Want to come?"

"We'd love to have you," Jack said.

"You look far too lovely to hang around here," Hugh said, grinning.

If they were all leaving, this might well be her best chance to get into Michael's laboratory. She yawned. "Actually, I'd love to take you guys up on that, but at a later date? I'm just getting accustomed to my new surroundings, and I'm feeling pretty tired."

"You really should come," Michael said, placing a hand over hers.

She smiled at him, as if enjoying the contact. "I will. Next time," she said sweetly.

Mary arrived with her salad. The men remained politely waiting for her to eat, then rose together when she was done. Lorena said that she would walk them out to the parking lot, then head for her room.

The three men climbed into Jack Pine's Range Rover, and she waved.

As soon as they were gone, she headed for the inner workings of the museum.

And Dr. Michael Preston's lab.

LARS AND ABE stood by Jesse on the embankment, watching as the M.E. bagged the remnants of Billy Ray.

At the moment, Jesse felt the weight of the world on his shoulders.

There was no one else who could go to see Ginny. This was going to be his responsibility, and with the Metro-Dade force on the scene, that meant he could go to her now.

But he hesitated, seeing the floodlights illuminate the immediate darkness and feeling the oppressive heat of the ebony beyond.

"I don't believe it," Lars said, staring in the direction of the M.E., shaking his head.

"I'm not quite sure I do, either," Jesse said. He pointed. "The best I can figure it, Billy Ray was in his boat. His shotgun was still in it, and it had been fired. It looks as if an alligator actually rammed the boat, Billy fell out, and...well, you know how they kill; shaking their prey, then drowning it."

"Alligators don't ram boats," Lars said.

"Looks like this one did," Jesse said.

Abe frowned, staring at Jesse. "Alligators may follow a boat, looking for a hand out—literally." He smiled grimly. "But they don't ram boats. I'd say maybe someone was out here with Billy Ray. Maybe they fought. Maybe Billy Ray even shot at him. Then the fight sent him overboard, and a hungry old male might have been around. A really hungry old male, since we all know gators don't choose humans."

"Gentlemen, this is my neck of the woods, and God knows, I want tourists out here as much as anyone, but I'd say it was time we get some kind of warning out," Jesse said.

"Warning?" Abe protested. "Like what? Don't head into the Everglades? Killer alligators on the loose?"

"Yeah, something like that," Jesse said flatly.

Abe shook his head. "Jesse, you're nuts. What do you want to do, destroy the entire economy out here?"

"I'll tell you this, I intend to issue a warning," Jesse said.

"Hey, you do what you want," Abe said.

"What the hell are you saying?" Jesse demanded, his temper rising. "We all know that Billy Ray was killed by a gator."

"How do we know that?" Abe demanded. "Seriously. You do an autopsy I don't know about?"

Jesse stared at him, incredulous. "What?"

"We have a ripped-up body. You said yourself that Billy Ray's gun had been shot. Maybe someone shot back at him, he wound up in the water, bleeding, and then the gator attacked him. That's a far more likely scenario."

"Stop it," Lars protested. "Both of you. We've got a bad situation here."

"Yeah, we do. A couple shot to death—with the remains of an alligator found nearby. Now a fellow who knew this place better than any living human being, killed by an alligator. If that isn't enough—" Jesse said.

"That couple were killed because they saw something going on in the swamp—I'd lay odds on it. And alligators don't shoot people," Lars argued. "These incidents are totally unrelated."

Jesse just stared at him, so irritated he longed to take a jab at Abe's out-thrust, obstinate jaw. Instead, he turned and walked away. "You do what you want. So will I."

"Hey!" Lars called after him.

Jesse turned back.

"Jesse…you may want to be on the lookout for a… well, I don't know. A rogue alligator. A big one," Lars suggested.

"Yeah. Are you going to contact the rangers, or should I?" Jesse asked.

"I'll see that they're notified," Lars assured him grimly.

Abe snorted. "Yeah. We'll handle this one by the book. This is your neck of the woods, Jesse. Billy Ray was one of yours. Homicide only comes in when we've got a murder. We'll see that the site is investigated, and then we'll sign off on it. This is your ball game."

"And I'll get warnings out on Indian land. And I also intend to arrange a hunt."

"It ain't season, Jesse," Abe said.

Jesse crossed his arms over his chest. "Maybe not, but it *is* tribal land. Like you said, it's my call. At the least, we're talking about a nuisance animal. I'll be taking steps."

Abe threw up his hands.

"This one is your call, Jesse," Lars told him.

"Fine. And you know the call I've made. You put out the warnings in your territory."

"Because of one alligator?"

"How do we know it's just one?" Jesse demanded.

"And how do we know Billy Ray didn't just drink himself silly, then irritate the creature—a normal, everyday predator that happens to live out here—and make the mistake of going in right where a big boy was hungry?"

"What was an alligator limb doing out where Hector and Maria were killed?" Jesse demanded.

Abe shook his head. "People murdered with big guns—and a natural predator attack. There's no damned connection!"

"Hey," Lars said. "The matter will be under investigation."

"Abe, I'm warning you, there could be a lot more trouble," Jesse said.

"Great. I'm warned," Abe said.

"Jesse, no one is going at this with a closed mind," Lars assured him. "Hell, I'm a cop, not a kindergarten teacher. We're professionals. We'll complete our investigation of the scene and sign this one over to you. Abe, dammit—you know as well as I do that anything is possible. All right, children?"

"Sure," Abe said.

"Yeah," Jesse said. "You're right. And now I have to go talk to a woman about the fact that her husband is dead."

Abe snorted. "She should be relieved."

Lars exploded, swearing.

Jesse turned away.

He couldn't put it off any longer. He had to go to see Ginny.

And then...

Then he would have to talk to Julie.

The night ahead seemed bleak indeed.

CHAPTER FIVE

SINCE SHE WAS carrying a lock pick in her purse, Lorena had no problem waving with a smile as the car drove away, then heading straight back inside and down the hall to Dr. Michael Preston's lab.

She stood for several seconds in the hallway, but the place was entirely empty.

There were guards on duty, of course. But they were outside, protecting the alligator farm. She had made a point in the beginning of seeing whether there were cameras in the hallways, but there weren't—not unless they were exceptionally well hidden.

She headed for the door, reaching into her purse.

"Lorena!"

Stunned, she spun around. Michael was there in the hallway, right behind her.

"Hey!" she said cheerfully, approaching him quickly.

"I thought you were going to get some rest tonight?" he said, frowning.

"I changed my mind. I was hoping to find you."

"In the hallway? You just waved goodbye to us."

"I don't know—sixth sense, maybe. You're back, and I'm so glad. I can still go with you. If you're still going."

He nodded. "I forgot my cell phone, so I came back to get it."

"Great. I'll wait for you."

He nodded, still appearing puzzled, but she kept her smile in place, following him into the lab.

The hatchlings squeaked from their terrariums.

Lorena stood politely by the door, waiting. As she had before, she inventoried what she could see of the lab.

The file cabinets. Michael's desk. The pharmaceutical shelves. The computer.

He took his cell phone from the desktop, then joined her. She linked arms with him, and felt the tension in him ease.

"Are you a poker player?" he asked her.

"Not really," she admitted.

"There's not too much else," he warned.

"I love slot machines," she assured him.

He smiled back at her. Apparently her attempt at flirtation was working. He slipped an arm around her shoulders. He was a good-looking man, with a sense of humor, and though it seemed he sometimes wondered if he were too much of an egghead in comparison with the rugged handlers, he apparently also had faith in his own charisma. "Let's head out, then, shall we?" he asked, and there was a husky note in his voice. If she was happy in his company, it apparently wasn't too big a surprise to him.

Then again, she'd been trying to keep the right balance. Flirt just the right amount with the bunch of them.

"Let's head out," she agreed, and she fell into step with him, aware of his arm around her shoulder—and also aware that the lab was where she really needed to be.

JESSE HAD A feeling that Ms. Lorena Fortier from Jacksonville would be quite surprised when she learned that the Miccosukee police department currently consisted of a staff of twenty-seven, nine of them civilian employees, the other eighteen officers deployed throughout the community in three main areas: north of the Everglades in Broward County; the Krome Avenue area, encompassing the casino and environs; and the largest center of tribal operations, on the Tamiami Trail. The pay was good, and the Miccosukee cops were a respected group. The department had been created in '76, because most of the tribal areas were so remote that a specific force was necessary to protect the community, and to work with both the state and federal agencies in tracking down crime.

Jesse wondered if Lorena was under the impression that he was working as the Lone Ranger.

Before he made his dreaded trip to Ginny's place, he returned to the station. His crews were up on everything that happened in the jurisdiction, but he hadn't been back in himself yet, and he disliked being in a situation where communication wasn't tight as a drum.

The night crew was coming on, but he was in time to catch the nine-to-fivers and give everyone his personal briefing on both the double homicide and the death of Billy Ray.

He liked being at the office; he wasn't a one-man show, but the department was still small enough that every officer and civilian employee knew that they mattered, and that their opinions were respected. He got the different departments researching activities in the area, possible drug connections, the backgrounds of Hector and Maria, and anything that might strike their minds as unusual, or any kind of connection.

Barry Silverstein, one of the night patrolmen, was

especially interested in the alligator limb that had been brought to the veterinarian for examination. "Strange that you found only a piece," he said. "Think maybe we're looking for a poacher?" he asked.

"Could be," Jesse said. "But it's not likely. We have an alligator season, and a license is easy enough to obtain. Besides, the alligator farms have pretty much taken the profit out of poaching."

"Kids?" Brenda Hardy, the one woman on night duty, inquired. "You know, teenagers, maybe. Or college students. Say that the piece of the alligator has nothing to do with the murders. Maybe some kids pledging a fraternity or just making ridiculous dares to one another."

"I sure hope it's not a trend," Barry said. "They may have gotten that gator, but you start playing around with some of the big boys out there...well, hell, we know what they're capable of."

"Poor Billy Ray," Brenda said sadly, shaking her head. She was a pretty woman, tall and slim, and all business. She was light-skinned and light-haired, probably of Germanic or Nordic descent. You didn't have to be Native American to be on the force. Barry, who was Jewish and had had ancestors in the States so long he didn't know where they'd originally come from, always liked to tease her that she was an Indian wannabe. Brenda had once gravely shut him up by assuring him that she had been a Native American in her previous life.

"I'll tell you frankly that this situation scares the hell out of me. These people are brutal and ruthless. Everyone has to be alert," Jesse warned.

George Osceola, one of the Native officers on the force, a tall man with huge shoulders and a calm, controlled way of speaking that made him even more imposing, had been watching the entire time. He spoke then. "Jesse, you think these incidents are related, don't you. How?"

"That's what I can't figure. Murders that cold-blooded are usually drug related. And we're not ruling that out," Jesse said.

"Could we be dealing with some kind of cult?" George asked.

"I don't know. What I do believe is that we've got to get to the bottom of it fast. George, ask questions, see if anyone has seen anything out of the ordinary. People coming through who aren't out to enjoy nature or a day at the village. Strangers who hang around. Anything out of the ordinary. *Anything.* Metro-Dade homicide is working the murders. I'm afraid we may find the killers closer to home."

"We'll all be on it," Brenda said.

Jesse nodded. "Brenda, do me a favor. Get background investigations busy for me, will you?"

"On the Hernandez family?" Brenda asked, sounding puzzled.

"No. On a woman named Lorena Fortier. I just wrote her a ticket, so we'll have her driver's license information. Find out more about where she comes from, what she's been doing."

"Lorena Fortier?"

"She just started working at Harry's."

"All right," Brenda said, still puzzled, but asking no more questions.

"You going out to Ginny's now?" Barry asked.

"Yeah," Jesse said. "And then to see Julie."

No one replied. No one offered to take on the responsibility. He didn't want them to, and they knew it. These were things he had to do.

He left to see Ginny, and it was rough. As rough as he had expected.

Eventually he left Ginny with her sister and niece, both of whom apparently thought that Billy Ray had come by accident to an end that he deserved. Thankfully, they weren't saying that to Ginny, though; they just holding her and soothing her. Anne, Ginny's niece, had told him that as soon as possible, she was going to take her aunt away for a while. For the moment, they had called the doctor, who had prescribed a sedative for her.

Before he left, Ginny had gripped his hand. Her large dark eyes had touched his.

"Help me, Jesse—please. Find out…find out what happened."

"Ginny, he met with a mean gator," her sister said.

But Ginny shook her head. "Billy Ray knew gators. Jesse, you have to help. I have to know…*why*. Oh, God, oh, God…Jesse I need to know, and you're the only one who can help."

With her words ringing in his ears, he had gone on to meet Julie.

Hell of a night.

So now he sat with his old friend in the upstairs bar of the casino hotel where she had chosen to stay. Julie had told him that she appreciated his offer to let her stay at his place, but she had wanted to be closer to the city and couldn't quite bring herself to stay in her parents' house.

He agreed that she shouldn't stay at her folks' house—certainly not alone. Neither he nor the Metro-

Dade police had any idea what had happened, and the houses in that area were way too few and far between for him to feel safe with her there.

"I'm telling you, Jesse, there's no way my folks were connected to anything criminal," Julie said, at a loss. "I'd give my eyeteeth to help. In fact…I think I could kill with my own bare hands, if I knew who did this. But they were as honest as the day is long."

"I know that, Julie."

She sighed, running a finger around the glass of wine she had ordered. "I'm glad you're on this, Jesse. The other guys…they didn't know my folks."

"Lars is a good man. So is Abe. A bit of an ass, but a good detective."

That brought a hint of a smile to her lips. "Still, no matter what you tell people…everybody seems certain that my dad had turned a blind eye to some drug deal, at the very least. The thing is, you and I both know that there was no such thing going on."

"Of course." He patted her hand. "Did your mom or dad ever say anything to you about anything strange going on out there?"

Julie shook her head. "No." She hesitated, frowning. "Actually, once…" She fell silent, shrugging.

"Once what?"

"Oh, something silly. It can't have anything to do with what happened," Julie said.

Jesse touched her hand. "Julie, I don't care how silly you may think something sounds. Tell me what it is."

"Um, well, I lose track of time, but a few days ago, maybe a week, when I was talking to my mom, she was getting into talking about ETs. You know, extra-terrestrials."

"Oh?"

"She said there were weird lights. I'm sure it was just someone out in an airboat, but…"

"But?"

"Well, my mom was getting on in years, but her vision was good. She thought the lights were coming from the sky. That's why she got it into her head that aliens were searching the Everglades."

"A lot of planes come in that way," Jesse pointed out.

"The lights from planes don't stay still."

"Helicopters," Jesse said.

Julie shrugged. Then her face crumpled and she began to cry. Jesse didn't try to tell her that it would be okay. He just came around the table and held her.

Helicopters. If anything big had been going on—the police searching for someone, for instance—he would have known about it.

Maria had had fine eyesight, no more fanciful than the next person. And she had seen lights.

Jesse knew that there had been an airboat behind the house the night Julie's parents had been killed. That wasn't surprising. Airboats abounded. But helicopters…

They were uncommon, especially in that area. Not unless someone was looking for something.

But in the middle of the night?

"Jesse, what could it have been?" Julie whispered, as if she had been reading his thoughts.

"I don't know. But I swear, Julie, I will find out."

THE CASINO DIDN'T compare with a place in Las Vegas or Atlantic City—there were no roulette tables and no craps—but it was nice, and it was apparently quite convenient for people in Miami with a free night but not the time to really get away.

It was thriving when they arrived.

The three men tried to encourage Lorena to try her hand at one of the poker tables, but she managed to convince them that she preferred slots and would be happy wandering around, just getting to know the place. There were several restaurants, and though there were tables offering free coffee, she opted for café con leche at the twenty-four-hour deli. She noted the numerous security officers and stopped to chat with one young man. His name was Bob Walker, and he had bright blue eyes, thanks to a dad who had come to the States from the Canary Islands, and superb bone structure, thanks to a Seminole mom. He told her that casino security departments and the Miccosukee Police were two separate entities, but of course they worked together, just as Security would work with the Metro-Dade police or any other law enforcement agency. He'd sounded a little touchy at first, but as they spoke, he explained with a grin, "Too many gamblers drink, lose and get belligerent. And they think we can't take care of them. We do. We have the authority."

She grinned. "I don't intend to get rowdy," she assured him.

He flushed, and she thanked him and went on.

The place was big, and she wandered a while before finding a slot machine that looked like fun. It had a little mouse, and a round where you got points for picking the right cheese. She liked the game—it might be stealing her money, but it was entertaining.

Out twenty bucks, she left to walk around some more.

It was fascinating, she thought. The crowd was truly

representative of the area, running the entire ethnic gamut. Miccosukee, Hispanic, Afro-American, and whatever the blend was that ended up as Caucasian on a census form.

She could see the poker tables and was aware that, from their separate poker games, the guys were also keeping an eye on her.

She was frustrated, throwing away quarters when she should have thought of a better lie when she had run into Michael in the hallway. This would have been the perfect time to have gotten into the lab. Still, since the mouse game was diverting, she went back to it. She was just choosing her cheese bonus when she was startled by an already familiar voice.

"What are you doing here?"

She looked up to see Jesse Crane, leaning casually against her machine. It made her uneasy to realize that his scent was provocative, and that he looked even better in his tailored shirt, khakis and sport jacket. When she glanced up, the bright green of his eyes against the bronze of his face was intense. She wouldn't want to face him at an inquiry, that was certain.

She wondered what it was about certain people that made them instantly attractive. About certain *men,* she corrected herself, and the thought was even more disturbing. Michael Preston was definitely good-looking; Hugh was charming; Jack Pine exuded a quiet strength. But Jesse Crane…just the sound of his voice seemed like a sexual stimulant. The least brush of his fingers spoke erotically to her innermost recesses. She was tempted to touch him, because just the feel of crisp fabric over muscled flesh would be arousing.

A blush was rising to her cheeks. She looked away

from his eyes, but her gaze fell on his chest. And then below.

She closed her eyes.

"Hello?" he said softly.

What *was* she doing here? She forced herself to focus. To shake off the ridiculous sensation of instant seduction and sensuality.

Nothing, frankly, accomplishing nothing. "Um… gambling," she murmured.

She arched a brow, shrugging as she looked at him and hit the button on the machine again. "Losing money. What about you?"

He shrugged. "I live in the area."

"So do I, remember?"

"Who did you come with?"

"A group from Harry's."

"And who would that group be?"

"Michael, Jack and Hugh." She stared at the machine, trying not to let him see her mind working. "Are you out for a night on the town? Or just passing through?" Her machine did some binging and banging—three cheeses in a row. She had a return of ten dollars. Not bad.

"Why?" he asked.

"Just curious. Well, actually, if you're heading out…" She yawned, moving away from the machine. "I'm not much of a gambler. I was thinking of going back, but I came with the guys."

"I'll give you a ride," he told her. "Who should we tell you're leaving? Michael?"

"Um…any of them, I guess," she murmured. *Not Michael. He might get suspicious.* "Hugh is right there—we'll just tell him."

She slid off the stool, ready to head for Hugh's poker table.

"Aren't you forgetting something?" Jesse asked.

"What?"

"Your money."

"Oh. I didn't lose it all?"

"No. There's more than a hundred dollars there."

"Oh. Of course I want it," she said.

His eyes seemed to drill right through her. "Do you?" he inquired lightly. "I didn't think money means a thing to you."

She ignored him and gave her attention to the machine, hitting the "cash out" button.

"You have to wait for an attendant," he told her. "I'll let Hugh know you're leaving."

"Sure. Thanks."

The place was busy, the wait for an attendant long. She was ready to leave her winnings for some lucky stranger, she was so antsy, but she didn't know whether she was being watched. By the time they actually left, she fumed silently, the men might well be right behind them.

Finally, money stuffed into her bag, Lorena hurried past the slots and found Jesse waiting for her at the end of the row.

She quickly checked to make sure that the three men from the alligator farm were still at their tables.

They were.

"Sure you want to go?" Jesse inquired.

"Yes, thank you."

As they turned to leave, he set his palm against the small of her back, nothing more than a polite gesture.

Even so, she felt that touch as if she had connected with a live electric current.

Outside, Jesse didn't speak as he politely seated her on the passenger side and slid behind the wheel.

She felt the silence.

"Thanks for taking me back," she said nervously.

"Not a problem."

Again there was silence. Uncomfortable silence. It should have been a casual drive. It wasn't. It felt as if the air between them was combustible.

"Is our casino a little too tame for you?" he asked at last.

"No. Honestly, I liked it a lot. All I ever play is slots, anyway. I don't understand craps, so it doesn't matter to me if there's a table or not. I guess I'm just not that much of a gambler."

"I'd say you were."

"Pardon?"

He glanced at her sharply. "Oh, you take chances. Racing out here like the wind. Working at Harry's. Going out with three men you've barely met. Especially when there have just been two truly gruesome murders in the area." His tone was amazingly matter-of-fact.

"I hardly think I'm in danger with my co-workers."

He didn't say any more until they had taken the turn into Harry's. She was digging in her purse for the pass that would open the door after hours when he startled her by leaning over and gripping her shoulder. The force was electric, and when she looked at him, she was certain she had guilt written all over her features.

"I really don't understand why you're lying to me. Or what makes you think I'm such a fool that I believe you. What are you doing here?" he demanded roughly.

"Working!"

"You know I'll have you checked out by morning," he said.

She prayed that he couldn't feel the trembling that was suddenly racing through her.

"Go right ahead. Check me out. I'm an RN. You'll find that to be a fact." She reached for the door handle.

"You're playing with fire."

"I'm working. Earning a living."

"Two people, shot. I'd bet everything I have that the killer or killers didn't even know them. It was cold-blooded murder, as cold as it gets."

"Look, I know you're going to check me out. Believe me, you won't find a criminal record. I'm out here to work."

"Right." The green of his eyes was sharp, even in the dim light. "You've come down here to start over, start a new life, that's all."

"May I get out of the car now?"

He released her. The sudden loss of his touch created a chill.

Tell him the truth!

But she couldn't. She had nothing to go on. And he couldn't help, not if she couldn't offer him some kind of proof. And, anyway, could she be certain, absolutely certain, that he wasn't in any way involved?

Actually, yes. Somewhere deep inside, based on instinct, she simply knew the man was completely ethical.

But she didn't dare speak. He would send her packing.

"I'll tell you what you're not," he said softly.

"Oh?"

"A very good liar. So whatever you're up to, God help you."

She stared straight at him. "I am a registered nurse."

"And what else?"

"I dabbled in psychology, but a lot of those classes went toward the nursing degree."

"So you came down here to bandage knees and psychoanalyze the great American alligator?" he inquired dryly. "What else should I know about you?"

"There's this—I'm really tired," she told him.

"And stubborn as hell. You've barely arrived and everything has gone insane. So I'm going to hope that you're not dangerously stupid—or carelessly reckless."

She wondered how he could simply look at her and be able to read everything about her. Or was she that transparent to everyone?

It's just him, she thought with annoyance. Even when he wasn't touching her, it somehow felt as if he was. And even when he grilled her, she was tempted to lean closer to him, to do anything just to touch him, feel a sense of warmth. Even with so much at stake, no matter how she tried to control her mind, it kept running to thoughts of what it would be like just to lie beside him....

"May I get out of the car now?" she asked again, once more feeling drawn to tell him that she actually wanted to stay. Put her head on his shoulders. Tell him the whole truth. But she didn't dare.

"Well, I can't arrest you. At the moment." He turned away from her, shaking his dark head. "Good night, Ms. Fortier. And lock your door," he said.

"I intend to," she assured him, then exited the car as

quickly as she could. Her fingers slipped on the little plastic ID entry card. She had to work it three times.

At last the door opened.

Jesse waited until she was inside, then drove away.

When he was gone, she didn't bother heading toward her own room. She walked straight to Michael Preston's lab. With no one around, she surprised herself with her ability to quickly pick the lock.

She knew it was dangerously stupid as she checked the big wall clock over the door, but she didn't stop. The hatchlings began to squeal the minute she entered the room.

Almost as if they sensed prey.

She ignored the sound and started with the desk drawers, then the computer. She knew that she would need a password to access his important files, but she hoped to study his general entries and discover whether he was involved or not.

The clock ticked as she worked. She read and read, keeping an eye on the clock.

Almost an hour since she had left the casino.

Regretfully, she turned off the computer and made a last survey to assure herself she'd left nothing out of order.

Then she left the room, quietly closing the door behind her. She listened for the lock to automatically slip into place.

Just in time. As she hurried down the hall, she heard voices. She quickly turned the corner, out of sight.

"If you're not bright enough to ask that woman out on a real date, I will."

Lorena recognized the voice. It was Hugh.

Michael answered, laughing dryly, "Yeah, well, I

kind of thought that she was interested. But she lit out like a bat out of hell once Jesse arrived."

"She's not a poker player. One of us should have stayed with her."

"Is that it?" Michael said dryly. "Women *have* been known to find Jesse appealing."

"Yeah, and then they find out that they're lusting after the unobtainable."

"He won't be grieving forever," Michael said. "And either she went with him because she wanted to, or..."

"Or what?" Hugh demanded sharply.

"Or she wanted to get back here without the three of us."

She heard the rattle of the lab doorknob then. "Locked," he murmured.

"I'm asking her out," Hugh said. "For an airboat ride. That's innocent enough."

"Hey, every man for himself, huh?" Michael said.

Hugh laughed. "Yep, every man for himself."

She heard the lab door open and shut. Not knowing if Hugh had joined Michael or would be heading on down the hallway, Lorena fled.

As soon as she reached her own room, she thought of Jesse's warning and made sure her own door was locked.

Then she dragged a chair in front of it, wedging it tightly beneath the knob.

Still, it was a long time before she slept.

JESSE SAT OUTSIDE the alligator farm complex, watching.

He'd left, parked on the embankment, and waited.

Once he'd seen Preston's car return, he'd counted

the seconds carefully, then slipped his car back into gear to follow.

Just in the shadows, off the drive near the main entrance, he parked.

He spent the night in the car, his senses on alert.

The grunts of the gators, loud in the night, sounded now and then, sometimes just one or two, sometimes a cacophony.

Strange creatures. He'd been around them all his life. They were an amazing species, having survived longer than almost any other creature to have walked the earth.

Their calls and cries could be eerie, though.

He stayed until daybreak, waiting, though for what, he wasn't certain. Something. Some sign of danger.

Dawn broke. Light came softly, filling the horizon with pastels. There was a breeze. Birds cried and soared overhead.

He began to feel like a fool.

Then he heard the scream.

CHAPTER SIX

LORENA BOLTED OUT of the bed, stunned and disoriented. The first sharp, staccato shriek that had awakened her had been followed by other screams and cries.

She threw on a robe and went flying out of her room, down the hall, and then burst out back to the ponds, the area from which the sounds of distress were still coming.

Then she heard the distant sound of sirens.

It was far too early for the gates to have opened to tourists, and she couldn't imagine what had happened. Her heart was thundering as she saw that most of the employees had gathered around the deep trench pond where Old Elijah was kept.

The biggest, meanest alligator in the place.

At first she stood on the periphery of the crowd, trying to ascertain what had happened, listening to the shouts that rose around her.

"How in hell did *he* fall in?" one of the waitresses asked, incredulous.

"Roger has been a guard here from the beginning… what would make him lean far enough over to fall in?" asked one of the ticket-takers.

"Jesse's in there now. He'll get him out," a feminine voice said.

Lorena swung around to see that Sally Dickerson

was there, threading her fingers through her long red hair. She turned to stare at Lorena. Where everyone else seemed to have eyes filled with concern, Sally's had a gleam. She was enjoying the excitement.

"What?" Lorena said.

"Jesse's gone in. He'll get Roger out."

Lorena wasn't sure who she pushed out of the way then, but she rushed to the concrete rim of the great dipped pond and natural habitat that held Old Elijah.

There was a man on the ground, next to the concrete wall. Jack Pine and Hugh Humphrey were there at the side of the wall, maneuvering some kind of rope-rigged gurney down to the fallen guard, who was apparently unconscious.

There was Jesse.

And there was Old Elijah.

The way the habitat was set up, there was the concrete wall and rim, a pond area, and then a re-creation of a wetland hummock.

The great alligator had so far remained on the other side of the water. He watched with ancient black eyes as Jesse Crane moved with care to manipulate the body of the fallen guard with the greatest care possible onto the gurney.

Jesse was no fool. He kept his eye on the alligator the whole time.

"Where the hell is Harry with that tranq gun?" Jack demanded hoarsely.

"Got him!" Jesse shouted. "Haul him up, haul him up!"

Tense, giving directions to one another as they brought up the gurney, the men were careful to raise it without unbalancing the unconscious figure held in place by buckled straps. Jesse helped guide the gurney until it was over his head.

And all the time, Old Elijah watched.

Motionless, still as death, only the eyes alive.

Others jumped in to help as the gurney rose. Jesse reached for the rope ladder that he'd come down and started up.

And then Old Elijah moved.

He was like a bullet, a streak of lightning. Someone screamed.

The massive jaws opened.

They snapped shut.

They caught the tail end of the rope ladder, and the great head of the beast began to thrash back and forth.

Jesse, nearing the top, teetered dangerously. A collective cry rose; then he caught the rim of the concrete barrier and hauled himself over.

At the same time, they heard the whistle of a shot.

Harry had arrived, holding a huge tranquilizer gun on his shoulder.

The dart struck Old Elijah on the shoulder.

At first, it was as if a fly had landed on his back, nothing more.

The gator backed away, drawing the remnants of the rope ladder with him. Then, as if he were some type of blow-up toy with the air seeping from him, Old Elijah fell. The eyes that had blazed with such an ancient predatory fervor went blank.

The crowd was cheering Jesse; med techs were racing up, and more officers had arrived to control the space and let the emergency techs work.

Jack slammed a hand on Jesse's shoulder. Hugh

shook his head and fell back against the barrier, relieved.

Jesse looked down into the enclosure, shaking his head as he stared at Old Elijah. Then his gaze rose, almost instinctively, and met Lorena's.

She stared back, oddly frightened to see the way his eyes narrowed as he regarded her, filled with suspicion. His mouth was hard. She flushed; he didn't look away.

Someone caught his attention, and he turned.

"Damn, Harry, it took you long enough to get that gun," Jack called, shaking his head.

"Jack Pine, you're the damned handler, so get a handle on what happened here," Harry shouted back.

"Calm down. We're going to have an inquiry," Jesse said.

"Inquiry?" Harry snorted. "Roger was out here by himself. What the fool was doing leaning over the concrete, I don't know. We'll just have to wait until he's regained consciousness to find out."

"Yeah, *if* he regains consciousness," Jack snorted. He was tense, and his features were hard as he stared at Harry.

"Hell of a thing—" Harry began, and then realized that he had an audience, more than a dozen employees hanging around. He stopped speaking and shook his head again. "This show's over, folks. Back to work, everybody back to work." Then he turned to Jesse. "Hell, Jesse, what kind of questions could anybody have?"

"That will come later. I'm getting in the ambulance copter with Roger," Jesse said, brushing past Harry.

He stared at Lorena again then. His features remained taut and grim, and his eyes now held…

A warning?

He hesitated, speaking to a couple of officers who had arrived along with the med techs, then hurried after the stretcher.

A man in one of the Miccosukee force uniforms spoke up, his voice calm and reassuring, yet filled with authority. "Go ahead, folks, get going. We'll be speaking with you all one by one."

The crowd slowly began to disperse. Harry was complaining to the officer. "I don't get it. What could your questions be? For some fool reason, Roger got stupid and leaned too far over the barrier. No one else was out here. Security was his job."

"Harry, we have to ask questions," the officer said. "Hey, if there were an outsider in here, giving Roger or anyone a problem, you'd want to know, right?"

"Well, yeah," Harry said, as if the idea had just occurred to him. "You boys go right ahead. Question everyone. Damned right, I'd want to know."

He turned to walk away, then saw that several of his employees hadn't left.

"Get going, folks. It's a workday, and this isn't a charity. So get to work. And everyone, give these officers your fullest cooperation." Then he walked away himself, followed by one of the officers.

Lorena nearly jumped a mile when she felt a hand on her shoulder. She swung around. Michael was there, looking sleepy, concerned but foggy, also clad in a robe.

"What the hell happened?"

She explained.

He shook his head. "Well, that's about as weird as it gets. Roger has been here forever. He should have known better."

"Would that alligator...Old Elijah...would he have eaten the man, do you think?" Lorena queried softly.

"He's really well fed, so...who knows," Michael said. "Eaten him? Maybe. More likely he just would have gotten angry, taken a bite, tossed him around, drowned him. Who knows. I don't question Old Elijah. There's only one thing I can say with certainty about alligators."

"And that is?"

Michael's eyes met hers directly. "That you'll never really know anything about them," he said flatly. "You'll never know what goes on behind the evil in those eyes."

JESSE SAT IN the back of the emergency helicopter, doing his best to keep out of the way of the men desperately working to save Roger's life. He didn't need to ask questions, not that they would be heard above the roar of the blades, not from where he sat. A glance at the med tech who had taken the man's vitals and affixed his IV line told him that Roger had not regained consciousness.

As soon as they reached the hospital, Jesse paced the emergency room waiting lounge. Hell of a place. He knew the hospital was good; one of the best in the nation for trauma. But it was also the place where those without insurance came for help, and the place was thick with the ill, the injured and those who had brought them.

He wasn't the only law enforcement officer there. As he waited, two drug overdoses and a man with a knife in his back were rushed in, escorted by cops. Strange place, he thought. Stranger here, in the heart of the city, than out in the Glades. The wealth to be found in the area was astounding; movie stars, rock stars and celebrities of all kinds had multimillion-dollar mansions out on the islands, in the Gables and scattered throughout the county. At the same time, refugees from Central and South America abounded, many who slept under bridges, or lived in the crack houses that could be found not so far from the million-dollar mansions.

At length, one of the doctors came out. "Well, we've got him stabilized. But he's in a coma. He's not going to be talking."

"Will he come out of it?" Jesse asked.

"I don't know," the doctor told him honestly.

Jesse nodded, and handed the doctor his business card.

"I'll call you first thing, and I mean first thing, if there's any change at all," the doctor promised.

Jesse thanked him. There was a Florida Highway Patrol officer in the waiting room who had just finished with an accident victim. He offered to drive Jesse back. It was a long way, and Jesse thanked him for the offer.

"Heard you've been having some bad business around here," the officer, Tom Hennesy, said as they drove. "Anything new on those shootings?"

"No. Metro-Dade Homicide is handling that case, though."

Hennesy nodded. "You had a fatal gator attack, too."

Jesse nodded.

"Strange, huh?" Hennesy said. "Usually that kind of thing only happens when someone wanders into the wrong place." He shrugged. "Of course, the 'wrong' place is getting harder to avoid these days, what with developers eating up the Everglades. Still, it's usually only the big gators that will attack an adult. It's usually toddlers. Or pets." He cast a sideways glance at Jesse and flushed slightly. "I was reading up after the attack the other day. Since 1948, there have been fewer than 350 attacks on humans in this state, and the number of fatal attacks is only in the teens." He laughed. "I remember when the creatures were endangered, and when the first alligator farm opened in 1985. My uncle used to come out to the Glades, sit in a cabin and drink beer, and go out and hunt gators—till they made the endangered list. And now…my wife wanted to move close to the water. Now, after the latest incident, she wants to move out of state and up into the mountains somewhere."

Jesse smiled at the man, offering what he hoped was polite empathy.

"Hell, you're down here all the time," Hennesy said. "Think about it. How many attacks have you seen?"

Jesse looked at him. "Well, my uncle Pete lost a thumb, but he was one of the best wrestlers the village down there ever had. He was proud of it, actually. I don't think you can call that an attack, though."

When they at last reached the alligator farm, Jesse was disturbed to realize that more than half the day was gone.

The place was full of tourists, as if nothing had happened. A discreet inquiry assured him that Lorena was busy, helping out with Michael Preston's hatchling speeches.

He took a glance into the lab and saw that there were at least twenty people on the current tour. Lorena didn't see him. He watched her, watched the way she smiled, seemingly at ease. But in reality she was moving around the lab looking for something, he realized. She was subtle, leaning against a cabinet, a desk, casually assessing the contents, but she was definitely searching for something.

He was tempted to shout at her. *Stupid!*

Was she stupid, or dangerously reckless? Why? What was driving her?

A little while later, when he drove away from the farm, he realized that he'd been afraid to leave, afraid to head home for a shower. He was tired as hell, but the shower was necessary. Sleep would have to wait.

LORENA HEARD THAT Jesse had returned to Harry's. That he had spoken with a number of people.

Just not her.

The next morning she met Thorne Thiessen, the veterinarian. He had come to take a look at Old Elijah.

He was a distinguished-looking man, weather-worn, with a pleasant disposition, very tall, very fit. He had his assistant with him, a huge guy named John Smith. They both looked like extremely powerful men, in exceptional shape.

Maybe that was a requirement for survival in the swamp. Or else something in the genetics of the men in the area.

Watching Thiessen examine Old Elijah had been a real education. They had pulled out a lot of equipment—Elijah was one big beast—and they had snared him, something that had taken Jack Pine, Hugh, John Smith and two part-time wranglers to manage. The gator had thrashed, even when caught, and sent several of the handlers flying. Between them, however, they got the creature still, with Jack making the leap to the animal's back, shutting the great jaw and taping it closed.

Only then did Thiessen go into the pit. He took blood samples, checked the crocodilian's eyes, did some kind of a temperature reading and checked out his hide.

Despite the time she'd spent in school, Lorena really didn't know how the vet was determining if the ancient creature was in good health or not. Personally, she thought that the way he had been able to toss grown men around as if they were weightless seemed to prove that he was doing okay.

Jesse showed up right when Thiessen was leaving. Lorena, who had been watching from the pit area, did her best to eavesdrop. The men greeted each other cordially enough, but then Jesse pressed the vet, who in turn became defensive.

"I'm working on it, Jesse. But come on, Homicide doesn't see any connection between the alligator limb and the murders. Something ate the rest of the thing, that's all. Poachers don't kill people with high-powered rifles."

Jesse shrugged. "I can see where this may not be at the top of your priority list, but it *is* high on mine. If you don't want to deal with the responsibility, I can just take it to the FBI lab."

Thorne frowned, even more indignant. "No one knows reptiles the way that I do!"

"That's why I brought the specimen to you. Another day or so, Thorne, then I'm going to have to go for second best."

As he finished speaking, Lorena realized that he'd noticed she was there. She had forgotten to eavesdrop discreetly.

But there were others around, too. Jack and Hugh were speaking together, just a few feet away. Sally was standing politely to the rear, obviously waiting for a chance to have a word with Jesse.

Even Harry was still by the pit, calling out orders to

the two wary part-time handlers, who had been left to free Old Elijah from the tape on his snout.

Michael Preston was there, too, sipping coffee with a thoughtful frown as he watched all the activity.

Jesse, however, was gazing thoughtfully at *her*.

"Ms. Fortier," he murmured. "I need to see you later," he said.

He turned to leave. Sally tapped him on the arm, asking a question that Lorena couldn't hear. As Jesse walked away, Sally was still at his side.

"Hey!" Harry called. "Doors are opening."

LORENA REALIZED THAT although she was always distracted when she brought visitors through Michael's lab, she actually enjoyed his talks. He had a nice flair for the dramatic. That morning, though, she felt the frustration of not being able to find anything out of the ordinary. Except for the eggs with the cracked shells. That was where changes—or *enhancements*—might take place. But they were out in the open. Part of the show.

In the afternoon, she watched as Jack and Hugh both put on their own demonstrations. Jack wrestled a six-foot gator to the amusement of the crowd. Hugh brought out gators in various stages of growth, thrilling the children, who were allowed to touch the animals. After the last show, Hugh approached her.

"How about an airboat ride? See some of the scenery up close and personal?" he suggested, his grin charming and hopeful.

She agreed, and soon, they were out in the Glades. She had been afraid, at first, when it had looked as if they were trying to take off over solid ground. But it wasn't ground at all.

The river of grass. That was what it was and exactly the way it looked. As they traveled, Hugh educated her about their environs, shouting to be heard over the motor. The Everglades really wasn't a swamp but a constantly moving river; it was simply that the rate at which the water moved was so slow that it wasn't discernible to the naked eye.

Hugh obviously loved the area. Before they started out, he had explained that he was an Aussie, would always be an Aussie at heart, but that he had come to love this place as home.

Trees on hummocks seemed to rush by with tremendous speed. Ahead of them, brilliantly colored birds, large and small, burst out of the water and into the sky. At last Hugh cut the motor, and the airboat came to rest in the middle of what seemed like a strange and forgotten expanse of endless water, space and humid heat.

"So how do you like the airboat?" Hugh asked. He had a cooler in the rear of the boat and edged around carefully to open it. He produced two bottles of beer.

She accepted one.

"The feel of the wind is great," she told him.

He took a seat again, grinning as he looked at her. "You like it out here?"

"It's strange. A bit to get used to. But yes. I don't think I've ever seen more magnificent birds. Not even in a zoo."

"Around the early 1900s, some of them were hunted into extinction. Their feathers were needed for every stylish hat," Hugh said, leaning back. "But they *are* fabulous, aren't they?"

She nodded. "So, Hugh, were you a croc hunter back home in the Outback?"

He laughed. "Actually, I was born and raised in Sydney, but I always wanted to find out about the wilds. We've got some beautiful country at home, but there's just something here…the loneliness, the trees, the birds, the…I don't know. Some people simply fall in love with the land. Despite the SST-size mosquitoes, the venomous snakes and the alligators."

"Have you been a handler ever since you got here?" she asked. "I mean, did you ever help with the research side of things?"

He laughed. "Research?" He shook his head. "I know enough about gators without that. I know when they mate, know that a mother gator is one of the fiercest creatures known to man. And I know about the jaws, and that's what counts."

He sat back easily, adjusting his hat. He was attentive and clearly glad to be with her. In fact, he really seemed like a nice guy.

And he knew nothing about research.

Or so he claimed.

But here they were, in the middle of nowhere, and if he had wanted to cause her any harm…

"Damn!" he said suddenly.

"What?" she asked.

He lifted his beer, indicating something west of them. She peered in that direction, squinting, trying to see what he was seeing.

She realized that there was an embankment, and that they were in a canal. Trees grew at the water's edge, and it seemed that there was a small hummock in the direction he was pointing.

Limbs were down here and there, no doubt a result

of the early summer rainstorms she had heard came frequently here.

"There… They really are amazing creatures. They blend perfectly with their environment," Hugh said, his voice a whisper touched with awe. "See him?"

Suddenly she did. Just the eyes and a hint of the nose were visible above the water. And then, way behind the head, she could see the slight rise of the back.

"He's huge!" Hugh continued softly. "I've never seen one that big. I've never even seen a croc that big."

"How can you tell his size?" she asked, whispering, too, though she didn't know why. Actually, she did, she realized. She didn't want to attract the creature's attention.

"Well," Hugh said, "if you look at the water—"

"The water looks black," she protested.

He laughed softly. "It's not the water, it's the vegetation. But look closely. You can see the length of the body. We're talking huge. Maybe twenty-something feet."

"They don't get that big here!" she heard herself protest.

As they watched, the alligator suddenly submerged. Lorena felt a sharp stab of fear, sudden and primitive. She was certain that the creature was coming for them.

The airboat was small and built for two, with both seats at the rear. The nose of the vehicle offered only a small bit of space for supplies. The boat was fairly flat-bottomed, and it would be hard to knock over, but…

How much could a creature like that weigh?

"Man, I would have liked to see him up close," Hugh marveled.

Lorena couldn't speak. She was certain that Hugh

was going to get his wish, that the gator would be there, beneath them, in a matter of seconds.

Frowning, Hugh rose. Despite the rocking of the airboat, he moved easily and confidently. She was about to scream to him to sit down, that he needed his gun, that...

She heard it then. The motor of another airboat.

Just then something brushed by their boat. Just touching it. Nosing it.

Testing it?

Then the other airboat came into the picture, whipping over the water. It was a much larger vehicle, with the motor and giant fan far in the rear, and with more storage space and six seats in front of the helm. She noticed that it bore a tribal insignia.

Then she saw Jesse.

She released a long breath, aware that she wasn't afraid anymore, that even his airboat seemed to shout of authority.

The creature had disappeared; it was no longer touching their airboat.

"Hey!" Jesse shouted, cutting his motor as his vehicle drew next to theirs.

"Hey, Jesse," Hugh said dryly. It was apparent that his romantic plans had just been shattered.

"What are you two doing out here?" Jesse asked with a frown.

Hugh cocked his head, his hands on his hips. "I asked the lady out, and she agreed."

Jesse looked impatient. "Hugh, I don't know how you missed my notice. We've got a man-eater out here. We're going to get a group of hunting guides out here and go after it. The medical examiner says that Billy

Ray was bushwhacked by one big son of a bitch. We're going after it. It's not safe out here right now."

Hugh snorted. "Jesse, I've been dealing with gators for half my life. I'm armed, and I can take care of Lorena. I carry more than one big gun."

Jesse shook his head. "Hugh, you're one of the best. But Billy Ray knew alligators, too. Take your airboat on back. Lorena, step over here."

"Now, wait a minute!" Hugh protested. "Lorena is with me."

"She's coming in for questioning," Jesse said.

"What?" she and Hugh asked simultaneously.

Those startling green eyes leveled upon her hard. "Lorena needs to answer some questions about an incident at the alligator farm the other day."

"Jesse, you are crazy—" Lorena began.

"I can put the cuffs on you," he assured her.

"What the hell are you talking about?" Hugh demanded.

Jesse leveled his eyes on Lorena as he answered Hugh's question. "Something to do with a little kid getting a bite. I'm sure Harry wants it kept quiet. Therefore, I need a few answers."

Hugh frowned, staring at Lorena. "You don't have to go with him. What are you trying to pull here, Jesse Crane?" Hugh demanded.

"I think that Lorena wants to come with me," Jesse said, staring at her meaningfully.

Her skin prickled. It wasn't with the kind of panic she had felt when she believed that a monster gator was stalking her, but with an overwhelming sense of unease. *He knew.*

And maybe he was giving her a chance to talk to him before he blew the whistle on her.

She sighed, rising. The boat rocked.

"There was a bit of a problem with one of the children the other morning, Hugh. Easily taken care of. I'll just go with Jesse now," she said smoothly.

Panic seized her once again when she was ready to step from boat to boat. Where had the gator gone?

Whatever ruffled male feathers had begun to fly, the situation was suddenly eased as Hugh, holding her arm as she moved to join Jesse, said, "I think we just saw your alligator."

"Here?" Jesse asked.

There was about a foot and a half of empty space between the boats as they rocked gently in the water. Lorena looked down.

Her heart slammed into her throat.

There it was. Submerged, and moving in fluid silence, just beneath the surface.

She nearly threw herself into Jesse's arms.

"There!" she said. "Underneath us."

He frowned at her, dark brows drawn, eyes narrowed. He forced her into a seat and strode back to the edge of the airboat. "Where? Hugh, you see it?"

Hugh was also searching the water. He had a shotgun in the back of the airboat. He reached for it and stood still, watching.

Time passed.

It felt like an eternity to Lorena, who heard the drone of a mosquito but was afraid to move, too frozen even to swat at the creature.

At last Jesse sighed.

"It might have been here, but I don't see it now," he

said. "But this might well be its territory, so we'll start here tomorrow."

"Sunset?" Hugh asked.

"Right before. You gonna join us?"

"Yeah," Hugh said. "I travel around here all the time, though. I haven't seen that gator before."

"What was left of Billy Ray's body was tangled in the trees not too far from here. You know, right around the bend, where he had his favorite fishing spot. Yes, this is its territory. I'll pick you up at Harry's, six o'clock sharp tomorrow evening."

Jesse started up his motor.

The sound was like the sudden whirr of a thousand birds, rising from the swamp.

She gripped her chair, still feeling cold. Hugh waved.

She couldn't wave back.

The wind lashed around her, whipping her hair around her face. She closed her eyes.

She was startled when the motor died, along with the forward motion of the boat.

She opened her eyes. They still seemed to be in the middle of nowhere.

There was a hummock where they had come to rest, land that wasn't covered in the deceptive saw grass that grew where the water ran, making a person believe that there was terra firma beneath.

And yet in all directions, she still saw only wilderness.

There was no sound, except for the cries of birds, the rustle of foliage.

She swallowed, frowned, and stared at Jesse uneasily.

"Where are we?"

"My place," he said. "And you can talk to me here, tell me the truth, or we'll just head downtown, to the FBI office. Here's your chance, Lorena. Truth or dare. What do you know, and what the hell are you really doing here?"

CHAPTER SEVEN

DESPITE THE FACT that there was a well-maintained dock, Jesse could see that Lorena was more than a bit concerned about where they were going when he helped her out of the airboat.

His house had been built on a hummock and, he thought, combined the best of tradition and the modern world. There were still members of his tribe who made their homes in chickees, but for the most part, beyond the village and the other tourist stops, tribal members lived in normal houses, concrete block and stucco, sturdy structures that offered the same comforts as those enjoyed by everyone else.

He was lucky to own the land, which had been his father's. And it was a good stretch of hummock, rich with trees and foliage, and high enough to keep it from flooding during hurricanes or the rainy season. As they came in from the rear, winding along the path from the canal, the first sight was a chickee. Chickees had first come into being when various tribes—once grouped together under the term "Seminoles"—had moved deep into the Everglades to escape persecution and the white determination to export every last Native American to the western reservations. High above the ground, the chickee offered protection from snakes and gators. The open sides allowed the breezes to pass through continually, keeping the inhabitants cool year round.

Lorena gave the chickee a nervous glance, and he saw the relief on her face when they rounded a bend and she saw the house.

There was a screened-in patio with a pool, and sliding glass doors that led from it into the house. He owned a fairly typical ranch-style dwelling, with the large rear, "Florida room" extending the width of the back. He had a good entertainment center and comfortable sofas and chairs, which often led to him being the one to host Sunday football get-togethers. His home probably differed from some in that it was filled with Indian artifacts: Miccosukee, Seminole and others, including South American and Inuit. He had totem poles, lances, spears, shields and buffalo skulls, all artistically—at least in his mind—arranged, and he had come to love the feeling that he was surrounded by both past and present, tradition and the need for all Americans to be aware of the modern world. He considered education the most necessary tool for any Native American, and finding the path between prosperity and ethnicity was not an easy one.

"Thank God for bingo," he murmured aloud.

"What?"

Her eyes were wide; he could tell that she was decidedly uncomfortable, yet apparently relieved at the same time.

"Coffee? Tea? Soda? Beer or wine?" he asked. "Sorry, that's all I keep around." He left her standing in the Florida room and walked through the hall, hanging a quick left into the kitchen, where a bypass over the counter opened to allow him to keep an eye on her.

She shook her head uneasily. "I'm fine."

"Then I'll have coffee."

He reached into the cupboards for the paraphernalia he needed, watching her as he did so.

Some of the trepidation in her face had eased. She was walking around, studying the various pieces on the walls. She turned suddenly, as if feeling him watching her.

"Have you always lived here?" she asked, trying to sound casual.

"In the general area, yes. This house is new, though."

"Ah."

"And, let's see…you were raised in Jacksonville. Attended the University of Florida. Where you did indeed earn a nursing degree."

"Yes," she murmured, looking away.

"And a law degree."

Her eyes flew to his again. Belligerent, defensive.

"All right, so I've spent the last few years with a law firm. My nursing credentials are still good. You seem to know everything, so you must know that, too."

"I do," he assured her grimly. "Sure you don't want a cup of coffee?"

"All right," she murmured.

She walked around to join him in the kitchen. He wondered how she could have spent the late afternoon in an airboat in the swamp and still manage to retain such an alluring scent.

"Sugar…cream," he said, indicating the containers.

She added a touch of cream to her cup, not looking at him. Her fingers were shaking as she stirred, but she quickly returned to the Florida room, taking a seat on one of the sofas that looked out over the pool.

"All right," he said, taking a seat next to her. "We need to start communicating here. This is serious. Shall I continue, or do you just want to talk to me?"

"You're going to try to get me out of here," she said, not looking at him. Then her eyes shot to his. "And I'm not inept. Actually, I'm a crack shot."

"Your life seems filled with accomplishments," he said with obvious irony.

She blushed, looking away. "I thought I wanted to go into nursing…but then I wound up taking some legal courses related to medical ethics and I found out that I liked the law. I was able to work part-time in a hospital while I went back to college. I was lucky. My dad was associated with a firm that was known for going to bat for the underdog. They hired me right out of law school."

"Which has nothing to do with why you're here," he said softly.

"Actually, in a way it does," she murmured, staring down again. Then she looked up at him. "One thing about studying the law is that you learn you need proof to go to court."

He shook his head, looking at her, then taking the cup from her and setting it on the coffee table. He took both her hands. "All right, here's the rest of what I know. You're going under the name Fortier because that was your mother's maiden name. Your father was Dr. Eugene Duval, working for Eco-smart, a company that, among other facilities, ran an alligator farm. He died last year after a fall down a stairway. So why does that bring you here?"

She shook her head. "He didn't fall."

"Lorena, I've read the police reports. He was alone in the building at the time."

"No. He did *not* just fall."

Jesse sighed, squeezing her hands. "Lorena, I know what it's like to desperately seek something behind the obvious. Your father fell down a stairway. He broke his neck."

"No," she said stubbornly.

"Why are you so convinced it wasn't an accident?"

"Because he had something. Something that his killer wanted."

"And that was?" Jesse persisted.

She hesitated, realizing that he didn't know everything.

He squeezed her hands more tightly. The lingering scent of her cologne wafted around him, seemed to permeate his system. He realized that his own heart was pounding, that the blood was rushing in a hot wave through his system. He was torn between the desire to gently touch her face and the equally strong desire to draw her into his arms, shake her, tell her none of this was worth her life.

He desperately wanted to hold her. And more. The texture of her skin was suddenly so fascinating that he longed to explore it with the tips of his fingers. Her features were so delicate, elegant and determined that he was tempted to test them with the palm of his hand.

He fought the desire that had begun to build in his system the first time he had seen her. She was angry, lost, determined…and trusting. He knew he should pull his hands away. He didn't. He couldn't. He had to get answers from her—now.

"Lorena, what did your father have?" he demanded.

She stared back at him, clenching her teeth; then she shook her head. "You mean you don't know? It's obvious. He had a formula."

"A formula for what?"

"Well, basically, steroids," she said flatly. "There were other ingredients, but the formula was based on steroids." She inhaled, exhaled, looking away but not drawing away. "My father was a great man. He wanted to feed the world. He worked with all kinds of animals, trying to find a way to improve the amount and quality of their meat without creating the chemical dangers you so often find in farmed meats. He saw alligators as the wave of the future. A creature that had been endangered—nearly wiped off the face of the earth—then raised in captivity to return with a vengeance. In his mind, we were going to be looking to a number of basically new food sources, new to the American public, at least. Emu. Beefalo. Different fish. Eels. And alligators. He thought they were magnificent creatures, with hides that could be used for all kinds of things and meat that could be improved in taste, quality and quantity. So he began working on a formula. Now he's dead and someone else has it—and I think Harry's place may be involved."

Jesse stared at her blankly, wondering why something like this hadn't occurred to him. *Because it was right out of a science fiction novel, that was why.*

"Lots of people work with alligators," he said, his tone sharper than he had intended. "Lots of scientists work with formulas to improve breeding and supply."

"Maybe, but my father had found one that improved the creatures' size to such an extent that…that he destroyed his own specimens."

Jesse felt frozen for a moment. It was all beginning to make sense. Too much sense. He was accustomed to drug-related crimes in the Everglades, or illegal immigrants, and the big money and guns that came with both. He knew the tragedy of greed, gangs, and the jealousy and fury behind domestic violence, and the tribulations brought on by the abuse of alcohol. And now industrial espionage might well be exactly what they were looking for. *A formula that was dangerous, but that could take a business to the top of the heap?* It made way too much sense. A couple killed for what appeared to be nothing had probably seen something they shouldn't see. A man who knew the Glades like the back of his hand, dead, killed by an alligator. But what kind of an alligator? Perhaps one scientifically induced to grow bigger—and more dangerous?

"All right, your father was working on a formula, but he's been dead for more than a year. There are all kinds of establishments working with alligators, all through Florida, Georgia, Texas and more. What brought you here?" he asked.

She hesitated. "I finally cleaned out all my dad's business communications. An old e-mail I found from Harry's Alligator Farm and Museum seemed to point in this direction."

"Was Harry Rogers ever in Jacksonville? Did he know your father?"

She shook her head. "Not that I know of."

"I assume your father communicated with a lot of other institutions."

"Yes, but…none of the others were…well, located in such a wilderness. A place where it's possible to hide so much."

"Exactly what did the e-mail say, and who was it from?"

"I don't know. It wasn't signed. It was just a query, but there was something off about it. Something greedy. My father wrote back that he couldn't help."

"Then…?"

"It came right after there had been an article about my dad that mentioned the kind of research he was doing. So I came here, and…that couple got killed, and you found a piece of an alligator there, and then that poor man was…eaten."

"Still…"

"Jesse, I'm telling you, there was nothing else to go on, nothing."

"What about the other employees where your dad worked? What did they say?"

She shook her head in disgust. "According to everyone, my father had destroyed his research, the formula and his specimens. He worked for a very aboveboard corporation. When he said his research had taken a dangerous turn, they gave him the freedom to start over. So now they're all sorry, and they all understand that I'm upset. But as far as they're concerned, it was an accident."

She stared at him, then grasped his hands. "But it *wasn't* an accident. I know it. Harry—or someone here—got my father's formula, and they killed him to do it. You have to believe me! And now they've lost a few of their specimens, and those gators are running around the Glades killing people. They're trying to track them down, but they don't want to get caught, and I think that's why your friends were killed. Whoever was out there picking up the specimen decided that

Hector and Maria had seen too much. But what really scares me is that I think they're still trying to use the formula. Jesse, please, think about it. You said that Hector and Maria were wonderful people, that they couldn't have been drug-running. So you have to go to the next conclusion—that they were killed for something they saw, for what they might know. Come on! Why else would anyone kill your friends? They were shot because they saw the alligator. And the killers dared to murder them because they knew everyone would just assume it had something to do with drugs. Jesse, I'm right, and you know it."

He drew away from her at last, then stood and walked to the glass doors, looking out at the pool and the deep, rich green of the hummock beyond, not seeing. "Lorena, your dad has been dead more than a year, right?" he said softly.

"Right."

"And his research went back several years. But alligators, even pampered hatchlings, only grow about a foot a year. To get a creature big enough to kill a man would take well over a decade."

"Jesse, you don't understand just what can be done once man starts messing with nature. My father began his studies about five years ago, and with the alterations he could create, a gator could grow as much as four feet in a year. You figure it out. Do the math. See where we'd be right now," she said softly.

"I don't believe it," he said, but he wondered, *Was it possible?*

"You've got to get out of here," he said flatly. "This is about the wildest theory I've heard in my entire life, but if there's any truth in it whatsoever, someone is going to find out who you are. You've got to get away." He spun on her. "And another thing. Why the hell didn't you tell me about this when you arrived down here?"

"Hey! The second time I ever saw you, you were *at* Harry's. Sally told me you come there all the time. How could I know for certain that you weren't involved somehow?"

He sighed, looking down. "I'm a cop, Lorena. And just like I said at the beginning—a real one."

She rose, staring back at him. "And you're going to tell me that there haven't been dirty cops?"

He lifted his hands; then his eyes narrowed, and he strode over to her, taking her by the shoulders, ready to shake her for real. His fingers tensed where he held her, his teeth locked. He fought both his temper and his fears for her. At last he said, "You couldn't tell? You couldn't tell by *getting to know me* that I wasn't crooked?"

She inhaled, staring at him, eyes wide. She parted her lips, ready to speak, but words didn't come. She moistened her lips, ready to speak again, then just shook her head and, to his surprise, leaned it against him.

He wrapped his arms around her. Time ticked away as they stood there and he felt the soft force of her body against his, his own emotions washing through him with the force of a tidal wave. Heat began to fill him. He was torn, ready to rush out and pound his fist into anyone who would so coldly kill and let loose such a danger. But he was a police officer, sworn to uphold the law. He'd been a detective, trained to find out the truth before ripping into something like a maniac.

But he was also simply a man.

And here *she* was, in his arms. She had elicited emotion and longing in him from the first time he had seen the green-and-gold magic in her eyes, heard the tone of her voice. He'd been irritated, angered, enchanted. He'd seen the empathy in her eyes for others, the spark of fire when she was angry.

This wasn't the time.

He had taken her away from Hugh, and Hugh would be angry now, telling the tale to everyone.

And at Harry's, they might be suspicious....

"You can't go back there," he said, and he lifted her chin, his thumb playing over the flesh of her cheek.

Her eyes met his. Her fingers moved down his back, dancing lightly along the length of his spine. "I *have* to go back," she whispered.

"No," he said. And he brought his lips to hers. She didn't protest or hesitate for a second. It was as if they had both been simmering, awaiting the boiling point, and when they touched at last...

She melted into his arms, breasts and hips fitting neatly into his form. Her fingers threaded into his hair; her mouth tasted of mint and fire.

They broke apart. "I have to..." she said, and her meaning was unclear, because they fused together again, and her hands worked down to his hips, then below, cupping his buttocks, drawing him closer.

At last he caressed her face as he had longed to, exploring texture and shape. Then his fingers fell to the buttons of her shirt, and the fabric obediently parted. His fingers slid along the flesh of her throat, stroked, then careered down the length of her neck. Beneath the cotton of her shirt, he found her bra strap, slipped it away, and his lips dropped to her shoulder, while his fingers continued to disrobe her, baring more flesh for the eager whisper of his tongue. He felt her hands at his belt, then realized his gun was there. He released her long enough to discard his gun belt, then drew her back quickly, fevered, heedless of anything then but the wanting and the heady knowledge that she was just as hungry as he was.

Her skirt and delicate lace bra fell to the floor, and the sleek length of her back was available to be savored by the touch of his fingers, while his lips found the hollows at her collarbone, then moved steadily down, finding her breasts. He felt the quickening of her breath, and that, too, was an aphrodisiac. She was smooth and soft, erotic, hot, vibrant. Her lips and teeth on his shoulders, bathing, biting, aroused him. Her hands, deft and seductive, were at the waistband of his trousers. It was then he realized that, remote as his house might be, the glass panes opened to the glory of the Everglades—and the eyes of anyone who might wander by. He caught her up into his arms, heedless of the clothing they left scattered behind, and strode down the hallway to his bedroom. As he did so, her eyes met his, dazed and mercurial, fascinating, poignant pools. And then her fingers swept back a dark lock of his hair, touching his face as he had so tenderly touched hers.

Night was coming to the Everglades. Coming in hues of crimson and purple, red and gold. The light shone dimly into the room, illuminating them as they fell onto the bed and came together again in a fury of naked flesh. Every little nuance of her seemed to touch and awaken and arouse him. Whispers and soft moans escaped her lips, a siren's song, as he reveled in the discovery of her, the tautness of her abdomen, the length of her legs, the firm fullness of her breasts. And in return...her hands were on him, touching without restraint, fingers no more than a whisper, and then a tease that brought the blood thundering through his veins again, his own breath a drumbeat, the tension in him unbearable.

And yet the anguish was sweet. As if the moment would not come again and had to be cherished, savored. He felt he died a thousand little deaths, not willing to allow it to end, hands upon her everywhere, lips tasting, teasing, giving homage, demanding response. He held himself above her, found her mouth, his tongue thrusting within, gentle at first, then almost angry. Finally he allowed his body to slide slowly against hers as he eased himself lower, again finding the fullness of her breasts, the rose-tipped peaks of her nipples, and below, his tongue stroking a rib, delving into her naval, the lean, low skin of her midriff, then…a kneecap, outer thigh, inner thigh, and the crux of her sex.

He heard the anxious, heady sound of her whispers and moans, protest, encouragement. She writhed against him and into him, and he felt the pulse of her body, until at last he rose above her again and thrust into her, his eyes locked with hers, his soul needing to encompass the length and breadth and being of her with the same searing need that ruled his body. The world rocked in the colors of the sunset, soaring, shooting reds, golds that burned into heart and mind. He moved, and she moved with him, a fit as sweet as it was erotic. Fever seized him, and the rhythm of their union became staccato and desperate. The sounds of their breathing rose to storm pitch, hearts attuned in physical cacophony. Searing lava seemed to rip through his veins, and he fought it, until he felt her surge against him, and then his own climax seized him with violence and majesty.

He moved to her side, and felt the thundering in his chest decrease to a steady beat, the pulse slow, the air move. The colors of sunset faded. Mauve darkness settled over them as she curled against him. He touched her hair in wonder, but his voice rang harsh again when he spoke. "You can't go back there."

The wrong words. She pushed away from him.

"I have to."

"No."

"Jesse…"

"Shh."

"I have to go back. And I have to go back soon."

"Not now."

"They'll know I'm with you."

"It's early."

"But…"

"Shh."

"Jesse, you can work with me or against me," she whispered.

He didn't reply. He was fascinated by the color of her hair against his sheets in the dying light. She went rigid beside him, so he smoothed her hair, then her brow. Then he kissed her forehead, her lips.

And then it began all over again, and this time, when the final thunder came, the black of night had descended fully.

They didn't speak, just held each other for the longest time, her head on his chest, their legs entwined. At last she pushed away from him, rose and found the shower.

He found her there. And in the spray of heat and steam, he found himself exploring anew, touching, tasting, licking tiny water drops from her flesh….

Feeling them licked from his own skin, feeling himself touched, taken, stroked.

Soap upon flesh, flesh upon flesh, a night in which he found he could not be sated, in which he soared, in which he was afraid. And he didn't want it to end, because, when it did...

Eventually they managed an actual shower. The lights on, they moved in silence, finding all the scattered pieces of their clothing. And then, a new cup of coffee in his hand, Jesse told her firmly, "You can't go back."

She was rigid and determined; he could see that immediately. She regally smoothed back a piece of wet hair and said, "I told you, you can work with me and keep me safe, if that's what you feel you have to do. But I *am* going back."

"I can stop you," he told her.

She lifted her chin. "You'd really arrest me?" she demanded. "For what?"

His teeth grated.

"I can tell Harry that you're acting suspiciously. That I think you're dangerous." He lifted his hands in frustration. "Lorena, your being there is pure insanity. You've told me that someone killed your father. An innocent couple was shot down in cold blood. A man was eaten by a gator. If someone at Harry's is involved, that someone is ruthless."

She set her hands on her hips, indignant, eyes narrowing dangerously. "What? I'm a woman, and that means I have to be incompetent?"

"I didn't say that. But I'm not letting you go back there."

"Then you'll never find the killers you're after!" she told him.

He stared back at her, feeling anger rise in him again.

"I need to go back. And I need to go back now. I'm already going to have to think of something to say when everyone wants to know why you detained me."

"I told both you and Hugh that I was going to talk to you about the incident at the farm," he said flatly. He shook his head in disgust. "You're playing a dangerous game. You haven't just entered a pit of vipers, you're asking them to bite."

"What?"

"Oh, come on. You're flirting with the pack of them."

"I went for a ride in an airboat," she said. "So what?" But there was no conviction in her tone.

He stared at her, torn, impotent, and furious because he knew that, on the one hand, she was right.

He had no proof of anything. So…what? Wait until something else terrible happened and hope he was there to save her? Find some reason for a search warrant, a legal way to get into Harry's, and rip the place apart?

"No one was suspicious of me except you," she reminded him. "Honestly, Jesse, I told you I'm a crack shot. I carry a gun, and I'm licensed."

"Great. And do you walk around armed all day?"

She let out a sigh. "Do you really think anyone is going to hurt me in front of dozens of witnesses?"

"Two days," he said.

"What?" she asked him, frowning.

"Two more days. That's what I'll give you. And you have to swear to me that you'll go nowhere alone with any of those men. When it's night, you lock yourself in. When it's morning, you get where you need to be—fast."

"I need to get back into the lab," she said.

"You can do that when I'm there."

She cocked her head to the side, wary. "And we'll manage that how?"

"Easy. I'm around enough."

She hesitated. "Jesse—"

"That's the deal. Take it or leave it." He shook his head angrily. "You toe the line, and I mean it. It's going to be busy as hell right now, too, because I have to arrange hunting parties to find your scientifically mutated alligators—assuming they even exist. Every one of them has to be caught and killed. God knows how many people could die if some super race of huge, aggressive gators starts breeding out there."

"Two days, then," she said softly. "But, Jesse…that's my point, don't you see? I have to find the truth. I have to find out what they know and just how they've altered the alligators, not to mention just how many of them are out there."

"I need enough evidence to get a search warrant, nothing more," he said.

She nodded, then said softly, "I really have to go back now."

"I need a minute to get a few things," he told her.

"For what?"

"For the morning."

"You can't stay out there," she protested.

"Yes, I can."

"They'll know! Someone will definitely get suspicious if you start staying out there."

"No one is going to know."

"And how can that be?"

He smiled grimly. "Because you're going to sneak me into your room at night."

Her breath seemed to catch in her throat as she stared at him.

"Jesse, I've told you, I'm a crack shot."

"So was my wife," he informed her softly.

Then he turned away.

CHAPTER EIGHT

HARRY WAS BESIDE the canal, looking both anxious and edgy, when they returned in the airboat.

Lorena cast Jesse a quick frown to warn him that they had clearly made the man suspicious.

"What are you two doing out this late at night?" he demanded.

Jesse managed to look a little sheepish as he tied up the airboat and helped Lorena to the embankment. She was surprised that he bothered, and that he could sound so casual as he said, "Just trying to avoid a problem."

"Maybe you want to let me in on it?" Harry said.

"We had a complaint, Harry," Jesse said. "But don't worry, it's all been nipped in the bud."

"What do you mean, don't worry? I thought I owned this place!"

"Just some kid said he'd been bitten by a hatchling. Turns out, it was the kid's fault. He was trying to steal it," Jesse explained.

"Steal one of my hatchlings?" Harry looked enraged.

"Yep, and that's why the parents have dropped the whole thing. I just needed Lorena's account of the problem. There's nothing to worry about, Harry. I thought it would be a minor thing, and it was. If there had been anything to worry about, naturally I would have spoken with you immediately."

"This could mean a lawsuit," Harry protested.

"It might have, but it isn't going to," Jesse said.

Harry was still glowering. "It's my place. I need to be apprised of everything that happens here."

"Harry, chill. The complaint has been dropped. Lorena told me everything I needed to know. There was no reason to upset you."

Harry stared hard at Lorena. She tried to decide if he looked worried or not. Mostly he just seemed concerned about his place. And angry with Jesse. "You're not doing your job right, Jesse Crane," Harry said angrily. "Cutting corners, kidnapping my nurse."

Lorena was instantly aware that Harry had said the wrong thing. Jesse stiffened, and the look in his eyes turned chilling. "Harry, two good people have been shot to death, a tribal member has been killed by an alligator, and you've got a security guard in the hospital, hovering between life and death. Drop it," he said icily.

Harry backed down, instantly. "I, uh, I just checked on Roger. He's still in a coma," he said gruffly. "You found out anything else on the murders?" he asked.

"No," Jesse said simply. "Nor can I tell you anything else about Billy Ray. But we're going out gator-hunting from here tomorrow evening around six. The office will set things up with the guys who run the licensed hunts. I'll be needing Jack Pine and Hugh. We know we've got a man-eater out there, and it's got to be put down."

"Now you're going to take my handlers?" Harry said incredulously. "Like hell! This is a business."

"And you can do business tomorrow. You'll just be minus a couple of handlers come six o'clock."

"Dammit, Jesse—"

"How many tourists do you think you're going to

have if this rogue gator attacks more people?" Jesse demanded.

Harry waved a dismissive hand. "Are you going to need my nurse again, too?" he demanded.

"Hopefully not," Jesse said calmly, not raising his own voice to meet Harry's indignant tone.

"You coming in for dinner?" Harry asked Jesse, clearly changing the subject to avoid an argument.

Jesse glanced at Lorena. "If there's still dinner, might as well," he murmured.

Harry made an unhappy snorting sound, and they walked together toward the main building. As they went, they could hear the bellowing of the alligators in their ponds.

Soon they reached the cafeteria. "I've eaten," Harry said curtly. "You two go on."

Lorena murmured, "Thank you," and stepped in ahead of Jesse.

Sally was seated at one of the tables, with Jack Pine and Hugh.

Hugh rose when he saw them enter.

"Well, that took a while," he said dryly.

"We got to talking, that's all," Jesse said.

Sally set a hand on his arm. "Jesse, how are you doing?" she asked, real concern in her voice.

Jesse frowned at her. "I'm worried," he said flatly.

Jack Pine waved a hand in the air. "Jesse, there may be one big gator out there, but face it, Billy Ray was a drunk. Do we really want to cause a panic out there when for all we know he passed out, fell in the water and drowned, and *then* got eaten by that gator?"

"No panic. Just a hunt," Jesse said.

"Let me get you all some food," Sally said sweetly,

flashing a smile at Jesse, then Lorena. "It's late, they're closing down, so I'll just make sure you two get to eat."

"Thanks, Sally," Jesse said, smiling back at her.

Lorena found herself remembering how Sally had talked about Jesse earlier. *Devastated, but not dead!* She felt at a loss for a moment, realizing that she knew so little about him. The night had been strange. Intimacy had been sudden and yet…she felt as if it had been something that, unbeknownst to herself, she had actually been awaiting. But she didn't know anything about whatever might have gone on with him—and Sally?— before she got here. She did know that he'd had a wife, and that she was dead….

And that she'd been a crack shot.

"Harry teed off about the hunt?" Hugh asked.

Jesse shrugged.

"Harry's all about the bottom line," Jack said. "He doesn't even give a damn about Michael's research. He just wants to please the tourists, grow the gators, harvest the meat and hides."

"Yeah, but if we catch the rogue that killed Billy Ray, he'll want it on display, don't you think?" Sally said, returning to the table. One of the waiters was behind her, carrying two plates piled with something Lorena couldn't identify.

"Jesse won't be letting Harry have that old gator, will you, Jess?" Jack said.

"Why not?" Harry asked.

"It should go to the village, to the Miccosukee," Jack said flatly.

"Let's catch the thing first," Jesse said.

"Hey…you're not going soft, are you? Thinking it's just a good ol' predator doing what comes naturally, and planning to transplant it somewhere deeper in the Glades?" Hugh asked.

Jesse shook his head. "No. It's dangerous. We have to put it down. There's one thing I'm really hoping, though."

"What's that?" Sally asked.

"That it *is* an 'it.' That we're not searching for more than one really dangerous alligator."

"There's one thing *I'm* wondering," Jack said.

"And what's that?" Lorena asked.

He stared at her. "Where the hell did a bugger that big and vicious come from?"

There was silence at the table. Lorena found herself intensely interested in her meal.

The conversation never really recovered after that.

Jack left the table first, a few minutes later. Then Hugh. Sally didn't seem to want to leave, though.

But finally Jesse stood. "Ladies, I've still got some work to do, so I'll bid you good night."

Sally watched him go, obviously appreciating the view.

Lorena cleared her throat. Sally glanced at her, her eyes sparkling with amusement. "Well, I see that you're coming to enjoy our local…wildlife, shall I say?"

Lorena ignored the other woman's teasing tone. "What happened to his wife?" she asked.

Sally didn't seem to mind dispensing information. "She was a cop, too. Some coked-up prostitute she was trying to help walked up to the back of her car one night and—on the order of her pimp—put a bullet into the back of her head."

Lorena let out a long breath. There was really nothing to say except "Oh."

"She was something, I'll tell you. An heiress determined to make the world better through law enforcement." Sally assessed Lorena carefully. "Don't go getting any ideas. He'll never marry again."

Lorena forced a smile. "Sally, I barely know the man."

"But you know enough, don't you?"

Lorena rose. "Like I said, I barely know the man. Thank you for making sure we could eat."

"He's interested in one thing, and one thing only. So you'd better play like a big girl, if you intend to play."

"Thanks for the advice," Lorena said lightly. "Good night."

As Lorena started walking away, Sally called softly after her, "Be careful."

Lorena spun back around. "Why?"

"Well, hell!" Sally laughed. "Old Billy Ray—eaten. And Roger… Just goes to show, you can never trust a gator. Believe me, I'm going to be very careful myself."

"Are you suggesting that Roger was helped into that pit?"

"Good God, no! He must have thought he heard something. Then leaned too far over the edge."

"So you think he fell in?" Lorena asked.

"Of course. Who would have pushed him?" Sally demanded.

"Hey, you're the one who warned *me,*" Lorena said lightly, then smiled and left.

On her way to her room, she paused at the door to Michael Preston's lab and started to test the knob. Then she heard his voice from inside and stopped, listening. She thought maybe he was on the phone. His voice was low but intense.

She tried desperately to eavesdrop, but she couldn't make out his words. Nothing other than *giant* and *hunt*. There was nothing suspicious about that. By now everyone knew that Billy Ray had been killed by an alligator, a big one, and that it had to be hunted down and destroyed.

Still, she lingered, listening, until the sound of footsteps down the hallway warned her that she'd better get going. Worried that he might eventually have said something useful and now she was going to miss it, she gave up and hurried on to her own room.

JESSE TOOK THE airboat back to headquarters and checked in with his staff.

Brenda Hardy was there, doing paperwork. She perched on the edge of Jesse's desk. "I don't care what anyone says. There's more going on here than just some big gator. Billy Ray had a shotgun with him, he could shoot dead drunk. I'd bet cash money you're thinking what I'm thinking. All this happening at one time is too much to be coincidence."

Jesse nodded to her, then excused himself as his cell phone rang. It was Julie.

"Jesse."

"Julie. You all right?"

"Yeah…yeah. You know what I've been doing? Playing bingo out at the casino. I bought about a million cards. You can't think when you're trying to put little dots on a zillion numbers at once."

"Good, Julie. I'm glad. Anything that works for you is what you need to be doing."

"Right, I know. I had to tell you, Jesse. I drove out by the house before, and…and I drove back here as quickly as I could. I didn't go in. I didn't even get out of my car. But I saw the lights. I saw lights…like my mother said. I know why she thought aliens were landing. It was creepy…the way they seemed to come out of the swamp and the sky at the same time."

"Julie, don't go back there. Stay at the casino, stay in the bingo hall, at the machines, or locked in your room, all right? And don't tell anyone you drove by the house."

"All right, Jesse. I just thought you should know."

"I should, and I'm glad you called me. But you have to keep yourself safe. You understand?"

"I will, Jesse. I guess I thought I needed to go back to believe it. But I'll stay away."

"Promise?"

"I swear."

Jesse hung up. As he did, George Osceola walked over to his desk. Jesse looked up.

"You're not going to like this," George warned.

"What?"

"Dr. Thiessen, the vet, just called," George said.

"And?"

"He went back into his office tonight to get some notes. He'd decided to send the specimen and his samples to the FBI lab."

"And?"

When he got there, his night security man slash animal sitter was out cold in the kennel area."

"And let me guess. The alligator specimen and all the tissue and blood samples were gone?" Jesse said.

George nodded. "I'm meeting some of the fellows from the county out there now."

"I've got a drive to make," Jesse said. "Then I'll meet you there."

He got in his car and started speeding along the Trail, only slowing as he neared Julie's parents' house. He turned off his lights before he entered the drive, knowing that, even for him, that was foolhardy, considering the terrain.

He parked on the embankment that bordered the property. The crime tape still hung limply around the house itself and the place where Maria had died. The whole area seemed forlorn, desolate.

Whatever Julie had seen, Jesse realized after about twenty minutes of watching from the front seat, it was gone now. Tomorrow night, if Lars couldn't send a man to keep watch, he would send one of his own men, or even keep watch himself.

He got out of the car, carrying his large flashlight, and walked toward the water. As he reached the wet saw grass area that fell away from the hummock toward the water, he saw that the long razor-edged blades were pushed down. Once again, someone had been through with an airboat. He looked around but didn't see anything else suspicious.

"When he got back to his car, he put a call through to Lars Garcia, despite the time. Lars already knew about the break-in at the vet's and was on his way out there.

When Jesse arrived at Doc Thiessen's, he found that the CSI team were already working, dusting for fingerprints, looking for footprints, searching for tire tracks, seeking any small piece of evidence.

Doc Thiessen had been born into a family of fruit-and-vegetable farmers in Homestead. He'd earned his veterinary degree at Florida State University and determined to come back to his own area to work. Now he had a head full of snow-white hair and a gentle, lined face. He worked with domestic as well as farm animals, and was known in several counties for his abilities to help with pet turtles, snakes, lizards, birds and commercial reptiles.

He was standing with Lars and the uniforms who had apparently been first on the scene when Jesse arrived. He shook his head as Jesse approached. "Jesse, I'm damned sorry. I was trying to prepare my samples properly, study them myself…I should have sent them straight out."

Jesse placed a hand on his shoulder. "It's not your fault. You couldn't have known this was going to happen. What about your night man? Jim? Did he see anything?"

"He's over there," Lars said, pointing. "Go on. I've already spoken with him."

Doc's night guard was a man named Jim Hidalgo, half Peruvian, half Miccosukee. He and Jesse were distantly related. They shook hands, and Jim looked at him, wincing. "Jesse, I didn't even see it coming. We've got a few dogs in the kennels, you know, belonging to folks on vacation. I heard something, went to check on the pups. One little beagle was going wild, and I walked over to it and…that's the last thing I remember until Doc was standing over me, taking my pulse."

"Thanks, Jim." The man had a bump the size of Kansas on the back of his head. Jesse stared at it and whistled softly. "You're lucky you're alive."

"They're insisting I go to the hospital," Jim said.

"Yeah, well…that's quite a bump. Let them keep an eye on you, at least overnight."

Jim sighed. "All right. If you say so."

Jesse walked back to Lars, who was waiting for him.

He told him about Julie's call and his trip out to the house.

"I had officers out there last night," Lars said with a sigh. "It's just that the department only stretches so far. But I'll send some men out again, twenty-four-hour watch. Anything else? You find your rogue gator?"

"Not yet. We're doing an organized hunt tomorrow night." He hesitated. "We may be on to something, though."

"What?"

"I need someone else to explain it to you."

Lars's partner, Abe, walked up then. "You know something, Jesse? If so—"

"Know something? Let's see. A couple is murdered, and there's an alligator limb at the scene. A man is attacked and killed by an alligator. A guard falls or is pushed into an alligator pit, and now the vet's guard has been attacked and specimens have been stolen. Gee. Think anything might be related here? Does the word 'gator' mean anything to you?"

"Go to hell, Jesse," Abe snapped. "I want to know what you've got to go on. I'm Homicide. I look for human killers. You're the alligator wrestler."

"An alligator is a natural predator, Abe."

"My point. I can hardly arrest one."

"If an animal is trained to kill, that makes the trainer a murderer, doesn't it?" Jesse asked dryly.

"I just said that if you've got something—"

Jesse ignored Abe and turned to Lars. "How about lunch tomorrow? The Miccosukee restaurant? On me."

"Yeah, we can make it," Abe answered for Lars.

Jesse shook his head. "I have someone who may

know something. But she won't talk if we make this too big a party. Abe, just let Lars handle it."

"Who is she?" Abe said angrily. "We can just bring her in."

"And do what? Issue a lot of threats and get nothing back?" Jesse asked angrily.

Lars set a hand on Abe's shoulder. "Partner, whatever I get, you know we share. So…"

Abe glared at Jesse. Jesse glared back. "Dammit, Abe, I'm not asking Lars to hide anything from you, and I'm not trying to hide anything myself. Hell, I'd invite anyone who could bring justice for Henry and Maria. But, Abe, you're not a guy with a gentle touch. Let Lars take this one. He can call you the minute he leaves."

"Fine," Abe grated.

With the crime-scene people busy at the vet's, Jesse knew there was nothing he could do there for the night. "I'm going to have a last word with Jim," Jesse said. "Lars, see you tomorrow."

They were almost ready to take Jim to the hospital for observation. He was being laid out on a stretcher.

"Jim?"

"Yeah, Jess?"

"You walked back to the beagle. You were hit on the head. Then nothing, nothing at all until Doc was there?"

"Nothing, Jesse. I'm sorry."

"That's all right."

"Does Doc usually come in at night?"

"No, but he'd been worrying about finishing up the work you wanted, 'cuz he hasn't been able to get to it during the day. We've been really busy lately. It's a bitch, huh?"

"Yeah, it's a bitch."

Then the med tech gave Jesse a thumbs-up and rolled Jim into the vehicle.

Jesse waved and headed out.

LORENA SHOULD HAVE been dog-tired, but she was nervous. Television couldn't hold her attention. She found herself prowling the room as the hour grew later.

He had said he would be here.

Irritated with herself, she sat down and tried staring at the television again. She thought she was just blanking on the screen, since she didn't understand a word that was being said.

Then she realized she was on a Spanish-language channel.

Insane.

She should work, she told herself.

Work, and not wonder if Jesse was really coming.

Work, and not feel on fire with such breathless anxiety, both physical and emotional....

What she'd told Sally was true: she barely knew the man.

It was also true that she needed to work. She hadn't managed much of her "real job" since she had come here. But then she had happened to arrive just when there had been terrible murders, and when a Native American who knew the canals better than his own features had met with his fate in those waters. There should have been time. Time to become trusted. Time to flirt, if necessary.

She needed to get into that lab.

She was convinced there were answers to be found there. She was usually so organized and analytical. But she was afraid to make notes, afraid that her room might be searched and her real purpose discovered.

She showered more to hear the sound of the water and feel the pounding of it against her flesh than anything else. Then she slipped into a cotton nightshirt and lay on her bed, but she still felt ridiculously keyed up.

Had he been serious? Was Jesse really coming back here?

Forget Jesse, she told herself.

She tried to fathom the truth from what she had been able to glean from Michael's files. As yet, nothing that was proof positive. He was experimenting with gator eggs, of course. The temperature at which they were hatched determined the sex of an alligator; that kind of manipulation was easy. Breeding was basic biology. And here, at an alligator farm, it made sense to weed out characteristics one didn't like and fine-tune those features that were favorable to farming. Sex, size, the quality of the meat and hide.

But selective breeding hadn't created the monster she had seen today. Steriods and a formula—one that her father had known was too dangerous to exist—were behind what she had seen. Still, even if she got back into Preston's lab and found out what he was working on, how could she prove he had stolen her father's work?

Two days. Jesse had given her two days.

Just as she thought of the man, she heard a soft rapping at her door. She glanced at her glow-in-the-dark Mickey Mouse watch. It was after 1:00 a.m. She leapt from the bed, her heart thundering, and angry because of it.

The tapping sounded again. Then, softly, "Lorena, will you open the door?"

She hurried over, threw it open. "It's after one in the morning," she informed him.

He closed the door. "Shh."

"I actually do sleep at night. I have a job to do here. I wake up and start early. I—"

He drew her into his arms. "Shh."

"Jesse, I have to tell you—"

"Shh."

There was warmth in the depth of his eyes as well as amusement. There was something possessive in his hold, and she felt him slipping into her heart even as he inflamed her desires.

He's devastated, not dead. He'll never marry again. He's interested in one thing, and one thing only, so you'd better play like a big girl, if you intend to play.

He started to frown, staring into her eyes. "What's wrong? Has something happened?"

Lorena placed her fingers against his lips. "Shh," she said, and moved closer to him. His flesh was rich and warm, burnt copper, vibrant, vital.

He groaned softly, pulling her to him, and his lips found hers, pure fire. When they broke, she heard his whisper against her forehead, felt the power of his touch against her. "Lorena."

Fumbling, she found the light switch. And once again she said very softly, "Shh…"

Then she was in his arms. And the hour of the day or night didn't matter in the least.

When the alarm rang, rudely indicating that morning had come and it was time for the workday to begin, he was gone.

CHAPTER NINE

IT SEEMED TO be business as usual at the alligator farm.

Lorena went through greeting the tourists and taking them to their first stop: Michael Preston's lab.

While working with a group of children, she tried to get a good look at the hatchlings and at the cracked eggs.

They appeared normal, as far as she could tell. She wished she had been more interested in her father's work at the time he'd been doing it, but she had simply never liked alligators.

It was the eyes, she was certain.

Two more groups of tourists came through. Michael was his usual self, valiantly trying to give a good speech, but obviously uncomfortable. Or maybe he only seemed so to Lorena because she knew he loved research and hated tourists. He did seem happy, however, to have her come through with the groups.

Happy to have her stay.

At eleven, her cell phone rang. It was Jesse. "I'm coming to get you for lunch," he told her.

"I'm not sure I'm supposed to leave during the day," she said.

"Everyone gets lunch. You won't even be ten miles away," he assured her.

At noon, he picked her up in front of the farm. He was in uniform. "Where are we going?" she asked.

He grinned. "A restaurant."

"Okay."

She had passed the place on her way out to Harry's she realized when they got there. It was directly across from the Miccosukee village.

Jesse glanced her way dryly. "Don't worry. You won't have to eat grilled gator or anything."

"I never thought I would," she responded. "You have a chip on your shoulder."

"I do not," he said indignantly, and she had to smile.

She balked when they reached the place and she saw that Lars Garcia was standing out front.

"What is this?" she demanded heatedly.

"You have to tell him what you think is going on."

"You gave me two days!" she said.

"There's been a complication. The vet's office was broken into. Another man was attacked. Thankfully, we have hard heads out here. He survived."

Jesse was grim, but she was still furious. She had nothing, no evidence at all, really, and he had brought her here to tell her story to another policeman. She was stiff and still angry when they went in.

Lars was as polite and decent as ever. He chatted about the weather while they waited for their food, and he and Jesse talked about an upcoming musical festival put on by the Miccosukee tribe in the Glades. "People come by the hundreds. It's great," Lars said.

When their food came—she'd ordered a very boring meal: hamburger, fries and an iced tea—Lars lowered his voice and said, "Jesse says I need to know why you're here."

She'd thought she was tense already, but now her muscles constricted to an even greater degree, and she shot Jesse a furious glance.

"Lorena, it's important I know."

"Then I'm surprised Jesse didn't tell you," she said.

"I need to hear it from you."

She clenched her teeth, set her hamburger down, shot Jesse one last filthy stare, and explained what she knew and feared to Lars. He listened without mocking or doubting her, though he glanced at Jesse several times, as if Jesse might have put him in the middle of a science fiction tale, but when she finished, he sighed and asked, "Your father's death was ruled an accident?"

"Yes. But I know it wasn't."

"That's going to be very difficult to prove."

"Maybe not now, when other people are dying," she said.

That caused a glance between Lars and Jesse.

"What was in the e-mail from the alligator farm?" Lars asked.

She shrugged. "It was vague. They were interested, of course, in learning about any developments to increase quality and efficiency. They suggested that they could pay well."

"What was your father's reply?" Lars asked.

"That he had nothing ready as of yet. And he explained that research was difficult, that all genetic scientists had to take the greatest care when playing with the makeup of any life form."

"Did other alligator farms contact your father?" Lars asked.

She shrugged. "Yes."

"So why are you concentrating on this one?"

"Every other e-mail was signed by a specific person. At Harry's, the same e-mail account can be used by almost anyone who works there."

"We can trace the computer," Lars said.

"If so, what will that prove?" Lorena asked.

"Whether it was in the office, in the lab or somewhere else," Lars said.

"Preston would have to be involved, wouldn't he?" Jesse asked.

"There are no 'have-tos,' Jesse. We both know that," Lars said. He looked at Lorena. "You need to get out of that place."

She tensed again, staring at Jesse. "I can't see how I can be in any personal danger. I had nothing to do with my father's work."

"Anyone can be in danger," Lars said softly.

Lars sat back, wiped his mouth and stared at Lorena. "I'll have to talk to the D.A.'s office about a search warrant. In the meantime, you shouldn't go back."

Lorena leaned forward, speaking heatedly. "My father is dead. A local couple have been killed. You don't know how many enhanced alligators you might have running around the Everglades. You need me, and you need my help."

"There's something I don't understand here," Lars said, and he glanced at Jesse, frowning. "This research has to be fairly new. Alligators take time to mature and grow. How could this one have gotten so big so fast?"

Lorena shook her head. "The formula causes an increase in the growth rate. Take people. Better diets, rich in protein, make for taller, stronger teens. Body builders bulk up with steroids. You'd be amazed at what chemicals can do to the body. That's why it's so important not only that we find out who was doing what but to just how many specimens."

"We need a search warrant," Lars said simply.

"Do you think you can get one?" Lorena asked anxiously.

He shrugged. "If I can argue well enough. And prove just cause. Well, I should get moving." He lifted a hand to ask for the check. Jesse caught his arm.

"I told you yesterday. This one is on the tribe."

"Thanks." He rose. Lorena and Jesse did the same.

When Lars had walked out, Lorena turned on Jesse. "You told me that I had two days."

"Lorena, what do you think you're going to find in two days?" Jesse demanded.

"More than anyone else?"

"Is biochemistry another of your degrees?"

She gritted her teeth, staring at him. "No. But I know what might have been stolen from my father."

"Lorena, face it, you're not going to be able to do anything if you're dead!"

She turned away from him and headed toward the door, clearly indicating that lunch was over for her, as well.

He followed. As soon as he came out, she got into the car. There was no possibility that she was going to walk back to work.

He didn't pull straight back onto the road but instead drove almost directly across the street. She gazed at him with hostility. "You have a few minutes left. I thought you might want to see the village."

She didn't have a chance to refuse. He had already gotten out of the car.

They entered the gift shop first. It offered Indian

goods from around the country. There were a number of the exquisite colorful shirts, skirts and jackets for which both the Seminoles and Miccosukees had become famous, along with dream catchers, posters, T-shirts, postcards, drums, hand-carved "totem" recorders and jewelry. Some of the unique beadwork designs on the jewelry might well have attracted Lorena's attention, but Jesse was already headed straight out the back. There was an entry fee, but Jesse just smiled at the girl, and he, with Lorena trailing behind him, walked on through. She offered the girl an awkward smile, as well.

Out back, there were a number of chickees, along with more items for sale. Women were there working on intricate basketry, sewing the beautiful colored clothing and designing jewelry.

Lorena, fascinated, would have paused, but Jesse was again moving on to one of the huge pits where alligators lived with a colony of turtles.

Looking into the pit, Lorena noted that a number of the gators were large, very large. But not one of them was more than ten feet.

"Jesse, what's up?"

A man with ink-dark hair and Native American features, wearing a T-shirt that advertised a popular rock band, walked up to them.

Jesse nodded to him. "Mike. This is Lorena Fortier. She's working at Harry's."

The man studied her with a smile. "Welcome."

"I thought she might want to see the village."

Mike smiled and shrugged. "Well, there's the museum, the pits, we do some wrestling, give a few history lessons."

"She's on lunch break. I just thought she should come

look around. And I wanted to make sure you'd seen the notice."

"About the hunt tonight? I'll be there," Mike said grimly. He shook his head. "Billy Ray…well, he wasn't the kind of man that gave us a lot of pride, but hell, I wouldn't have wanted my worst enemy to go that way."

"Right. Make sure everyone knows we're hunting something big, really big. Close to twenty feet, maybe even more."

Mike whistled softly. "We do know what we're doing, Jesse," he said. "But it's good to be warned."

"See you later, then. And extend my thanks to everyone showing up from the tribe."

Mike nodded. "See you then."

Jesse turned and headed toward the exit without a word to Lorena. She had been angry, but now he was the one who seemed irritated. They reached the car, where, despite his apparent anger, he opened her door.

"You're the one who betrayed me," she reminded him.

He shot her a scowling glance. "I'm trying to get you out of what might be a dangerous situation. But you know what? I don't usually have a chip on my shoulder, but today, I do. Chemists, biochemists, biologists! They're playing with life. Interesting, sure. Let's see how we can improve what God made. But, the thing is, people play God, and things can happen. Billy Ray was no prize specimen of humanity. But you heard it in Mike's voice. He was one of ours. We're a small tribe. We were forced down to this land, and we learned how to live on it. Billy Ray had every right in the world to be fishing. Hell, if he wanted to drink himself silly, that was his choice, too. He shouldn't have been attacked by an animal that was only there because someone decided to play God."

Lorena gasped. "My father wanted to help people," she insisted angrily. "And when he was afraid he might be on to something dangerous, he was willing to destroy years of research!"

"Too bad you couldn't have explained that to Billy Ray while he was being eaten," Jesse said.

Lorena stared at him incredulously. "Evil people come in all colors and nationalities, you know!"

The drive from the village to the alligator farm was short. Jesse pulled in just as Lorena finished her tirade, and she was out the door before the engine could die. She walked around to his window. "Thank you for your concern for my safety, but since you've turned things over to Metro-Dade now, I'm sure I'll be just fine. You can feel secure in the fact that I'll be safe without your assistance."

She spun around, her feet crunching on the gravel path, heedless as to whether he called her back or not.

Lunch was over. It was time to get back to work.

She did so, energetically, talking to the tourists, helping Michael, even going with the tours to the pits and watching while Jack wrestled one of the six-foot alligators.

It didn't matter what she did, as long as she did something. With Michael in his lab, she certainly wasn't going to get anywhere there, so she put her heart into the business of people. Anything at all to keep busy.

To keep from thinking.

She shouldn't have gotten so close so fast. Getting intimate with someone so unique, so unusual, so very much…everything she might have wanted in life…had

been more than foolhardy. She had let herself become
far too emotionally involved, and then…

She'd felt that wretched knife in her back. His bitterness against her father had been unexpected and deeply
painful.

That afternoon, she actually put her nursing skills to
the test. A little girl fell on one of the paths.

Nothing like a registered nurse to apply disinfectant
and a bandage.

As she tended the child, Lorena suddenly wondered
why Harry had decided that he needed a nurse on the
premises. It had made sense at first. The alligator farm
was in an isolated location. But she had seen the local
services in action. Help had arrived almost instantly
when Roger had been found in the pit. Helicopters provided a swift transport to the emergency room.

Of course, nothing so drastic was necessary for little
scrapes and bruises, but still…

Still, the question gave her pause. She forced herself to concentrate on it. It was good—no, it was *necessary*—to think about something—anything—other
than Jesse Crane and the startling color of his eyes, the
sleek bronze warmth of his flesh, the sound of his voice,
the way he touched her, the structure of his face and the
way she just wanted to be with him…

No! She had to think of something else.

He would be back at the end of the day, there to organize the hunt. As it veered toward five o'clock and
closing, she determined to spend some quality time
with Dr. Michael Preston.

BY THE TIME Lorena stalked off, Jesse had already
cooled down and realized that he'd been a fool, taking his frustration over what had happened out on her.

What was it about the woman? She made him forget everything the moment he was with her, even though she wasn't his type at all.

And why not?

Because she was blond?

Elegant, feminine…a powder puff, or so he had assumed at first.

But she wasn't. She was determined. Reckless, maybe, but determined and fierce, and she had told him that she was a crack shot. Not a powder puff at all.

But also not the kind to spend a lifetime in the wilds. Then he reminded himself ruefully that his "wilds" were just a forty-five-minute drive from an urban Mecca with clubs, malls, theaters and more.

What was he doing, arguing with himself, convincing himself that his lifestyle was a good one? Because…?

Because he hadn't felt the way he felt about her in a very long time. In fact, he'd thought he'd buried those feelings along with Connie, that as long as he threw himself back into his passion for the land and the tribe, he could learn to live without all they had shared, the tenderness and sense of being one, loving, laughing, waking together, sleeping each night entwined. There was the chemistry that brought people together, and, if you were lucky, the chemistry, excitement and hunger that remained. And more. The longing to see someone's eyes opening to the new day, the times when no words were necessary, the nights when life was good just because the world could be shared.

He lowered his head, wincing, feeling as if the scars that had covered his wounds were ripping open. As if they were raw and bleeding, all because of the promise of something, some*one,* else. But that promise brought with it the one emotion he dreaded more than anything. Fear. No wonder he'd pushed her away.

He clenched and unclenched his fists. This wasn't the right time. In fact, it was idiotic. And, anyway, she was furious with him, probably regretting the very fact that they'd touched.

He forced his mind onto the case.

He felt that they were closing in, that Lars would be able to get the search warrant after what he had learned from Lorena. There were, however, other alligator farms in the area. It might be tough for him to convince the D.A.'s office, without concrete proof, not only that there really were "enhanced" alligators in the Everglades, but that Harry's Alligator Farm and Museum was responsible, and that whoever had gone to the extremes of biochemical manipulation was also willing to kill for it.

He hesitated, then decided to take another drive out to Dr. Thiessen's place to see if the Metro-Dade cops had missed anything, though he doubted it. They were good.

Then again, this was a world he knew far better than anyone else, a world that could not be taught in any lab or classroom.

IN HER ROOM, Lorena found herself amazed to be carefully considering her wardrobe for the evening.

She hadn't been asked on the hunt, which made sense. Only experienced alligator trappers were going, and that definitely did not include her.

Nor, she suspected, did it include Michael Preston.

Which was good, because she wanted to spend some

time with Michael. She didn't want to appear as if she had dressed to seduce, but she *did* want to look attractive.

Not in an aggressive way. Just enough to be compelling, so she could conduct her own hunt this evening.

She opted for casual slacks and a soft silk halter top. When she was dressed, she headed for his lab, listened, and heard movement. She tapped on the door.

"Yes?"

Lorena slipped in. "Hey. Are you going on that hunt this evening?" she asked him.

He arched a brow, grimaced and shook his head. "I'm a scientist. The brains, not the brawn."

"Ah."

"I guess you're into brawn."

"I am?"

"Well…" He perched on the edge of his desk, still in his lab coat. "You've been spending a lot time with our bronzed-and-buff policeman, Ms. Fortier."

She shrugged casually. "Not really. I wound up driving with him when that poor woman freaked out over her friend having been killed. And I probably shouldn't have headed out to the casino to begin with, the night I left with him. Too tired. And then someone told him about the incident with the hatchlings, so he wanted to talk to me."

"Not me."

"Did you tell anyone here?" Lorena asked.

He lifted his shoulders. "I don't think so. Maybe the kid complained in the end, I don't know. Maybe we shouldn't have let the little brat off the hook."

"Maybe not," she agreed. She walked closer, then sat on the other corner of his desk. She frowned. "Michael, did you ever believe any of those stories about kids buying baby alligators and then their parents flushing them down the toilet, so they wound up in the sewers of New York, that kind of thing?"

He waved a hand in the air. "Science fiction," he assured her. "Alligators, even in a sewer, wouldn't last long in New York. They need the sun, the heat. You know that."

"Right," she mused. "But…down here, I wonder how many alligators wind up free after they've been lifted from a place like this one by a kid like that brat. I mean it's possible. We both know that."

He slipped from his position on the desk and approached her, a smile on his face. She was a bit unnerved when he came very close, leaning toward her, resting his hands on the desktop on either side of her. "Possible," he said softly, his face just a whisper away. "But no kid is going to steal a hatchling from here, then let it loose in the New York sewers to grow into a monster."

"But there's at least one monster alligator out in the canals right now," she said. "That's what they're hunting tonight."

She saw a pulse ticking in his cheek. He didn't move. "Just what are you suggesting, Ms. Fortier?" he asked very softly.

"What else could it be?" she asked innocently. "I think that alligator escaped or was stolen from a lab," she said, and shrugged.

"From here?" he asked.

"From somewhere," she breathed. He was close. So close. And he might be the brains and not the brawn, but he still had quite an impressive build, and she just might have taken things too far.

"If I could create a super-gator, I'd be rich," he said, sounding surprisingly disgusted.

But she could see the tension in his face, feel it in his muscles. Her recklessness could prove dangerous. This, however, had been the time to take chances. Dozens of men from around the area would be arriving shortly. If he came any closer…

If she felt a deeper surge of unease…

All she had to do was scream.

He was staring at her intently. Searching her eyes.

He started to raise a hand toward her face, smiling.

"Michael?"

The call and a fierce knocking were followed by the door simply opening.

Lorena slipped from the edge of the desk as Michael turned.

Harry was there.

"Michael, can you get out here and help with the equipment? This is insane, if you ask me. Half the guys have no supplies. Damn Jesse. Leave it to him to get the full cooperation of the Florida Wildlife and Game Commission for a wild-goose chase."

If Harry had noticed that he had interrupted something, he gave no sign. But maybe he hadn't noticed, she thought. He seemed much more upset about the hunt than that a man had been killed by a gator.

Lorena grimaced as she caught Michael's eye, then escaped in Harry's wake.

Hurrying out back to the canal, she saw an unbelievable lineup of airboats and canoes. Jesse was up on some kind of a huge tackle box, giving instructions. "Remember, folks, we're looking for something really large—not indiscriminately killing off a population for trophies."

"How big, Jesse?" a man shouted from one of the canoes.

"Bigger than the norm," Michael Preston answered for him, hurrying forward. "The biggest gator ever recorded in Florida was seventeen feet, five inches long. The biggest gator recorded in Louisiana was nineteen feet, two inches. So if you find anything smaller than that—wrong gator."

"Ah, hell!" the same fellow snorted. "We have to have something real to go by."

"You heard the man. We're looking for fifteen feet or over. All right?" Jesse asked.

"We get to harvest what we get?"

She saw Jesse defer to a man who looked like he was about to go on safari, in khakis and a straw hat. He was tall and lean.

Jesse reached a hand down and helped the man up on the box. "This is Steven Bear, Florida Wildlife and Game Commission."

"We can harvest the fellas, huh?" another man called.

"Gentlemen, the important thing is this—we're not out on a regular hunt. Make sure your quarry is over fifteen feet. Then the meat is yours. Nothing small is to be taken. Understood?"

She saw both Steven Bear and Jesse jump down from the box. Someone asked Jesse a question, and he answered, then headed for an airboat with a number of men already aboard.

Michael came up behind her. "Half those guys see this as a free-for-all," he murmured.

She turned to him, frowning herself. "I don't get it.

I mean, there are so many boats. Are they going to try to sneak up on it with all those lights, all that noise?"

"You'll see," Michael said.

And she did. It had seemed like chaos, but when the airboats took off, they headed in all different directions. Once again, she had forgotten that what appeared like solid ground in this area most often wasn't.

River of grass.

They were taking off over that river in a dozen different directions.

"Well, they'll be gone awhile," Michael said. "Why don't we have some dinner?"

"Sure."

They ambled to the cafeteria together, chose pork chops for their meals, and sat together.

The place was almost eerily empty. "Did Sally go on the hunt?" Lorena asked, curious that the outspoken, sexy redhead was nowhere to be seen.

"I didn't see her," Michael said.

"Does she help with the research here at all?" Lorena asked.

Michael laughed. "There's only one green thing that Sally would research—money," he told her.

"Oh?"

"Um."

Lorena smiled, smoothing back a lock of hair. "I don't get it then. Why is she working out here?"

"I think she's trying to be so indispensable to Harry that he makes her a partner. He owns land all over the place. And we're doing well here…but I think he'd like to open another facility, closer down by the Keys. He's already opened a few shops in Key Largo."

She frowned again. "Michael, this is a totally dumb

question. But Harry raises gators for their meat and hides, right? So where does he—"

"Lorena!" Michael said, grinning. "You don't 'harvest' animals where you show them off to the tourists! I told you—Harry owns a lot of land closer to the Keys, down in the Florida City–Homestead area."

"Ah."

"You really are interested, aren't you?" When she nodded, he said, "I can show you a few things, then. Are you done?"

"Um, yes," she murmured.

He wiggled his eyebrows in a manner suggestive of a hunched Igor in a horror movie. "Come, my dear, I'll show you my lab," he growled jokingly.

Lorena froze for a moment. She'd been doing everything in her power to sneak into the lab, and now he was making this offer.

While anyone who might have come to her rescue was off hunting for a rogue alligator.

No. There were more live-ins around the compound. And Harry hadn't gone on the hunt; he was around somewhere.

Besides, she had waited far too long for this opportunity. She could take care of herself.

And she was going in.

"Let's see what you've got to show me," she said with a smile.

He flashed her a smile in return, showing very white teeth. They rose and walked across the compound. She noted that there was another guard on duty.

She noted as well that he was spooked. When he heard their footsteps, his hand flew to the hilt of his gun, buckled at his hip.

"Just Ms. Fortier and me," Michael said.

"Evenin'," the guard replied.

When they reached the door to the lab, Michael drew out his keys and opened it, pressing the small of Lorena's back lightly to get her to proceed inside.

He followed, closed the door, then locked it.

Then he turned and stared at her. "I don't know why I bother. Someone picked it open the other day."

"Oh?"

He shook his head, approaching her. She cocked her head, looking at him. The guard had just seen the two of them together. He couldn't possibly be planning anything...evil.

Not unless he meant to go back out and kill the guard as well!

He was still smiling, as if his intent was to seduce, but she knew it wasn't. She found herself backed against the desk.

He was the brain, he had said, not the brawn. But he was a liar. She could feel the heat and strength of his muscles.

And his anger.

His menace...

"You picked the lock, Lorena, didn't you?" he asked softly.

"What?"

"Ah, the innocence. Like hell, Ms. Fortier. You're flirting madly with me, while it's more than obvious that it's Jesse Crane who's really stirred your senses. And yet you're charming as hell to Jack and Hugh, too. Are you just a little vamp, Ms. Fortier? I don't think so. I think you're up to something. You want something in this lab. Tell me what it is. Here we are, you and me, alone, finally. So…it's time. You want to see what's going on in here? You might as well. I think you should see exactly what you've been wanting to see. Now. *Right now*."

CHAPTER TEN

NIGHTTIME IN THE EVERGLADES, and it was eerie.

No matter how well a man knew the place, the near-total darkness hid the predators haunting the swamp and made this a dangerous place.

When light touched the gators' eyes, they glowed, as if they were demons from hell, not of this world at all.

Jesse was accustomed to the glowing eyes, and yet even he found them chilling in the dark of the night.

Despite his familiarity with the creatures, it was difficult for him to determine the size of one with only the eyes to go on. Sometimes, he knew instantly when he was looking at an animal of no more than five to eight feet, but with just the eyes above the water to go by, more often than not it was a crap shoot.

Twice they snared a creature only to realize that the specimen they had in their loops was no more than nine feet, ten tops.

Each time they released their catch. Enraged, the alligators made swift departures from the area once they had been freed.

The rest of the group on the airboat, Jack, Leo and Sam Tiger, were soaked and exasperated, but no one suggested giving up as they moved closer to the location where Billy Ray had been attacked and killed.

They had been out a few hours and had just cut the

motor, and only the noises of the night were echoing in the air around them, when Jack Pine said softly, "There," and pointed.

Jesse looked in the direction Jack was indicating.

The alligator wasn't completely submerged. The length of the head was incredible. He focused hard and saw the length of the animal as it floated just beneath the surface.

And he knew they had found the beast they were searching for.

Sam whistled softly. "I have never seen anything remotely near that size before," he said.

"Let's bait it," Jesse murmured.

Their bait was chicken. He tied several pieces on the line.

The alligator watched them as they approached. It didn't move; it showed no fear.

When the line was cast in the water, the animal moved at last.

It went for the bait. They were ready with their snares.

A massive snap of the mighty jaws severed the lines as well as securing the meat, but Jack managed to get a noose around the neck.

The alligator made one swing of that massive head. Jack went flying off the airboat, a shout of surprise escaping his lips. The animal instantly began to close in on him.

Sam quickly started the engine and headed in for a rescue. Jesse went for one of the high-powered revolvers. He aimed and fired, aimed and fired, as they neared Jack.

Sam swore, shouting to Jack.

In a frenzy, Jack moved toward the airboat.

Jesse, taking care to miss the man, fired again and again.

Ten bullets into the gator.

It kept coming, heedless of the men, heedless of the bullets that had pierced its hide.

They reached Jack. Sam and Leo instantly reached for him, and he reached back, grabbing their hands, the muscles bulging in his forearms and a look of dread in his eyes.

They were just dragging Jack over the edge of the airboat platform when the gator's head emerged, mammoth jaws wide with their shocking power.

Jesse aimed again, dead into one of the eyes.

The explosion ripped through the night.

The eye and part of the head evaporated.

And at last, with Jack's feet just clearing the water, the creature began to fall back.

Jesse fired again and again, aiming at what was left of the disappearing head.

He felt a hand on his arm. Sam's. "You got it," Sam said softly.

And from where he lay on the floor of the airboat, Jack said softly, "Dear God."

In the silence that followed his statement, they heard the whir of motors, saw approaching lights and heard the shouts of others.

More airboats and canoes arrived, and the area was suddenly aglow with floodlights.

"You got it?" Hugh called from another vessel.

Jesse realized that he was shaking. He nodded, turned, lowered his gun and found a seat.

The others began to haul the creature in.

"WELL, LORENA?" MICHAEL asked huskily.

Great, she thought.

She had a gun, and she was a crack shot. But she had let her eagerness to find the truth lead to stupidity, so here she was, boxed in by her main suspect, and he was challenging her....

She slid her hands backward on his desk. In all the old movies, there was a letter opener on a desk, ready to be used by a desperate victim as a weapon.

There was nothing on Michael Preston's desk but his computer and a few papers.

Not even a paperweight.

"Well..." she murmured, as he came closer. Closer.

There was nothing of use on the desk.

She told herself to scream!

It was all she had left.

"How could you?" Michael said suddenly, turning abruptly away from her.

She gulped down her scream.

"What?"

"How in the world could you suspect me of anything? Although what you think I've been doing, I still don't know. You've been on my computer. You've been searching this lab. What do you think that I've done? Or are *you* out to steal something from *me?*" he demanded.

She stared at him, a frown furrowing her brow. He seemed to be genuinely upset, and he also seemed to be as much at a loss as she was herself right now.

But if not Michael Preston...who? He was the scientist here.

The brains, not the brawn.

"What?" she repeated, stalling for time, rapidly trying to determine just what to say.

"Are you a thief?" he queried.

"Of course not!" she protested.

"Then what have you been doing?"

She sighed, looking downward. "Trying to understand," she murmured.

"Understand what?" he demanded.

"Well, you know, more of what's going on around here."

"Really. Didn't the concept of simply asking occur to you?"

Again she sighed. "Well…no. It's all so strange. This place, the people here."

"Except for Jesse Crane."

She stared at him, then shrugged. "He seems to be a decent guy. I like him," she murmured.

"In a way you don't like me?"

"Oh, Michael! You're great. You know that. Half the women you meet immediately start crushing on you," she told him.

He grinned ruefully, then shrugged. "The problem is," he said huskily, "it's the half of the female population I *want* that couldn't care less about me."

Lorena felt awkward then, not sure what to say. But feeling awkward was much better than feeling terrified.

"Michael…"

"Never mind. It's true. Women prefer brawn to brain."

She arched a brow. "Are you insinuating that men with brawn can't have brains? I have the impression that you spend a fair amount of time in the gym."

He sat beside her on the desk, crossing his arms over his chest. He sounded amused as he admitted, "Yeah, I go to the gym. But do I want to be out looking for a giant gator? Not in this lifetime. I like hatchlings. They're little. They might bite fingers, but it's unlikely that I'll become dinner for them."

"Michael...have you ever altered a hatchling?"

"Altered?"

"When you crack the eggs. Have you ever experimented?"

"Yes," he said flatly. His eyes narrowed sharply as he stared at her. "Is that what you're after? Trying to steal my vitamin compounds?"

"Vitamins? No."

"Well, that's about all I've worked with. Vitamins in the egg. You want my password? You want to get into the files you haven't been able to crack?" he asked.

She was uneasy again, thinking that he might have refrained from harming her only because he hadn't decided what she was really doing, why she had come.

Was this a trap?

"Just what kind of work are you doing?" she inquired.

"What do you think?" he demanded. "The same kind of research as everyone else! Alligator meat is already lean and high in protein. I'm trying to make it even better, so someday it can feed the world."

He sounded like her father. But she wondered if he was driven by the same true passion to help, or if he was seeking renown—or just money.

He shook his head with disgust suddenly and walked around to click on his computer. "What kind of work do I do? Research, and yes, experimentation. But you know what? Nothing I know about can create a giant killer gator. So you go ahead and take a look. I hope you're up on your enzymes, proteins, compounds, vitamins and minerals."

"Look, Michael," she began. "I—"

He was typing something when he suddenly looked up. "I just realized something. Why are you looking into *my* research? For a gator to have gotten as big as this one supposedly is, it would have to have been growing for years and years—while both of us were still kids, practically."

"Not that long," she murmured dryly.

He stared at her, then exhaled slowly. "Is there some kind of research out there that I don't know about? Some kind of discovery. That is…what you're saying is impossible."

"Hey," she murmured, keeping her eyes low. "I'm not a researcher. I'm not even an alligator expert."

"So what are you after?"

"I'm not sure. I'm just curious, I guess," she lied. She still wasn't certain she could trust Michael Preston.

He shook his head, studying the computer screen. "There have been big gators, but the biggest one on record wasn't even caught in this state. I suppose someone could have figured out a way to jump-start gator growth, or hybridize a gator with something else. I mean, we only have beefalo because of somebody's bright idea to breed a cow with a buffalo."

He seemed genuinely absorbed in seeking answers, but Lorena found that she was uncomfortable despite that fact.

"Come. Look," he demanded, staring at her belligerently.

She walked over to see the screen. He stood, urging her into the chair.

He had opened his research files. He had been telling her the truth—at least, as far as this proved. There were notes on the eggs with cracked shells. There was a study on albino alligators, with statistics regarding their life expectancy in the wild. There were side notes reminding him to speak to Harry about habitat changes, notations regarding the fact that he intended to set the temperature to create a male so they could eventually breed it with a number of females and track its genetic influence.

As she read his notes, she could feel him. He was standing directly behind her chair.

"Go on," he snapped, sounding angry again. "Keep reading."

Words began to swim before her eyes. She wondered how much time had passed.

It felt like forever.

She pushed the chair away from the desk, pushing him back, as well. "Michael, I told you, I'm not a researcher, so I don't even understand what I'm reading. I was just curious." She stood. "And I'm tired, really tired."

He shook his head. "You're not leaving here. Not until you tell me what you're up to."

"I'm not up to anything," she lied flatly.

"Then why break into my lab?"

She lowered her head, seeking a plausible explanation. She looked up at him again, knowing she had to be careful. "Michael...you're an attractive man."

"So?"

"I...well, frankly, I was interested in you. As a man. As a scientist. I was curious about you. I wanted to know what made you tick, why you're so fascinated with such strange creatures. But then…"

"Then you met Jesse."

She shrugged, not wanting to commit.

"You're sleeping with him," he accused her.

"Michael, that's really none of your business."

"Ah, I see. You break into my lab because of a crush on me—sorry, interest in my life, what makes me tick—but *your* life is none of my business."

She lifted her hands. "I'm sorry."

"I should report you to Harry."

"Do whatever you feel you have to," she murmured, looking down.

"You're making a mistake, you know."

He was close to her again. Just a foot away.

He reached out a hand. She nearly jumped.

He touched her face. "A big mistake," he told her.

"I'm afraid I've already made more than a few of those in my life," she murmured.

He tilted her chin upward, meeting her eyes earnestly. "No. You're making a big mistake with Jesse. You don't even know him."

"I know something about his past, if that's what you mean," she said.

"He's a loner, Lorena. Do you want to spend your entire life sitting on a mucky pile of saw grass? He belongs here. You don't. His passion is the land and the tribal council. He's decent enough as a human being. But he puts a wall up. He always will. Think about it."

She caught his hand and squeezed it. Like a friend. She was more anxious than ever to get the hell out of his lab.

"Michael, we've got a bigger problem than my love life right now. There's a killer gator out there."

"People have been killed by alligators before," he said flatly.

"Yes, but this is different. And we breed gators here. People are liable to think we have something to do with it."

He laughed a little bitterly. "You think? Who cares? Maybe that gator will make things better here. Think about it. People love to stop and stare at accidents. They love horror movies. People don't mind watching terrible things happen to strangers. I think the fact that there's a man-eater out there will draw even bigger crowds."

"Michael, that's horrible!"

He shrugged. "A lot that's horrible is true."

She hesitated for a moment, feeling another tremendous surge of unease.

"They should be coming back soon," she murmured. "Very soon."

"Are you trying to get away from me?" he asked her.

She straightened determinedly. "I want to see if they're back yet, if they've caught that thing," she said.

She headed for the door.

She felt him following her.

For a minute she was terrified that she wouldn't be able to open the door easily, since it was locked.

She twisted the knob, feeling his heat as he moved up close behind her, almost touching her.

She was certain he was reaching out, about to grab her, but the door opened easily, and as she threw it open, Sally was coming down the hallway.

"Sally!" she exclaimed loudly.

If Michael had been about to touch her, his hand fell away. "Hey, Sally."

"I think they're coming back," Sally was saying excitedly. "Harry was just on the radio with someone. They've got something."

"They caught it?" Michael asked.

"Well, I don't know if they caught 'it,' but they caught something. Come on."

JESSE FELT DRAINED and uneasy when they arrived back at Harry's. Jack Pine had come too damn close to being that alligator's last meal.

But he was apparently the only one who felt uneasy. Everyone else, including the hunters who had come back empty-handed, seemed to be on some kind of a natural high—amazed and excited by the size of the creature.

"It's a record," Harry said as the men made their way to land, a number of them dragging the nearly headless carcass onto the hard ground.

Harry was barking out orders, getting people to take measurements. He, too, seemed pleased and excited.

Jack, who had been given the tape measure, cried out, "Son of a gun, we just beat Louisiana. Twenty-two feet, three inches!"

"I don't care what it costs, we need the best taxidermist in the country. What's left of this sucker is getting stuffed. Hell, who shot the thing so many times? Never mind, never mind, the bullet holes are good. They make him look tougher than a *Tyrannosaurus rex*," Harry said.

"Harry, it's going to a lab. There's going to be an autopsy," Jesse said. He was drenched and covered in muck, and in no mood for the spirit of joviality going around. The thing had been a killer.

"An autopsy? On a gator?" Harry said.

Jesse felt his stomach turn. "We need to know for sure if this was the animal that took down Billy Ray."

Silence fell over the crowd at last as they all realized what Jesse was saying.

The gator would still have been digesting its last meal when it was killed.

"All right, Jesse. Have it taken to the lab." Harry sounded unhappy but resigned. "Do I get it when you're done?"

Jesse didn't answer, just turned away. Lorena was there, standing back in silence.

He felt a flip-flop of emotion.

In the heat of the hunt, he'd forgotten that he'd left her here. Alone.

But she appeared to be fine. More than fine. As ever, she was stunning. A rose in the midst of swamp grass.

"Are you taking the carcass to Doc Thiessen?" Harry asked.

Jesse kept staring at Lorena as he answered. "They'll have better facilities upstate, at the college," he said, turning away from Lorena at last.

Everyone had their cameras out now. They had hoisted the alligator up over one of the steel light poles. The thing was actually bending with the weight. Everyone had gone back to talking excitedly and having their pictures taken with the carcass.

The head…just the head…dear lord. The size of what was left was terrifying.

Lorena stayed apart from the crowd, but he saw

that Michael and Sally were posing, Hugh snapping the picture.

"Harry, we'll see about getting the gator to you when we're done, okay?" he said congenially.

"Folks, we got the cafeteria open!" Harry called out, beaming at Jesse's words. "There's just coffee and sandwiches, but you're all welcome!"

Still grinning broadly at Jesse, Harry walked away.

Lorena was still a good twenty feet away, but her eyes were on him.

"Hey," he said softly.

"Hey." She smiled, apparently having forgiven him, and walked toward him slowly.

Damn, but he was in love with just the way she walked. The slow, easy sway of her hips. The slight look of something secretive, something shared, in the small curl of her lips. The way her hair picked up the lights, burning gold.

She reached him and touched his face, apparently heedless as to whether anyone noticed or not.

"You know, Officer Crane, you look good even in muck," she told him.

"I'd be happy to share my muck," he told her.

"Not here," she whispered. He thought she shivered slightly. "Not tonight."

"Are you coming home with me, then?"

Her head lowered; then she looked up, and her smile deepened. "Yeah, yeah, I guess I am."

The feeling of dread and weariness that had taken such a grip on him as they returned seemed to melt away. Strange, how life could be, how human emotions could be changed by something as simple as the sound of someone's voice.

The sway of someone's hips. Her smile.

Chemistry. She had been fascinating but unknown, and now she was known. Everything he knew now made her slightest movement all the more seductive. The thought of touching her again was deep, rich, combustible.

"Should we take my car?" she asked.

He arched a brow with a rueful smile, indicating the state he was in.

"I told you, I like you in muck."

"Down and dirty, eh?" he teased.

"I was thinking of a shower," she murmured.

"Jesse!" someone called excitedly.

He was startled from the absorption that had made him forget that dozens of people surrounded them.

"Jesse!" It was Sally. She came over and gave him a big hug. "Aren't you excited? That's the biggest gator on record, and you're the one who bagged it."

"It was a killer, Sally."

"That makes you one big, bad hunter, then, doesn't it?"

There was innuendo in her voice. Once it had amused him, but now it was an imposition.

She suddenly realized she had her back to Lorena and turned. "Oh, I'm sorry, Lorena. It's just so exciting."

Exciting? Yeah, Sally was excited, Jesse thought. Sally was the kind who found sensual stimulation in danger.

He looked at Lorena, and at that moment he realized that he was falling in love. She was clearly amused by the situation. Her eyes didn't fill with anger, fear or suspicion; there was even a slight smile on her face. She was willing to let him handle it. And she would wait.

"It was an alligator, Sally. Thousands of alligators are killed on hunts. But I guess you're right. There are people who like the hunt. Frankly, I'm not a hunter."

"Jesse! Your people have lived off gators for over a century, hunting them, wrestling them."

For some reason, the way she said "your people" didn't sit right with him. He realized suddenly that Sally would always be fascinated with someone for what they did, not who they were. He hadn't really given it any thought before, but she'd never been more than someone with whom to enjoy a friendly flirtation. Tonight, he found that he was slightly repelled.

A wry smile came to his lips. That was, of course, because he'd never realized he could actually fall in love with anyone again.

"Isn't the casino the big moneymaker these days?" Lorena asked, her smile growing deeper as she and Jesse met each another's eyes.

"Oh, yeah. Bingo," Jesse agreed. "But we're all glad this guy's been caught. I think he's the one that got Billy Ray, and we'll know for certain soon enough. Good night, Sally."

He didn't actually step around her, just eased into a position that let him slip an arm around Lorena's shoulders.

"Good night, Sally," Lorena said.

The woman stared blankly at the two of them for a moment. Then she seemed to realize that they were leaving. Together.

"Oh! Uh, good night."

They avoided the cafeteria, where people had started massing. As they walked down the hallway, they could hear Jack talking. "I'm telling you, I thought I was a goner. If it hadn't been for Jesse, I'd have been chum."

Outside, Jesse protested again. "Lorena, this is swamp muck. Heavy, smelly dirt. The car—"

"There's a towel in back. You can throw it over the seat," she said. After rummaging for a moment, she found the towel and put it over the driver's seat.

"Hey, I'm the dirty one," he told her.

"And I don't know where I'm going. You need to drive."

She tossed him the keys. He shrugged. It was true. If you didn't know where to take an almost invisible road off the Trail, you were never going to find his house.

It was no more than a ten-minute drive, and both of them were too preoccupied to talk. And they were barely inside the door before she had slid into his arms, shivering slightly, clinging to him, her arms slipping around his neck, her body pressed to his, her lips seeking his mouth. It seemed an eon of ecstasy that they remained thus, and he felt a renewed sense not just of fervor and hunger, but of that deeper rise of emotion that came from the fact that they had made the subtle adjustment from wanting to needing, from carnal chemistry to a melding of body, heart and soul. She, too, was soon covered in swamp mud, and they made their way to the bathroom, where he managed to turn on the shower spray while disrobing himself and her, barely breaking contact the whole time.

Flesh, naked flesh, soap and suds, and hands. She touched him everywhere. He returned the favor. She had magic hands, taking a slow course of discovery. Light on his shoulders at first, and then with a pressure that both alleviated strain and created the sweetest strain of a very different kind.

Her fingers played down the length of his spine, over his hips. He touched her in return. The darkness of his hands over the pale roundness of her breasts was arousing, his palms rubbing over her nipples before his head ducked and his mouth caressed them. The water sluiced through her hair. He caught it and cast it over her shoulder, turning her against him so that his lips could fall on her nape, below her ear, on her shoulders, her back. He turned her in his arms, continuing his erotic ministrations against her abdomen, her thighs, then between them. She gripped his shoulders, quivered at his touch, moaned slightly, then cried out, sliding down in sudsy sleekness to meet his mouth with the furious hunger of her own once again.

Her hands were delicate, then fierce, stroking against his chest. They knelt together in a steaming spray that seemed almost fantasy, something keener, sharper, than he'd ever known before. She stroked his sex with her hands and tongue, and he wound his arms around her, bringing them both to their feet, bracing her against the tile of the shower, lifting her until she came back down on him and the hard arousal of his sex slid easily into her. He nearly whispered the words to her then, that he was more than physically one with her, that he was falling in love. But he would never have her doubt such words, as she would if they were spoken in the urgent desperation of the desire that drummed through him like a storm tearing the Glades asunder, so he whispered instead that she was beautiful, and the words she returned were ever more arousing. He became aware of the ancient thunder throbbing through his body, his lungs and his heart, and in a matter of moments they climaxed together in the steamy spray. The winds began to ease while they remained entwined.

Later, when they had sudsed again, then slipped into each other's arms to sleep, but wound up making love again, he held her, spooned against him. He lay awake, stroking her hair, in wonder. He had thought he would never find a woman like his wife again, someone who had loved him fiercely, been brave and funny, sweet and strong, an equal, but able to make him feel his own strengths, that he was very much a man.

And, of course, he hadn't found his wife again. In a place in his heart, he would love and cherish her forever.

He had found someone unique, who was passionate and righteous, confident, her own self. Different, and yet with qualities that resonated in his heart and soul.

He adjusted his position slightly. Pressed his lips to the top of her head. "I think I'm falling in love," he whispered.

She gave no reply. He wondered if he had pushed her too fast, if his great epiphany was not exactly shared.

But neither did she move or deny him.

Then he realized that he had found the words to say what he was feeling too late, at least for that evening.

Her breathing was soft and even, her fingers curled around his.

And she was sound asleep.

He smiled to himself.

It changed what he was feeling, deepened it, to know that she would sleep beside him, that they would wake together in the morning.

That he wanted to sleep this way every night of his life, and wake beside her again and again.

Would she feel the same? he wondered. Enough to really love this place, where predators roamed, the mosquitoes seemed elephantine and bit like crazy…and the sunsets were the most glorious man would ever see, and the birds that flew overhead came in all the colors of a rainbow.

He rose in the night and padded naked to the back window, looking out on the eternal darkness.

He heard her, felt her, before she came behind him, arms winding around his back as she laid her cheek against him.

Words failed him again.

He simply turned and took her into his arms. Though tenderness reigned, he found himself afraid.

Afraid to break the moment…

Afraid she didn't feel the same.

And later, still awake, he wondered if there was even more that had stopped him.

Fear…?

They had almost certainly killed the man-eater that had gotten Billy Ray.

They had not, however, captured the man who had created it.

CHAPTER ELEVEN

THE MASSIVE ALLIGATOR was being taken upstate for examination, but that didn't stop Harry Rogers from trying to use it to improve his tourist trade.

When Lorena arrived bright and early for work, she discovered that Harry knew how to move quickly. Out front, next to the ticket stalls, he had a mounted enlarged photo of the giant crocodilian—his own arm around it.

Lorena hadn't seen what had gone on overnight, so she was amazed to see that a number of the television stations had arrived, along with radio and newspaper reporters.

The monster was, as Harry and Michael had known, good for business.

The day moved rapidly, in a whirl of tours. Lorena took only a few minutes for lunch. Besides helping with the tours, she had to pull out an ammonia capsule to revive an elderly lady who stood in the heat a bit too long, patch up two little boys who scraped their knees, and treat an allergic reaction to a mosquito bite.

Michael was either too harried to bother her about the previous night or he had just gotten bored with the subject and didn't care any longer.

Sam and Hugh were both still a bit on fire, talking about the hunt the night before. Jesse had turned off his phone during the night, so Jack and Hugh, with Harry's blessing, were delighted to keep busy providing the reporters with what they needed.

The place was jumping.

The police waited until closing to make their appearance.

Lorena had just been saying goodbye to a group of tourists near the main entrance when she heard Harry's booming voice, alive with protest.

"A search warrant—for *this* place? What do you guys think that I'm doing here, feeding drug runners to my critters? What the hell are you after at an alligator farm?"

She noted that although a number of cops had arrived in vans with all kinds of equipment, Lars Garcia and Abe were the ones talking to Harry.

Lars sighed. "Harry, look, I'm sorry—"

"This is Jesse's jurisdiction, or so I thought!"

"Tribal law stands, unless the county, state or federal authorities have to step in," Lars said unhappily. He saw Lorena and studied her absently as he spoke. "Look, Harry, Jesse knows that we're here, and he's not feeling that his toes are being stepped upon. Harry, that was a monster they brought down. We have to search all the farms."

"For what?" Harry demanded.

"Evidence that someone's genetically engineering monster gators," Lars explained.

"What?" Harry seemed incredulous. "Look here, that was no creature from a horror movie. It was big, but it was just a gator. Jesse shot it, and it died."

"There has never been an alligator that size in Florida before," Abe said.

"There hasn't been one on record. Doesn't mean there hasn't been one out there."

"It was way beyond the norm, Harry," Lars insisted.

"Harry," Abe interjected, "God knows, you're an opportunist. Let's just hope you're not a crook."

Harry looked at Abe, enraged.

"Harry, please," Lars said, glaring at his partner. "Let us just clear you and your group so we can move on."

"You idiot!" Harry said, still glaring at Abe. "Clear me of what? Hell, am I an idiot? If I could manufacture a creature like that, do you think I'd let it out in the Everglades? Hell, no! I'd be making money on it."

Lars tried once again to explain. "Harry, we all know that a hatchling could get out. Someone could get careless, or someone could steal one, then lose it."

Harry threw up his hands, really angry. "You know what you can do with your search warrant as far as I'm concerned. But you go right ahead. You look into anything that you want to look into. Search yourself silly. I'm calling my lawyer. You know, if you wanted to see something at my place, all you had to do was ask."

Harry walked away muttering. Lars gave a slight smile to Lorena, shrugged and turned away to talk to a distinguished-looking man in a special-unit suit.

She hadn't realized that Michael had come up behind her. "The suspicious cops are your fault, I imagine?" he asked softly.

A shiver shot down her spine as he spoke. She spun around quickly. She didn't have to answer. He shrugged. "Not that I care. But if Harry finds out…mmm. You're in trouble. Big."

"Excuse me, Michael, I'm hungry," she said, and started for the cafeteria.

"I'm hungry, too," he said, trailing after her.

When they entered the cafeteria, Sally was rushing out. She didn't look at all amused. "Hey, sexy, what's up?" Michael demanded, stopping her.

She grated her teeth and cast Lorena what seemed like an evil stare, although she couldn't really be sure.

She might just be paranoid.

"They're inspecting everything, and Harry wants me there to explain the books. I don't get this—I don't get it at all! There was a giant alligator in the swamp—so we get *audited?* Not that there are any problems, I can assure you. My books are always perfect."

"I'm sure they are," Lorena murmured.

The woman might have been in a hurry, but she took time to glare at Lorena. "It's amazing, isn't it?" she murmured. "We were such a quiet place. Then you arrived and all hell broke loose. Did you have a nice time last night?"

"Yes, thank you," Lorena said evenly.

"What did you do last night?" Michael asked with a frown.

"Oh, come on, Dr. Preston! We have a budding romance in our midst, or didn't you know?" Sally asked.

Michael stared at Lorena. "You left with Jesse?"

"We're not required to stay on the premises," Lorena said.

"You're moving in with him?" Michael demanded. Lorena couldn't tell if he was angry or just surprised.

She looked at him incredulously, shaking her head. "That's kind of a leap, isn't it?" she demanded. She kept smiling, but the curve of her lips was forced. "This is my business, okay?"

"We're just trying to watch out for you," Sally assured her, suddenly saccharine. "I mean, well, you work here, so you're one of us. Jesse is…well, Jesse keeps his distance."

"Doesn't seem that he's keeping much of a distance now," Michael murmured.

"Hey!" Lorena protested again.

"Think of us as one big family," Michael told her.

"Okay, *bro.* I'm not moving anywhere. If such a thing ever happens, I'll be sure to inform my *family,*" she said.

"How lovely," Sally murmured. "I'm off to see to my books. You children have a lovely dinner." She waved a hand in the air and left them.

"You know, you are going to have to tell us what's going on," Michael said, a hand at Lorena's back as he directed her toward a table.

She was saved from having to answer at that moment when Jack Pine joined them, sitting down with a weary grimace. "Busy day," he said.

"Oh? At your end, too?" Michael said.

"A bunch of scientist types, or so I'm told, will be in tomorrow. They want to investigate all our stock," Jack explained.

Michael stared at Lorena again. "How come I haven't heard anything about this?"

"Maybe they just haven't gotten to you yet," Jack suggested.

Hugh came over just then, settling down at the table across from Michael. "This is nuts."

"Are we closing tomorrow for all this?" Michael demanded.

"Oh, no. They can work around us. They're taking samples, bringing chemists and vets in, that kind of stuff," Hugh said cheerfully.

"It's absurd," Michael said indignantly. "I mean, my research is…well, it's *mine*. Where are my rights in all this?"

"I suppose the problem has something to do with giant alligators eating people," Jack said with a shrug.

"There are alligators everywhere," Michael protested. "Alligator farms abound in this state. Entrepreneurs run hunts on private property that aren't sanctioned or controlled by the state or federal government."

"Well, Michael, maybe they feel that your research will help them," Jack said. "Who the hell knows? Has anyone ordered dinner yet?"

Looking across the room, Lorena saw that Jesse had arrived. She was both startled and pleased, and jumped to her feet before she realized that despite the fact that their affair was growing obvious, she might have been a little more circumspect.

"Well, well," Hugh murmured.

Lorena ignored him.

Jesse was already walking over to them. He offered her a smile, held out her chair for her, then chose one for himself.

"So you reported Harry's as a hot bed of…what, exactly?" Michael asked.

Jesse frowned. "What?"

Michael leveled a finger at him. "Cops and the people from Fish and Wildlife are going to be crawling all over the place."

"I heard they're checking out a bunch of places," Jesse said with a shrug.

"Why assume that Harry's has anything to do with a giant alligator?" Michael demanded.

"Maybe because Harry sponsors a lot of research—*your* research—into improving gator meat and hides?" Jesse suggested.

"Can we order now?" Jack asked as one of the waiters arrived at the table.

"Sure. We're in the middle of a criminal investigation. Let's eat," Michael snorted.

"I'm hungry," Jack snapped back.

The tension was definitely growing, Lorena thought.

"Michael, they've got to find out what is going on," Jesse said. "There could be more of those creatures out there. And if they don't find the sustenance they need in the wild, that would put people in danger. Come on, Michael. How many attacks on humans do you want to see?"

"There's no reason to think there are more alligators that size out there," Michael insisted. "Maybe our gators are just getting bigger all around, catching up with some of their counterparts in other places. Maybe they should start investigating that before they come out here on Indian land and start poking their noses into things."

"Hey, this may be Indian land, but when it's a county-wide problem—"

"The alligator was caught on Indian land, too," Michael said testily, cutting Jesse off mid-sentence.

Lorena saw Jesse tense, but he wasn't the one who answered. "So what are you suggesting, Michael? That it's all right because only Indians will be eaten?" Jack Pine snapped.

"Don't be ridiculous!" Michael argued indignantly. "I'm trying to be supportive of tribal law."

"Good of you to be concerned," Jesse replied.

"I think we should order dinner," Hugh murmured, nodding to the waiter, who had continued hovering in the background.

Fresh catfish was suggested and accepted all the way around. Most of the tension around the table eased, but a slight chill remained. Jesse seemed distracted, Jack stiff, and Michael annoyed. Only Hugh seemed oblivious to the general air of discomfort.

"So, any clues as to how our gator got to be such a monster?" Hugh asked Jesse.

"It's been sent off to Jacksonville. That's all I know right now," Jesse said.

"Hey, there's Harry," Hugh said. "He looks happy."

Harry, smiling broadly, breezed by the table. "Looking good, looking good," he told them cheerfully.

"What looks good?" Michael asked skeptically.

"This place. The phones have been ringing off the hook. People want to find out all about alligators. It's kind of like Jurassic Park meets the Florida Everglades. Hey, how's that catfish? Can't get any fresher."

"Harry, we don't know. We haven't got it yet," Hugh said, amused.

"Well, it's going to be great. We're on a roll, all of us. Keep up the good work."

Harry left just as their catfish arrived.

Lorena glanced at Jesse. Could Harry possibly be guilty of anything if he was this happy while the authorities were crawling all over his holdings?

Just as Jack remarked that the catfish was indeed excellent, a slender, balding man in a typical tourist

T-shirt and khakis walked up to the table. "Dr. Michael Preston?" he inquired.

Michael sat back tensely. "Yes."

The man offered a hand. "Jason Pratt, Wildlife Conservation. Can you give me a few minutes of your time? When you're done eating, of course."

"I guess I'm done," Michael said, throwing his napkin on the table.

"There's no reason for you to rush," Pratt protested. "I just wanted to catch you before you retired for the night."

Since it was still early, it was unlikely that Michael had been about to go to bed. Maybe Pratt was afraid Michael was about to flee?

Michael rose. "No. I'm done. How can I help you?"

He walked away with Pratt. Jesse rose, as well. "Want to take a ride with me?" he asked Lorena.

"Sure," she murmured, rising, too. Jack and Hugh were exchanging glances. She knew that along with the giant alligator, she was definitely a topic of conversation between them.

"See ya," Jesse said, nodding, taking Lorena's hand and heading out.

"Where are we going?" she asked as they got into his squad car.

"To see Theresa Manning."

"Theresa Manning?"

"The woman whose friend was…eaten," Jesse said.

"And what are we going to learn from her?"

"I'm not sure, but I called to see if we could speak with her, and she asked us over for tea and scones."

"Tea and scones?"

He shrugged. "Apparently she likes to bake."

"Jesse…do you think Michael is behind all this? I had the strangest conversation with him last night."

He scowled fiercely, looking at her in the rearview mirror. "You were alone with him?"

She ignored that. "He seriously believes that I'm here to cause him trouble."

"You need to stay away from him."

"But if he's doing anything illegal…he's about to face the music, right?"

Jesse shook his head. "Someone else has to be involved. Someone with money."

"Harry has money, but he seems as happy as a lark."

Jesse's cell phone started ringing. He answered it, then fell silent, frowning. Finally he said, "Call me as soon as you find out anything."

"What happened?" Lorena demanded.

He glanced quickly at her. "The alligator never made it to the university. Somewhere between here and Jacksonville, the truck it was on disappeared."

MICHAEL LEANED AGAINST his desk, scowling as Pratt and the other investigators—ridiculously casual in jeans and cotton island shirts or T's—went through his research records and his computer.

"What's this?" one of them asked.

Michael came around and looked over his shoulder.

"A record of the temperatures required to create the different sexes," he said patiently.

"And what's this?"

"Maturity level for the most tender meat," Michael said.

"And this…?"

"Breeding for the best skins," Michael said wearily.

The man rose suddenly. Others were still working in the filing cabinets, but most of his records were on the computer.

"I guess that's it for now," Pratt said, smiling cheerfully.

Michael realized that he had broken out in a cold sweat. Now he felt a debilitating rush of relief.

They hadn't found anything. Nothing. Nada. Zilch. Not a damned thing.

"You're done?"

"Yep. Thanks so much for your time and your patience," the man said.

"Hey, uh…sure," Michael said. "Anything to help. Not a problem. Anytime. Come back anytime you think I might be able to help." He couldn't seem to stop himself from babbling, he felt so relieved.

Pratt thanked him again as he and the others left the office. Michael sank into his chair with a sigh of relief.

"Yeah, any time," he muttered. Then he looked at his computer and quickly logged into his secret files.

"SUGAR? MILK? LEMON?" Theresa asked. "And…let me see. Those are blueberry in the middle, plain on the left side, and cinnamon on the right. I do so hope you enjoy them. I love to cook. My husband loved my cakes and pies."

Jesse had bitten into one of the blueberry scones. "It's wonderful," he told Theresa. "And it was so kind of you to make this offer. Delicious. Thank you. And for me, just tea is good."

"A touch of milk," Lorena murmured. "Thanks. And Jesse's right. These are just too good."

Theresa sat, beaming. "Well, I know you didn't come out for the scones. So how can I help you?"

"I know that this is painful for you, Theresa," Jesse said. "But you've heard all the ruckus about the alligator we caught last night."

Lips pursed, Theresa nodded grimly.

"Caught. It was caught," Lorena emphasized gently.

"That one was caught," Theresa said.

"So you think there are more?" Jesse asked.

"I think my friend was attacked by another one of your giant gators," Teresa said with assurance.

"Why?" Jesse asked her.

"They're territorial, aren't they? And yours was caught off the Trail. My friend was killed way out here."

Jesse cast a quick glance in Lorena's direction. "Was there anything strange going on at the time?" he asked Theresa.

"Strange?" Theresa repeated, then sat thinking for a while. "No. Nothing strange. Oh, now and then a few pets disappear, but…well, a small animal is natural prey, right?"

"I'm afraid so," Jesse said. "But you don't think there was anything else going on in the area?"

"Like what?" Theresa asked.

"Lights of any kind," Jesse said.

"Lights?" Theresa appeared confused. Then she gasped. "Why, yes, actually! There were lights in the sky several times right around the time when…" She paused, making a choking sound deep in her throat.

"Did they ever kill the alligator that took your friend?" Jesse asked. "Did animal control or the nuisance-animal division ever find the right gator?"

She shook her head, then returned to his previous

question. "We had been joking about aliens arriving," she murmured.

By the time they left, Jesse looked grim. He was silent when they got back in the car, and silent as they drove. At last Lorena asked him, "So...you believe that several of these creatures have grown up in the Everglades, and that big money is behind it. Enough big money so that someone is out in helicopters searching for their missing gators?"

"Yes," he said simply.

"But Harry is probably the one most involved with alligators who also has the most money," she said, lifting her hands in confusion. "And Harry is so happy he's practically singing!"

"We're moving forward," he said tensely. "The noose is tightening, and we will catch whoever we're looking for."

He didn't head back for the alligator farm but wound his way down the road that she would never have found herself, the road that led to his house.

As he parked, he looked at her, arching a brow. "Stay here tonight?"

"I should go back," she murmured.

"No, you shouldn't. Ever."

She sighed. "Jesse—"

"You want to catch a murderer. Well, you've done all the right things. The authorities are involved now. You don't need to go back."

She decided not to argue with him for the moment.

As they got out of the car, she glanced his way with a small smile. "You really are in the wilds out here."

"Pretty much," he agreed, watching her.

"It's been a long, hot day," she said.

"And...?"

"And the last one in is...a fried egg, I suppose!" she said, and dashed toward the door.

She began shedding her clothing once she had reached the patio. And she was definitely the first one in the pool.

The water hit her with a delicious sense of refreshing coolness. She swam from the deep end to the shallow, enjoying the cleansing of her flesh.

To her amazement, he was there, waiting for her, when she surfaced.

As she came up against the length of him, she was elated to feel the strength beneath the sleek flesh. His ink-dark hair was slicked back, and the green of his eyes seemed brilliant. His arms wrapped around her. "Skinny-dipping, Ms. Fortier? How undignified. Is this something you do frequently?"

She smiled and said softly, "Actually, no. This is the first time I've ever been skinny-dipping. In my whole life."

"I'm flattered. And honored."

He smoothed back a length of her hair, his lips brushing hers, hot and warm beneath the faint scent of chlorine. His arms tightened around her, bringing the full length of her body against his. Her breasts were crushed against the powerful muscles of his chest, her hips molded to his, and the perfectly placed thrust of his sex against hers was a titillation that thrilled and warmed her with a heady sense of anticipation.

"Does that mean," he asked huskily, "that the entire concept of sex in a pool is equally new?"

She started to answer, but his lips moved down the length of her neck and the words evaded her. He kicked away from the wall, the force slamming them more tightly together. She was scarcely aware of the slick feel of the tile steps when they landed there. For a breathless moment she met his eyes. Then she felt the full brunt of his body as he lifted her high against him, then thrust himself deeply inside her. She wrapped her limbs around him, and the fire that suddenly seemed to burn between them was an intoxicating contrast to the coolness of the water. She cast her head back, felt again the fury of his lips on her throat, breasts, the hollow of her collarbone.... Her lips met his again as they moved in the water, the night sky high above them, the whisper of the foliage around them, and the thunder of pulse and breath taking over. She buried her head against his shoulder as the power of need, and the agony-ecstasy of longing seemed to seep through her, spiral and grow, seize her and shut away the world. Her arms stroked his back; her fingers dug into his buttocks. She arched and writhed, and wondered that she didn't drown, but he kept them afloat, and in a cauldron of searing carnal mist until it seemed that the world exploded right along with the night stars, and she collapsed against him, still held tight and secure. Then she began to shiver, for the night, without the fire of him, was strangely cool.

"If I'd had any warning, we might have had towels," he said, amused, his lips handsomely curved as he pulled ever so slightly away.

"I was simply seized with overwhelming desire," she told him, and she smiled herself. "Quite frankly, I'm not sure I could have planned skinny-dipping."

"Stay, I'll get the towels," he said.

"But it's just as cold—"

She fell silent. He had already leapt out and, naked and dripping, headed for the house.

She realized that it was colder outside the water than in it, so she waited.

At first she eased her head back and simply smiled. She felt so wonderful that she refused to let herself wonder if she wasn't being a fool, falling in love with someone who made no promises, who was so distant.

But there wasn't a thing she would change, even if she could.

Her eyes opened suddenly, and she wondered why, aware that she was feeling the first twinge of unease.

She glanced around. Lights shone in and around the house, but beyond...

Beyond was the Everglades. Miles and miles of darkness and foliage and swamp, a land that was deep, dark and dangerous. A place where a million sins could be hidden.

She froze, aware then that she was in the light, that any eyes could be looking on from the darkness.

She was suddenly afraid, certain that the night could see.

"Here we are," Jesse murmured.

A towel was wrapped around his waist, and he had one for her in his hands. The sight of him seemed to turn back the darkness.

"Thanks," she murmured, rising, allowing him to wrap her in the soft fabric.

"Thank *you*," he murmured, and kissed her lightly on the lips.

The brilliance of his eyes touched hers, and he repeated the words very softly and tenderly. "Thank you."

He lifted her up, and they headed for the house.

In his arms, she forgot the darkness, and any thought that eyes might have gleamed at her from the black void of the night beyond.

CHAPTER TWELVE

JESSE WAS GONE in the morning. So was his car.

And she was furious. Despite the night they had spent together, she had no intention of listening to him about not going in to work. She was in no danger at the alligator farm. It was alive with officials—local, state and federal. Nothing was going to happen to her while she was working.

She walked around, fuming, for several long minutes while she brewed coffee.

Just how long would it take to get a taxi out to the middle of nowhere? In fact, was it even *possible* to get a taxi out to the middle of nowhere?

Come to think of it, she didn't know exactly where she was. What did one say? Come out and get me. There's a dirt road off Tamiami Trail, and it looks as if it leads into nothing but saw grass and a canal, but there's really a house out there. Quite a nice house, actually. Swimming pool, state-of-the-art kitchen…

She swore aloud and hesitated, wondering if she should call in to work or just pray that Jesse would show up and drive her to work.

She pulled out her cell phone and stared at it, ready to put through a call to his cell, tell him what she thought of his high-handed tactics and demand that he come back immediately so he could take her to work.

He might, of course, simply refuse. He might even be involved in a situation from which he couldn't extract himself. Too bad. There were others on his day crew. He could send someone for her, and damn it, he *would*.

Just as she was about to punch his number in, her cell rang. Caller ID said the number was the office at Harry's.

"Hello," she said quickly, expecting Harry, though a glance at her watch showed her that she wasn't late yet.

"Hey" came a soft voice. Male.

"Michael?"

"No, it's Jack. We didn't see you at breakfast. We were getting a bit worried."

"We?"

"Hugh, Sally and me."

"That was nice of you, but I'm fine."

"Glad to hear it. Not that you shouldn't be," he said hastily. "Things are just a bit strange around here right now, you know? I mean, who'd ever think *I* would be in any real danger from an alligator? So…we were worried."

"No, I'm fine, just…" She hesitated for only a second. "Jesse seems to have gotten caught up in something. He's not here, and I'm afraid I'm going to be late."

"We'll come get you."

"No, I'm sorry. You don't have to."

"No, no, it's fine. One of us will come. Fifteen minutes."

Jack hung up.

She clicked her phone shut. The hell with Jesse and his high-handedness. She was running her own life. No matter how much she cared for someone, she wasn't going to be ordered about or dissuaded from her course.

Her father had been murdered, and she had never felt so close to capturing the killer. No way was she going to back off now.

Inside, she poured a last cup and turned the coffeepot off. And waited.

GEORGE OSCEOLA REPORTED on the missing van. It wasn't much of a report—the van was still missing. It had been on I-95. The driver had spoken to his wife at about ten-thirty in the morning, just after fueling up.

And then...

He and the van had just disappeared. County law enforcement throughout the state had been notified, along with the highway patrol, but so far, the van hadn't been spotted.

A call to Lars provided no further information.

Jesse looked at the phone and thought about calling Lorena. She was going to be really angry. But she hadn't called him to demand that he come back and take her in to work. Maybe she had fumed for a while, then decided on her own that the smart thing to do now would be to stay away from Harry's.

As he stared at his desk phone, it rang. A female voice greeted his ears, but not Lorena's. "Jesse, it's Julie. I was just calling in to see if...well, if anything else had happened."

"We're working on it, Julie, but I've got nothing to tell you."

He could sense her hesitation, then she said, "Jesse, I know it was probably foolish, but I went by the house last night. I mean, I have to go back inside eventually."

"I'd be happier if you'd stay away a little longer," he told her. "Just a few more days."

"A few more days," she echoed. "The police have asked me to wait a few more days, too. Before…before claiming the bodies. They're afraid the medical examiner might have missed something. But about the house…I'm going to need clothes."

"Julie, when you go, I'll go with you. And if you need my help at the funeral home or with the church…"

"It's all done, Jesse, thanks. I knew what they wanted," Julie said. "I didn't call you to cry."

"Sweetheart, you have the right to cry as much as you want," he assured her softly.

"Thanks, Jess, but what I need is to…to bug you and make sure no one stops until my parents' killer is caught. And also, I called because I keep thinking about the lights I saw out at the house."

"Plane lights? Helicopter lights? Men on the ground with flashlights?" Jesse asked. "What do you think?"

"I know they didn't come from anyone on the ground," Julie said. "To tell you the truth…I know why my mother thought aliens were landing. They hovered right above the trees. I didn't hear any noise. Of course, I was in the car, and they were at a distance."

"Thanks for calling, Julie. I'll look into it. Trust me. I want to help you. I loved your parents."

"I know you did, Jesse. And they thought the world of you. So do I. And I'll wait till we go inside together, okay?"

"Perfect."

He hung up after a minute, then called Lars back. "We need to start checking the airfields. More specifically, we need to find out who has been taking helicopters up."

Lars groaned. "Every television and radio station

out there has a traffic and weather copter! And when
we were out at Hector and Maria's, you said an airboat
had been through."

"So?"

"So we've been talking to a lot of people with airboats, Jesse."

"Yes, and that was a move that needed to be made.
Now we need to find out about helicopters."

He heard an even louder groan.

"Lars, I keep hearing stories about lights wherever
there's been an event with an alligator. You have more
resources at your disposal than I do. Can you get on it?"

He heard the deep sigh at the other end, but then Lars
agreed. "All right. I'm on it."

Satisfied, Jesse hung up. He drummed his fingers
on the desk. Something had been bothering him, and
he wasn't quite sure why.

He looked at the phone and thought about calling his
house, then decided not to.

He rose suddenly, since he wasn't getting anywhere
sitting at his desk.

He grabbed his hat from the hook by the door.
"Where are you going?" George asked him.

"To check with Doc Thiessen or Jim Hidalgo. See
if anything else has happened over at the vet's. I'm
pulling into his drive now, so call me if you hear anything," Jesse said.

LORENA EXPECTED EITHER Hugh or Jack to show up at
the rear of the property with an airboat. Instead, it was
Sally who finally tooted her horn from the front. Lorena clicked the front lock and hurried out.

"Jesse's trying to keep you away from Harry's, huh?" Sally said.

"Why would he do that?" Lorena asked, hoping she wasn't giving anything away.

"Why? Killer gators, feds all over the place, something fishy in the air," Sally said with a laugh. "Actually, you should be happy. If he didn't care about you, he wouldn't be acting so much like an alpha dog. Well, maybe he's just the alpha-dog type. I don't know."

Lorena shrugged. "Thanks for getting me. I don't know what he got involved in, or when he might get back, but I don't like being late."

"Aren't you even a little bit worried about everything that's going on?" Sally asked her.

"Should I be?" Lorena asked.

Sally laughed. "Michael thinks you're a suspicious character."

"Michael is paranoid," Lorena murmured.

"Maybe. He's a scientist. Maybe all scientists get paranoid. They think their research is better than gold."

"Maybe it is. Sometimes."

Sally waved a hand in the air. "I don't think Michael has created a strain of giant killer alligators."

"Oh?"

Sally shook her head. "He always seems frustrated. He's a good-looking guy. I think he had the hots for you. Actually, until Jesse stepped into the picture, it kind of looked like you liked Michael."

"I like everyone at the farm," Lorena murmured.

"Just the slutty type, huh?" Sally queried.

"What?" Lorena snapped.

"Well, you *were* flirting pretty hard with everyone until you settled on Jesse."

Lorena stared out the front window. "Did you come to get me just so you could give me a hard time?" she asked.

Sally looked at her, eyes wide. "No! Of course not." A small smile curved her lips as she shook her head.

DR. THORNE THIESSEN wasn't in when Jesse arrived at the veterinary clinic.

Jim Hidalgo was there, though. "Hey, how are you feeling?" Jesse asked him.

"Fine. Just fine," Jim assured him.

"How come you're here? I thought you had the night shift? And where is the doc, anyway?" Jesse asked.

"This is the day he does calls. He covers a few of the alligator farms, you know. And he does cattle, as well. There are even a couple of folks with real exotics, snakes and things, and for them, he makes house calls. One day one week, two days the next. I guess it works for him."

Jesse chewed a blade of grass and nodded. "You still don't remember anything about what happened that night, huh?"

"Nothing. You still haven't caught the thief, huh?"

Jesse shook his head. "Tell me if I've got it right. You were in the back, then…wham! And then nothing, nothing at all, until Doc was standing over you?"

"Yeah, yeah, then lights, sirens, cops, med techs… You know the rest. You were here."

"Right."

Jesse shrugged. "So when will the doc be back?"

"Tomorrow morning," Jim told Jesse.

"Where is he?"

"Don't know. He works lots of places."

"And you're in charge until then? What about the day guy?"

"He works with Thiessen, travels with him. Weird goose, if you ask me."

"Because he's white?"

Jim laughed, shaking his head. "Because he never talks. Hey, lots of folks live and work out here who aren't part of the tribe. We all get along. His day guy, though. John Smith. Who ever heard such a name for real? He's a big goon. Never talks."

"To each his own," Jesse said. "Thiessen must trust him. Anyway, you feel safe enough out here alone now?"

"I'm not alone."

"Oh?"

Jim gave a whistle. A huge dog came crawling out from beneath the desk where Jim sat. He was quite a mix. Evidently a little bit shepherd, chow and pit bull. Whatever else, Jesse didn't know, but it made for one big beast of a canine.

"I just got him," Jim said happily. "I call him Bear."

Bear wagged his tail.

"He likes you," Jim continued.

"I'm glad," Jesse said.

"Anyway, he makes me feel safe. He was sniffing and woofing before you got out of your car. When I told him it was all right, he sat right back down. Got him from the animal shelter."

"Great."

"Doc isn't too fond of him," Jim admitted. "But he knows I'm not happy anymore about holding down the fort by myself on the days he's gone and at night, so…" He shrugged happily.

Jesse nodded. "See you. Don't forget—"

"Yeah, I know the drill. If I think of anything, I'll call you."

"Yep. Thanks."

When he reached his patrol car, Jesse put a call through to the office.

The van with the alligator carcass was still missing. And nothing had been found of the samples taken from the vet's office.

There were no known leads on the murders.

He clicked off, hesitated, and at last called his house.

She wasn't answering. He hung up, then called back, and spoke when he heard his own message. "Pick up, Lorena, please. It's Jesse."

But she didn't pick up. She might have been in the pool, in the shower or in another part of the house.

Or she might have called someone to take her in to work.

He tried her cell phone.

She wasn't picking up.

Okay, so she was angry.

He put a call through to the alligator farm. Harry answered. "Hey, Harry. I'm surprised to hear your voice."

"It's still my place, you know. Despite the goons crawling all over it," Harry said. But he sounded cheerful.

"You just don't usually answer the phone."

"This place is doing twice the business we used to. No one here but me to pick up. The feds said I didn't have to close, just as long as they could go through what they wanted. Hell, they can go through anything, as far as I'm concerned."

"I'm glad you're happy, Harry," Jesse said. "I guess it would be tough for you to find someone to search the throng of tourists and find Lorena for me, huh?"

"Yes, it would be. But I can put you through to the infirmary, in case she's there."

"So you've seen her?"

"Not this morning. But I'm sure she's working, no thanks to you."

"What do you mean?"

"You're trying to seduce my help away from here, aren't you, Jesse Crane?"

"Harry—"

"Hang on, I'll put you through. How do you work this ridiculous, pain-in-the-ass thing?" he muttered.

Harry didn't put him through. He hung up on him. Irritated, Jesse snapped his phone closed.

His house was between the vet's and the alligator farm, so he decided to make a quick stop, see if she was there fuming and swearing at his furniture, then head out to the farm.

A sense of genuine unease was beginning to fill him. It was as if puzzle pieces were beginning to fall together, yet they didn't quite seem to fit.

He closed his eyes for a moment. Someone from Harry's was definitely involved. There had to be a money connection. And someone who knew the Everglades well.

There was more than one person involved, for sure. A connection through Harry's, a money man, someone with a knowledge of genetic engineering, and someone else, a hired goon.

Thoughtful, he picked up the phone to make one last call, then hit the gas pedal.

THE PHONE RANG, and Sally answered it.

"Hey," she said cheerfully. Then she glanced sideways at Lorena. "Sure...No...Yes, of course."

She clicked off, then offered Lorena a rueful smile. "Jesse," she said.

"Jesse?"

"Yeah, he wants me to make a quick detour."

"Uh-uh. No way. Let's go in to work."

"I think he's found something."

"What?"

"I think he's made a discovery. Something to do with...if I heard him right, your father."

"My father!" Lorena said, startled.

"Yeah. I didn't know Jesse knew your family. Hey, it's your call. He wanted me to bring you out to what they call Little Rat hummock. It's barely a piece of land, but they have names for every little hellhole and cranny out here. From the days when they were running and hiding out here, I guess. Anyway, what should I do? Jesse sounded all excited."

Lorena's heart flipped; her pulse was racing. She was still furious with him. But if he had discovered something and needed her in any way, she had to be there.

"If Jesse were calling me," Sally said, sounding wistful, "I'd sure be going."

"I'm supposed to be working," Lorena murmured.

"Okay, we'll go to work."

Lorena lifted her hands. "No. Little Rat hummock it is."

"Good thing I brought the Jeep," Sally said. "There's no real road out there."

There wasn't. Lorena thought they were going to sink in mire once and, if not, be swallowed in the saw grass.

But Sally knew the terrain. Right when Lorena was gritting her teeth, certain they were about to perish in the swamp, the wheels hit solid ground. Ahead, she saw a cluster of pines.

"You're not scared out here, are you?" Sally asked her. "You don't need to be. Well, maybe you should have worn boots, but don't worry—the snakes won't get you, not if you leave them alone. Besides here, in the pines, all you really have to worry about are the Eastern diamondbacks and the pygmy rattlers. Well, and the coral snakes, but they don't have the jaws to bite you unless they get you just right." She glanced at Lorena, who could feel herself turning pale. "Sorry. I'm out in the Everglades all the time, and I've never been hit by anything more vicious than a mosquito."

Sally brought the Jeep to a halt.

Lorena looked around.

There was nothing. Nothing but a patch of high ground, a bunch of pines and the saw grass beyond.

"I don't see Jesse."

Sally was frowning, staring ahead.

Lorena heard the noise, too, then. A throb of engines.

"Airboat?" she murmured.

"Yeah. What the hell…?" Sally murmured.

"It's probably Jesse," Lorena said, getting out of the car.

Sally got out, as well. She walked around the car, staring ahead, still puzzled.

"It's not Jesse," she murmured after a minute.

The airboat came around the cluster of pines that lay ahead. "It's Jack. Jack Pine," Sally said.

"So it's Jack. Maybe Jesse asked him to come out here, too," Lorena said.

But Sally shook her head. "No…no…something's wrong here."

Jack brought his airboat to a halt and leapt out.

"Oh, man," Sally murmured. She turned again. Lorena realized that they had walked some distance from the Jeep.

"Hey!" Jack called. "Hey, Lorena! Stop!"

Sally shook her head wildly. "Run!" she advised, and immediately took her own advice.

Lorena stared from Jack to Sally, then back again.

There was a large machete hanging from Jack's belt.

"Run!" Sally called back to her.

"Run where?" Lorena cried, chasing after Sally.

"Follow me. I know where I'm going!"

THERE WERE TIRE tracks in front of his house. Jesse hunkered down and studied them.

A Jeep. Harry's had a number of Jeeps. Any of the senior staff had access to them.

He checked the house quickly, but he knew the minute he entered that she wasn't there. He paused in back, though.

There were tire tracks in the front, but the broken foliage in back indicated an airboat had been by, as well.

At that instant, his heart seemed to freeze in his chest. He headed back for the car, already flipping open his cell phone.

"George, I've got Lars checking on a few things, and I've asked him to get men out here. But we know the area better than they do. I want everyone available out here. Something is going down *now*. Cut a swath from the vet's to Harry's, pie-shaped, fanning south."

"Jess, what the hell…?"

"Do it. Just do it."

LORENA STOPPED BECAUSE she couldn't run anymore. Sally, ahead of her, had stopped, as well.

She looked back at Jack Pine, who'd been closing in on them.

Jack had stopped, too.

"What are you doing out here, Sally?" Jack demanded.

"Jesse called," Sally said.

Jack shook his head. "No."

"What the hell are you doing out here, Jack?" Sally demanded in return, sounding frightened.

"Following you. I saw the car from the airboat. I was on my way out to pick up Lorena, so I couldn't help but wonder why you were heading out there, too. What's going on, Sally?"

"Jack, you're a liar and a murderer!" Sally cried, her tone hysterical. "I couldn't let you get Lorena. I couldn't let it happen."

Jack shook his head, looking puzzled. "Lorena, get away from her. She must have been listening on the phone. She had to get to you before I did."

Lorena looked from one of them to the other.

Sally wasn't armed.

Jack was carrying one frighteningly big knife.

She had no idea where she was, only that she was far from the car.

"I have an idea," she said. "Let's all head back to the alligator farm and discuss this whole thing."

"Lorena, don't be ridiculous," Sally said.

Lorena realized that Jack was moving steadily closer to her.

"Get away, Jack," she said.

"Don't you get it yet?" Jack said.

"You're going to kill her—and me!" Sally cried. "Lorena, don't you see? He's going to chop us up and feed us to his alligators."

"No!" Jack cried. "You've got it all wrong. You have to listen."

"Come on," Sally cried. "Lorena, move! One swing of that machete…"

"Lorena," Jack pleaded as he took another step toward her.

"This way!" Sally cried to her.

Lorena tried to maneuver around the three pines that separated her from Sally.

"No!" Jack cried. "No!"

He was coming after her.

She turned to run more quickly.

But as she did, she was suddenly running on air. There was no earth.

No hummock, no ground.

She was falling through space.

Falling, falling, into the darkness of a pit.

She hit the ground with a thud, but after a moment of breathless shock, she realized that she hadn't broken any bones. The ground was not hard. It was muck and mire. Of course. They were below sea level. It would be impossible to dig a dry hole.

She let out a sigh of relief, then heard the thud next to her.

Someone else was in the hole.

And then…

She heard the noise. Loud. A grunting sound, like a pig. No, not a pig. A huge, furious boar. Or…

An alligator.

CHAPTER THIRTEEN

JESSE CHOSE TO take his own airboat, trying to follow the broken foliage across the Everglades, certain that time was of the essence. His heart felt heavy. There was so much ground to cover. The river of saw grass seemed endless. He'd already seen so much evil done out here. You could search forever to find a body.

No, he refused to think in that direction. She had to be alive. He was certain that Lorena had been lured somewhere, but where, he didn't know. Or even why. Except that she was a piece of the puzzle; she'd been the first to know that something very wrong was going on, and that they were talking technology.

Dangerous stolen technology.

They weren't going to find anything at Harry's Alligator Farm and Museum.

Because Harry wasn't guilty.

And if all went as the thieves had planned it, they wouldn't find the van or the alligator carcass, nor the specimens from Doc Thiessen's lab.

He still didn't have all the facts, but he was certain of one person who might be involved. And that person didn't intend for any of this to be discovered, and it wouldn't matter just how many people died. The frightening thing was that no matter how many people died, mysteriously or otherwise, the techno thief clearly believed he couldn't be caught.

Ahead, he saw one of the airboats from Harry's. And there was someone beside it, gesturing madly.

He cut his engine.

Sally.

"Jesse, Jesse! Help! Quickly. It's Lorena…. Help!"

His heart remained in his throat. "Lorena…?"

"Come with me. For the love of God, hurry. And be careful. It's Jack…he'll kill her!"

Jack? Jack Pine?

Sally was running. Jesse ran after her in a flash. She circled around the pines, then shouted to him.

"Hurry!"

He did. And then he plunged into the hole.

He should have seen it. Even concealed as it had been with bracken and brush, he should have seen it. Hell, this was his country. This god-forsaken swamp was his heritage. He knew it like the back of his hand. He should have seen the damned thing, and realized that it wasn't any natural gator hole.

No. This one had been dug intentionally. And it was deep. In the rain, it would flood. But in the dry season…

He landed hard. The hole was deep, and the thatch covering above kept out all but a hint of light.

"Oh, God, Jesse!" Lorena cried, recognizing him in the meager light. In a second she was next to him, warm and vital. He held her, damning himself a thousand times over. She'd come flying into his arms with such trust.

And he had no idea how to get them out of this mess. He pulled out his cell phone. No signal. Damn!

"Jesse?" Jack Pine moaned.

"What the hell?" Jesse said. He eased himself away from Lorena.

It was pitch black, and he wasn't a trigger-happy kid or a rookie, but Jesse pulled his gun, just in case.

"Stay where you are, Jack. I'm armed."

"I'm not your problem," Jack said.

Jesse blinked, trying to accustom his eyes to the eerie lack of light.

"Stay back," he said softly, his mind going a hundred miles an hour as he tried to figure out what the hell was going on.

Lorena backed up until she and Jack were both flat against the wall of earth and muck.

Above them, Jesse suddenly heard laughter.

Sally's laughter.

"What a pity I can't see you all down there. Sorry, Jack. You were really kind, likable. You shouldn't have been so determined to help Lorena. And Jesse…so gallant. See, Lorena? You were the problem. Everything was going just fine until you appeared. But it doesn't matter. They'll rip Harry's apart, but they won't find a thing. They'll just have to accept the fact that we've grown some big gators in the Everglades—and that they ate you all up."

She sounded as if she were happily reading a children's fairy tale.

"I have to go now. I have to get rid of both those airboats. Goodbye. Nice knowing you."

Jack exploded. "Dammit, Jesse. Do something. She's insane. I mean…she's not the brains behind things, I'd swear it, but when I realized she had Lorena, I knew something wasn't right."

It was then that Jesse heard it. The grunt…the grunt followed by the roar.

He'd been listening to alligators since he'd been a kid. He'd learned a lot about the sounds they made.

Those that had to do with mating.

And those that had to do with territoriality…and hunger. Or both.

"Hell," he muttered under his breath. He could barely see the other two. "Stay back," he warned them.

"Jesse," Lorena said softly. "What are you going to do?"

"I'm armed," he reminded her. But he was worried. Bullets at almost immediate range had barely pierced the tough hide of the alligator they had bagged two nights before.

He wanted to rush over to Lorena. He wanted to hold her, to place his body as a barrier between her and the creature in the darkness. He wanted to say a dozen things to her. He wanted to tell her that he loved her.

He stood dead still, listening, waiting.

The animal was moving. He heard it moving slowly at first, but he knew just how fast a gator could be.

Then there was the rush.

He spun, blinded, but going on instinct. He emptied the clip. The sound was deafening.

The animal bellowed and paused, then slammed into him.

In the dark, he heard the jaws slam shut.

Close. So close that he felt the wind the movement created.…

He jumped back.

"Jesse!" It was Lorena, shouting his name.

"Jack, we've got to straddle it!" Jesse yelled.

"Are you insane?" Jack shouted back. "These are monsters. They can't be wrestled down like a five- or six-footer."

"Do you want to be eaten?" Jesse demanded.

The animal had apparently been wounded, because it continued bellowing. Its senses were far better than his own, Jesse knew, but it seemed to be disoriented. He tried desperately to get a sense of its whereabouts.

Then he threw himself on the animal.

He aimed accurately, hitting the back just behind the neck. But the creature was powerful and began thrashing. Right when Jesse thought that he was going to be tossed aside like blown leaf, Jack landed behind him.

"What now?" Jack shouted.

"I've got to get on the jaws."

"I can't hold the weight!"

"You've got to."

"Wait! I'm here!" Lorena cried.

"Lorena, you don't—" Jesse began.

"We've done something sort of like this before," Jack panted. "Kind of."

There was a flurry of motion as the alligator gave a mighty bellow, tossing its head from side to side.

Lorena landed on the animal's back behind Jack.

"Now what?" Jack demanded.

"The jaw," Jesse said.

"You're mad," Jack responded.

"What? We can't ride this damned thing forever," Jesse said.

"But—"

"Big or little, if I can get the jaw clamped, we'll be safe."

"Yeah, yeah…if you don't get eaten first. Go for it."

He did. He had no choice. He tensed, feeling every inch of the creature beneath him, sensing with all his might, trying to ascertain what the creature's next twist would be.

And then he moved. He leapt forward, landing heavily on the open jaw, snapping it shut. The creature was mammoth; the jaws extended well beyond his perch.

He'd snapped the jaws shut, and still the animal was trying to fight him off. Its strength was incredible. It would shake them all off if they weren't careful.

Trying to maintain his seat, he reached into his pocket for a new clip. The animal bucked. He nearly fumbled the clip.

He tried again.

"Hurry," Jack breathed.

The alligator made a wild swing with its tail.

Lorena screamed. Jesse heard the whoosh as she flew through the air, the thud as she slammed against the mud wall of the pit.

The alligator bucked, fighting him wildly, beginning to get its jaws open, despite his weight.

"Jack, hold him!" he cried.

"Damn it, I can't. I can't!"

Then he heard Lorena, rising, breathless but as tenacious as the creature beneath him. "I'm coming."

"Watch it!"

The alligator swerved, knowing exactly where Lorena was, trying for her.

She moved like the wind, flying past him, landing behind Jack once again.

He could barely hold the gun, much less insert the clip. He had to. He had to, and he knew it.

He locked the clip into place.

He felt for the eyes, and he fired.

The ferocity of the bellow that erupted from the creature nearly threw him. The sound of the bullet exploding was terrible, almost deafening.

But he shot again.

And again.

At last the gator ceased to move.

For long, awful moments, none of them moved.

Jesse's ears were ringing when he finally said huskily, "Lorena, try getting up."

She did so, slowly, carefully.

The creature remained dead still.

"Jack."

Jack moved, but Jesse stayed. He groped around and found the base of the skull, then warned them, "I'm shooting again."

He delivered two more bullets into the creature.

Then, at last convinced that the creature had to be dead, he moved, too.

In the darkness, he felt her. But she didn't collapse against him the way a lesser woman might have. She strode over to him, and her arms wound around him as his wound around her.

Only then did she start to shake.

He heard Jack sink to the ground. "I think I'm moving north," Jack muttered. "Somewhere with ice and snow and no alligators."

Jesse allowed himself a moment to revel in simply holding Lorena, in feeling her, breathing her scent above the gunpowder and the muck.

"What the…?" Jack said suddenly. "Hell."

"What?" Jesse demanded sharply.

In the darkness, they could hear Jack swallow.

"What?" Jesse demanded again.

"There, uh, there was someone else down here," Jack said very softly. "There are...body parts."

"Oh, God!" Lorena breathed.

"Hey, we've got to keep it together," Jesse said sharply. "It's not over yet. We've got to get out of here. Quickly. They'll be back."

"They?" Jack said dully. Then he added, "Of course. They."

"Come on, Lorena," Jesse said. "I'll hike you up first."

He lifted her, and with Jack's help, he got her to his shoulders. From there, a shove sent her out of the pit.

"Hey! I found a big branch," Lorena called. "You guys can use it as a ladder."

She nearly hit Jesse in the head with it, but as soon as they got it in place, Jack reached upward, bracing against it. Jesse gave him a push.

They heard the tree limb cracking, but Jack was nimble for his size, and grasping for both the ground and Lorena's hand, he managed to throw himself to the edge of the pit. He turned then, ready to help Jesse. "Come on!"

Jesse eyed the height of the pit, the broken branch, and the length of Jack's arms. "Back off," he said.

"What?"

"Back off."

He gave himself a few feet, then ran at the tree limb, using it as a stepping-stone and no more.

He just made the rim of the pit, then hung there.

His grip slipped in the muck.

"Jack, where the hell are you?"

Jack didn't answer.

Jesse dangled. Then he got a grip, and at last, straining, he dragged himself over the rim of the pit. He rolled, then lay panting in the bright sunlight.

"Damn you, Jack," he said, turning.

And then he fell silent, knowing what had happened to Jack.

Both Jack and Lorena were still there. Completely covered in black muck and mire.

But the true killer, the thief, the one determined on getting rich at the expense of so many lives, had at last arrived himself.

Jesse made it to his feet, aware of the Smith & Wesson pointed at his face, and the grim features of the man he had once respected.

"Doc," he said. "Doc Thiessen. I've been expecting you."

"Damn, Jesse, why do you have to be so hard to kill?" Thorne Thiessen demanded.

"Hell, I don't know. I just like living, I suppose."

Sally was standing right behind Thiessen. Jesse noticed that she hadn't gotten rid of both airboats. There were two on the little hummock, his own and the one Doc had come in.

"So, Doc...I kind of figured you were involved in this," he said smoothly. He was playing for time now, but Doc didn't know that. Doc didn't know that the troops were already on the way.

"Oh, bull! You didn't have the least idea," Doc Thiessen said.

"Yeah, I did, Doc, but I was awful damn slow putting it all together. At first I thought it was Harry, because Harry has money. But so do you. I admit, I didn't figure out right away who you had working for you, and I sure as hell didn't suspect Sally, but after I talked to Jim Hidalgo a few times, I knew you had to be involved. He gets whacked on the head, and the first one he sees is you. And those samples… You should have had them all prepared and studied and on their way somewhere else. You had to steal your own samples. And I'm willing to bet that by now Lars Garcia has found out that you own a helicopter, though I doubt you were the one flying it around, looking for your gators. That was probably John Smith. I'm willing to bet that the altered gators are marked somehow. They would have found out just exactly how if the one I shot had reached the veterinary school, as it was supposed to. I didn't suspect Sally at first, but I should have. She was the one who gave Roger a shove, wasn't she?

"So let me see if I've got it worked out. You were the leader, and Sally and John were working for you. Who did all the dirty work for you? The killing, Doc. Who killed Maria and Hector—and Lorena's father?"

"I really don't have time for this," Thiessen said, shaking his white head. The face that had always seemed so kindly was now twisted in a mask of impatience and cold cruelty.

"Come on. You beat me." Jesse tried to assess the situation. Doc was the only one with a gun, and it was now aimed at him. Jack and Lorena were standing to one side, where they'd been forced in the last seconds while he'd been getting himself out of the hole.

But neither Jack nor Lorena looked as if they were about to collapse. As if they had been beaten. They were survivors. Lorena had a steely strength to have gotten this far.

In fact, she looked both defiant and angry. She wasn't going to go down easy.

And he couldn't count Jack out, either.

Thiessen smiled. "Actually, you'll find out who does my dirty work in just a minute or two. But first I've got to decide how to do this. You killed my gator, Jesse. In fact, damn it, you've killed two of them."

"C'mon, Doc, what else could I do?" Jesse said. "But listen, since I'm going to die anyway, do me a favor. Explain it all to me first, will you?"

Doc shrugged. "Easy enough. Sally heard about the research, made the contacts and came to me, since she didn't have the expertise to work with what she'd found. I've worked my fingers to the bone out here, and you can't imagine the millions to be made off a formula that can create an animal this size. The old man up in his research lab panicked. He didn't have to die. But he found out I'd gotten hold of a few of his specimens. Found out that they were growing, and he didn't keep his mouth shut, the old fool. He had to go and confront me about it. He hadn't figured out Sally's role yet, but I couldn't take the chance he would. She'd worked for him briefly, and if she'd been caught, that would have led back to me. So he had to die. Just the way things go," he said coldly. "Now, as to Lorena being the old man's daughter, well, it took me a while to make the connection, I'll admit."

"You bastard!" Lorena said softly.

For a moment Jesse thought she was going to fly at Doc, but she controlled herself, tense as a whip.

Her eyes touched Jesse's. He realized that she was trusting him to get them out of this.

He couldn't fail her.

Thiessen was on a roll. "You should have accepted that accident, Ms. Fortier. The cops would have gone on believing that Hector and Maria had been involved in drugs. As to old Billy Ray, well, I didn't kill him. The old drunk ran into one my gators, that's all."

"Just how many killer gators are there?" Lorena asked tightly.

Thiessen appeared amused. "There were four. One died on its own—near Hector and Maria's. You killed two, Jesse. There's still one of these beauties out there somewhere, and trust me, I'll find it. I've had Sally eavesdropping all along, and as soon as there's word, I'll know. None of this was as hard as you're trying to make it look, Jesse."

"And getting away with it won't be as easy as you think, Doc," Jesse said. All he needed was a distraction. He was certain that Doc knew how to shoot, but he was no ace, no trained officer. A distraction, and...

He swallowed hard. Did he dare? He'd be risking Lorena's life. And Jack's.

Lorena was staring at him, waiting. She still seemed to trust in the fact that he intended to do something.

And if he didn't?

Then they could all be dead anyway, unless the cavalry got here pronto.

"Lars Garcia will put all these pieces together, Doc."

"Don't be ridiculous. Other people out here have helicopters, and airboats? They must number in the thousands."

"People who know reptiles as well as you do are harder to find," Jesse commented. "And I've already mentioned your name to Lars. What was it, Thorne? Not enough money in what you were doing, or not enough glory?"

"The world is changing, Jesse. Genetic enhancement is being made on a daily basis. Clones are a dime a dozen now. You're got to be at the front of the flock."

"I'm telling you, Lars is on to you," Jesse said softly. "And you think that Metro-Dade Homicide will let go? You're out of your mind."

Thiessen looked troubled for an instant. "He has no proof."

"He will. I figure you marked those gators, tagged them in some way, and then let them loose on purpose, trying to see how they did in the wild. But you wanted to protect them from discovery at the same time, so you tracked them by helicopter, as well as by airboat. They're territorial creatures, so you probably shouldn't have let that one get so close to a populated area. That was a stupid-as-hell reason for Hector and Maria to die. Whoever killed Hector and Maria came on their property with an airboat. So tell me, Doc. Who did it?"

"I did," Sally offered, stepping around from behind Thiessen. "I did it, you fool. You thought I was nothing more than an attractive piece of ornamentation, a numbers cruncher. Background and nothing more. Well, get this. You underestimated me. You were friendly... you were even warm sometimes. But I could always see it in your eyes. I was nothing to you. But you were wrong. So wrong about me. I know how to be a mover and a shaker."

"And a killer," he said huskily.

She smiled. "And a killer."

She was slightly between him and Thiessen at that

point. Jesse cut a quick glance toward Lorena and realized that her eyes were on him.

She was afraid, but not panicking. She would fight until her last breath. He had never felt such a connection to another individual in his life.

A diversion. He needed a diversion.

She was staring at him so intently, he was certain she knew what he needed, how to help.

He prayed.

Then he gave a slight nod.

"Hey!" Lorena cried.

Startled, both Sally and Doc turned slightly.

And he made his move. He threw his body hard against Sally's, slamming her into Thiessen, bringing them all down to the ground.

The gun went off. A scream sounded sharply.

Still smoking, the gun lay on the ground in Thiessen's hand. Nearby was a pool of blood.

Jesse slammed his fist down on the man's wrist, and Thiessen released the gun. Jack Pine stepped forward, kicking it far from the man's grasp.

"Lorena!" Jesse cried, and leapt to his feet. She was standing. Unhurt.

Unbloodied.

She rushed into his arms.

He held her, shaking, feeling as if the world itself had begun to spin madly.

"Get up," Jack Pine was saying harshly to someone.

Jesse pulled away from Lorena long enough to turn and look.

Thiessen was getting up.

Sally lay on the ground, her eyes open but sightless.

A hole in her chest was surrounded by crimson.

"Is it over yet, Jesse?" Jack asked.

Jesse let out a sigh. "Not exactly. I imagine that, in a few minutes, John Smith will be arriving. He'll have been alerted by now to the fact that we're out here. If he does show, he'll be picked up. And I would also say that within minutes half the Miccosukee force will be out here. They'll be followed by the Metro-Dade cops. I can hear the airboats now."

Lorena looked up at him, then down at Sally. She shuddered, but only for a minute. Then she spun on Thiessen.

"Who killed my father?" she demanded.

"Ah, that," Thiessen murmured.

"Who actually killed my father!" Lorena repeated.

"Not me. I didn't kill anyone." He paused, and Jesse could see his mind working, trying to find a way out, to make himself look less guilty. "Sally...the whole thing was her idea. That woman was bloodthirsty. I was beside myself when I learned about the death of your poor father. And Hector and Maria. If she hadn't killed them... But she was certain they knew something and would get Fish and Wildlife in."

"Rather than Metro-Dade Homicide?" Jesse asked dryly.

"She was the one who forced me into everything," Thiessen said.

"Tell it to a jury," Jesse said.

"I intend to."

They heard the whir of an airboat motor coming closer. Jesse spun quickly, ready to dive for the gun if another of Thiessen's accomplices was arriving.

But it was George Osceola at the helm, and a number of tribal officers were with him. In seconds, they were rushing forward, shouting, going for Thiessen.

Seeing that the matter was in hand, George walked over to Jesse. "Everyone all right?"

"Except for Sally. She's dead," Jesse said.

"Sally!"

"Sally killed Hector and Maria," Jesse explained. "Were you able to pick up John Smith?"

"They're still looking for him. But, Jesse, you were right. Lars put out the APB, and Smith was spotted upstate. I'd bet money he abducted the van driver. We'll know more as soon as we get hold of him." George studied Jesse, then went silent. "Meanwhile, we need to get you all out of here."

"Hey!" Lorena cried suddenly. "Stop him! Doc's heading for the water!"

George Osceola swore; so did Jesse. They should have cuffed the man immediately.

Doc Thiessen was fast, and he knew the Everglades. He was tearing across the hummuck, heading for the water.

"Stop or I'll shoot!" George shouted.

Thiessen made a dive into the water. Jesse didn't think the man could make it—not with a trained force on his heels, several of them Miccosukees who had grown up in the area. It was a last desperate attempt at freedom by a desperate man.

They raced toward the canal. Thiessen had plunged deep, apparently hoping to surface at a distance, then disappear into the saw grass.

Jesse streaked toward the water himself, then stopped.

Everyone stopped behind him.

There was a thrashing in the water. Droplets splayed high and hard in every direction.

They were all dead still, watching the awful scene playing out before them.

Alligators were territorial.

And Thorne Thiessen had disturbed a large male in his territory. The dance of death was on.

There was no helping Thiessen.

He'd been caught in the middle of the abdomen, and now the mighty creature was thrashing insanely, trying to drown his prey.

Thiessen let out one agonized scream.

Then the alligator took him below the surface.

Gentle as dewdrops, the last glistening drops of water fell back on the surface of the canal.

And then all was still.

Jesse heard a soft gasp, but even without it, he had known she was there. He knew her scent. Felt the air tremble around her.

He turned, and her eyes were brilliant and beautiful and filled with tears. She had wanted justice, not vengeance, he realized.

It had been a fitting end to Thiessen, he thought himself. But maybe he needed to learn a bit more about mercy.

He took her into his arms. Felt the vibrance and life in her body.

He drew her tightly to him. And he didn't care about the tragedy they'd just witnessed, the mud that covered them both, or who heard his words.

"I love you," he said softly. "And it's going to be all right."

EPILOGUE

IT WAS FALL. The sun beat down on the water, but the air was gentle. Birds, in all their multihued plumage, flew above the glistening canal. Trees, hanging low, were a lush background for the chirps and cries that occasionally broke the silence.

There had been a picnic. A week had passed since the events at the hummock. They had all spent hours in questioning and doing paperwork for both the tribal police and Metro-Dade.

Michael Preston and Harry Rogers had both been horrified to discover that they had been under suspicion.

Hugh had merely been indignant that he hadn't been in on the finale.

They had all attended the funeral for Hector and Maria. Julie and Lorena were fast becoming friends, just as she was a friend of Jesse's.

Now, with the picnic cleaned up, with the others having talked over everything that had happened and finally gone home, Lorena stared out at the strange and savage beauty of the area and smiled.

Jesse, a cold beer in his hand, came up behind her, then took a seat at her side.

She leaned against him comfortably, taking his hand, holding it to her cheek. "There's one more monster out there," she reminded him.

"Yeah. We haven't heard any reports about it, but we'll arrange more hunts until we get it."

"And when you do…will you capture it or kill it?" she asked.

He smiled at her. "When an animal is altered, it's man's doing, not the creature's," he reminded her. "But these things could mate. Undo the balance in the Everglades. I don't like to make judgments, but if it's up to me…I think the creature is too much of a risk. Too many people have died already. Your father died to protect people from creatures like it, and so…"

"At least they didn't kill the van driver," Lorena said.

"They thought they did, though," Jesse said grimly. "John Smith thought the man was dead when he stole the carcass and drove the van into a canal. It's a miracle that he came to and escaped."

"Every once in a while, we get a miracle," Lorena said.

"So…" Jesse murmured.

"So…?"

"So somehow I doubt that you plan to keep your position at Harry's."

"I was thinking of doing something else."

"You want to leave," he said very softly.

"Actually, no."

"No?" His face seemed exceptionally strong then, handsome and compelling, his eyes that startling green against the bronze of his features.

She sighed. "I know it's soon, but I had been hoping you would ask me to stay here. My real love is the law. And causes. I'm great at causes, Jesse. It occurred to me that the tribal council could probably use a good lawyer now and then. And living here, with you…"

He laughed. "I love you. You know that. I have to admit, I've had my fears."

"You? Afraid?"

"This isn't just where I live. It's part of what I am. And you come from a world that's…glittering. Clean. Neat. Sophisticated. Not that we don't have our own 'Miami chic' down here, but…I'm not knocking anything, it's just that here…well, there are alligators in the canals. Water moccasins, and saw grass hardly stands in for a neatly manicured lawn. And my nearest neighbor is…well, not near."

She laughed softly. "Hmm. Water moccasins."

"I'm afraid so. Though they're not the vicious creatures they're made out to be. They're afraid of people."

"And alligators."

"Normally, they leave you alone if you leave them alone."

"Muck, mud, mosquitoes and saw grass."

"I'm afraid so."

She turned to him, touched his face. "But they all come with you," she said softly.

He caught her hand, eyes narrowing, a smile curving his lips. "Then you really would considering staying? I'd love a roommate, but I'd much rather have a wife."

Her heart seemed to stop. "Are you asking me?"

"I'm begging you."

She threw herself into his arms.

"Is that a yes?"

"A thousand times over."

He gently caught her chin in his hand, thumb sliding over the skin of her cheek. Then his lips touched hers. The breeze was soft and easy. The birds went silent. The night was as breathtaking as his kiss.

THE WEDDING WAS a month later. They chose the Keys.

The bride wore white. The groom was dashing in his tux.

They were both barefoot, married in the sand at sunset.

They'd taken the whole of one of the mom-and-pop motels, as well as rooms in one of the nearby chains. The attendance was huge, with Seminoles, Miccosukees, whites, Hispanics and, as Hugh, the token Aussie, commented, a bit of everyone in between. Even Roger had made it out of the hospital in time to attend.

The sunset was glorious.

The reception was the South Florida party of the year.

And when the night wound down, they were alone in their room that looked onto the ocean, feeling the gentle breeze, aware of the salt scent on the air...

And then nothing else, nothing else at all...

Except for each other.

* * * * *

Books by Tara Taylor Quinn

Harlequin Superromance

Where Secrets are Safe

Wife by Design
Once a Family
Husband by Choice
Child by Chance
Mother by Fate
The Good Father

Shelter Valley Stories

Sophie's Secret
Full Contact
It's Never Too Late
Second Time's the Charm
The Moment of Truth

It Happened in Comfort Cove

A Son's Tale
A Daughter's Story
The Truth About Comfort Cove

MIRA Books

Where the Road Ends
Street Smart
Hidden
In Plain Sight
Behind Closed Doors
At Close Range
The Second Lie
The Third Secret
The Fourth Victim
The Friendship Pact

And coming soon from Harlequin Heartwarming,
Once Upon a Friendship

THE SHERIFF
OF SHELTER VALLEY

Tara Taylor Quinn

For me.

CHAPTER ONE

"MAMA! MAAMAA!" RYAN'S scream tore through her fog of sleep.

Beth Allen was out of bed and across the room before she'd even fully opened her eyes. Heart pounding, she lifted her two-year-old son out of the secondhand crib, pressing his face into her neck as she held him.

"It's okay, Ry," she said softly, pushing the sweaty auburn curls away from his forehead. Curls she dyed regularly, along with her own. "Shh, Mama's right here. It was just a bad dream."

"Mama," the toddler said again, his little body shuddering. His tiny fists were clamped tightly against her—her nightshirt and strands of her straight auburn hair held securely within them.

"Mama" was what he'd said when she'd woken up alone with him in that motel room in Snowflake, Arizona, with a nasty bruise on her forehead, another one at the base of her skull. And no memory whatsoever.

She didn't even know her own name. She'd apparently checked in under the name Beth Allen and, trusting herself to have done so for a reason, had continued using it. It could be who she really was, but she doubted it. She'd obviously been on the run, and it didn't seem smart to have made herself easy to find.

She didn't know how old she was. How old her son

was. She could only guess Ry's age by comparing him to other kids.

Stoically, Beth stood there, rocking him slowly, crooning soothingly, until she felt the added weight that signified his slumber. Looking at the crib—old brown wood whose scars were visible even in the dim August moonlight coming through curtainless windows—Beth knew she should put him back there, should do all she could to maintain some level of normalcy.

But she didn't. She carried the baby back to the twin bed she'd picked up at a garage sale, snuggled him against her too-skinny body beneath the single sheet and willed herself back to sleep.

In that motel room in Snowflake, she'd seen a magazine article about a young woman who'd run away from an abusive husband. Like someone drawn in mingled horror and fascination to the sight of a car crash, she'd read the whole thing—and been greatly touched to find that it had a happy ending. The woman had run to someplace called Shelter Valley, Arizona.

Desperate enough to try anything, Beth had done the same.

But after six months of covering her blond hair and hiding her amnesia, she was no closer to her happy ending.

Neither, apparently, was her son. Spooning his small body up against her, she tried to convince herself that he was okay.

Ryan had only had a nightmare. Could have been about monsters in the closet or a ghost in the attic. Except that the one-bedroom duplex she was renting had neither a closet nor an attic.

No, there was something else haunting her child, giving him these nightmares.

It was the same thing that was haunting her.

Beth just didn't have any idea what it was.

NEARLY BLINDED BY the sun-brightened landscape, Sheriff Greg Richards scanned the horizon, missing nothing between him and the mountains in the distance.

A young woman had been rear-ended, forced off the road. And when she'd rolled to a stop, two assailants had pushed her into the rear of her Chevy Impala. She'd never even seen the car that hit her; she had been overtaken too quickly by the men who'd jumped out of its back seat to notice the vehicle driving off.

Stillness. That was all Greg's trained eye saw. Brownish-green desert brush. Dry, thorny plants that were tough enough to survive the scorching August sun. Cacti.

Another desert carjacking. The third in three months. A run of them—just like that summer ten years before. Yet…different. This time, instead of ending up dead or severely injured, the victim, Angela Marquette, had thrown herself out of the car. She'd flagged down a passing car and used a cell phone to call for help.

Greg continued to scan the surrounding area, but there was no sign of the new beige Impala. Not on the highway—patrols had been notified across the state— nor in the form of glinting metal underneath the scarred cacti and other desert landscaping that had witnessed hideous brutalities over the years. In the places it was thickest, a hijacked car or two, even an occasional dead body, could easily slide beneath it undetected.

Patrol cars and an ambulance ahead signaled the location of the victim. Pulling his unmarked car off the road and close to the group of emergency personnel, Greg got out. The immediate parting of the crowd always surprised him; he hadn't been the sheriff of Shelter Valley long enough to get used to it.

As he approached the victim, he noticed that she was shaking and in shock. And sweating, too. The young woman, her brown hair in a ponytail, leaned against one of the standard-issue cars from his division. One of the paramedics shook his head as Greg caught his eye. Apparently she'd refused medical attention.

"Angela, I'm Sheriff Richards," he said gently when her gaze, following those of his deputies, landed on him.

"We've got her full report." Deputy Burt Culver stepped up to Greg. "We just finished." Burt, only a few years older than Greg, had been with the Kachina County Sheriff's Department when Greg had first worked there as a junior deputy. Other than a short stint with Detention Services—at the one and only jail in Kachina County's jurisdiction—Burt had been content to work his way up in Operations, concentrating mostly on criminal investigations. He was one of the best.

Culver had never expressed much interest in administration, had never run for Sheriff, but Greg was hoping to talk him into accepting a promotion to Captain over Operations. No one else would be as good.

Greg glanced down at the report. "This is a number where we can reach you during the day?" he asked.

"Yes, sir," the young woman replied, her voice as shaky as her hands. "And at night, as well. I'm a student at the University of Arizona. I live at home with my parents."

"The car was theirs?" Greg asked her. Chevy Impalas weren't cheap. Certainly not the usual knock-around college vehicle. She would probably have been perfectly safe in one of those. These hijackers didn't go for low-end cars.

"No, sir, it's mine. I also work as a dance instructor in Tucson."

Greg looked over the pages Burt had handed him, confident that everything was complete. That he wasn't needed here, at the scene of the crime. Still, he thumbed through the report.

Two men had done the actual hijacking. Young, in their late teens or early twenties. One Caucasian. A blonde. The other had darker skin, brown eyes and black hair. They'd both been wearing wallet chains, faded jeans—in the one-hundred-and-ten-degree heat—ripped tank T-shirts, medallions. The blond—the driver—had a tattoo on his left biceps and he'd been wearing dirty white tennis shoes. They'd had her radio blaring.

"Neither of them spoke to you?"

The young woman shook her head, the movement almost spastic. Other than a couple of bruises, she'd escaped physically unharmed. But she'd probably carry mental scars for the rest of her life. Greg stared into the distance for a moment, focusing his concentration. He was the sheriff now. Personal feelings were irrelevant.

The carjackers of ten years ago had been silent, as well. No accents to give any clue that might imply one social group or school over another.

"I just remembered something," the girl said, her brown eyes almost luminescent as she struggled against tears and sunshine to look up at him. "Just after they pushed me...over the seat...one of them said something...about this 'counting double.' They turned the radio on at the same time and I was so scared… I could be wrong.…" She shook her head, eyes clouded as she frowned up at him. "Maybe I'm not remembering anything at all."

"Are you sure you wouldn't like the paramedics to take a look at you?" Greg asked.

She shook her head again. "I'm fine…just a little sore…" She attempted a smile. "I called my parents." Her words suddenly came in a rush. "They're on their way to get me."

Nodding, Greg handed the report back to a sweating Culver. "See that I have a copy of this on my desk ASAP," he said, then added, "Wait here until her folks arrive. I want them to be able to get the assurances they'll undoubtedly need from the man in charge, not from a junior officer."

"Got it, Chief."

Unsettled, dissatisfied, glad only that Culver was in charge, Greg gave the young woman his own card with the invitation to call if she needed anything now or in the future, and headed back to his car.

He could keep trying to pretend that this case wasn't personal, but either way, he was going to get these guys. There was simply no other choice. With every carjacking that went unsolved, there was a greater chance that another would follow.

That was the professional reason he wasn't going to rest until the perpetrators were caught.

And the personal one…

His father's death had to be avenged.

He entered Shelter Valley city limits an hour later and drove slowly through town, glancing as he always did at the statue of the town's founder, Samuel Montford, that had appeared while he'd been away.

There was no reason for Greg to stop by Little Spirits Day Care. Bonnie, founder and owner of the only child-care facility in Shelter Valley—and Greg's only sibling—would be busy with all the "little spirits" in her care, doing the myriad things an administrator at a day care did.

He pulled up at Little Spirits, anyway. It was Friday. After a week of day care, maybe Katie, his three-year-old niece, needed to be sprung.

Even if she didn't, Bonnie would pretend she did. Bonnie understood.

Sometimes Greg just needed a dose of innocence and warmth, sweetness and love, to counteract the rest of his world.

"Dispatch to 11:15..." The words came just as Greg was swinging shut the driver's door. With an inner groan, he caught the door, sank onto the seat again and listened.

Two minutes later, he was back on the road. There was a warrant out for Bob Mather's arrest. As far as Greg knew, the man he'd graduated from high school with hadn't been in Shelter Valley for more than five years, but his parents' place was listed as his last known address.

Which meant Greg had to pay the sweet-natured older couple yet another unpleasant visit, when he should've been watching ice cream drip down Katie's dimpled chin.

This was not a good day.

TOILETS WEREN'T HER SPECIALTY. But Beth made the white porcelain bowl, the fifth she'd faced that day, shine, anyway. A job is only worth doing if it's done right.

Beth squirted a little glass cleaner on the chrome piping and handle to make them glisten, then wiped efficiently, satisfied when she saw an elongated version of what she supposed was her chin in the spotless flush handle. She ignored the pull she felt as the quote ran through her mind again. *A job is only worth doing if it's done right.*

How did she know that? Had someone said it to her? Many times? Her mother or father, perhaps? A boss?

There was no point traveling in that direction. The blankness in her mind was not going to supply the answer. And Beth didn't dare look anywhere else.

But she made a mental note to write the thought down in her notebook when she got home that night. Because these obscure recollections were her only link with a reality she couldn't find, she was cataloguing everything she remembered—any hint that returned to her from a past she couldn't access.

And making up new rules to live by, as well. Creating herself.

Bucket full of cleaning supplies in hand, Beth blew at the strand of hair that had fallen loose from her ponytail. Only one more bathroom to go, and Beth's Basins could chalk up another good day's work. She still had to vacuum the Mathers' carpets and water mop the ceramic tile in the kitchen and baths, but those jobs weren't particularly noteworthy. Beth measured the progress of her day by bathrooms.

The doorbell rang in the front of the house. Stopping only to rinse her hands in the sink she had yet to clean, Beth wiped her palms along the legs of her overall shorts and hurried to the door. The Mathers had told her they were expecting a package, and she didn't want to disappoint them by failing to get to the door in time.

The man waiting outside was uniformed in brown, but he wasn't the UPS deliveryman she'd been expecting.

"Sheriff?" Between the hammering of her heart and the fear in her throat, she barely got the word out. His face was grim.

Ryan! He has to be okay! They can't take him! Have they found me out? What do they know that I don't? The thoughts buzzed loudly, making her dizzy.

"Beth!"

She almost relaxed a notch when Greg Richards's stern expression softened.

"I didn't know the Mathers were one of your clients."

"Just this month," she said. He hadn't known she was working there. So he hadn't come after her.

Thank God.

But then…that meant he was there to see the sweet older couple she'd met in the lobby of the Performing Arts Center at Montford University six weeks before.

"I take it Bob, Sr. and Clara aren't home?" he asked.

He had the most intense dark green eyes.

Still holding the door, Beth told him, "They went to Phoenix to have lunch and see a movie." She frowned. "Is something wrong?" Bob, Sr. had lost both his parents during the past few months. Surely they'd had their share of bad news for a while.

Greg shook his head, but Beth had a feeling that it was the "I'm not at liberty to say" kind of gesture rather than the "no" she'd been seeking.

"I just need to ask them a couple of questions," he

added, "but it sounds like they'll be gone most of the afternoon." His gaze was warm, personal.

"I got that impression."

Hands in his pockets, Greg didn't leave. "I'll catch them later tonight, then. If you don't mind, please don't mention that I've been by."

"Of course not." Beth never—ever—put her nose in other people's business. She didn't know if this was a newly acquired trait or one she'd brought with her into this prison of oblivion. "I won't be seeing or talking to them, anyway. I just leave their key under the mat when I'm through here."

"So what time would that be?"

Beth glanced at her watch—not that it was going to tell her what jobs she had left or how long they would take. "Within the hour." She was due to pick Ryan up from the Willises at five.

Ryan couldn't be enrolled in the day care in town. Not only was Beth living a lie, without even a social security number, but she couldn't take a chance on signing any official papers that might allow someone to trace her.

Especially when she had no idea who that someone might be.

So she left the toddler with two elderly sisters, Ethel and Myra Willis, who adored him. And she only accepted cash from her clients.

"How does an early dinner sound?"

That inexplicable headiness hadn't left her since she'd answered the door. "With you?" she asked, stalling, putting off the moment when she had to refuse.

He nodded, the movement subtly incorporating his entire body. It was one of the things that kept Greg on her mind long after she'd run into him someplace or other—the way he put all of himself into everything he did. You had to be sincere to be able to do that consistently.

"I have to feed Ryan," she said, only because it was more palatable than an outright no. It still meant no.

Pulling a hand from his pocket, he turned it palm upward. "The diner serves kids."

Beth's eyes were automatically drawn to that hand and beyond, to the pocket it had left. And from there to the heavy-looking gun in a black leather holster at his hip.

"Ry's not good in restaurants." Her mouth dry, Beth knew she had to stop. Too much was at stake.

Yet she liked to think she was starting a new life. And if she was, she wanted this man in it.

If he weren't a cop. And if she weren't afraid she was on the run from something pretty damn horrible. If she were certain she could trust him, no matter who she might turn out to be, no matter what she might have done.

"He's two," Greg said. "He'll learn."

"I have no doubt he will, but I'd rather get him over the food-throwing stage in private."

Greg stared down at his feet, shod, as usual, in freshly shined black wing tips. "In all the months I've known you, I've never done one thing to give you reason to doubt me, but you always brush me off," he said eventually.

"No, I…" Beth stopped. "Okay, yes, I am."

"Is it my breath?"

"No!" She chuckled, relaxing for just a second. With the truth out in the open, the immediate danger was gone.

"My hair? You don't like black hair?" He was grinning at her, and somehow that little bit of humor was more devastating than his earlier intensity.

"I like black just fine. Tom Cruise has black hair."

"Dark brown. Tom Cruise has dark brown hair. And he's the reason you've come up with an excuse every single time I've asked you out?"

"No."

"It's the curls, then? You don't like men with curls?"

"I love your curls." Oh God. She hadn't meant to say that. Her throat started to close up again. She couldn't do this.

And she couldn't *not* do this. Beth's emotional well had been bone-dry for so long she sometimes feared it was beginning to crumble into nothingness. She had no one else sharing her life—her fears and worries and pains; worse, she didn't really even have herself. She was living with a stranger in her own mind.

"Ryan has curls," she finished lamely.

Greg's expression grew serious. "Is it the cop thing? I know a lot of women don't want to be involved with cops. Understandably so."

His guess was dead right, but not in the way he meant. "I'm not one of them," she said, compelled to be honest with him. About this, at least. "I'd consider myself lucky to be involved with a man who'd dedicated his life to helping others. A man who put the safety of others before his own. One who still had enough faith in society to believe it's worth saving."

"Even though you'd know, every morning when you kissed him goodbye as he left for work, that you might never see him again?"

"Every woman—and man—faces that danger," she

said. "I'll bet that far more people die in car accidents than on the job working as a cop."

"Far more," he agreed.

"And, anyway," she said, feeling a sudden urge to close the door, "who said anything about kissing every morning?"

"I was hoping I'd been able to slide that one by you," he said.

"Nope."

"So—" his gaze became challenging "—if it's not the cop thing and it's not my breath, it must be *you* that you're afraid of."

"I am not afraid."

He sobered. "If you need more time, Beth, I certainly understand. We could grab a sandwich as friends, maybe see a movie or something."

More time? She frowned.

"It's been—what?—less than a year since you were widowed?" he asked, his face softening.

Widowed. Oh yeah, that. It was the story she'd invented when she'd come to town. She was a recent widow attempting to start a new life. You'd think she could at least manage to keep track of the life she'd made up to replace the one she couldn't remember.

"Look," she said, really needing to get back to work. Ry was going to be looking for her soon. Routine was of vital importance to her little boy. "If you were serious about the friend thing, I could use some help."

She was testing him. And felt bad about that. But not bad enough to stop herself, apparently.

"Sure."

"I just bought a used apartment-size washer and dryer." Taking a two-year-old's two and three changes a day to the Laundromat had been about to kill her—financially and physically. "I need someone with a truck to go with me to pick it up and then help me get it into the duplex."

He'd know where she lived, then. But who was she kidding? He was the county sheriff—a powerful man. And Shelter Valley was a small town. He'd probably known where she lived for months.

"I have a truck."

"I know."

She'd passed him in town a couple of times, feeling small and insignificant in the old, primer-spattered Ford Granada she'd bought for five hundred dollars next to his beautiful brand-new blue Ford F-150 Supercab.

"If I offer to help are you going to brush me off again?"

"No."

"You aren't just setting me up here?" He was smiling.

"No!" Beth said indignantly, but she was smiling, too.

"I'm tempted to force you to ask, just to win back a little bit of the pride you've been quietly stripping away for months. But because I'm afraid to chance it, I'll ask you, instead. May I please help you bring your new appliances home?"

Beth laughed out loud…and was shocked by the sound. She couldn't remember having heard it before. Couldn't remember anything before waking up in that motel room in Snowflake, Arizona, with bruises and a child who called her Mama crying on the bed beside her.

"If you're sure you wouldn't mind, I could sure use the help," she said, all laughter gone. She had no business even *thinking* about flirting with the county sheriff, but she and Ryan needed those appliances. And she couldn't get them to the duplex alone.

"What time?"

"Tonight? After dinner?"

"Sure we couldn't do it before dinner and just happen to eat while we're at it?"

"I'm sure."

Beth hated the conflicting emotions she felt when he gave in with no further cajoling and agreed to pick her up at six-thirty that evening for the ten-minute drive out to the Andersons'. They were remodeling the one-room apartment over their garage and no longer needed the appliances, which, while five years old, had hardly been used.

Conflicting emotions—one of the few experiences Beth knew intimately. Intermittent relief. Disappointment. Resignation. Fear.

Peace. That was, and had to be, her only goal. Peace for her. And health, safety and happiness for Ryan.

Nothing else mattered.

CHAPTER TWO

HE'D SEEN HER DOWNTOWN, coming out of Weber's Department Store, at the grocery store, the gas station, and in the park just beyond Samuel Montford's statue. Seen her at Little Spirits once or twice when he'd stopped in to visit Bonnie or spring Katie. According to his sister, Beth Allen never left her son at the day care, but she volunteered once a week so he could have some playtime with the other kids.

He'd seen her at the drugstore once, and at Shelter Valley's annual Fourth of July celebration.

But he'd never seen her at home.

The duplex was not far from Zack and Randi Foster's place. But it didn't resemble that couple's home with its garden and white-picket fence. Her place was very small. One bedroom—the door was shut—a full bath squished into a half-bath space, a living room with a kitchen on the other end. And a closet that would fit either coats or the stackable laundry unit Beth had purchased. But not both.

The closet had washer-dryer hook-ups, and a clothes bar and single door, both of which had to be removed to fit the washer and dryer. The door he could rehang. The clothes bar's removal would be permanent for as long as the closet remained a laundry room.

The entire house was meticulous.

"Where'd you say you lived before coming to Shelter Valley?" Greg asked as, pliers in hand, he attached a dryer vent to the opening on the back of the appliance.

"I didn't say."

"That?" Beth's two-year-old son was standing beside Greg's toolbox.

"It's a hammer," Beth said.

"That?"

"A level."

"That?"

"A screwdriver."

Glancing between the top rack of the toolbox and the little boy, Greg frowned. "How do you know which tool he's referring to?"

Ryan hadn't pointed at anything. His index finger had been in his mouth ever since Greg had collected Beth and her son more than an hour before.

She shrugged, hoisting Ryan onto her hip. "I could see where he was looking," she said.

"You don't have to hold him." Greg returned to the metal ring he was tightening on the outside of the vent. "He's welcome to help."

She held the boy, anyway, as defensive about her son as she was about herself.

Greg still liked her.

"Here, Ryan," he said, standing to give the little boy his wrench. "Can you hang on to this and give it to me when I ask for it?"

After a very long, silent stare, the toddler finally nodded and took the tool. He needed both hands to handle the weight of it, meaning that finger finally came out of his mouth—but he didn't seem to mind the sacrifice.

"You changed."

Beth's words threw him. "Changed?" he asked. "How?"

"Out of your uniform."

"I'm off duty."

"I've never seen you out of uniform."

He hadn't thought about that, but supposed she was right. He'd been on duty the Fourth of July. And just coming off duty each time he'd stopped in at Little Spirits. She hadn't been there the afternoon he'd spent building the sandbox on the patio of the day care.

"You look different."

Giving the dryer vent a tug, satisfied that it was securely in place, Greg moved down to the washer. "Good different?" he asked. The jeans were his favorite, washed so many times they were faded and malleable, just the way he liked them.

"Less…official."

He screwed the washer tubing to the cold-water spigot. "So, you going to tell me where you're from?"

"You going to tell me why you're so nosy?"

"I'm a cop. It's my job to be nosy."

"I thought you were off duty."

"Touché." Leaning around the edge of the washer, he grinned at her.

Beth wasn't grinning back. Her expression showed both anger and hurt. And defensiveness—again. She hugged Ryan closer, almost knocking the wrench out of the little guy's hands, but the boy didn't complain. He just held on tighter.

Ryan Allen was one of the quietest toddlers Greg had ever met.

"You think I'm some kind of threat to the people of Shelter Valley?" she asked.

"Of course not!" Greg would've laughed out loud if he wasn't so surprised by the tension that had suddenly entered the room. "I'm interested, okay?" he said, eager to clarify himself before the evening dived into dismal failure. "As a guy, not as a cop."

"Interested." Her hold on the boy loosened, but not much.

"Yeah, you know, interested." He went back to the job at hand, thinking it was probably his safest move. "Men do that," he grunted. He could tell the water spigots hadn't been used in a while. If ever. He was having one helluva time persuading the faucet to turn. "They get interested in women who attract them."

"I attract you?"

An entirely different note had entered her voice. Though the sound of battle hadn't left, he was no longer sure he was the target.

"I haven't made that perfectly obvious by now?"

The room had gone too still. Greg glanced around the washer once more, half thinking he might find he was alone, and his gaze locked with Beth's.

"I need to be more obvious?" he asked. He'd never worked so hard for a woman in his life. Not that he'd had that many. His life had taken unexpected turns, been filled with unexpected responsibilities, but when he'd wanted a woman, he hadn't had to work at it.

"No," she said, looking down. From his silent vantage point, Ryan stared up at her, as though following the conversation with interest. "I, um…guess—" her eyes returned to his "—you have to be *looking* to see the obvious, don't you?"

"You're trying to tell me you aren't looking. Period." He couldn't deny his disappointment.

"No. Yes." She set her son down. "I'm saying maybe I didn't notice your, um, interest because I wasn't looking."

The woman challenged him at every turn—something he particularly liked about her—and yet she'd never, until that moment, been difficult to follow. Just difficult to get any information from.

Of course, she'd been hurt, was wary. Probably loath to risk letting anyone get close again. Greg could understand that. It had taken him a long time to open up after Shelby left.

"And now that I've pointed it out to you?"

"I know."

"And?"

"I don't know." As Ryan toddled toward Greg to see what he was doing, Beth leaned over the washer. "How's it going back there?"

Greg twisted the faucet again and it gave immediately. Probably because exasperation had added strength to his grip. "Good," he told her. "Another five minutes and you can throw in your first load."

"Can I have the wrench, Ryan?" he asked, surprised when he turned his head to see the little guy so close to him, staring him right in the eye. Without blinking, the boy handed over the wrench.

"He's a man of few words," Greg said to Beth.

"We're working on that."

With his only living relative in the day care business, Greg knew a lot about kids. "He'll talk when he's ready."

"I hope so."

Greg made one more adjustment. "Here you go, little

bud," he said, handing the wrench back to Beth's son. "You want to drop that in the toolbox for me?"

Ryan put the tool down on top of the hammer.

"I'll bet he has more to say when it's just the two of you," he said as he slid the appliances in place against the wall.

"Not really."

She sounded worried. Greg figured it had to be hard for her, a single mother—all alone in the world, as far as he could tell. She had no one to share the worries and heartaches with, to calm the fears, to share the mammoth responsibility of child-rearing.

More than ever, he wanted to change that.

If she'd let him.

"Did you get to the Mathers'?" she asked as he packed up his toolbox.

Greg nodded. It had been just as difficult as he'd expected.

"Bad news?"

"A sheriff rarely gets to deliver good news."

"Clara told me they lost a daughter."

Resting a foot on his toolbox, Greg leaned his forearm on his leg. "It's been almost twenty years," he told her, nowhere near ready to leave. Ryan was sitting on the floor a few feet away, a toy on his lap, pulled from a neat stack of colorful objects in the bottom drawer of the end table. The boy was obviously occupied, but Greg lowered his voice, anyway. "She and some friends were in a boat on Canyon Lake. They hit a rock. She was thrown and ended up underneath the boat."

Beth's eyes clouded. "They have pictures of a boy in their bedroom. I'm assuming they have a son, too?"

Greg nodded.

"Is he still around?"

"He's still alive." Greg sighed. The Mathers had physically deflated as he'd told them about the latest trouble Bob had gotten into. "After Molly, their daughter, was killed, they focused everything they had on Bob. He became their reason for living. He was a rebellious kid, but they pinned all their hope, love and energy on him."

"You knew Bob?"

"We graduated in the same class."

"Is he good to them?"

Greg wasn't surprised by the compassion he read on Beth's face. He'd been touched by her natural warmth the first time he'd run into her at the day care. He hadn't needed his sister's priming—her point-blank match-making attempts—to get his attention. Odd how someone could be so closed off and yet emanate such caring.

"Bob somehow came out of it all believing that the world owes him a living. He's a conniver who works too little and drinks too much."

"He's not good to them."

Most of what Greg knew, he wasn't at liberty to say. "He hasn't been home to see them in over five years." He could tell her that much.

"What a shame. They're such nice people."

"They are."

"It's not right, you know," she said softly, her arms wrapped around her middle as she leaned back against the wall, facing him and the room where her son played.

"What's that?"

"Life, I guess. You have people like the Mathers, filled with unconditional love, great parents in an empty house, and their son, a jerk who's completely wasting one of the greatest gifts he'll ever get in this life. I'd literally give a limb to have what he's just throwing away."

She stopped, stepped away from the wall and busied herself with closing the closet door and picking up the packaging from the dryer vent, the papers she'd been given with the appliances.

She'd said more than she'd meant to. He could tell by the stiffness in her back. The way she wouldn't look at him. Greg knew the signs well. He'd seen them again and again over the years as he'd questioned suspects. Could tell when just another push or two would wring the confession he was seeking.

"How about we take this little guy out for ice cream?" he asked, walking toward Ryan.

"Cweam?" the boy echoed, staring up at his mother.

"He's messy," Beth warned.

It wasn't a no. Greg was elated. Probably far beyond what the situation warranted.

"Messiness is an unwritten rule when you're two," he said lightly.

He could read the uncertainty in her face. Which only made him want her capitulation that much more.

If he was a nice guy, he'd give up. Go away and leave her alone, quit bugging her, as she seemed to want. Except, Greg didn't feel at all sure that *was* what she wanted. From the very beginning, whenever their eyes met, which she didn't allow often, he'd felt the communication between them.

Something about this woman kept bringing him back, in spite of her refusal to have anything to do with him. And he had a pretty strong suspicion that she was drawn to him, too.

Her mouth said no. But he wasn't convinced the rest of her agreed.

"Aren't you worried about what people will think?" she said in a low voice.

As excuses went, it wasn't one of her better ones. "It isn't against the law for sheriffs to eat ice cream with messy kids."

"Cweam?" Ryan asked again. Beth picked him up.

"Greg—" She stopped abruptly.

It was the first time she'd called him by his first name. He liked it. Too much.

"You know what I mean," she said, her shoulders dropping. "I've only been here six months and don't know many people, but I've certainly seen how well-oiled the gossip wheel is in this town. It might make things uncomfortable for you if you're seen with the cleaning lady."

"We aren't snobs in Shelter Valley."

"I know, but I'm a nobody who cleans houses and you're the boss of the entire county."

"I don't think Mayor Smith would be too happy to hear you say that."

"Even I know that Junior Smith is just a figurehead in this town."

"Cweam?"

The boy might not talk a lot, but he was persistent. Greg liked that.

"Why don't you tell me the real reason you're so hesitant to be seen with me," he said.

She didn't. But he had a pretty good idea that she wanted to. Her eyes were telling him so much, frustrating him because, as hard as he tried, he couldn't translate those messages.

She'd mentioned gossip. "You're worried that they're going to see us together once and start planning the wedding."

"I might worry about it if I believed for one second that anyone would think I was good enough for you."

"Bonnie's been trying to hook us up for two months."

"No way!"

"Yes, way. She's invited you to dinner every Sunday for the past five weeks."

"So?"

"I was invited, too."

"Cweam?"

"Just a minute, Ry," Beth said softly, kissing the top of the boy's curly head.

"That's just a coincidence," she told Greg, adjusting her son on her hip. Ryan slid a finger into his mouth.

Katie would've been crying by now, demanding ice cream. Beth's son didn't seem to demand much at all. Something he had in common with his mother.

"Trust me, there are no coincidences with my sister," Greg told her, prepared to stay there arguing the point all night if necessary. "And she wouldn't leave something as important as this to chance, anyway. She's not the least bit subtle or embarrassed about how adamant she is to change my marital status. Nor has she been subtle about telling me what a fool I'd be if I let you get away—I'd be missing my chance of a lifetime." He mimicked the little sister he adored.

"So you're doing this for her."

Greg took more hope from the disappointment he heard in her voice than any other thing she'd said or done since he'd met her.

"No."

He had no idea what had tied Beth Allen up in knots so tight they were choking her, but it bothered the hell out of him. She shouldn't have to fight this hard all the time.

"I noticed you before Bonnie said a word," he said, telling her something he would normally have kept to himself. "In fact, I'd already tried to get you to go out with me before she told me there was someone I 'just had to meet.'"

"Oh."

"Cweam?" Ryan said around the finger in his mouth.

Greg's eyes met Beth's and that strange thing happened between them again. As though something inside her were conversing with something inside him....

"Not tonight, Ry," she finally said, breaking eye contact with Greg.

But she hadn't looked away fast enough. He'd seen the pain in her eyes as she'd turned him down. It was the most encouraging rejection he'd had yet.

"Another time, then," he murmured.

He could've sworn, as he said goodbye and told her he'd be in touch, that she seemed relieved.

Yep, there was no doubt about it.

Beth Allen wanted him.

"BONNIE, CAN WE TALK?" Monday was not her usual day to volunteer at the day care, but Beth had come, anyway. She'd been thinking about this all weekend.

"Sure," the woman said, giving Beth one of her signature cheery smiles. Other than the dark curls that sprang from all angles on her head, thirty-four-year-old Bonnie looked nothing like her older brother. Short where he was tall, plump where he was solidly fit, she could be, nevertheless, as intimidating as he when she got an idea.

Beth knew this about her and she'd only known the woman a few months. Until now, she'd liked that trait, identified with it somehow.

With Ryan in clear view, Beth followed Bonnie into her windowed office and, canvas bag still over her shoulder, sat when Bonnie closed the door.

"What's up?"

"I want you to quit bugging Greg to ask me out."

"Why? Greg's great! You two would have so much fun together."

In another life, Beth was certain she'd agree. It was precisely because she wished so badly that this *was* another life that she had to resist. She'd thought about it all weekend and knew she had no choice.

Yet, how she longed to be able to confide in this woman, to talk through her thoughts and fears, benefit from Bonnie's perspective.

Almost as badly as she longed to go out with Bonnie's brother.

"I just don't want to be a charity case," she said, hating how lame she sounded. "I don't want anyone asking me out because he feels sorry for me or he's forced into it or—"

Bonnie cut her off. "You don't know Greg very well if you think I could force him to do anything he didn't feel was right. Nor would he ever date a woman simply because I wanted him to. Otherwise, he wouldn't be thirty-six years old and still single."

"He told me you've been trying to get us together for months."

"And if he's asked you out, it has absolutely nothing to do with me."

Bonnie's green eyes were so clear, so sure. She was the closest thing Beth had to a friend in this town. Although she knew it would probably shock the other woman, Beth's relationship with Bonnie meant the world to her.

"Well, just stop, okay?" she said, standing. Somehow she'd convinced herself that if Bonnie quit pushing, so would Greg.

Or was it because she secretly hoped he wouldn't that she'd been able to take this stand?

"Sure," Bonnie said. "But it's not going to change anything. If Greg asked women out because I pushed them at him, he wouldn't have had eight months—at least—without a real date."

Beth sat back down. "He hasn't had a date in eight months?"

"I said *at least* eight months. That's how long I know about. That's how long he's been back in Shelter Valley."

"Back? I thought he grew up here." She didn't care. Wasn't interested. Ryan was playing happily with Bo Roberts, a three-year-old with Down syndrome. Bo, a high-functioning child, was a favorite at Little Spirits and particularly a favorite of Ryan's.

"He did. We both did. But Greg moved to Phoenix ten years ago."

"To be a cop?"

Hands clasped together on the desk in front of her, Bonnie shook her head, eyes grim. It wasn't something Beth had seen very often.

"He was already a cop," Greg's sister said. "Our father was severely injured in a carjacking and required more care than he could get in Shelter Valley. Greg moved with him to Phoenix and looked after him until he died."

Beth's heart fell. A dull ache started deep inside her. She didn't want Bonnie—or Greg—to have suffered so.

"What about your mother?"

"She died when I was twelve. From a bee sting, of all things. No one knew she was deathly allergic."

"I'm so sorry."

"Me, too."

Beth needed to say more. Much more. And couldn't find anything to say at all.

"So it was just you and Greg and your dad after that?"

Bonnie nodded, and the two women were silent for a moment, each lost in her own thoughts. Bonnie, Beth supposed, was reliving those years. Beth was searching desperately for anything in her life that might help her to help Bonnie. But, as usual, she found nothing there at all.

"Anyway," Bonnie said suddenly, spreading her arms wide, "Greg moved back here to run for Sheriff last January and hasn't had a single date since he was elected. And it hasn't been for lack of trying on my part, either."

"So I'm just one in a long line to you, eh?" Beth asked, trying to lighten the tension a bit, make sure Bonnie knew there were no hard feelings, and the two women chuckled as they returned to the playroom.

Bonnie went back to supervising and Beth to finding crayons and engaging little minds in age-appropriate activities. On the surface, nothing had changed. But Beth was looking at her friend with new eyes. She'd had no idea Bonnie had led anything other than a blessed life.

There was a lesson in this.

Bonnie had suffered, and still found a way to love life. The other woman's cheerfulness, her happiness, could not be faked. It bubbled from deep inside her, and was too consistent not to be genuine.

Beth had a new personal goal. Peace was still what mattered most—behind Ryan's health and happiness, of course. But she didn't plan to completely scratch happiness off her list. At least, not yet.

The next time Bonnie asked her and Ryan to Sunday dinner, she was going to accept. What was she accomplishing by denying herself friends? She literally didn't know what she had to offer, so there was no way she could embark on an intimate relationship. But where was the harm in taking part in a family dinner? How was she ever going to create a new life for Ryan and herself if she didn't start living?

CHAPTER THREE

LOOKING AT THE photos was grueling.

"I think we're wasting our time here, looking in the wrong places," Deputy Burt Culver said. Greg studied the photos, anyway.

It was the third Friday in August, and there'd been a fourth carjacking the night before. This time the victim hadn't been so lucky. A fifty-three-year-old woman on her way home from work in Phoenix had been found dead along the side of the highway. There was still no sign of the new-model Infiniti she'd been driving.

"I understand why it's important to you to tie these incidents together with what happened ten years ago, Greg, but you're letting this get personal."

Anyone but Burt would be receiving his walking papers at that moment. Eyes narrowed, Greg glanced up from the desk strewn with snapshots. "I appreciate your concern," he said, tight-lipped, and turned back to the pictures—both old and new—of mangled cars. Of victims.

"But you're not going to stop," Burt said. In addition to obvious concern, there was a note of something bordering on disapproval in the other man's voice.

Studying a photo of the smashed front end of a ten-year-old Ford Thunderbird, Greg shook his head. "I'm not going to stop." The front end of a year-old Lexus found abandoned earlier that summer, its driver nearly dead from dehydration, unconscious in the back seat, looked strangely similar to that of the Thunderbird. They hadn't started out looking similar. "Neither am I going to let my personal reasons for wanting this case solved interfere with the job of solving it."

His trained eye skimmed over the image of the nearly nude young woman found in the desert ten summers before. The carjackers had become rapists that time. Her car, a newer-model Buick, had turned up twenty miles farther down the road. Also smashed.

Greg frowned. Another front-end job.

"My instincts—" He paused. "My cop instincts are telling me there's some connection here."

"Why?" Culver asked, barely glancing at the photos. Of course, he'd seen them all before. Many times. As had Greg. "Why these two sets only? Why not look into the rash of heists down south?"

"Those cars were being put to use."

"So?"

"Whoever's doing this is taking brand-new or nearly new cars, expensive ones, and smashing them up."

"Joyriders."

Yeah. It happened. More often than Greg liked to admit.

And yet... "Look at these front ends," Greg said, lining up a few of the photos on another part of the desk.

Burt looked. "They're mangled."

"They're identical," Greg insisted.

"They're smashed, Greg." Burt wasn't impressed.

Hell, maybe he *was* letting it get personal. Maybe he should agree with his deputy and back away. Still...

"They all look like they hit the same thing at the same angle and speed," he said slowly.

Pulling at his ear—something he only did when he was feeling uncomfortable—the deputy leaned his other hand on the desk and gave the photos more than the cursory glance he'd afforded them earlier. "Could be," he said.

It would be pretty difficult, especially after the hard time he'd just given Greg, for the older man to admit he'd missed something that might be important. Greg had no desire to belabor the issue. His eyes moved to the table behind his deputy and the partially constructed jigsaw puzzle there, which gave Burt a moment to himself.

"Let's not write off the past just yet" was all he said.

"I'll order some blowups of these...."

Burt didn't meet Greg's eyes again as he left the room. Standing over the puzzle, pleased to fit in the first piece he chose, Greg sympathized with his friend and co-worker. There was nothing a cop like Burt— or Greg—hated more than to have missed something important.

WHY HAD SHE thought this was a good idea? With her canvas bag clutched at her side, Beth stood in Bonnie Neilson's sunny kitchen on the third Sunday in August, watching Ryan and Katie ignoring each other as they played quietly in the attached family room. She longed for the dingy but very organized interior of her rented duplex. Better the hardship you knew than one you didn't.

The duplex wasn't much, but for the time being, it was hers. She was in control there. Safe.

"Keith just went to town for more ice," Bonnie was saying as she put the finishing touches on a delicious-looking fresh vegetable salad. Already in a basket on the table was a pile of homemade rolls. Really homemade, not the bread-machine kind she used to make...

Beth froze. She'd had a memory. A real one. She had no idea where that bread machine was, no picture of a kitchen, a home, a neighborhood, a town or state—but she knew she'd had a bread machine. And she'd used it.

And been chastised for it?

"Can I do something?" Beth asked, probably too suddenly, reacting to a familiar surge of panic. She needed something to occupy herself, calm herself.

Staying busy had worked for months. As far as she knew, it was the only thing that worked.

"You can—"

"Unca!" Katie's squeal interrupted her mother.

The ensuing commotion as Katie tossed aside the magnetic writing board she'd had on her lap and jumped up to throw herself at her newly arrived uncle—and Ryan dropped the circular plastic shape he'd been attempting to shove into a square opening on the shape-sorter to make his way over to his mother's leg—served to distract Beth. She was so relieved, she didn't have nearly the problem she had anticipated with the arrival of Greg Richards.

Instead, she was almost thankful he'd come.

LATER THAT AFTERNOON, Beth had very mixed emotions about Greg's presence at his sister's house. Bonnie and Keith, her husband, had left to drive over to his grandmother's. Katie was asleep in the new trundle bed in her room. Ryan was also asleep, his little body reassuring and warm against her. He'd climbed in her lap after lunch, when they'd all migrated to the sitting room before trying the new chocolate cream cheese dessert Bonnie had made that morning.

That was when Keith's grandmother had called and Beth had suddenly found herself alone with a man who launched her right out of her element.

Not that she had any idea what her real element was. These days, all she had to go by was the Beth Allen Rules of Survival. A notebook with frighteningly few memories. Plus the perceptions she'd had, decisions she'd made, since waking up in that motel room.

He lounged on the leather couch, dressed in jeans and a cotton-knit pullover that emphasized the breadth of his chest. He was surveying her lazily, and appeared content to do so for some time to come. Beth didn't think she could tolerate that.

"Bonnie said you'd explain about Grandma Neilson," she reminded him. His younger sister had begged that Beth stay, insisting they'd only be gone a few minutes and she'd hate it if their day was ruined.

"She refuses Bonnie's invitation to join us for dinner on a fairly regular basis, insisting she doesn't want to impose, and then, inevitably, has some kind of mock crisis that's far more of an imposition than her acceptance of the dinner invitation would've been."

"Mock crisis?" Soothed into an unusual sense of security, Beth leaned back against the oversize leather chair she'd fallen into after lunch.

"Something that seems to need immediate attention, but that she could handle perfectly well by herself—or that turns out to be nothing at all. A toilet that *might* be clogged, for example. Or a strange noise in the attic, due to a loose shingle." Greg was smiling.

"But today's call—a seventy-five-year-old woman who's lost electricity in half her house, including her refrigerator—sounds pretty legit to me."

"Most likely a blown fuse."

"Still, for a woman her age…"

"Baloney," Greg exclaimed.

Ryan stirred, but settled back against her, his auburn curls growing sweaty where his head lay against her.

"She might be seventy-five years old, but she's as feisty and as manipulative as they come—and I've loved her as long as I can remember."

"You knew her before Bonnie and Keith got married?"

"She used to be the librarian at the elementary school. Every kid in town knew Mrs. Neilson. And loved her, too, I suppose. She's been a widow since Keith's dad was little. She's also the strongest person I've ever met. She'd go to the wall for any one of us if she believed in our cause. Nothing as trivial as a blown fuse is going to get in her way. Lonna Neilson could rewire that whole house if she put her mind to it."

"Then, why do Bonnie and Keith keep running over there?"

Greg's shrug drew her attention to the width of his shoulders. Shoulders a woman could lay her head against…

If that woman wasn't Beth Allen. Or Beth Whoever-she-was.

"In the first place," he said, "because they never know whether she's crying wolf or whether it might be the real thing."

She liked that. A lot. That they didn't give up on the old woman.

"And more importantly, because what's really driving her to call is the need to know she's loved. That's why Bonnie always goes, as well. It takes both of them to either make her feel good enough to be happy at home, or to convince her to join them here."

Beth smiled, praying he couldn't see the trembling of her lips. "So you're used to being left here with Katie every Sunday?" she asked. *Keep talking, don't think. Don't envision a vacant future, or, maybe worse, one that isn't vacant, only intolerable.*

"Nah, Grandma Neilson comes over about half the time she's asked, and then there's the occasional Sunday when no crisis arises."

His words were something to focus on. Something to take her thoughts away from the fact that her past held a threat so great she'd taken her baby and run.

"But I'm used to time alone with Katie," Greg continued lazily. "She's a big part of my life."

"Have you ever thought about having kids of your own?"

Beth's gaze shot down to Ryan as soon as she heard her own words. She'd broken a major Beth Allen rule. *Never ask personal questions.* Doing so was often taken as an invitation by the recipient to ask questions, too.

Damn. Give her a good meal, a comfortable chair and she lost all sense of herself. Which was scary when one didn't have much of that to begin with. When one was making things up as one went along…

Lifting an ankle to his knee, Greg slouched down farther. He looked more like a college kid than the head of an entire law enforcement organization. "I used to think I'd have a whole houseful of kids by now," he said. "You've probably noticed that Shelter Valley families tend to be rather large. You don't have to live here long to figure that out."

His grin was sardonic, half deprecating, half affectionate, as he spoke about the people he protected day in and day out.

"Especially if you spend any time at Little Spirits," Beth said, his easy tone allowing her to continue a conversation she'd meant to shut down. "It seems like everyone in Shelter Valley is related."

"Either by blood or by a closeness of the heart," Greg agreed. He sounded proud of the fact. "Everyone in Shelter Valley has family of one sort or another."

It was the perfect opportunity to ask why he didn't have that houseful of kids he'd envisioned. She badly wanted to know.

Only the very real threats she lived with every second of her life kept her silent. The threat of being found out. And of never finding out. Never learning who she was. What she was hiding from.

And why she hadn't been strong enough to solve her problems rather than run from them.

The threat that he might ask questions she couldn't answer. Or find answers she didn't want him to have.

"Did you and your husband plan to have more children?"

Blank. That was the only way to describe the mental picture his question elicited. But there was nothing blank about the instant panic that accompanied the emptiness. As the dull red haze blotted out her peripheral vision—a reaction she'd long since recognized as her body's danger signal—Beth again looked down at her son.

She could do this, get through whatever life required, for Ryan. Without a single memory, she knew he was the reason she'd run. And she'd keep running forever, from her memory, her needs, her heart, if that was what it took to keep him safe.

"I'm perfectly happy with Ryan," she said.

"So you'd planned for him to be an only child?"

"Not necessarily."

"Did your husband spend a lot of time with the boy?"

I don't know! "What's with the inquisition, Sheriff?" Guided by survival instincts, she stared at him, chin raised, as she offered the challenge.

And then turned quickly away. Those dark green eyes scared her with their intensity. When he looked at her, Greg Richards saw more than she could allow. She didn't know how or why; she only knew it had to stop.

"I'm just trying to get to know you, Beth, but for some reason you make that very difficult. I can't help wondering why."

Because if she told him the smallest thing—truth or lie—he'd be able to find out more. Because she couldn't afford to trust. Not even him. No matter what her heart said.

The red haze was back. "I notice you didn't answer my earlier question about your own empty house," she said, making a quick amendment to Beth Allen's Rules of Survival. Avoiding personal questions was no longer the issue. Sidetracking him was.

"A couple of things happened to change my plans."

"What things?" The fact that she really wanted to know made the query a dangerous one. But she had to keep him talking—about him. And not her. It wouldn't be much longer before Bonnie and Keith returned. "You haven't met the right woman?"

It was a common enough excuse.

"I met her."

Oh. Beth frowned. "Was she from Shelter Valley?" Had the woman died? Why hadn't Bonnie told her?

"Born and raised," Greg said, his thumb tapping a rhythm on the couch beside him. "Shelby and I met in grade school. Dated all through high school. I think I always knew I'd marry her someday."

"What happened?" And why was she taking this so personally?

"I asked her to marry me, but I wanted to wait until after I graduated from Montford and the police academy."

Beth didn't think she'd have agreed to wait—and was bothered by that thought. Did it mean she was impatient by nature? She certainly hadn't had any indication of that up to this point. But she'd been so busy surviving, self-discovery hadn't been much of an option.

As life in Shelter Valley grew more routine, things were starting to slip out from her hidden past, her hidden mind. She wanted that so badly.

And yet…she didn't want it at all.

Ignorance allowed her to stay safe in Shelter Valley and raise her son.

Of course, maybe the reason she wouldn't have agreed to wait had nothing to do with her; maybe it was just because of Greg. She couldn't imagine having him in love with her and agreeing to wait a week, let alone years.

"During my last year of college, Shelby went to Los

Angeles to visit a girl who'd lived with her grandparents in Shelter Valley during our senior year in high school. Shelby met some guy in California and was married within a month."

"What?" Beth sat forward, completely forgetting that Ryan was sound asleep. Disturbed, the child lifted his head, eyes unfocused as he opened them. He fussed for a second and then settled against her and went back to sleep.

"She wanted out of Shelter Valley. Didn't want to be trapped in this small town, raising a bunch of kids. She just hadn't bothered to tell me that."

"She was an idiot." The words weren't conciliatory or polite. Beth honestly couldn't think of any dream better than a real home in this town, shared with a loving man. One who'd love Ryan, teach him the things a son should know. One who'd give her another baby or two...

But was it the *real* Beth thinking these thoughts? Or were they simply the desperate longings of a lost woman on the run?

"I like to think so," Greg said, grinning at her. "Anyway," he added, growing more serious, "that kind of put a kink in my plans for home and family."

The softly spoken words lured her further into the dangerous conversation.

"That must've been at least ten years ago," she said. "I can't believe there haven't been opportunities since then."

"I spent the past ten years taking care of my father."

"Bonnie told me," Beth said, compassion welling up so strongly she wasn't sure what to do with it. "I'm so sorry."

Tight-lipped, Greg didn't say anything. Beth could almost feel his frustration…and pain.

Which was ridiculous. She barely knew this man.

She adjusted Ryan, moving him to her other shoulder. His sweaty hair had left a damp spot where his head had lain.

"So you didn't date for ten years?" The superfluous words were probably all wrong, but what else could she ask?

"I dated," Greg answered with a dim version of the grin he'd given her earlier. But he looked relieved, too, to have been rescued from whatever thoughts had been hounding him. "I just couldn't find a woman willing to take on a paraplegic senior citizen."

And Greg was not a man who would put his father in a full-time care facility unless there was no other choice.

Beth had never wished more than she did in that moment that she was free to like this man—and maybe let something develop between them. Something more than liking…

DR. PETER STERLING and Houston prosecuting attorney James Silverman faced each other in the elegantly furnished waiting room of Sterling Silver Spa, in the newly incorporated town of Sterling Silver, Texas. The spa's last client had just left for the evening.

"Damn, it's hot." Dr. Sterling pulled at the collar of his pristine white shirt. He'd just walked over from visiting a new resident in the apartment complex a couple of blocks away. "August has got to be the worst month of the year."

Silverman didn't agree. He thought January's cold

was pretty miserable. But it wasn't worth an argument to say so. Loosening his tie, he unfastened the top button of his dress shirt. How did Sterling do it? Just keep going every day, always looking perfect?

Didn't the man ever get tired?

And what did it say about Silverman that he was damn exhausted?

"It's time to hire someone new," Sterling said, his eyes black points of steel as they pinned Silverman. "Winters isn't working out. We should've heard something by now."

"I know." James undid a second button. He'd been unhappy with the private investigator for weeks. But he didn't know whom he could trust. There was too much at stake.

"Every day that goes by puts us all in more jeopardy."

"I know."

"We can't think only of ourselves," Sterling reminded him, as he did in just about every conversation the two men had these days. "We have many, many good people relying on us."

"I know." No one knew that better than James Silverman. He didn't need Sterling reminding him, pressuring him. He carried the burden of his mistake every waking—and sleeping—moment of his life.

He wasn't going to fail his new family, his friends. If nothing else, he believed in the cause. In them. He might have lost his faith in most things, but he still believed in a better tomorrow, a world free of negative energy and aggression.

They'd worked too hard, for too long, and come too far to let a traitor ruin everything for them now.

"Beth's dangerous."

"Yes." James felt sick.

"There's no telling what she's capable of."

Silverman nodded.

"She has to be stopped," Sterling said, his voice colder than any of his patients had ever heard. "At all costs."

"I know."

Satisfied, Sterling got to his feet. The meeting was over.

"We'll get through this together," he said, his tone softer. "Together we always find the cure, don't we?"

James nodded, more because it was expected of him than because he was in a trusting mood that night. As he locked up, he wondered if the doctor's cures were losing their effectiveness. For him, anyway... And that made Beth's defection more dangerous than ever.

CHAPTER FOUR

AS HE LOCKED the door of his office, Greg thought about how he couldn't lock away the impressions that continued to bombard him. There were puzzle pieces that definitely fit together—as clearly as the myriad jigsaws he'd worked on over the years. If only he could figure out how... Culver was right, there'd been many carjackings in the past ten years. No reason to believe that this year's series had anything to do with the ones that had happened ten years ago. Except that in both cases, there had been a series.

Of course, Burt was also right in his claim that the occurrences near the border had been a series, too.

But...

The pieces floated in and out, settling, moving around, changing location without offering him a single answer.

He was outside Beth's nondescript apartment on one of the older streets in Shelter Valley. Greg chuckled to himself. Considering where he was, his thoughts seemed fitting. Because, judging by past experience, he wasn't going to find out any of the hundred things he wanted to know here, either.

And just as he did with any other puzzle, he kept looking at all the pieces. Turning them this way and that, trying to fit them here or there to create the whole picture. When something mattered enough, when the feeling was strong enough, there wasn't any other choice.

"Greg. Hi." It wasn't the most welcoming tone as Beth opened her door to him that Wednesday night. He hadn't seen or spoken to her since she'd left his sister's right after dessert, late Sunday afternoon.

She'd blamed her early departure on Ryan's grumpiness on waking, but Greg wasn't convinced that was the only reason.

Maybe he should've taken time this afternoon to stop at home and change out of his uniform.

"I knew that if I asked you to dinner or a movie—or anything else, for that matter—you'd say no, so I decided to just come by."

Face softening, though not quite into a smile, Beth leaned against the door. She was wearing a black tank top and black sweats cut off just below the knee. One of the sexiest outfits he'd ever seen.

"If you know I don't want to go out with you, why bother?" she asked.

She hadn't shut the door. Nor did her question seem nearly as off-putting as it could've been. As a matter of fact, she sounded curious.

Good.

"I don't think we've established that you don't *want* to go out with me. Only that you'd say no if I asked."

"Isn't that the same thing?"

Glad he'd come, Greg shook his head. "I don't think so." He paused, pretending to consider. "Nope, not at all."

She straightened. "Well, it seems like the same thing to me," she said.

She'd tensed again.

"It would be a good idea to ask me in," Greg said quickly, before she had a chance to dismiss him. "You know, before the neighbors see a uniformed officer at your door and start to talk."

Beth grinned, looking out at the street in front of her house where he'd left his car. "Oh yeah, like that thing with the big 'Sheriff' emblazoned on the side isn't going to raise any suspicion?"

"Hell, no." He grinned, too, hands in his pockets as he stood his ground. "They'll just think the sheriff's sweet on you."

"And that won't cause talk?"

"Well, not the kind I was referring to. You know, the kind where everyone whispers about the possible secret life you're living and they start to weave fantasies about bank robberies or jewel thefts and lock their windows and doors at night and give you a wide berth anytime they run into you at the grocery store."

"Oh, that." Beth started to pale at the ridiculous situation he was describing, but then she laughed. "Yeah, that's about as likely as the sheriff being sweet on me."

"I sure hope not," he said, almost under his breath. And then wished he hadn't. That was good for a slammed door in his face.

Because he didn't know what else to do, Greg met her eyes. And that was when *it* always happened with them. From the first time he'd met her, he'd recognized something in that deep blue gaze. And until he knew what *it* was, what *it* meant, he had to keep coming back.

She didn't shut him out or close the door.

"May I come in?"

Beth just stared. Her eyes were trying to tell him something...if only he could decipher what it was.

"I won't stay long."

Still without a word, she stood back, holding the door wide. Greg quickly stepped inside and followed her into the small living room. It was as neat as it had been the last time he was there. Neat and bare.

"Where's Ryan?" he asked. He'd expected the boy to be playing quietly on the floor, had expected to see some toys out, stacked along the wall, something.

As far as he could tell, Ryan Allen hadn't discovered the terrible twos yet.

"He's asleep already. Normally bedtime isn't until seven-thirty, but I had a cancellation today and we spent the afternoon at the day care. He was beat."

"Did he and Katie acknowledge each other?" Greg asked, taking a seat on the edge of an old but relatively clean tweed couch, elbows on his knees.

"Nope."

"Your son doesn't like my niece?"

"More likely, your niece isn't interested in giving my son the time of day." She had a challenging glint in her eyes.

God, he loved it when she was feisty. And wondered why he saw that side of her so infrequently.

"No way," he said, shaking his head as he grinned up at her. "Katie'll make friends with anyone."

"You make it sound like she shows no discrimination at all."

He shrugged. "She's a day care kid," he said. "She really will play with anyone. So the problem has to be Ryan. The boy's stuck on himself." He was being outrageous and didn't care. He'd made her smile.

"Or maybe Katie thinks since she's *so much older,* it would be beneath her to play with a two-year-old."

"Were you that way in high school? Too good to go out with the younger guys?"

"Probably not."

"Why just probably?"

She looked away, her shoulders hunched as she rested her arms along the sides of her chair, an old but sturdy rocker. "Oh, you know," she said, "you never see yourself in quite the same way other people do."

True enough. "Tell me what you think you were like in high school."

It took her a long time to answer. "Not one of the stupidest kids in class, but not one of the smartest, either."

"I'll bet you never failed a single test."

"Not that I can remember."

"And you had dates every weekend."

"Well, I don't recall a single weekend without one." She grinned, but was still evading his eyes.

"Did you have a steady boyfriend?"

"Nobody who stayed with me."

She was finally talking to him. Sort of. He wondered what she'd been like before the loss of her husband, before his death had locked her so deeply inside herself.

But Greg wasn't going to let her reticence deter him. He understood the grieving process—from personal experience—but he also knew you didn't stop living.

"What do you enjoy doing?" For someone who interviewed people regularly, he was doing a pretty lame job of gaining his subject's trust.

But then, Beth wasn't a subject. She was a woman who had insinuated herself into his thoughts so thoroughly that she was interfering with his calm, predictable life.

"I'm good at business. Numbers. That kind of thing."

Not quite what he was looking for. And yet, perhaps the first piece of personal information she'd given him.

"So did you go to college?"

He'd just assumed she had no higher education—based solely on the fact that she was cleaning houses for a living. Yet Greg knew better than most how often things turned out to be exactly the opposite of the way they appeared. He knew what a mistake it was to assume anything. To judge anything by appearances.

"I sure didn't learn about business law in high school."

"You majored in business?"

"As long as I can remember, I've wanted to own my own business." She was so passionate in what she was saying that Greg almost missed how adeptly she'd sidestepped his question.

"I don't know how we got that far off topic," she added, before he could attempt to wade any further through the vagueness surrounding her, "but maybe Katie just doesn't like kids who are a little more serious in their endeavors and that's why she won't play with my son."

No matter how beautiful the teasing grin she shot him, it didn't cover the fact that she had, once again, completely turned the conversation away from herself.

From his probing.

"I still think Ryan's the problem," he said, quite purposefully egging her on.

"My son is *not* a problem." The teasing glint remained in her eyes, but she'd crossed her arms over her chest. Usually a defensive gesture.

At least, when you were a suspect being questioned.

"Okay, *problem* is the wrong choice of word. But if the kid's anything like his mom…"

"Ryan plays with other kids," she said. She'd lost the glint.

Sobering, Greg said, "Bonnie told me the reason you volunteer at the day care in exchange for playtime is that you're trying to draw the little guy out more."

"I want him to have a homelike environment during the day when I work, but I did think being around other kids his age might encourage him to talk."

Greg nodded. He knew how much Bonnie and Keith—and he, too, for that matter—ached over every little glitch in Katie's life. A measurement that wasn't right in the middle of the chart. Teeth coming too soon, steps taken too late. Fevers, ear infections, runny noses. An aversion to vegetables. Shouldering all those worries alone had to be hard.

And that on top of losing the man you'd meant to spend the rest of your life with…

"If there's ever anything I can do—teach him to play catch, empathize with you when he's sick—you know I'm here, right?" he asked, certain that he was crossing a line he shouldn't cross.

"Thanks." Beth smiled again. A sad, very real smile, instead of the quick assurance he'd been expecting.

It wasn't agreeing to a date. But in Greg's book, it was far better than that.

And even though she'd given him more information about herself than he'd ever had before, he still didn't have a clear picture of who Beth Allen really was.

"So what did you do today?" Beth asked Greg when silence fell between them and she was afraid he might take that as a sign to leave.

She felt buoyed up and wasn't ready to be alone.

He sat back, his uniform creased from a day in the August heat. That uniform made her uncomfortable. It reminded her of everything she couldn't have. Freedom from fear. Freedom to speak openly. Sex.

"I can't be sure, but I might have wasted the majority of it." The words, accompanied by a tired sigh, completely surprised her.

Greg always seemed so on top of things. In control. Able to handle anything.

She couldn't believe how quickly she wanted to help when she found out that wasn't the case.

"Anything you can talk about?"

"I'm attempting to find a connection between some recent carjackings and the one involving my father ten years ago."

Knowing how close Greg and Bonnie were, how much family meant to them, that couldn't be an easy job. "You think there is one?"

He clasped and unclasped his hands. "I'm sure of it. Problem is, the deputy in charge—the best man in the whole damn department, as far as I'm concerned—doesn't agree with me."

"What does he say?"

"That I'm making it personal."

"Are you?"

"I don't think so."

Beth didn't know much about herself, but thought she had a pretty good sense of this man. The type of person he was. "You're a smart man, Greg. And an honest one. I don't think you'd kid yourself about something as serious as this."

His eyes were grateful when he looked over at her, making Beth feel elated for no reason at all.

"I don't think so, either," he murmured.

"So what are the similarities you're finding? Anything you're free to discuss?"

"In the first place, we're dealing with a *series* of carjackings in both cases. There are other random occurrences, but these fit an identical pattern—several assaults with the same MO over a relatively short period of time. Two guys, late teens—early twenties, just after rush hour—either morning or evening."

"It's the same two guys every time?"

"No." Greg looked more than frustrated when he shook his head. "In fact, they aren't always even from the same ethnic background."

"So what else?" There had to be more. Greg wasn't the type to be this concerned over flimsy evidence.

"They only take place in the summer, for one thing. I have no idea what that means, but it has to mean something. They start midsummer, there's a rash of them, and then, inexplicably, they stop. No arrests. Not even any real suspects. They just stop."

"What about the drivers?" Beth asked. "Could they be the tie-in somehow?"

With another shake of his head and a raised brow, Greg said, "I don't find a single thing to connect them. Not age. Not where they work or live. Not their religion, where they bought their cars or even their injuries." A shadow of pain crossed his face.

She winced inside, thankful suddenly for the blessing of amnesia. "They weren't all hurt?"

His brows drawn together, Greg gave her an apologetic glance. "You don't have to do this."

"What?" she asked, a bit afraid of how important it had suddenly become to talk this through with him. To do something to help him. "Talk to a friend?"

"Is that what we are? Friends?" His expression lost none of its seriousness.

"I don't know." Beth had to be honest. After a pause, she returned to her earlier question, "So, they weren't all hurt?"

"Of this current group, all but one," Greg said. His voice was tightly controlled but she could hear the anger.

"Most were killed," he went on. "But not in the same way. One was shot. Another raped and strangled. One was left unconscious in the desert to either succumb to the heat or die of dehydration, whichever came first."

Beth swallowed.

"I can stop now."

"No, go on," she said. "It's okay, really. I'm not squeamish. I'm just sorry for these people and their families."

She wasn't squeamish. Another characteristic to add to the list she was keeping in her memory notebook. This was a good one. The kind she liked to add. Rated right up there with orderly.

"This summer, a college girl chose to throw herself out of the back seat of her moving car rather than submit to whatever else her abductors had in mind. She was a dancer and knew how to land and roll. She was miraculously unhurt."

Beth frowned, struck by an uncomfortable thought. Could something like this have happened to her? Had she merely been the victim of a random crime and not the runaway she supposed herself to be?

Of course, that didn't explain the canvas gym bag, obviously grabbed in a hurry with a couple of diapers and a change of clothes for Ryan stuffed in with various sweats, T-shirts and socks that fit her, or the two thousand dollars. Not many people traveled with that much cash. And no identification.

Not smart people, anyway.

Beth didn't know what that bag signified. But she always kept it close. As though it somehow connected her to the self she'd lost.

As for the two thousand dollars—part of it she'd invested in equipment and supplies to set herself up in business.

"There's something else," Greg said slowly. "The front ends of all the stolen cars—ten years ago and now—were smashed in such a way that no matter what make or model, they look remarkably the same."

"Like they all hit the same thing? Or something similar?"

Greg's brow cleared as he nodded. "Yeah. Odd, huh?"

"Very. Your deputy didn't think so?"

"Didn't seem to. Nor did he seem impressed by the fact that they were all new-model cars. Most carjackers are looking for quick transportation. They aren't usually so picky."

"You're sure this guy knows what he's doing?" Beth asked, somehow not surprised at the thought that this deputy might not be all that he seemed.

What she found startling was that she was so cynical. She'd just naturally assumed the man was up to no good. People didn't think that badly of the human race without reason, did they?

Oh God. She was cynical. Two things for the list in one night. This second one was not a characteristic she was particularly eager to have.

These past months of almost no self-revelation at all weren't looking as bad as they once had...

"I know he does," Greg said somberly, his words rescuing her from the familiar dark hole she'd been sinking into.

"WERE YOU IN the middle of work or something?" Greg asked, pointing to the piles of papers, receipts and ledgers on the scarred desk at one end of the room. Beth had grown silent, and he was kicking himself for bringing up such a personal subject. But then, it was difficult to tell *what* she considered personal. He'd worked so hard for so long to get in the door, and he hated the idea of losing the little trust she'd given him.

"Just doing my books," she said, sounding completely relaxed. Maybe for the first time in their acquaintanceship.

He smiled. "Looks like you've got enough stuff going on to be running a business the size of the Cactus Jelly plant."

"I told you I liked numbers. I'm actually keeping a tally of month-to-month percentages on the variance in cleaning supply costs. I check at the local Wal-Mart and at several places in Phoenix. I then keep track of how much cleaning I can do per ounce of solution. I'll bet you didn't know, for instance, that Alex Window Cleaner does linoleum more cost-effectively than any of the ammonia-based floor cleaners."

"No, I didn't know that." There was apparently much more to cleaning than he'd ever realized.

But what was of far greater interest to him was the woman who was rattling off dollars and ounces as easily as he did police radio codes.

"I take it your business is doing well," he said, when she'd given him a rundown on the benefits of bulk purchasing versus storage costs. Not just for cleaning supplies, but for business in general. Beth hadn't been kidding. She knew her stuff. More than any business student he'd ever known.

"As a matter of fact, this is the first month that Beth's Basins—and the Allens—are completely in the black! The bills are paid, money's put aside for emergencies and Ryan's education, and I even have some to spare. Ry's been wanting this balsa wood airplane he saw downtown, and even though it's really for older boys, I'm going to get it for him."

"He told you he wants an airplane?" Greg couldn't believe the change in her. She could have been any normal woman.

Certainly she was a beautiful one. Beth's loose auburn hair falling over shoulders left bare by the tank top she wore was driving him just a little crazy.

"Ryan hasn't said so, of course," she was telling him, her bare feet pushing off the floor as she rocked gently. "But his eyes light up every time we pass it. Hopefully I'll have time to take him tomorrow."

"You really love that little guy, don't you," Greg said. About that, at least, she was completely open.

"More than life itself."

Somehow one hour became two and Greg was still there, sitting on Beth's couch while she rocked in her chair. She'd gotten up once to get them both cans of soda and to check on Ryan, but that was all. Greg, who usually had a hard time staying in one place, was surprised by how much he enjoyed just sitting there looking at her.

Maybe that was why he didn't push his luck with any more personal questions. He didn't want her to show him the door.

Even now that she was more relaxed, Beth's eyes were still inexplicably expressive. Was it just her intelligence he saw there? He didn't think so.

The woman was a contradiction. Vulnerable one moment, and completely in control the next. Able to accomplish anything. Needing no one.

Teasing—and instantly defensive.

Insecure. And then confident.

And those breasts. He was ashamed of how much he was noticing them, how many times he thought about touching them.

Greg stayed long into that night, talking, mostly about growing up in Shelter Valley—including his college years at Montford University, the Harvard of the West, Shelter Valley's pride and joy. Beth had a million questions, making him wonder if she'd been storing them up for the entire six months she'd lived in town.

A million questions, but very few answers.

He got to know nothing at all about the circumstances and facts, the history, that made up Beth Allen's life.

CHAPTER FIVE

SHE WAS GOING to have to lie. Driving her old Granada to Bonnie's for her second Sunday dinner in three weeks, trying to distract her thoughts with the grand beauty of the mountains surrounding them, Beth finally accepted that she'd have to make up a past—not just the couple of lines she'd recited anytime anyone asked about her. Up until now, the fact that she was a grieving widow had sufficed. Recognizing that her recent past was painful, people were sensitive enough not to ask further questions.

But that was when those people were only acquaintances.

Bonnie Neilson and her family—her brother— wanted to know Beth Allen. Where she came from. Where she went to school. Her most embarrassing moment. Happiest moment. The men she'd dated.

The man she'd married.

They wanted to know it all.

They had no idea how badly she wanted to know all those things herself.

What she didn't want was the rest of the memories that would come as part of the package. She was scared to death to find out she might have stolen her son.

If that was the truth, and if she remembered it, she'd be forced to give him back.

Still, before she'd left home today, she'd read over the few entries in her memory notebook, trying to piece together a picture she could give people.

"We're going to Katie's house, Ry," she told her son, sending him a big smile. His feet, hanging over the edge of the sturdy beige car seat, were still. But his eyes were alert, intent, as he looked back at her, straight-faced.

"You remember Katie from Little Spirits," she continued, knowing that Ryan understood everything she was saying, even if he wouldn't respond. "We went to her house for dinner a few weeks ago and you fell asleep on Mommy's shoulder. You played with Katie's blocks. And she has a Magna-Doodle, too."

Ry's little voice filled the car, but Beth couldn't make out the words. From his intonation it sounded like a question.

So Beth replied to what she could only assume he'd asked. "Yes, I think she'll let you play with the Magna-Doodle, but I want you to promise something, okay?"

Ryan nodded.

"I want you to promise that you'll play with Katie today. Okay? Just like you play with Bo and Jay and Bethany Parsons."

Ryan watched her lips and then her eyes.

"Okay?" she repeated.

He nodded again. Slowly, deliberately, his little chin moved up and down. The chin that had the same cleft in the middle as hers.

Ryan might not say much, but when he agreed to something, she could count on it. Soon after they'd arrived at the Neilsons he picked up one of Katie's puzzles and took it over to sit by the little girl. He dumped the wooden pieces and, with the hand-eye coordination of a two-year-old, he started putting them awkwardly back on the board. Within seconds Katie turned around and placed another piece. Not a word was spoken between them.

Beth wished her own interactions could be so clean and simple. She spent the first five minutes staying out of the way, clutching her canvas bag.

Dinner was excellent—another cold main-course salad in deference to the weather. It was the first Sunday in September, and still too hot to even think about turning on the oven. Or eating anything warm, for that matter.

She was saved from having to sit next to Greg by Katie's last-minute insistence that she get to sit by "Unca" which resulted in Grandma Neilson and Greg switching chairs to accommodate Katie's booster seat.

"Lou can lose my high chair, Wyan," the little girl said importantly as she climbed up and set her little bottom down in her new blue plastic booster.

Well before the end of dinner, Beth had fallen in love with Grandma Neilson. The white-haired, barely five-foot-tall woman didn't let anything—not age, infirmity nor death—get in her way. She'd reduced life to its simplest terms. Being loved and loving others were what mattered. Anything else was simply an inconvenience to be dealt with as quickly as possible.

"So, Bonnie says you've got a cleaning business here in town," Grandma said to Beth as she chomped on her Chinese chicken salad.

Dressed in a long-sleeved button-up blouse and pair of navy slacks in spite of the heat, Keith's grandmother looked like she was ready to go to the office.

"I do," Beth said, on edge that afternoon as she waited for a question she couldn't answer.

Maybe this was too much of a life for her—having friends, trying to have family experiences. And yet, seeing Ryan sitting there in his high chair, pulled up to the table as though he belonged, watching him grin at Keith and babble a sentence to Bonnie, she wasn't sure she had any choice.

She had no idea what she'd taken Ryan away from. Aunts, uncles? Maybe a grandmother or two like Grandma Neilson?

A father?

How could she not do everything possible to provide him with some of the same now?

"Good for you," Grandma was muttering. "Get on with it, that's what I say."

Head bent over her plate, Beth nodded.

"Use your spoon, Katie, not your fingers," Keith said. Greg leaned over to help his niece do as her father directed.

"Losing a husband is hard," Grandma said. "I'll grant you that, but you still have to get on with it, or the Good Lord would've taken you, too."

"Sorry about that," Keith said. "Grandma just tells it like she sees it."

"I don't mind," Beth said. She had a feeling that if there was ever a time she needed someone to confide in, Keith's grandmother would probably be her most sympathetic audience.

The least judgmental, anyway.

She'd understand how a woman could love her baby so much she'd do anything for him.

"Do you have room for another customer?" Grandma

asked. "I've gotten myself on so many committees, I sure could use some help keeping up the house."

Beth didn't miss the way Bonnie, Keith and Greg shared surprised looks. But she didn't really care.

"What committees?" she asked.

She gave up even trying to keep them straight after Grandma described the fifth one. The woman seemed to run the entire town single-handedly.

With a little help from Becca Parsons, apparently. Little Bethany's mother had been mentioned several times during Grandma's dissertation. Beth had yet to meet the woman who was not only a prominent member of Shelter Valley's city council, but wife to the president of Montford University, as well.

"So, you got the time?" Grandma asked.

"I do," Beth said. She didn't really, but she'd make time. She really needed to be putting away more for Ryan's education than she was currently able to allot each month.

If she were anyone else, she could just hire an employee or two. But she wasn't. She was Beth Allen, nonexistent person. While she was diligently figuring out her taxes and setting aside the money to pay them if she was ever free to do so, she couldn't actually file. She didn't even know her social security number.

"I don't accept checks or credit cards," she said.

"Smart woman." Grandma nodded approvingly. "Cuts down on bank fees."

"You want to do my house, too?" Greg asked. "I could—"

"Forget it, buddy," Beth interrupted before she was somehow trapped, in front of the sheriff's family, into doing something she knew would be far too dangerous.

Greg Richards was in her thoughts too much already. She didn't need to see where or how he lived. Didn't need to know where his bedroom was, what his sheets looked like.

Didn't need to know if he kept his refrigerator clean. If it was empty. If he picked up his clothes and left open *TV Guides* lying around.

But Grandma Neilson's house was a different matter. Beth had a feeling there was a lot she could learn from Keith's resilient grandmother.

THERE WASN'T SEATING for everyone in the family room, with Grandma Neilson added to the Sunday party. Conscious of the fact that she was the one who didn't belong in that house, Beth quickly pulled out the piano bench and sat down after dinner when they all trooped in to watch a movie on Bonnie and Keith's new LCD flat-screen TV.

"Afraid you might have to sit by me?" Greg whispered on his way to the couch.

It was only because he was carrying Katie, who would have overheard, that she refrained from calling him a name she wouldn't have meant, anyway. But it sure would've been good to say it. To at least pretend she wasn't aware of every move the man made.

If she didn't get control of her reactions to Greg, she'd have to stop coming to Sunday dinner. She could not be influenced by the woman inside her who wanted to love and be loved. Too much was at stake.

"You know how to play that thing?" Grandma asked, settling herself in the armchair next to the piano. Her wrinkled face was alight with interest as her watery blue eyes rested on Beth.

"Maybe."

A rush of tears caught Beth by surprise, she blinked them away and turned to face the keyboard. Lifting and pushing back the wooden cover with practiced ease, she wished so badly that she had a mother or grandmother of her own. Someone to love and comfort her, someone who'd counsel and watch over her... She wondered if she'd left either—or both—back home. Wherever home might be.

No, she decided. Surely if she'd had someone like Grandma Neilson to run to, she'd have done so. She certainly wouldn't have awakened, badly bruised and alone, in that nondescript motel room. Registered under the name of Beth Allen but with nothing to prove who she really was.

Unless she *did* have a Grandma Neilson someplace, and she'd had to run to protect her, too?

The ivory and black keys did not look strange. Or feel strange, either, as she rested her fingers lightly upon them.

"You know how to play?" Bonnie asked, stopping beside the piano bench. "Keith's parents bought that for us when Katie was born, but none of us play."

"A little, I guess," Beth said, confused. She caressed the smooth white keys with the pads of her fingers, comforted by their coolness.

And their familiarity?

Did she know how to play? Have lessons as a child?

"All I can play is chopsticks," Keith said, standing beside his wife.

"Mama. Uh. Mama. Uh." Ryan toddled over to the bench, both hands grabbing hold of it.

"You want to watch Mama play?" Greg asked. Handing Katie to Keith, he picked the boy up.

"Pway," Katie said.

"You heard her." Grandma's voice brooked no argument.

Beth looked down at the keys—and panicked. She had no idea what to do. The people around her faded as the red haze filled her peripheral vision. She recognized the feel of those keys. Didn't think she could take her hands off them, her need for them was so intense.

And yet...what was she supposed to do now? No picture came to mind of ever having done this before, of what keys to press to make anything close to a song.

Did she use two fingers? Or all ten?

"Mama," Ryan said, not quite whining. But he sounded close.

Heart pounding, Beth knew she had to do something. Some force in her, deep and elemental, wouldn't let her get up without doing *something*. And Ryan wasn't going to give her much time.

Closing her eyes, Beth took a deep breath and stopped thinking. Focusing on that inexplicable drive buried deep inside her, she poised her hands and pushed down. The first sound that came crashing from the instrument was harsh. And yet—right. Completely right. The sounds that followed were perfection, flowing together in a rush of turbulent and compelling music. Beth's hands moved over the keys—flew over them—of their own accord. She hadn't listened to music in months. Never turned on the radio in the car. Had that been on purpose?

Someone gasped just behind her right shoulder, but she was only vaguely aware of it. Only vaguely aware of herself. Again, without her prompting, or even her understanding, tumultuous chords gave way to poignant ones, filling the room with sweet longing. And filling Beth with a longing she barely understood.

She couldn't stop. Music flowed out of her, gushing, it seemed, from every pore, the notes chasing each other almost faster than she could release them. She didn't know what was happening. Didn't know how.

She only knew she'd just discovered something very vital. For the first time in six months, Beth Allen was alive. Living.

The person she was meant to be.

She had no idea how much time had passed before her fingers, sore and almost raw, dropped to her lap. She was afraid to turn, to break the spell.

"My God." The whisper was Keith's.

Embarrassed, Beth glanced halfway around. Ryan was asleep on Greg's shoulder. Another pang of familiarity shot through her. Her son had done that before. He'd fallen asleep while she played to him.

She'd soothed him with her music when he was sick.

The knowledge came and went so quickly—just a brief impression, really—that she wasn't sure, in her oversensitized state, whether she'd imagined it.

Wishful thinking?

It was hard to know what was real when you didn't know your own mind.

"Thank you." Grandma Neilson's voice, soft and uncharacteristically reverent, broke the long silence.

Somehow, Beth wasn't surprised to see tears in the stalwart old woman's eyes.

"You're a concert pianist." Greg, standing just off

to her left, was staring at her, his expression a mixture of awe and scrutiny. He was going to want answers.

And that was something she couldn't give.

Beth turned, and started to play again.

GREG WAITED ONLY long enough to be sure Ryan was in bed that night before parking his truck outside Beth's duplex. He leapt over the couple of steps leading to her front porch before delivering a purposeful knock.

"I had a feeling you'd come," she said, holding the door open for him, resignation in the droop of her shoulders, her bent head. Sinking down into her rocking chair, she grabbed a pillow, angled perfectly in the corner of the couch, and hugged it.

She glanced over at him as he slumped on the couch, looking as dazed as he felt.

"Why?" He didn't bother with preliminaries.

"Why am I not surprised you came? Is that what you mean?"

Greg bit back a curse. Even now she was delaying, avoiding a response. What was it with this woman? And why in the hell did he care?

"Why didn't you tell me you're a pianist?"

"I play the piano," she said, although there was an odd note in her voice.

He didn't understand it. Doubt? Where there should've been confidence?

"That doesn't mean I'm anything more than a lady who cleans houses and once took piano lessons."

"That was more than piano lessons. It was an entire repertoire. A concert. Pieces very carefully chosen and arranged to express every nuance of emotion. The peaks and valleys, the passion—it was the most incredible musical experience I've ever had."

Beth met his gaze for a moment. He thought she might cry. And then she looked down, saying nothing. Her foot pushed gently against the floor, slowly rocking the chair.

"Why, Beth? Why hide such a remarkable talent?"

"I don't know."

Her eyes, when she looked up at him, were tortured. Tearing at him.

Greg sat forward, needing to touch her, yet knowing he couldn't—although he wasn't sure why. "Help me understand," he said gently.

She wanted to. Greg could see that in the way she held his gaze, honestly, hiding none of the pain or compassion she was feeling.

"I…can't. I just have to keep me to myself."

What the hell was driving her? What had happened to trap her so deeply inside herself? Was it the shock of losing her husband? Or something more?

"Can't or won't?" He deserved that much, at least.

"I don't know, Greg," she said. "I…" She swallowed, closing her eyes. "I hurt…"

Every word was difficult. Greg wanted to tell her it was okay. That she didn't have to do this.

But he couldn't.

It was too important.

"So badly," she continued. "But I'm still here, you know?"

Tears glistened in her eyes. And suddenly Greg did know. He'd had that feeling, too. Of having something essential taken away from him, and yet enduring because there was no other choice. First with Shelby. And then for the ten years he'd looked after his father or, more accurately, the shadow his father had become.

"I have Ry to think about," she said. "I have to go on. And somehow, in the process of making that happen, I just froze inside.

"It wasn't anything I consciously chose. Or even recognized at the time." Her voice was a whisper, each word an obvious effort.

He nodded. "Self-preservation," he said. He'd seen it dozens of times on different levels. Had experienced it himself.

Beth's arms rested on the sides of the chair as she rocked. The pillow was in her lap. Greg had a sudden and very unusual urge to lay his head there, too. Just for a moment.

To know that she was there, watching over him. To take comfort, for once, instead of offering it.

Unusual reaction. Odd. Embarrassing. *She* was clearly the one in need of comfort. Not he.

"I don't know how to get out," she said. The duplex was quiet. The street outside empty.

"Isn't that what you did today? Playing like that?"

"Maybe." Drawing up her legs, she pulled the pillow to her chest.

"Can you tell me a little about yourself?" he asked, hoping with a hope he thought he'd lost. "About the things that made Beth Allen the person she is now?"

His heart plummeted when she shook her head. "I'm not ready for emotional risk, Greg. If I don't open up to people, I can stay safe."

"Just tell me where you're from."

She peered at him above the pillow, her eyes moist. "I came here from Snowflake."

Instantly at attention, Greg forced himself not to budge from his relaxed position. "You lived there with your husband?"

She shook her head again.

"Is that where you grew up?"

"No."

"So where *did* you grow up?"

"In the south."

"Alabama? Louisiana? Georgia?"

She nodded.

He could sense how hard she was trying. And he didn't want to push her. "Did you have brothers and sisters?" he asked mildly.

Beth shook her head for the third time. Greg wondered if it was merely reaction to being questioned or an actual answer.

"Are your parents still alive?"

Another brief shake of the head.

God, it was worse than he'd realized. He couldn't imagine how horrendous it would be to face life knowing you were so totally alone. Even in the worst of times, he'd always had Bonnie. And Shelter Valley.

"You can trust me," he said.

"I know."

"I want to help."

"Then, please be my friend, Greg. Be my friend until I can work through this."

Her words brought him a surge of joy. Yet he couldn't take a chance on being mistaken. "You're sure that's what you want?" he asked, his gaze direct, probing.

"Yes."

"You wouldn't rather I just disappeared and let you get back to the business of surviving?"

"No."

"Why?"

Beth grinned; her eyes filled with tears that pooled but didn't fall. "I'm afraid I'm going to freeze to death and not even know it."

He had no sense of what he should say. What he should do.

"You make me *feel,* Greg. For the first time in six months, I'm feeling."

He needed her to continue. To explain herself. He waited.

"And the feelings are…good."

"I'm attracted to you." He wasn't going to pretend.

"I know."

"And I think you're attracted to me, too."

"I know."

She knew she was? Or that he thought she was? Somehow it didn't matter. Either way, they'd just established something important.

"I'll be your friend for as long as it takes." The words were a promise. One he was determined to keep.

"Thank you."

Her tremulous smile was beautiful. And young. Almost innocent. It planted itself in Greg's heart.

"I'd like one thing, though," he said.

She frowned. "What?"

"I'd like you to be my friend, too."

"Oh." Her brow clearing instantly, Beth met his gaze with clear eyes. "I can do that."

He felt hopeful. Capable. Strong. "Does a friend get to do any touching?"

The frown was back. "What kind of touching?"

"Any kind," he said. He was willing to take anything.

"A hug. Maybe—" he paused, reached over and took her hand "—just this." Her hands were slim, feminine. And had elicited such intense and powerful music from Bonnie's piano that it still reverberated in his head.

Looking down at their joined hands, Beth smiled. There was hesitation in the tentative way she turned her hand, taking hold of his. "This is okay," she said.

Then, he'd leave it at that. For now.

CHAPTER SIX

DEPUTY BURT CULVER shut his office door when the number popped up on his caller ID. It was Wednesday. He'd been waiting since Monday morning.

Picking up the receiver, he leaned against the edge of his desk, staring out at the Native Reservation that stretched for miles on the other side of the road. "It's not good," he said in lieu of hello to the retired sheriff on the other end of the line.

"Tell me."

"Richards is looking at those photos from ten years ago."

"There's nothing for him to find."

Culver relaxed slightly at the lack of hesitation in the older man's reply. Everything he cared about—his job—was at stake. And for once, he wasn't in complete control. He was being driven to do things, make choices, he wouldn't ever have thought he'd make.

But he couldn't lose his job. Being a cop was his only reason for living.

"We're talking about the magic man here," he reminded his ex-superior, tugging on his ear. "Richards is always pulling stuff out of thin air."

"Only if it exists. Richards is a great cop. He won't waste taxpayers' money looking for something that's not there."

"He's studying the front ends."

"Don't wimp out on me now, Culver. I'm telling you there's nothing for him to find."

"You'd better be damn sure about that." Culver didn't usually talk to his mentor like that. Remorse silenced the rest of what he'd been about to say. "I'm a good cop," he said instead, by way of apology.

"You'd give your life to see justice upheld. Same as me. And Richards, too. Relax, Deputy. You've done nothing wrong. You have nothing to fear."

Culver nodded, gritting his teeth. All he'd ever wanted was to be a cop. If he loved anything at all, it was his work. With a dissatisfied grunt, he dropped the phone back in its cradle.

Reaching behind him, he yanked out his top drawer, grabbed the bottle of antacids and gulped down a couple.

All he'd really done was plead the Fifth. He wasn't going down for that.

BETH WOKE UP SWEATING. Her eyes immediately went to the night-light by Ryan's crib, then to the mattress where her son lay sleeping. His breathing was even.

Thank God.

Heart pounding, shivering, Beth stumbled from the bed. Scrambled for the notebook in her underwear drawer, but couldn't make herself do more than hold on to it.

A glass of water might help. Might bring reality into focus, chase away the demons of a darkness she didn't understand.

She'd had the dream again. Not that she remembered it. Ever. But it always left her with this debilitating sense of impending death. She carried around a fear she couldn't conquer. Couldn't even identify.

The dime-store plastic tumblers were neatly arranged in two colorful rows on the bottom shelf of one of the three kitchen cabinets. She would've preferred glass, but wasn't going to waste money on purchasing two sets. And Ry needed plastic. She supposed this told her something about herself—that she didn't like mixing and matching, craved complete sets. Something to write in her notebook.

A half bag of ice remained on the shelf she'd designated for ice in the freezer. She'd have to buy more in the morning. It seemed odd to her, this practice of buying ice. She was pretty sure that where she came from, they just used the ice most freezers produced automatically. And those who were in less financially advantaged situations like hers and didn't have a newer refrigerator, made ice by filling trays with water from the kitchen faucet and freezing it.

In Shelter Valley the water didn't taste right for drinking directly from the tap.

Ice in the glass, water from the gallon jug she'd purchased at the grocery, a sip. Then two.

And still, book in hand, Beth found her limbs were shaky, her skin tingling with unease. She could only take one sip at a time, needing to stop between swallows for air.

"Nights are the worst," she said aloud. Sometimes hearing a voice helped bring her back. Even if it was her voice. "In the morning, when the sun's shining and the sky is blue, you'll be okay."

She wanted to believe herself.

Except…did the light really make a difference to

anything other than her sense of total isolation? It didn't change the loneliness, the fear and the uncertainty. Daytime only made it easier to be distracted from them.

Rubbing her arms, Beth stood barefoot and nearly naked in her kitchen. She couldn't afford to turn the air-conditioning up very high and although it was the second week in September, the heat was still unbearable. So were the shivers.

She'd watched an action-adventure movie once where the hero was thrown into a dungeon crawling with bugs. She had no idea when, where or with whom she'd seen that movie, but she remembered the scene, the character's horrific panic. His inability to cope.

That was how she felt. Surrounded by stone walls crawling with black things. And the walls were moving in on her, getting steadily closer.

No one could help. She'd done a lot of reading on memory loss and she knew there was nothing anyone could do. Her assumption was that she was suffering from some kind of retrograde psychogenic amnesia. There was a combination of factors; the damage was organic in nature due to the blows to her head and psychosomatic in reaction to acute conflict or stress. Retrograde in that "events preceding the causative event" were forgotten.

Slowly sipping water she didn't want, Beth silently recited the words she'd read in the *Encyclopedia Britannica* many times over the past months. *Causative event*. Scary words.

The imaginary bugs started to fade as she concentrated on the things she'd read. Her type of amnesia was reversible. But it had to happen in its own time. Amnesia was a coping mechanism, the mind's way of giving her time to heal or grow strong enough. When her mind was ready to cope with whatever it was hiding from, she would remember.

In the meantime, she was supposed to keep her life as stress-free as possible. To fill herself up with as many positive feelings and "events" as she could.

A tall order for someone living all alone, in fear, not knowing if she was in trouble with the law, if she belonged in prison. Or if there was a maniac out there looking for her. Wanting to hurt her or Ryan.

Not knowing who she was or where she came from.

And not sure she wanted to know. As much as she hated the darkness, she wasn't sure it was any worse than what she'd left behind. It must've been something pretty terrible for her mind to have resorted to such drastic measures. She couldn't escape the instinctive thought that she should just trust her own mind and leave things alone.

But could she?

After washing the cup, Beth dried it and put it back in the cupboard. How much longer was she going to be able to cope if she couldn't sleep a full night? If the nightmares continued? Every morning now, she got up exhausted—in mind *and* body.

It had been just over a week since she'd played that piano at Bonnie's house, and Beth still hadn't recovered from the traumatic emotions the incident had stirred inside her.

She didn't understand the emotions. Didn't know why they were so disturbing. But they were eating away at her insidiously, mostly at night when she was trying to sleep. Driving her slowly insane…

What if she lost her mind completely? What was going to happen to Ryan then?

Sitting on the floor of the bedroom by her son's crib, her knees pulled up to her chest, Beth opened the notebook and read by the dim glow of the night-light.

And forced herself to think.

SHE KNEW NOTHING about finding missing persons. There was the Internet. And in Phoenix, birth records. But the first thing asked at either of those places was *Name, Last.* It was a piece of information she didn't have.

Still, Beth was desperate enough to try. There had to be a reason she'd used the name Allen; maybe it would lead her to her past.

Leaving Ryan at the Willises' on Thursday afternoon, the second week in September, she finished her last cleaning job and drove over to the university. The place had become like a favorite vacation spot during the past few months. A second home of sorts, as she searched for answers to unending questions. The shelves of books seemed like a lifeline, offering information her mind withheld from her.

It was in that library, browsing the business shelves, that she'd discovered she had more than a passing knowledge on the subject. She'd recognized titles and authors. She'd found, upon pulling out some books and reading a bit, that she was familiar with many of the facts and theories.

She'd done most of her amnesia research at the famous Montford University Library, too.

Today, canvas bag tucked securely on her lap, she was there to use the computer. To log on to her free Internet account, set up with bogus personal information, trying to find out if there was a Beth Allen living in Snowflake, Arizona.

She got 144 hits when she typed in the name. But when she perused all of them, none of the corresponding addresses meant anything to her.

She wasn't really disappointed because she hadn't expected much.

She just knew that, safe as anonymity was to her, she was no longer sure it was completely safe for Ryan. As long as she was here to protect him, he'd be fine. But what if she wasn't?

There were ways of providing a guardian for him in case something happened to compromise her life or stability, but to be legally effective they had to be filed.

And without a name or a background—without a legal identity—she couldn't file.

The red haze had been with her almost constantly since that afternoon at Bonnie's house, more than a week before.

Beth looked up from the computer screen, needing to connect with the life around her for a moment—to remind herself that life was going on. She experienced a moment's respite from her panic when she saw the couple who'd just come into the library. Ben and Tory Sanders. She'd never actually met them, but she knew who they were. She had, in fact, made it a point to find out who Tory Evans was when she'd first come to town. It was the article about Tory that had brought her to Shelter Valley, Tory's happy ending she had held on to all this time.

She watched as the couple chose a table and sat down together, and took comfort from the intimate smile they shared before opening the books they had with them.

And then Beth returned her attention to the computer screen in front of her. The news hadn't gotten any better.

Frustrated, she closed the people-finder screen. She knew someone who could help her. Who'd know just where to turn next.

She'd seen him a couple of times since that Sunday night after her impromptu piano concert. Once they'd run into each other at the day care. And he'd stopped by for an hour this past weekend.

Both times she'd felt a confusing onslaught of comfort and unease. She needed his unconditional friendship more than he'd ever know. And yet she feared everything about having him in her life. Feared his job. His intelligence. His desire to know about her. His affection.

His sexuality.

Snowflake. She should look up newspaper articles on Snowflake, Arizona. Maybe her advent, while apparently unnoticed, hadn't occurred without incident. Quickly typing, clicking and searching through files, Beth read carefully, diligently, looking for any mention of a car accident, an attempted rape or murder, a robbery, a domestic disturbance. Anything that might have occurred about the time she'd found herself alone in that motel room.

Searched, too, for any mention of a woman named Beth. And ran a search on the names Allen and Ryan.

All turned up nothing relevant.

So, how about a missing person report? Either an article or a mention in a police log. On a woman. A child. A kidnapping.

Hits flashed up with links. Glancing at her watch, Beth grimaced, her sweaty palm tightening on the mouse as she clicked on the first one. She was running far later than she'd meant to, but she couldn't stop now.

"What's a woman like you doing in a place like this?"

The wireless mouse flew from her fingers and landed on the carpeted library floor.

"Greg!" Beth said, seeing red everywhere as she pushed keys, removing words from the computer screen before the Kachina County sheriff had a chance to read them and start asking questions.

Greg was a smart man. Who was already suspicious.

Picking up the mouse, he set it on the pad and sat down at the computer beside her. He was in uniform. Which always made her just a little more uncomfortable around him.

"I didn't realize you'd discovered our hidden treasure here at Montford," he said, surveying the library.

The entire facility incorporated many floors and separate areas, which included meeting rooms small and large, conference rooms, a couple of different computer labs such as the one she was sitting in, group study areas, no-conversation areas, and rows and rows of books on every subject imaginable.

She nodded. Had he seen the child custody article she'd been perusing? "I've been coming here for months."

It was because of far too many sleepless nights that she couldn't come up with a plausible reason for her library visits. "To find myself" didn't work.

But it was the truth.

While most people were there to learn new things, Beth had been visiting to find out what she already knew.

"We've got a state-of-the-art computer lab at the SO," he said.

He couldn't have seen what she'd had up on the screen. He wouldn't be making small talk otherwise.

"SO?" she asked.

"Sheriff's Office." He grinned at her, a devilish light glinting in his eyes. "I have a system in my shop, too."

"Your shop."

"My place of business," he said, nodding at an older woman dressed in a skirt and blouse, who walked by with her hands full of folders. "In other words, my car."

"So what are you doing in here?" she asked him. There were no reference books in the computer lab.

"I was returning a book and I saw you."

His eyes were warm. Familiar.

"Oh."

She loved that look. As though he had a right to know her, to ask questions, to be with her. As though they belonged together. And she was deathly afraid of it, as well. The tightrope she was inching her way along was getting more and more frayed, and she was afraid the person who'd really be hurt when it broke was a little boy who had no ability to help himself.

"Why are you looking up custody cases?" Greg asked, casually leaning his forearms on the computer table beside him.

Shit.

She'd closed the screen she'd been on. But behind it had been the original search request.

"I wasn't…originally," she said, focusing her energy. Focusing on what mattered most: being calm, keeping Ryan safe.

"I'm here looking for options for Ryan," she told him, deciding that honesty was the best way out of this one.

"Custody options? With his father dead, isn't that a given?"

"Unless something happens to me."

They were speaking quietly, in deference to their surroundings, and Greg stood suddenly. "Let's go for a walk," he said, taking her hand.

Beth shut down the computer and picked up her bag—the canvas gym bag she'd found with her in Snowflake—allowing herself to be led out into the Arizona sunshine.

Montford's campus was beautiful. The cultivated grass was as green and manicured as any golf course. The big old trees, pretty uncommon in this part of the country, threw shade on benches placed all over the university grounds.

Greg led them to one such bench, not releasing her hand as they sat. Beth was more than a little embarrassed by the cut-off sweats and T-shirt she was wearing.

"I love a woman who polishes her toes to clean house," Greg said, grinning as he stared down at her flip-flops.

"I polish them for me," she murmured. "They just come along when I clean house."

Polishing her toenails was almost a ritual for Beth. She'd had red-polished toes when she'd awakened in Snowflake. Keeping them that way seemed like a way to keep herself—the old self she didn't know—alive. It seemed disloyal, unfaithful to that woman, not to do so.

He rested his arm along the back of the bench. "So, why the sudden worry about Ryan?"

And that was one of the reasons she was uncomfortable around Greg. He had a way of jumping from topic to topic with absolutely no warning. From serious to comic. And back again.

It was a trait she had a feeling she'd have liked if she'd met him in another lifetime.

Greg waved at a distinguished-looking man striding purposefully on a sidewalk across from them.

"Who's that?" she asked.

"Will Parsons. He grew up in this town, went to school here, and is now the president of Montford."

"His daughter is at Little Spirits with Ryan...." Which brought her right back to the question he'd asked her. Why was she worried about her son?

Flicking her hair over her shoulder, Beth resisted the urge to lean into the crook of his arm. She straightened, looking directly ahead of her.

"I've been worrying about what would happen to him if anything happened to me. I don't know what took me so long to think of it, but now that I have, I'm not going to rest until I've made some kind of arrangements."

And that meant she might not be resting for a good long time.

"Your husband's been gone, what—eight, nine months? A year?"

"Yeah."

"Not such a surprise that you're just thinking about this now. Starting over is tough. It can only happen a little at a time."

He was speaking as someone who knew. Who'd been there. "Was it hard for you, coming back here after so much time away?" she asked. "Or did growing up in Shelter Valley make the transition easier?"

Greg shrugged, gazing out over the expanse of lawn. He seemed to be watching a couple as they made their way hand in hand down a walkway that cut through the middle of campus.

"Change is always hard," he said eventually. "And Shelter Valley was a double-edged sword. It's my home, and it welcomed me."

"But?" Beth loved the curls at his forehead. She'd always longed to run her hands through his hair. Sensuously, seductively…

Right now, though, she had the urge to run her fingers through those curls as she would Ryan's, to offer comfort. Solace. A promise of peace…

"My life here was with Shelby," he told her. "We'd been friends since kindergarten."

"You must have known her very well."

She couldn't imagine the luxury of having someone know her that well. But she imagined she'd love it.

"I thought I did. Almost as well as I knew myself."

Hurting for him, wishing she were stronger, more in control of life, Beth met his eyes. "I remember you said she didn't want to wait to get married. That she met someone else in L.A."

He shrugged. "I guess what I saw in Shelby and what was really there were two different things. I trusted her to be honest with me. She wasn't."

"So you…created an image you fell in love with?"

"Worse than that," he said, looking over at her, his eyes lacking their usual spark. "The things I loved about her were real enough to keep that love alive and burning. And to work against me, blinding me to the ways she was changing. What I didn't want to see."

"Maybe she helped that along by hiding them from you."

"I don't think so," Greg said. "I almost wish she had,

because then I could just chalk the whole thing up to the fact that she was a jerk. But it wasn't like that. Shelby's a good woman who tried her best to do what was right. And what turned out to be right for her—leaving Shelter Valley—wasn't right for me." He shook his head. "When I left, it wasn't by choice. But Shelby decided she wanted a different kind of life."

"So the moral of the story is that you can't trust anyone?"

"I don't want to believe that."

"What, then?"

"Maybe what you can trust is that people will change. No one's going to stay the same forever."

She could attest to that. "Just living changes people," she said slowly, watching a girl who was reading a book under a tree. She'd been highlighting so much, Beth had to wonder if she should even have bothered. From a distance, it appeared that she was including everything on the page, so none of it was going to stand out from the rest, anyway. "Each decision, no matter how small, each interaction, can have repercussions that affect your whole life."

"Living in a town like Shelter Valley," he said, "sometimes you forget that."

"Maybe it's different in a town like Shelter Valley. There are an awful lot of people here who've known each other all their lives and are still happy living side by side, supporting and loving each other. I don't think I've ever seen so many happily married couples."

"In a perfect world, people grow together, flowing along with each other's changes, rather than letting those changes tear them apart."

"Could you and Shelby have done that?"

"Maybe," he said. "I know I sure would've tried if she'd given me the chance."

For a split second, Beth was sick with jealousy. Who was this woman that had evoked Greg Richards's eternal love?

And was there any hope that she, Beth Allen, would ever be able to grasp even a crumb of it for herself?

She couldn't even be honest with him about the most basic realities of her life. If she told him the truth, he'd have to start looking for her identity. And if he found something bad, she'd be forced to run before he could turn her in.

But in that moment she wanted him to know her.

Better than she knew herself.

CHAPTER SEVEN

GREG WALKED BETH to her car in the visitors' parking lot. She was late picking up Ryan or he'd have tried to get her to stay longer.

"This is your alma mater, isn't it?"

"Yeah," he said, his hands in his pockets as he walked beside her. "Got a degree in criminal justice."

"I try to imagine sometimes what it would've been like going to school here. It makes me yearn to be twenty again."

"They were good times." Greg thought back to some of the parties. The friendships. The feeling that the world was waiting at his feet.

Beth nodded, a yearning look on her face. It puzzled him.

"Probably not much different from wherever you went," he said. "Unless you studied business at New York University and did Juilliard at the same time."

He was baiting her.

She didn't bite.

He pretended that her reticence didn't bother him. He couldn't figure out how telling him where she'd gone to school, grown up, been born, involved any kind of risk.

But then, he'd never been so completely alone in the world. And he'd given her his word....

"Ryan doesn't have any other family, besides you?"

he asked as they left the classroom buildings behind and walked across the gravel that led to the free parking lot.

"Not that I know of."

An odd answer.

"Wouldn't you know if he did?"

"I don't know much about my husband's family."

"He wasn't close to them?"

"I guess not."

Greg frowned. Beth was too warm, too intelligent, not to have probed more deeply than that.

"Is there anyone who could serve as his guardian? A close friend from home, maybe?"

"No." She stopped at her car, looking up at him, eyes filled with concern. "There's no one, Greg, and it's scaring the hell out of me. If something happens to me, he'll become a ward of the state, won't he?"

He wished he could tell her differently, but he couldn't. "Yes."

"And because he's not an infant, that probably means he'd be in and out of foster homes."

She was scaring herself. And yet, there was some truth to what she was saying.

"Maybe."

"The thought of that's been making me sick for two days."

"Foster homes aren't all evil," he said. "Don't borrow trouble, Beth. You're young, healthy, and you live in a town where law enforcement has substantial success in keeping down crime and keeping citizens safe."

She grinned, as he'd meant her to. But sobered quickly.

"Promise me something?"

"Of course."

"Promise me you'll take him if anything happens to me."

She wasn't kidding. Nor did she appear to be reacting to runaway emotions.

"You really think there's a possibility something might happen." It wasn't a question.

Beth looked away—her evasion a sickening confirmation of what he thought he'd just read in her eyes.

"It's always a possibility, isn't it?" she whispered.

He grabbed her arm, forestalled her as she started to climb into the driver's seat of the old Ford Granada. "Beth, look at me."

"What?" Her demeanor was suddenly that of a defensive child. She couldn't get away from him fast enough.

And he hadn't yet granted her request. Hadn't made the promise she'd asked.

"Are you in some kind of trouble?"

"No! Of course not."

The denial came too fast. Was too effusive.

"I'm not, Greg," she said, meeting his eyes. "Or put it this way—if I am, I certainly don't know about it."

He believed her—which made the entire conversation, the woman, that much more confusing.

"You'd tell me if you were, wouldn't you?"

"Of course."

"Come to me for help?"

Her expression completely serious, she stared up at him. "I think that's what I've just done, isn't it?" she said softly. "Please promise me you'll take Ryan if anything happens to me."

"Of course, but…"

"Thank you." She interrupted him before he could tell her there was little he'd be able to do, that he'd have no power whatsoever to keep the boy unless she put something in writing.

But almost as though she knew it was coming, she forestalled even that. Standing on tiptoe, she pressed her lips to his in a kiss so tentative it was almost virginal.

And before he could do more than soak up the flood of intense desire her touch had evoked, she'd climbed in her car and was gone.

"WHAT DO YOU mean the photos are ruined?" Greg yelled into the phone. It had been two days since he'd seen Beth. Which only added to his frustration.

"I'm sorry, sir, the developer overheated and when I jumped up to tend to it, I knocked the envelopes into the sink...."

"But you've got the originals," Greg said. He was at home, hadn't yet left for work when the lab technician called.

"Well, that's just it, Sheriff. We used the pictures you asked for, but the images weren't clear enough to get the exact marks you highlighted. The only way to—"

"Tell me it wasn't the originals that were just demolished."

"Yes, sir, they..."

The expletives that flew from his mouth didn't make Greg proud. Didn't help his temper much, either. He pounded his fist against the wall, restraining himself enough to prevent punching a hole in the plaster—but not to save his hand from a well-deserved bruise.

"What about negatives? Previous prints? Even if you can't produce the exact image I want, we can take them somewhere else. Get them digitally restored."

"They were all in that pile, Sheriff."

Jaw clamped against scathing words he'd regret, Greg stared out the huge window over his kitchen sink to the landscaped pool and barbecue in his backyard.

"You're telling me we don't have one single image left of any of those cars? Not from ten years ago?"

"Or this summer."

Greg frowned, every nerve on alert. "What were you doing with the ones from this summer? I marked only the four from ten years ago. And the ones from the summer were digital."

"Deputy Culver brought the disc, too, sir. Said something about comparing measurements of the horseshoe-shaped dents in the lower right front ends."

So Culver was suspicious, too.

"We have a back-up disc of photo evidence. Always."

"Deputy Culver thought so, too, but he couldn't find it."

"What you're telling me is that we've somehow managed to lose all visual record of those cars."

"The victims, too."

Greg hung up before he fired the bastard on the spot. He'd have to deal with this incompetence—if incompetence was all it was. But not before he'd had a chance to powwow with Culver. They might want to have the technician remain on staff just to keep track of him.

One thing was for sure.

Something was very wrong.

GREG ASKED BETH out twice that month. Both times she refused. He'd wanted to take her to Phoenix, to the theater. And to a campfire steak dinner in Tucson. Beth didn't dare leave Shelter Valley. Not until she had some idea of who might be looking for her.

And what *she* should be looking for. Prepared for.

Not while she was still so obsessed with the feeling that she didn't want to be found. Until she'd regained her memory, she had to trust that her mind, even while it withheld information, was telling her something.

She just couldn't take any chance on anything happening to her. Or leading anyone to Ryan.

Of course, there was no guarantee that she was safe in Shelter Valley. But after more than seven months in town, she felt an aura of security here.

It was the only home she knew.

And then Greg asked her to a concert at a casino on the Indian Reservation that bordered Shelter Valley. She was familiar with the band, knew the lyrics to their songs, but didn't have a single memory attached to them.

She wanted to go. She was afraid that if she kept turning Greg down, he'd give up on her. It shouldn't matter. But it did.

There were days when thinking about him, about the hopeful anticipation he sometimes instilled in her, about the warmth she felt when he was around, were the only things that kept her sane.

The casino was set in the middle of nowhere, and while it was bound to be crowded, it wasn't a crowd she'd need to fear.

She was still planning to refuse. Until Bonnie offered to keep Ryan for the night and Ryan, having heard that he might get to play at Katie's house again, looked at her and said "pwease?" Just like Katie did when she wanted something.

Beth was too busy blinking back tears to say no.

And that was why, on the fourth Friday in September, she was sitting beside Greg in the lounge of the Kachina Grounds Casino. She was dressed in her only pair of nice slacks—black stretch denim she'd bought at Weber's Department Store, just for the occasion—and a new gauzy red-and-black top. She had no idea if the outfit was anything she'd have worn in her previous life, but she felt good in it.

The cigarette smoke, on the other hand, felt like death to her.

"Will it bother you if I tell you how beautiful you look?" Greg asked, his arm around the back of the booth. The lonely woman inside Beth wished he'd touch her.

She was relieved he didn't.

"No," she answered honestly. "I'm the only other one who'd tell me something like that and it sounds much better coming from you."

"You tell yourself you're beautiful?"

"Only when I'm feeling desperate."

She was only half joking. "Times like those, I'll believe just about anything." She grinned at him. She'd had a glass of wine, the first she could ever remember. Maybe it had gone to her head more than she'd realized.

"Let me know next time it happens. I've got a few other things to tell you," he said. He looked so good sitting there in jeans and a navy-and-white plaid button-down shirt. The top button was undone and the shirt kept drawing her eye to what it covered.

She wondered if the hair on his chest was as thick and black and tightly curled as that on his head.

"Like what?"

"Uh-uh." He shook his head, taking a sip from the beer he'd ordered.

His grin made her warm in places that had no business feeling warmth.

"I'm not giving them up until you're in a believing mood," he said.

Thankfully she was saved from any further flirtation when the lights went down and then, on the stage, a single white spot appeared. In the shadows there were instruments set up. Really expensive-looking drums. Some guitars and amplifiers. An alto sax.

But on center stage, beneath the white spotlight, was a beautiful black baby grand.

Beth's heart started to beat so hard she could feel its rhythm. In the semidarkness, Greg's shadow took on a reddish hue. She could hardly breathe. Felt surreal, disconnected. Weak.

And very, very frightened.

She had to get out of there. Find a safe place.

She had to breathe.

"What is it?" Greg's whisper in her ear startled her so much she jumped.

"N-n-nothing," she said, her voice loud, competing with the sudden thunder of applause as the band took the stage. "I need some cool air."

Without another thought, Beth slid from the booth and hurried out. She had no idea where she was going or what she'd do when she got there. She didn't know how she'd explain herself. Or how she'd even get back inside the lounge.

She didn't care.

She had to get out.

Just outside the lounge wasn't far enough. Beth barely heard the cacophony of slot machines, coins dropping, people cheering, bells ringing as she searched, frantic yet completely focused, for a way out.

Fresh air. That was all she needed. She'd be fine as soon as she had air.

It might've made more sense to stop long enough to seek a door, to read a sign, to remember the way she'd come in. Beth didn't have time to stop. She charged in one direction and then the next, cutting through rows of slot machines, behind a tuxedoed woman dealing blackjack, through a series of roulette tables, back to what might have been the same slots. The room was filled with smoke and noise. She bumped into people and hardly noticed.

Finally, she found a revolving door. She shoved through in her haste to get out.

And then she was free. Outside. Sucking in balmy desert air. And choking back a deluge of tears she neither recognized nor understood. Beth didn't ever sob. As far as she knew...

Gasping, she ran down the sidewalk, not sure if she was heading toward the desert or the parking lot. Not caring. She didn't have a destination in mind. She'd arrived. Nothing else mattered.

"Beth!"

Greg came running up behind her, and she realized then that it wasn't the first time he'd called out to her.

"What?" She turned.

"What happened? What's wrong?"

"Nothing's wrong. I'm fine."

"I see more than my share of adrenaline rushes," he said, keeping pace beside her. "I know it when I see it."

She should slow down. Act normal. And she would. Just as soon as she got some air.

"I'm seeing it now," he went on.

"You're imagining things." Her voice was too high. Too fake. She'd work on that next.

"Should we check your pulse and see just how much I'm imagining? My guess is it's running at about 220."

"I'm fine." She was hyperventilating.

Grabbing her arm, Greg pulled her to a stop, cupped his hand over her nose and mouth and commanded, "Breathe."

She had no choice.

After a few seconds, she was no longer seeing stars. Red, maybe, but no stars.

"Where'd you learn to do that?" she asked, not pretending quite as hard that she was in complete control.

"I'm a sheriff, Beth. I know CPR."

"Oh." Yeah. She started to walk again, but more slowly now.

Maybe, if she was really lucky, she could wipe away the impression of a raving lunatic she'd obviously given him.

"It's a nice night, isn't it." Her voice was sounding more normal.

"Yes."

"I've grown to love the nights these past few weeks. The days are still hot, but the nights are more temperate than they were during the summer. Reminds you of summer days as a kid, doesn't it? Carefree. Playing hide-and-seek until ten o'clock."

"Is that what you did?"

She didn't know. "Yeah." She hoped so. Had no idea why she'd said such a thing or where the thought had come from. It didn't feel personal.

But then, at the moment, her own feet and hands felt like they belonged to someone else.

They walked for a while, neither of them speaking. Eventually Beth calmed down. She no longer felt as though she was going to be sick any second.

"So what happened?"

"Sometimes I have...memories." She chose her words carefully.

A double-wide sidewalk ran a large circle around the grounds of the casino. They strolled slowly through the darkness, not touching, but close enough to give her strength.

"Memories of your life before you came here?"

"Yes."

"And they're painful?"

"Very."

"So that's what happened back there? A painful memory?"

Beth couldn't think about what had happened back there. Not until she was safe at home, in her duplex, where she could fall apart in private.

She'd remembered something important. Or at least she'd started to. Until panic had taken over and shut her down again.

She'd been on a stage before. Much larger than the one in there. There'd been a piano similar to that baby grand. No other instruments, though. Only a piano.

And then the spotlight had come on....

Beth stumbled. She couldn't go any further than that. It wasn't there. Maybe she'd already lost the rest of what had come storming back.

"I'm really sorry," she said now, proud of how normal her voice sounded. "I told you I wasn't ready—"

"You miss him that much?"

She shook her head. "I think I just hurt that much. It's not all about him. At least, I don't think it is. It's just about the uncertainty, you know?"

"The 'no guarantee' clause that comes with life?"

"Yeah, only they don't put it on your birth certificate. They wait until you're in all the way before they let you know about the risks...."

"But if we knew up front, we'd never take risks."

"Sounds good to me."

"If life involves change, it involves risk, too. Doesn't it?"

Beth didn't, couldn't, respond. Brushing against him as they turned a corner, she took his hand. "Thank you."

"For what?"

"Not hauling me away in a straitjacket."

"There was no reason to. You were upset, not insane."

It sure *felt* insane.

"It's just that I go through so much of my life these days not feeling anything at all, and then suddenly I feel something so intensely, it hurts so intensely, and I don't think I can stand it."

She couldn't believe she was telling him these things. And yet, she felt completely safe doing so.

"I think I get that. Only, instead of feeling hurt, I'm overwhelmed with anger."

"About Shelby?"

"No, that mostly just hurt." He sent her a wry grin. "I was talking about my father."

"Bonnie told me he'd been injured in a carjacking."

Greg nodded. "He was on his way home from Phoenix one evening after a round of golf with some of the guys he served with."

"He was a cop, too?"

"Volunteer fire department. My father was an economics professor at the U."

"Wow." She'd had no idea.

"As far as we've been able to piece together, he was rear-ended about twenty miles outside Phoenix. When he pulled over, he was jumped. He remembered nothing else until he woke up in the desert, unable to move. The bastards had broken his neck and left him there to die. By some miracle, a couple of teenagers had gone out to the desert and stumbled upon him." He stopped, and Beth, walking close beside him, squeezed his hand.

"They were afraid to move him, but even more afraid to leave him there. Between the two of them, they got him to their car and drove him into Phoenix. He didn't have any ID on him, but one of the guys I'd gone through the academy with answered the call."

"Were you close by?"

"I was at his house, waiting to drive him to Tucson to see a choral performance Bonnie was in."

They rounded another corner and reached the back of the casino. Just the two of them among Dumpsters, empty boxes thrown out the door, the rancid smell of trash that should have been emptied.

Beth figured that was a true metaphor for life.

"I'm so sorry," she said. It was weak. Useless. But there wasn't anything else.

"They never caught the bastards."

"Did they find the car?"

"Oh yeah. So far, we've always found the car—eventually. But the interior had been burned out leaving no clues. Dad couldn't remember anything. And eventually the case, considered a random carjacking, was closed."

"But it's not anymore."

"It's not anymore," he said, conviction in every line of his taut body. "I'm going to get those guys, Beth."

"I believe you."

She tripped, a smaller surge of fear darting through her. She was pretty certain Greg Richards always got his man—even if it took him years.

If the need ever arose, she hoped that would work in her favor. Not against her.

CHAPTER EIGHT

GREG WAS WALKING beside Beth, talking to her about his job again. And then he wasn't.

A movement between two of the Dumpsters caught his attention. He'd just barely glimpsed a shadow in the dark, out of the corner of his eye, but whatever was there was too big to be a rat. With an arm in front of Beth to prevent her from walking into the path of whatever was just ahead, Greg slowed and put his finger to his lips. It could be a javelina down from the nearby mountains, and he didn't want either of them to startle it. The four-hundred-pound wild pigs were not known for their placid nature.

Motioning for her to back up, he slid his hand in hers and took a couple of steps with her.

"Hold it." A gravelly voice came from behind them.

Greg froze, his only thought of the woman beside him.

Beth stopped, her hand squeezing all the circulation out of his. He could feel her trembling and willed her his strength.

He didn't have to see the blade to know that he had a knife at his back.

"What're you doin' back here, man?"

"Trying to have a private conversation," Greg said, shifting just a fraction of an inch, concentrating on his peripheral vision as he tried to determine whether there was only one knife.

There was.

Greg moved without further deliberation. Giving Beth a shove to get her safely out of the way, he spun around, his hand locking immediately and with force around the arm that was stretched toward his back.

His assailant was young. Strong. Fast. Greg wasn't intimidated. Martial arts, street-fighting, hand-to-hand combat, shooting—he could do them all. His body seemed to move instinctively, twisting, blocking, maintaining his iron hold on the hand wielding the knife.

The man grunted, used the force of an attempted spin to knock the two of them to the ground. Hitting the hard earth with his shoulder, Greg rolled with the fall, knowing that if he was going to keep Beth safe, he had to make sure this man did not get loose.

He couldn't think about her beyond that.

On the ground, he kept his eye on the potentially lethal six-inch blade gleaming in the darkness. The knife came close to his chest, and Greg rolled again, pinning the man beneath him. Then, with a swift lunge, he knocked his attacker's hand against the dirt. The knife flew. Greg twisted, rolled one more time, and the man was facedown in the dust, his arm twisted behind him.

Greg had his belt off and around the man's wrists in one swift action.

"Move and you die."

Heart pounding from exertion, Greg turned at the sound of the strange female voice.

Beth was standing there, discarded knife in hand, pointing it at a second figure crouched and trembling beside the Dumpster.

A teenager. Obviously strung out. A quick search of his prisoner revealed a vial of amphetamines that told Greg he'd just interrupted a drug deal. It was a classic. Some poor frightened kid, in too deep, and the intimidating dealer who owned him. There were few questions left to ask.

Except where Beth had learned to be so tough.

And how a woman who'd barely been able to stand half an hour before was suddenly single-handedly holding a drug addict at bay.

Emotional battles knocked her off her feet, but apparently physical ones did not. He couldn't help wondering what that said about the past Beth was so adamantly hiding.

"You sure you're okay, ma'am?"

Standing on the outskirts of the small crowd that had formed around the blinking police lights, her arms crossed, Beth nodded. Greg was there in the middle of the fray, giving his report.

"If there's anything we can get for you—a drink, an extra sweater…"

"Really, I'm fine." Beth smiled at the casino manager, hoping to convince him she wasn't going to fall apart. Or worse, sue him.

Frowning, he maintained his protective position next to her.

The truth was, at that moment, Beth felt better than fine. She'd been in danger and come up fighting. A huge entry for her notebook. But more, an enormous reassurance. She could count on herself; she could safeguard her child. She wasn't some weakling who collapsed at any sign of trouble.

She'd actually, without conscious thought and without hesitation, held someone at knife point.

The impact of that realization was huge. Suddenly, the unknown dangers lurking in the darkness of her mind weren't so threatening. There was a chance she was equipped to handle them.

"What's going to happen to that kid?" she asked the manager, as the Indian police led away the kid she'd found huddled by that Dumpster. He was just a fourteen-year-old boy.

"If it's his first offense, he'll probably just be handed over to his parents." The man shook his head. "You see this so much. These jerks hit up kids in schools with the promise of a cheap and completely harmless good time. Before they know it, the kids are addicted and doing anything for their next fix."

The harsh-looking man Greg had apprehended elbowed an officer as they led him to a patrol car. In one swift movement the officer had his hand on the back of the drug dealer's neck and had shoved his head against the car.

"He'll be back on the streets before school starts on Monday," the casino manager said, shaking his head again.

Beth hoped he was wrong—and feared he was right. She had a feeling that was the way the world worked. So often, evil prevailed.

"You, Sheriff Richards, are one hell of a fun date," Beth teased later that night. He'd talked her into coming back to his house where he could take a shower and continue their evening. Maybe with dinner or a movie in Phoenix.

Somehow they'd ended up staying at his place instead, grilling steaks in the backyard.

"Yeah," Greg said sarcastically, still kicking himself for how close she'd come to being hurt. He flipped the steaks, needing them to cook quickly. The potatoes he'd put on the top rack of the grill were almost done.

Sitting on a lounge beside the pool, Beth sipped from a glass of wine. Her slim body was beautiful, and the landscape lighting spread a silvery glow over her, giving her a mysterious, almost fairy tale aura.

"Next time I'll just take you down to the prison and let you have your pick of criminal action."

"With you there to protect me, I wouldn't worry a bit."

The night air was soft, cool against his skin. He was too agitated to enjoy it.

"I'm flattered you think that, Beth, but what I did tonight was so dumb I can't even come up with an excuse." He rubbed his shoulder. "Never, never, never is it wise to walk into a dark alley at night. And especially not on a mostly deserted reservation."

"It was hardly deserted with three hundred cars in the parking lot out front."

"Which was why we had no business not staying out front."

He absolutely did not understand what had gotten into him. Being aware of his surroundings was second nature—or should have been. He'd allowed them to stray into danger.

"Let up on yourself, Richards." Beth's soft voice held no humor, just a hint of affection. "You risked your life to save mine. Enough said."

Taking a sip of beer, Greg checked a steak; the middle was still too red. He'd let the night's fiasco go, but not before he made a silent vow never to lose perspective like that again. And to make sure that if Beth's life were ever in danger, he would not be the cause.

He vowed to protect her always—even if that meant protecting her from himself.

He'd let it go, but he wasn't going to forget.

"I HAD NO IDEA that Indians have their own law enforcement and legal system," she said later, as they sat at the white patio table eating steak and baked potatoes.

He'd turned on the waterfall on the far side of the pool, and the gentle lapping of the water added a romantic ambience to the classical music playing softly from the outdoor speakers.

"In some ways, the reservations are like countries unto themselves," Greg said. "Thanks for waiting while I handed the guy over to them."

"No problem." Her voice was light. Almost cheerful. Amazing considering the evening they'd had.

He topped off her glass of wine. She was no heavier a drinker than he was; he was still nursing his first beer.

"You've got this place looking great, especially since you've been here less than a year," she said, looking at the desert landscaping surrounding them.

Greg cut a big bite of filet mignon, ignoring the twinge in his shoulder. "Thanks."

All she'd seen of the house was the front hallway and kitchen, which they'd walked through on their way to the patio. She'd opted to wait outside while he showered.

Greg rubbed at his shoulder. "It was like this when I bought the place," he admitted.

"You could have some great parties out here."

"That's one of the reasons I bought it. With three bedrooms, it's a little bigger than I needed, but I liked the idea of being able to have my deputies and their families here to kick back now and then."

"How many times have you done that in the nine months or so you've been sheriff?"

"Three."

"I'm impressed."

"Cops are a close-knit group. We have to be. Our lives rest in each other's hands."

Beth sighed, the dim lighting giving her a wistful look. "A family."

He supposed that was what they were. "In terms of unconditional trust, I guess you're right. Though—" he grinned "—I certainly don't love those jokers like I love my sister."

Gazing pensively at him, Beth said, "But then, if you had a brother you probably wouldn't love him in the same way you love Bonnie, either."

She had him there. "So what about you?" He didn't expect an answer.

"I don't have a lot of memories of my family."

Well, it was an answer but not much of one. "You're adopted?"

"Just not very close." She put down her fork. Took a sip of wine. "I'm sorry you didn't get to hear the band tonight."

As upsetting as the incident at the casino must have been to her, speaking of it was preferable to speaking about her life before Shelter Valley. Greg couldn't help but file that information away.

"I've got a couple of their CDs and they probably sound better on those, anyway." The band had met with substantial success a decade or two ago, but their music was soft rock. As far as Greg was concerned, they were music's version of a chick flick. He'd chosen the date for her, not himself. "I'll bet you've got more than just two of their CDs," he said, smiling at her. Last he knew, Bonnie and every one of her friends had the entire collection.

"Nope."

"You didn't spend your high school years crooning with them?"

Beth's look was blank. "I don't think so. I don't croon." And then, "You've been rubbing your shoulder a lot. Is it bothering you?"

He hadn't realized he'd reached for it again. "Not really."

"You hurt it in that fall tonight, didn't you?"

Greg shrugged, determined not to wince as the movement pulled on the muscles just above his shoulder blade. "Bruised it a little, maybe." It wasn't a big deal.

Beth's expression was just short of a glare. "It's your trapezius," she said. "From watching that fall you took, I'll bet it's got one hell of a knot."

"I don't feel anything," he said. Her fussing made him uncomfortable; getting bruised was just something that happened—if not at work, then when he went to the gym or had a good sparring with a fellow black belt. A guy straining a muscle was as much a part of life as eating, sleeping and going to the john.

"It's gotta be spasming, too."

That sounded painful. "No. It's fine."

"Whatever you say, macho man."

Greg wasn't sure he liked the way she'd said that. But he was willing to let it lie.

Pachelbel's "Canon" came on. One of the few pieces of classical music Greg recognized by name.

The music was haunting. Evocative. Sensual. Mixed with the cool night air, the semidarkness and Beth, it bordered on dangerous.

And then, suddenly, he was reminded of that Sunday at Bonnie's. Beth could probably play this song.

He wanted her to play it for him. That piano tonight…

"Tell me what happened at the casino. When you ran out."

"Nothing, I—"

"Don't, Beth," he interrupted. "Tell me it's none of my business, but don't insult me with a lie."

Beth looked out over the pool toward the waterfall. "I don't lie."

"Never?"

"Not if I can help it."

"So what happened?"

Her gaze, filled with so much he couldn't decipher, locked with his. For a moment neither of them spoke. Greg braced himself not to say a word when she told him it was none of his business.

So why did he feel it was?

"I can't tell you exactly what happened," she said, her eyes steady on his. "I'm not sure I even know."

When he looked into those beautiful blue eyes, there was no doubting the truth of what she said. "What can you tell me?"

"When I saw the piano… I don't know…"

Wanting to reach for her hand, he reached for his beer instead. "What?"

"I used to play the piano professionally."

Her performance at Bonnie's had made that rather obvious. He wanted to ask why she'd denied being a concert pianist that night at her house.

"Seeing that piano there tonight, in the spotlight, brought it all back to me so forcefully…"

"It's okay," Greg said, although he didn't know if that was true. He didn't know what "it" even was. What kept her so locked inside herself? Her hand lay on the table next to her wineglass, and he covered those talented fingers with his own. "After dinner at Bonnie's you said you were starting to come out of a deep freeze. I imagine this was just more of the same. Starting to feel again. Reacting to all the particulars in your life."

"I guess."

Her brows lowered, not quite into a frown, just into a lost look that made Greg feel powerless. He was afraid of no one. But how could he fight what he didn't know?

"It's just so overwhelming…." Her voice trailed off.

There was so much more Greg needed to ask. And, just as badly, he needed her to tell him without his having to ask. He needed her to trust him.

SHE WASN'T GOING TO SUFFOCATE. Not out here in the cool evening air. Not twice in one night. Blocking her mind to the memories that had overwhelmed her earlier, Beth wondered if she should leave.

"You're doing that thing with your shoulder again," she said instead, watching as Greg rubbed ineptly at the knot that had to be tightening his trapezius.

Just how she knew that, she had no idea. And didn't dare investigate, either. Not at the moment.

She'd write everything down later. All the glimmers of memory. And all the internal enemies that had attacked her that evening, rendering her virtually help-less for perhaps the most frightening half hour of her life, would get their time.

When she was home alone, in the safety of her bed-room, she'd write everything down in her journal.

And then would come the responsibility of trying to make sense of it. To search further and see what she knew, what she remembered.

Until then...

"Let me do that," she said. Jumping up, she stood behind Greg's chair. A couple of minutes and she could ease his suffering.

"Right here?" she said, her hands instantly finding the knot in his upper back. Measuring its size, the exact point in the muscle where it lodged, Beth began to mas-sage. Her fingers worked automatically, moving over Greg's body as mindlessly as they'd moved over the piano keys a couple of weeks ago.

"Oh yeah," he said, "that's the spot." His head dropped.

Beth grinned, surmising that he must be too macho to grimace. Or say *ouch*. What she was doing had to hurt like hell.

But it wouldn't for long.

"Deep muscle spasms, just like I thought," she said, rubbing from the outside in.

"Mmm." Eventually Greg started to move with her. "That feels good."

"It would feel a whole lot better if you'd take off your shirt," she said. She was used to doing this on bare skin. With the proper oils within reach.

Beth's fingers faltered. Where? *Where* was she used

to doing this? On whose bare skin? And what oils were the proper ones?

Apparently taking her limp fingers as a command, Greg slid out of his shirt. And because she didn't know what else to do with that bare expanse of smooth back, she began to administer a deep-tissue massage.

When she was done, she kept right on massaging. The waterfall, the music, the soft lighting were all part of a distant scene, a vague background, as Beth continued to use skills that belonged to a person she didn't know.

"You can stop now." Greg's voice came from far off.

Beth kept working the musculature of his back. Sometime during the past few minutes she'd moved from his right shoulder to his left, and was now down to his latissimus dorsi.

"I guess it probably wouldn't do any good for me to ask where you learned to do that?" His voice sounded strained.

Nope. No good at all. She'd already tried and there'd been no answer forthcoming.

"Piano players have strong fingers." Beth found herself saying the words. Thought they were words she'd heard before. Some kind of explanation for the skill she was now displaying?

Or a defense of it?

A concert pianist. Masseuse. Other than the obvious requirement of strong fingers, the two professions had absolutely nothing in common, as far as she could tell.

Knotted bruise aside, Greg's back was beautiful. The muscles textbook perfect. In placement. In size.

And his skin...

As her thoughts took her in unprecedented directions, Beth's fingers worked harder. She knew one thing: she couldn't have done *this* as a profession. She was far too aware of the skin beneath her fingers, far too lacking in emotional detachment, not enough professionally removed to have done this very many times.

But then, how had she become so adept?

WHETHER IT WAS the beer that made him take the chance or the adrenaline still pumping from the evening's events, whether it was the night and water and soft music or the sheer torture of her fingers against his body, Greg didn't know. He just quit thinking.

Reaching back, he grabbed Beth's burning hand, placing his palm over hers as he guided her fingers through the hair on his chest and held them against the taut pectoral muscles straining for her touch.

Gently pulling, he brought her around until she was standing between his spread thighs.

"I…" Her eyes were wide, filled with uncertainty.

And with something else.

The something else was all he saw. "Shh," he said softly. And before she could say anything, he tugged once more, bringing her down to his lap, and covered her mouth with his.

If she'd resisted, even for a second, he would have stopped. Could have stopped. But when Beth's mouth opened over his, his reactions no longer seemed to be under his control. He took his time with slow, soft kisses, exploring her. Her taste. Her softness. The shape of her lips.

Her kisses started out hesitant, though by no means resistant. But as he continued to move his mouth against hers, her response grew tantalizingly ardent. There was no doubt that Beth was a hungry woman. Hungry to be touched. To be loved.

He forgot where they were, pretty much forgot *who*

they were. He was thinking with his senses. Feeling her. Driven by a desire more intense than any he'd experienced before. Lost in a sensual fog.

"Hold me." Beth's words pierced the fog. And then became the fog. Greg held her as close as he could. And when the chair hindered his attempts to deepen their closeness, he picked her up and carried her to the padded chaise longue she'd been lying on earlier.

It might have been made for one person, but it accommodated two quite nicely. Greg laid Beth down and then lay down between her legs, bolstering his weight on his forearms on either side of her. Cradling her.

"You are so beautiful," he whispered.

Her tremulous smile scared him a little, and Greg bent to her lips. Doing what he knew he could do well. What he already knew she wanted.

He kissed her.

And kissed her again. His lips trailed to the corner of her mouth. To her chin. Onto her eyelids. Down to her neck. He had to know every part of her, had to have some kind of claim on this woman who held everything back from him.

His groin ached with a tension far worse than he'd felt in his shoulder. Knotted and spasming and crying for attention.

Moving his hips against hers, Greg let her know what he wanted.

"Greg?"

"Yeah?" His voice sounded dry, parched.

"I want you so badly I'm aching."

He groaned. Ready to throw away everything he had for one night in this woman's arms.

With all his weight on one elbow, he caressed her side. Her neck. Burning hotter as she moved her head, eyes closed, making herself more accessible. Her gauzy top made it easy to slide his hand beneath the neckline and down, until he had one perfectly rounded breast in his palm—

"But I can't."

Greg shook his head, wondering what he'd missed. Somehow Beth's eyes had opened, were staring straight at him.

His hand still on her breast, he ran a mental slow-down over his body.

"Can't what?"

"Can't do this." She shuddered. "I want to so badly, but I can't. Not yet. Not while I'm still trying to figure things out. It's not fair to either of us...." Only the fact that she sounded as devastated as he felt allowed Greg to handle the situation like the man he purported to be.

"Okay."

"I'm sorry."

"It's okay."

"Greg?"

"Yeah?"

"You're...um...still holding my breast."

Damn. She was right.

Using far more physical strength than he'd needed when capturing the drug dealer, Greg dragged himself off Beth. And then, because he didn't trust himself not to fall down on top of her again and because he was in almost unbearable pain, he turned and dived, headfirst and fully clothed, into the swimming pool.

Even the brutal plunge into sixty-degree water didn't cool his ardor.

Of one thing he was certain. Beth Allen was more than just a woman.

She was a need.

CHAPTER NINE

THE SUBJECT GRADY MULLINS was ready. He sat straight and tall on the leather sofa in a private back wing of the spa, a big, athletically fit man in his late twenties. He'd shaved off his beard and cut his hair.

Tired as he was, Dr. Peter Sterling still felt the surge of renewed energy as he took in their newest recruit. This was what people on the outside wouldn't understand. It wasn't that they did anything evil—or even secret—at Sterling Silver. It wasn't that they wanted to be exclusive. Exactly the opposite, in fact. Their goal was to have everyone in the world live as they lived at Sterling Silver. Positively. Happily. Productively.

People in the outside world just didn't understand. But they were beginning to. Slowly. One soul at a time.

They had another worthy soldier for the cause in Grady Mullins. All the hard work, the fatigue and the frequent loneliness were worth moments like these.

Peter might not be able to save the world, but in his protected little corner of it, life was damn near perfect. Clean and free from hostility and negativism.

After weeks of relaxation training, Grady had fallen into an altered state of consciousness, almost without Peter's help.

"Grady, you believe in Sterling Silver, don't you?"

Peter asked, his voice low as he sat facing the man who'd declared his readiness for cleansing.

"I do. I know that the work here is right and good."

Peter smiled. *Right and Good.* That was one of several sets of key words used at Sterling Silver. Continually repeated trigger phrases that helped them all stay focused, lest they be wooed by the ways of the world.

"Why is it right and good?"

Grady's eyes met his. "Today's world is full of evil," he said, his voice ringing with the intensity of sure knowledge. "It's everywhere. In white-collar lives and blue, corporate structures and the ghetto. Gangs. Road rage. Terrorism. In politics. The Bible promises us that if we let evil forces—which we know to be manifested in negative energy—rule our lives, they will overtake us. The only way for any of us to overcome it is to rid ourselves of the negative energy. The hostility."

Yes. Heart thumping, Peter nodded. He'd sensed from the very beginning that this young man would be a powerful convert. Grady's fervor was validation for Peter's own faith in the rightness of his work.

Outsiders wouldn't understand what was going to take place there that day; they would probably be horrified by the things Grady was subjecting himself to. But that was because outsiders saw only the surface. They didn't understand the meaning, the purpose, the benefit, the motivation.

"The Bible also promises that good will win out over evil if we make right choices. The best choice is to rid ourselves of the negative energies we were born with."

Grady understood. And after him, there would be more. Slowly they were reaching the world.

"You're sure you believe that?" Peter had to ask.

Beth's lack of faith had been disastrous. He couldn't take a chance on having that happen again.

"With all my heart," Grady said, looking him straight in the eye. "I want cleansing more than anything, Dr. Sterling."

Peter believed him.

"You have faith that it will work?"

"I know that it will."

"My son, we've talked a little about the process, but there is much that you cannot know until you actually experience it. The mind is a curious thing and—given the chance—while still filled with negativity, it can take a right and good concept and turn it into something evil. We can't risk this or we've lost all power to do our work. We become devoid of influence and the rituals become meaningless."

"I understand."

"Then, we shall begin." Peter stood, anticipation filling his lower belly. "You must permit no doubt to enter your mind from this point forward. You do not question. You have to trust me completely. Negative energy does not give up easily. We have to render it powerless." The words lost none of their ardor even as Peter repeated them for the three-hundred-and-forty-ninth time.

Grady didn't even hesitate. "I'm all yours, sir."

That was just what Peter had been hoping to hear since first meeting the young man several weeks before.

"And you've made arrangements for afterward?"

"Yes, sir." Grady nodded. "I'll be working twelve-hour days just as prescribed so that my endorphins flow and fill my body with positive energy. I have always understood that hard work produces positive results."

"Prosecutor Silverman tells me you've moved out here to our little community."

"Yes, sir," Grady said. He smiled as he described his new apartment—in the complex Peter and James Silverman had contracted to have built just eight months before. It was already at capacity.

"I've given up my old job, as well."

This was something Peter already knew. He and James discussed each applicant in depth before ever letting things progress this far.

"I was a high school teacher and football coach. Pay wasn't much and the levels of testosterone-induced aggression couldn't have been higher. Instead, I'm going to be working in the cannery here. And doing some things with Prosecutor Silverman, as well."

While James put in many hours at Sterling Silver, he still worked for the D.A.'s office. His contacts there were too important to give up.

Moving closer to the door he'd indicated as the beginning point of the ritual, Peter paused. "And your outside activities?"

There was much to sacrifice in order to be part of the Sterling Silver community.

"I'm fully content to find my recreation right here," Grady said. "I know the more I move among nonmembers, the faster I regain negative energy, which would require more work from you. I intend to do all I can to protect your time, sir. You need to be helping outsiders enter our community, not wasting time on those of us who've already been cleansed."

Hand on the door, Peter stopped. "You'll still need cleansing, son. It's part of life. Evil forces are constantly trying to win us back."

"I know, Dr. Sterling. But I'm going to strive every day of my life to someday be like you."

"Like me?"

"You don't need cleansing."

"I don't get the benefits of cleansing, Grady," Peter said, injecting every bit of pain he'd ever felt into that statement. "There's no one else to perform the procedures. And even if there were, it takes two full days. Think of the number of people I'd miss helping every time I participated."

"I know, sir." Grady bowed his head. "I have to tell you how thankful I am for your willingness to do this. We all owe our lives to you."

Peter hoped so. He needed to make that much of a difference. He resisted the urge to hug Grady. Not everyone appreciated the power of touch.

"You have no illnesses?"

"None."

"Remember, after today you will never seek conventional medicine." Peter had to control the natural antagonism he felt at that moment. "Physicians take ownership of patients' bodies and interfere with energy forces. They prescribe medicines and treatments that pollute the body with negative influences, which makes my work here that much more difficult as I must then rid you of those influences."

"I understand."

"Okay, son." Peter finally opened the door, allowing Grady a brief glimpse of the darkened room. "Wait," he said, just as Grady was about to step through the doorway. "You haven't eaten today, have you?"

"No, sir."

"There will be no food for the next forty-eight hours."

"Fasting is good for the soul, sir."

With a nod, Peter moved aside, inviting Grady to enter the room. There was nothing but dark walls, a medical examining table and a dialysis machine. On the far side was a blackened door, through which Peter would come and go.

For the next two days, Grady was going to get the benefit not only of physical cleansing, but of thought reformation, making it easier for him to follow the mandates. He'd be reminded of the loyalty he'd promised, the contract he'd signed, stating that he had not been forced into anything against his will, that he was of sound mind and body and certain that he wanted the benefits of membership in Sterling Silver. During the two-day session it would be repeatedly stressed that he'd agreed to pay Sterling Silver two hundred thousand dollars, collectible throughout his lifetime, if he were to break any of the rules either then stated or in the future agreed upon.

Those rules would be repeated to him over the next hours until they became virtually hypnotic suggestions, orders that he simply followed while living life with the appearance of complete normalcy. He would never eat excessively—a benefit that the majority of the worldly population spent billions of dollars a year trying to obtain. There would be no consumption of alcohol or tobacco—both negative substances that weakened the body.

And henceforth, Grady—like all men at Sterling Silver—must engage in sexual activity twice a week—no more, no less—as scientific studies had proven that biweekly orgasm would build disease-fighting energies, but that any more activity would begin to diminish them. Grady had agreed that, if at any time he was not in a relationship, he would take care of that last requirement himself.

There was a lot to do during the next two days. Among other things, Peter was going to remove and replace Grady's energy, something that could only be done in this sterile atmosphere, devoid of outside influence.

"I'm going to leave you now to disrobe. Put all your clothes, including underthings, in the drawer by the door.

"I'll be back in ten minutes," Dr. Sterling said. "And remember, what you're about to do is right and good. Those who belong to Sterling Silver are above the rest of the world. Due to our diminished negative energies, our superiority is a given. We are 'as angels.'"

James Silverman was waiting for Peter out in the corridor. He didn't speak. After all their time together, he didn't need to. His raised brow was enough.

Peter didn't speak, either. He merely nodded.

And both men smiled.

BETH MIGHT NOT know where she'd come from, but she didn't have to be out in the world to know that Shelter Valley was exactly the type of place she wanted to be. Which was why, twice a week when she'd finished cleaning houses, she spent a couple of hours in the library at Montford University, while the Willis sisters looked after Ryan.

Until she knew what she was running from, she wouldn't know if she could stop running.

And until she knew what she was running from, she couldn't tell anyone she wasn't free. She couldn't take the chance that someone—especially the sheriff, who was starting to play a rather prominent part in her make-believe life—might put out feelers. Not until she had an idea where they might lead.

She had no idea if Greg's finding out who she was, where she came from, would put her and Ryan, or even him, in danger. No idea what kind of pain and hardship were waiting for her back where she'd come from. Indications were pretty clear that she'd been on the run from something serious—filling her with the vital need to hide. From everyone.

And yet she wanted so badly to tell him the truth. To tell him she wasn't *choosing* not to share information about herself, but that she simply didn't know the answers to his questions. Or her own…

But if she told him she had amnesia, he'd need to find out who she was. It would be his duty as a lawman to determine whether or not she was wanted somewhere, by someone. It was his nature as Greg Richards, fix-it man, to take matters into his own hands.

Unless she asked him not to. Could she trust him that much? Could she expect him to take a chance on her, harboring her, when she might, indeed, be a criminal? Could she be certain he'd even do it if she asked?

Could she stay in this town, putting them all in danger, if it turned out she was on the run from a maniac?

Beth didn't know. And she hated that.

Whether it was right or wrong, she was on her own and she had no idea where else to look for information. With days' and days' worth of research, she'd exhausted every Internet source she could think of.

The hours spent searching had netted her one thing. The knowledge that on or about the day she and Ryan had awakened in that motel room, there had not been one single article in the United States about a missing child fitting Ryan's description, a missing woman fitting hers, or an accident involving victims of either description.

She'd also discovered she needed glasses. After all the reading, her eyes were killing her.

SHE'D DONE NOTHING to warrant a background check.

Watching Beth's cute butt in the saddle in front of him, Greg gave himself a firm talking-to. It was a continuation of the conversation he'd had while shaving that morning. Okay, so the woman he was falling in love with refused to give him any personal information. That was not a good reason to invade her privacy.

So what if she was the first woman he'd felt instinctively able to trust since Shelby? A fact made more incredible by the secrets she kept...

No matter that she was everything he'd always dreamed of in a mate. She loved Shelter Valley as much as he did. Clung to the little town in a way he'd need his woman to cling after Shelby's defection. She had an adorable little boy who needed a father almost as badly as he needed a son.

He knew it hadn't been long enough, but he wanted to marry her. He'd always been a man who knew what he wanted.

Other than Shelby, he'd always been a man who got it, as well.

"Hey!" he called out to her, as her horse cantered away in front of him. If he couldn't get her to talk about her past, maybe he could interest her in the future. "I thought we were going for a relaxing ride," he said, catching up.

"She wanted to run," Beth said, nodding at her mare. "I didn't have the heart to tell her no."

"You have a thwarted compulsion to run now and then?" he asked, finding her comment far too ironic, considering the thoughts he'd just been having.

"None whatsoever. I honestly think I'd be happy never to leave Shelter Valley."

"That's because you've never tried to get all your Christmas shopping done here," he said. "I'm a firm believer in malls for that."

"Okay," she amended with a sideways grin. "I'll amend my remark. I'd be happy never to leave Shelter Valley except to go to a mall in Phoenix once a year."

"Ryan was okay when you left him at Little Spirits?" he asked, enjoying the quiet of the desert trail they were riding. Beth had had a cancellation that morning and she'd found herself with a free day.

Beth nodded, her bobbing ponytail making her look like a teenager. "It's Wednesday, which means Bethany Parsons was there playing with Katie."

"Ryan's two favorite women in the world."

"Next to his mother, you mean." She stuck out her tongue at him.

He'd seen cowboys grab women off horses in movies. He'd never had the desire to do it himself.

Until now.

"So, you'd be happy to stay in Shelter Valley. What do you see yourself doing here? Expanding the cleaning business?"

"That, and maybe other things," she said slowly, as

though she might actually be thinking about confiding in him. "It's as though, for the first time in my life, I'm exploring my options. Finding out what I want to do when I grow up."

"You were pressured as a kid?" The question simply emerged. Followed by a silent expletive. He'd promised himself he wasn't going to push her.

In case he pushed her right out his door.

"Yes," she said, staring out at the desert in front of them. "It feels like I've been pressured my whole life to *reach my potential*." She said the words in an ironic tone. "Funny thing is, I'm not sure I ever knew what I was reaching for. What *is* potential, anyway?"

Those blue eyes turned on him and Greg wondered if this was how a prisoner felt when he was being cuffed. Like his fate was sealed, somehow. Or his life had been irrevocably changed.

"I guess I've never really thought about it," he said. The October sun was warm without being too hot, shining down from a typically blue Arizona sky that was a daily gift, no matter how commonplace. "Maybe it's a combination of making the most of your physical and mental talents and yet doing what *you* want to do."

"If that's it, I don't think I've reached it." Her mare—or more accurately Burt's mare—broke into a trot, and Beth rode the saddle expertly, her jeans-clad lower body lithe and sexy.

"Take this, for instance," she said, grinning back at him. "I love to ride, but I know I haven't done it as much as I'd like."

"You've done it enough to get damn good at it."

"I guess." Beth's gaze grew distant.

"You think you'll ever get married again?" He

couldn't think of a quicker way to get her back from whatever past she was hiding from him.

Or maybe he just had marriage on the brain.

"I hope so," she said. And then wouldn't look at him.

Greg hoped so, too.

"I sure don't want to live the rest of my life alone."

She had no idea how damn glad he was to hear that.

"How about you?" Her body was tall and straight—a good rider's posture—but stiffer than it had been. She was no longer sending him sidelong glances.

"I don't want to live the rest of my life alone, either."

The response garnered him a nod.

"You think you'll ever want more children?" he asked.

"If everything else was in place, I know I would."

So how could he help her get things in place?

Of course, what was to say that even if he *did* help her, he was the one she'd want to be with? He knew so little about her. Had so little to go on, so little basis upon which to judge.

The thought did nothing to make his day.

"CAN I TALK to you?" Beth asked as they left Burt's small ranch and rode farther afield.

"Always."

Greg turned off onto a dirt path leading back to an old abandoned cabin. "Used to be an illegal distillery back here," he said by way of explanation. "Caught on fire when I was kid. My dad was in on the call."

"You don't talk about him much." Beth's voice softened.

Greg wondered if her eyes had done the same.

Wished for a brief second that he could just drown in them and get it all over with.

"I guess it's still hard to think about it without the rage."

"Because he was paralyzed?"

"It wasn't just that," he said. Even Bonnie didn't talk about their dad much. Those years had been so heartbreaking. "He lost his short-term memory, as well," he told Beth, the words sticking in his throat. He gave her a quick glance. Her eyes had softened just like he'd imagined they would. And they were encouraging him to tell her this. Promising in some unspoken way to share his pain.

It was an unfamiliar concept. Greg wasn't usually the recipient of anyone else's help. He didn't usually need—or want—help. "All that intelligence," he murmured. He pulled the horse to a stop in a clearing in front of the old wooden structure, or what was left of it. "He could give you dissertations on profit and loss, on market shares and the benefits of going public as opposed to staying privately owned. The information was all there. He just couldn't put it together. The man was a genius and spent the last ten years of his life sounding like a blithering idiot."

"Did he know?"

"What?" He looked back at her.

"Did he know he wasn't making sense?"

Greg shook his head, wishing he'd never brought this up. "It wasn't that he didn't make sense in a single moment. It was when you pieced the moments together that clarity disappeared. He'd say the same thing over and over and over again. Or string two completely unrelated thoughts together. And no, he didn't know."

"Then, you should be very, very thankful."

Beth's words shocked him. "How do you figure?"

"If he didn't know, Greg, he didn't suffer. He died feeling just as intelligent as he'd always been. And what are we, after all, except products of our own reality?"

For the first time in ten years, Greg felt a ray of real peace. He still hurt for himself and Bonnie—and the hundreds of other people who'd lost a great man too soon. But Beth was right. He was incredibly thankful that his father hadn't suffered his own loss. He'd just never thought of that before.

The woman was definitely a miracle.

"What was it you wanted to tell me?"

Her face twisted with what looked almost like a grimace of pain. "Speaking of our own realities…"

She didn't go on. As though she couldn't rather than that she didn't want to. Greg had a bad premonition.

"Yeah?" he said softly, bracing himself.

"I can't let you form a picture of me that isn't real."

"You're going to tell me what kind of picture we're talking about?"

"One in which a man and a woman live outside the present."

"As in planning a future?"

"Maybe."

"Any guesses as to who this man and woman might be?" he asked. But of course he already knew.

"You and me."

CHAPTER TEN

THE REINS WERE sticky between her fingers. Old leather and sweat. Beth loosened up on them.

Why was it so hard to do what was right? To *know* what was right?

"I like you." The words came out too loud, seeming to echo over all the shades of brown and green that were the desert, to the huge mountain in the distance and back again.

Greg didn't say anything. Just rode slowly and silently beside her.

"A lot," she added.

The trail narrowed, curved through a thicket of sagebrush. Greg let Beth go first. Pulling to the left on the reins, she nudged her horse—and then had to forcibly lighten up on the leather straps again.

She was losing the battle for words. Beth concentrated on the sound of the leather saddle and stirrups creaking, the smell of horse and old leather. They were comforting to her.

Was there a reason for that? Some memory attached to those smells?

Or was she just particularly drawn to the scent of old leather?

"I can't lead you on." She'd meant to deliver her message with a little more finesse.

"Meaning?"

She glanced over at him. The bright sun shining down gave his hair a blue metallic sheen. His face, eyes focused straight ahead, was stern.

"That night at your house…" Beth looked straight ahead, too. She felt uncomfortable. Wary. And turned on just by the thought of what they'd almost done out by his pool.

She'd been thinking about it ever since. Wanting him.

And wanting to run again, as fast and far away as she could get. Except that no matter where she went, she'd never be able to escape herself. Or the past that imprisoned her.

More and more she wanted to know about her past. Because she was finding it impossible to live with the constant fear, because she couldn't stand the dishonesty, because she wanted to be armed in every possible way to keep her son safe. And without knowing the enemy, she couldn't be sure of the risks.

She hated not being completely honest with Greg. Hated that she *couldn't* be. There was so little definition in her life that she held tightly to those things she knew to be important to her. Honesty was one of them. And Greg, she was afraid, was another.

So maybe the months in Shelter Valley had helped her heal enough to handle whatever she'd been hiding from.

Yet, if she *was* ready to handle it, wouldn't she just remember? From everything she'd read about psychosomatic amnesia, even when brought on by a blow to the head, regaining memory would be the natural course of events once the mind was ready to remember whatever it had blocked.

Should she trust her mind and just wait? Or...

"You've admitted you're attracted to me," she blurted out into the stillness. She felt as though she were riding next to a cardboard likeness of the man whose presence she'd started to crave.

"I am."

"And you keep asking me out."

"Can't argue with you there."

"I'm not saying no as much."

"I've noticed."

This wasn't going at all the way she'd scripted it in her mind. She was not supposed to be warring with herself at this point. The decision had been made. Beth's horse snorted, pulling on the reins. She'd been holding them so tightly she almost flew over the mare's head.

"Under the circumstances, a relationship could develop," she went on when she'd settled back in her saddle.

"Yeah."

"Though at the moment, I'm not so sure," Beth said, grinning at him in spite of the tension stiffening every muscle in her body. "You aren't being very kind here."

"I have a feeling I'm not going to like what's ahead," he said quietly, seriously. "I'm just waiting to find out."

His words spurred her on. "I don't want to presume anything," she said, "but because I know that, at least on my part, there's a real danger of wanting more from our relationship than friendship, I have to be honest with you and let you know that it isn't an option for me. No matter how much I want it."

She wasn't going to say any more. She wasn't. "Which I do," she said. And then, "But I can't, Greg."

She drew her horse to a stop and sat there facing him when he did the same. "I mean it."

His gaze locked with hers for several excruciating seconds. Then he nodded. "I believe you."

She was relieved and desperately disappointed all at once. The wasted possibilities seemed criminal. Especially in a life that offered no possibility, no love, at all.

"I need to know why."

The statement was soft, and so honest.

She didn't look away. He deserved much more than a partial answer to a statement that she should never have had to make. Sitting there, looking at him, she needed so badly to tell him. But there was too much at risk; she couldn't take a chance on making a mistake. More than anything, she was confused.

His horse lifted his head, then danced around for a couple of seconds before settling back. Beth's mare, standing placidly in the October sun, ignored him.

"I'm not free," she finally said.

"Not free how? You aren't married. You're a widow."

Beth shook her head. "Inside me, Greg, I'm not free. I'm trapped and afraid. I can't trust or find faith. There are so many things I don't know, so many things, I can't feel. I'm not whole."

When those intense green eyes darkened with compassion, Beth was afraid she'd be lost. Addicted to that look, she couldn't shift her eyes away from him.

"Sometimes, most times, it's relationships that are the cure for those kinds of wounds."

Beth shook her head. "Not when I feel like this, like I'm all chained up inside," she said, wishing he wasn't a cop. Wishing she knew what had made up her life before Shelter Valley, knew what she was going to be accountable for if they ever found her—or she found herself. "I can't stand the guilt, Greg. I can't stand not being fair to you. I can't let you think we're building something together when it's taking everything I've got just to hang on to me."

"Why don't you let me decide what's fair?"

"Because you're too nice for your own good. Someone has to watch out for you."

"I watch out for an entire county," he said sardonically. "I think I can manage to take care of myself."

"I don't. Not about this." She took a deep breath before plunging into the most dangerous territory of all. "I care about you. And with that caring, however tenuous it might be, comes responsibility. I can't let you walk blindly into something that's bound to hurt you."

"I'm walking in with my eyes wide open."

"No, you aren't. There's so much you don't know. So much *I* don't know."

"Why don't you know?" he asked with a puzzled frown. "It's your life."

Beth froze. She tried to find a quick reply that wasn't false without telling him a truth that was too precarious to divulge.

"I don't know why I'm handling the…tragedy—my husband's death—like I am. I understand grief, but this is more than that. I don't really understand why I'm so afraid. It's like I don't even know myself, anymore."

"So we'll discover it together."

Beth shook her head, bending over to pat her mare's neck. "This is something I have to do alone."

"I'll be here to cheer you on."

God, please don't be so cruel, Beth pleaded. The

things life required of her were already too hard. She turned her mare, intending to go back.

Reaching out, Greg grabbed her mare's bridle, preventing her from leaving. Pulling her closer.

"There's risk in every single thing we do, Beth. Pain is inevitable now and then. But if, in the between times, we find love and goodness, they'll sustain us through the hard times. It's worth the pain to have you in my life.

"Granted, Shelter Valley has a comparatively low crime rate, but what there is, I deal with. My job doesn't give me the opportunity to see much of the good stuff, and Lord knows, the last ten years with my father weren't chock-full of fun…."

"And before that was Shelby's defection."

His gaze was compelling. So earnest it would have broken her heart—if she'd still had a heart that was intact and whole and capable of love.

"Katie's been my only salvation in the past few years," he said. "When life gets too overwhelming, I go pick her up, spend a couple of hours with her, just soaking up that innocence—and then I return to work."

Tears filled her eyes. Beth wouldn't blink, wouldn't let the tears fall. How she wished she had the capacity to give this man the love he deserved. She might not remember much, but her heart was telling her there weren't too many men like Greg Richards.

"And then I met you," he said, leaning forward, putting his hand gently behind her neck. Caressing her for a tender moment before he straightened.

Her neck, her entire body, tingled from the too-brief contact.

"When I'm with you the world makes sense," he told her.

Beth chuckled. But inside she wept. "How can that be, when I don't even make sense to myself?" she asked.

"Because you make everything fit," Greg said, resolute. "You bring an inexplicable happiness to my life."

Her chest was so tight, Beth couldn't breathe. The desert brown was lost in a red haze.

"But I might not always," she finally managed to say.

"I'm sure you won't. That's human nature. There's balance in all things—and you know something? We value the good that much more when we've experienced its opposite."

He was right about that.

Could he possibly be right about some of the other things he'd said? Was it okay for her to let this relationship take its natural course?

"You've been honest with me," Greg said. He grabbed her hand, held it beneath his own against his thigh. "You're struggling. There are no guarantees for the future. You might be gone tomorrow…"

That was true enough.

"But you might not be."

It was her greatest dream. One she didn't dare dwell on.

"Chances are just as good that you'll wake up one day and find yourself healed and ready to marry me."

The jolt his words caused shot itself all the way from her stomach out to her fingers. Her hand would have fallen off his leg if he hadn't been holding on so tightly.

"Don't count on that."

"I won't."

"Don't hope for it, either."

"You can't dictate my hopes, Beth." His words were softly spoken, but assured. "And neither, it seems, can

I. Whether you leave town tonight or live here forever, I'm always going to hope that there'll be a day for us."

Oh, God, why? I begged you not to do this.

"You aren't planning to take no for an answer, are you?" she asked, trying again to blink away unshed tears.

"Not today, I'm not."

Then, she'd just have to try again another day.

And until then, she was going to revel in every bit of the joy being forced upon her.

THE DAY CARE was full of activity when Beth stopped in later to pick up Ryan.

"He went in the potty today!" Bonnie greeted her at the door.

The news almost made Beth cry again. "You're sure it wasn't just an accident?" she asked her friend. Bonnie knew how concerned Beth had been about Ryan's slow development.

"Positive," Bonnie said. "He grabbed himself, grabbed my finger and pulled me in the direction of the potty chair."

Beth's face almost hurt with the width of her grin. "I was starting to imagine all kinds of things," she said. "He's the biggest boy here still in diapers."

Shrugging, Bonnie walked with Beth through the groups of children playing contentedly—or not, as was the case with an older boy who was being comforted by one of the day care volunteers—toward the circle of two-year-olds. Ryan lingered on the outer edge as a child-care worker led them through a rousing rendition of "Old MacDonald Had a Farm." "Kids all develop at their own pace," she said. "Where is he on the growth chart for his age?"

"Average." Beth hated the lie, but she felt so light-headed with relief that she couldn't come up with anything else. She had no idea where Ry was on the chart. He hadn't been measured since she'd been here. And even if he had been, she still wouldn't know. The doctor needed a child's birth date to refer to those charts.

And Ryan's mother didn't know when that was. She didn't know how old her own son was....

"Hi, Bonnie!"

Startled, Beth turned with her friend as a well-dressed woman approached them. She was tall and slender. Dark-haired. She seemed to emanate an unusual combination of energy and peace, a quality Beth sensed—and responded to—instantly.

"Becca!" Bonnie greeted the older woman like an old and dear friend.

Becca Parsons. If she wasn't still reeling from the unexpected outcome of her afternoon with Greg and with Ry's news on top of that, Beth would've been intimidated.

"Have you met Beth Allen, Becca?" Bonnie asked, and then, before Becca could reply, she excused herself and went to greet another parent who'd just come in.

"Ryan's mom?" Becca stepped forward, a welcoming smile on her face as she shook Beth's hand. "I've heard so much about you. I'm glad to finally have a chance to meet you face-to-face," she said.

"I don't know what you've heard," Beth said, liking the woman immediately, "but it couldn't be anywhere near as good as what I've heard about you."

"I've heard that you're a single mom who's recently

been widowed and is raising a wonderful little boy while also single-handedly starting up a successful cleaning business. I'm very impressed." Becca surprised her by reporting all this.

With warmth spreading under her skin, up her body, Beth attempted to reply with some measure of confidence. "Thank you."

Becca made her sound like a strong, capable woman. Which sure as hell wasn't the way Beth saw herself.

"Bethany's decided she's going to marry Ryan."

"Until a few weeks ago, she was the only girl he'd play with."

Becca grinned. She was a beautiful woman whose composure Beth envied.

"Let's make a promise now," Becca said, leaning close as she lowered her voice. "If they like each other this much when they hit their teens, we'll watch them like hawks."

Becca's words implied Beth would still be in Shelter Valley then. "Got it," Beth said happily, deriving pleasure from that hope—or pretense.

"It's far too early to ask, of course, but Will and I host an annual holiday party up at our place every year. I'd love it if you could come. And bring Ryan. Bethany would have our hides if you came without him."

It was clear who ruled the roost in the three-year-old's home. But Beth also knew Bethany to be a very polite and well-behaved little girl.

"I don't know…" she started to say. A crazed cleaning lady partying with the town's elite? She didn't think so.

Maybe in her other life she could've held her own there, but…

"You can't possibly have another engagement planned this far ahead."

"No."

"Then, please say you'll come. We're planning to invite Sheriff Richards, too. He was several years behind Will and me in school, but we've always known his family and we're so glad he's back in town."

"He told me you helped with his campaign," Beth said, repeating something Greg had told her that Sunday night at her house when they'd sat and talked for so long.

"He was the best man for the job."

Beth grinned at the other woman's confident tone. "Because he's from Shelter Valley?"

Becca grinned back. "That, too. Now back to the party—you have to come! Bonnie tells me you're an incredible pianist, and we have a piano that spends its life being ignored."

Kids were playing and singing around them, the noise level was high, but Becca didn't seem bothered by it. For that matter, neither was Beth.

"I'd like to but—"

"Hey, lady!"

The woman Bonnie had gone to greet was standing behind Becca, holding two sleeping babies, one in each arm. Bonnie had disappeared into another room.

"Phyllis!" Becca said, immediately reaching for one of the two infants. "Let me have her."

"Only for a second," Phyllis said, smiling. "Matt gets impatient if he has to wait too long to see his babies after a long day at school."

"Give me a break," Becca sputtered. "Long day! Will says that man's out of there by three o'clock every day."

"I know—isn't it sweet?" Phyllis said. "Did you realize he used to work so late he actually slept there sometimes?" Phyllis glanced at Beth, who would have moved on except for her fascination with those two babies. And for the intensely cheerful redhead who was obviously their mother.

"I'm sorry, we haven't met," Phyllis said. "I'm Phyllis Sheffield."

"Oh, I'm sorry," Becca said. She quickly finished the introduction between the two women.

Phyllis offered her one free hand. "Beth Allen. You've got the new cleaning business," she said. "I've been anxious to meet you."

"Good to meet you, too," Beth said, overwhelmed by the other woman's friendliness, but entranced just the same. "How old are they?" She nodded toward the babies.

"Four months."

"Both girls?"

"Nope. One of each. This little fella's Calvin. And that—" she pointed to the sleeping baby in Becca's arms "—is Clarissa."

Though surprised by the depth of her envy as she thought of having not one but two babies to love, Beth smiled. "They must keep you busy."

"Which is why I've been wanting to meet you," Phyllis said. "My husband and I both teach at Montford, and between our students and these guys, I'm failing miserably at housecleaning."

"And Phyllis can't stand to fail at anything," Becca teased. "Her biggest problem has always been thinking she can do it all."

Phyllis playfully elbowed Becca in the side. "Shut

up," she said, her voice warm with familiarity and affection. Beth wanted a friend like that.

"And she's more than just a teacher," Becca continued, giving her a sly look. "Phyllis is not only the best psychology professor at the university, she's also Shelter Valley's resident psychologist."

The red haze slowly ascended. "You have a practice here in town?" She hadn't known there was anyone local.

"No." Phyllis laughed.

"Yes," Becca said at the same time. "It's just not official. Ask any of her friends. She's helped every one of us through pretty serious crises."

"I have not!" Phyllis said, jiggling her arm a little when Calvin frowned at her excited response to Becca. The baby settled back down. "I've done nothing more than be a friend."

"She's counseled every one of us, at one time or another," Becca said again. "Which is why there are so many happy women in this town."

Shelter Valley *did* seem to have an awful lot of happy people.

"That's the town's doing, not mine," Phyllis said.

The redhead did not look like a woman who'd recently given birth to twins. She was slim and almost as elegant as Becca in her business suit.

"It's *her* doing," Becca said to Beth. "Take our friend Tory. Phyllis rescued her from an abusive past that probably would've killed her."

"Tory Evans," Beth whispered.

"Sanders now," Becca said.

Both women were watching her closely. "You know

Tory?" Phyllis asked, protectiveness evident in her tone of voice, in her posture and even the look in her eyes.

"No," Beth quickly assured her. "I read an article about her in a magazine a while back. The article talked about the welcome Tory received here. It's why I chose Shelter Valley as a place to start over...."

"Not just Tory," Becca said, her gaze full of compassion. "Living in Shelter Valley seems to give all of us a renewed sense of confidence at one time or another."

"Including me," Phyllis said. "This place changed my life."

Beth glanced at the other woman, surprised. "You haven't always lived here?" Judging by Phyllis's closeness to everyone, her acceptance as a solid member of the community, her involvement, Beth had assumed the woman had grown up in Shelter Valley. That she and her friends had known each other all their lives.

"Unfortunately, no," Phyllis said. "I just moved here a little over three years ago."

"I was very pregnant with Bethany at the time," Becca said. "My marriage was on the rocks, and Phyllis flew in and immediately set Will and me straight."

Phyllis had only been here three years? And was a completely accepted member of the Shelter Valley family?

So there was hope.

Maybe.

"Then, how'd you get to know everyone so fast?" Beth couldn't help asking. Not that she could do the same. The fewer people she was close to, the better. For now.

"She and Cassie Tate do pet therapy together," Becca said. "That's part of it. They helped Cassie's stepdaughter talk again after more than a year of trauma-induced silence...."

Trauma-induced silence. Beth felt cold. And sick.

And very, very threatened. Was Ry's near-silence also trauma-induced? And was help for Beth standing right there in front of her? Did she have the courage to find out?

"She helped me save my marriage," Becca said, her voice softening as she smiled at her friend.

"She's making me sound like much more than I am, and I'll never be able to live up to it. Just take everything Becca says about me with an ear to the flattery involved. She wants my babies," Phyllis teased. "What I want to know is, do you have room for one more client?"

"Of course I do," Beth answered automatically. She'd put in longer hours. Make it work.

And if she took on one more client after this, she'd have to hire help.

Under the table, of course.

Meanwhile, she had to collect Ryan, go home and dye their hair—get herself to the safety of her own space, her regular routine—before the red haze became more than a warning. Her mind was overwhelmed, taking in too much to process at one time.

There were just far too many questions. And no answers.

CHAPTER ELEVEN

AT HIS KITCHEN table on that second Monday in October, Greg studied the four-foot-square collection of clippings and reports, plus the couple of photos he'd had at home—copies of the official photos taken of his father's accident. He scanned them and had them stored on his hard drive. And his staff was in the process of scanning all pictures entered in as evidence before the digital age. He and Burt had a meeting in the morning, and Greg knew Burt was going to recommend closing his father's case—all the carjacking cases—insofar as an unsolved case could be closed. Burt was ready to dismiss the incidents as random, continuing to be on the lookout for any information that might lead to suspects but not actively pursuing clues.

Greg refused to accept that verdict a second time. Not only had he assigned deputies to question people, but he and Burt had gone around interviewing everyone in the vicinity of the carjackings; they'd posted radio news announcements and put out requests on all of the Arizona television stations asking for anyone with information to call.

Burt had personally dealt with every single one of the hundred or more calls they'd received.

They'd turned up nothing. Burt had also, in deference to Greg's ambition to see this case solved, questioned most of the key witnesses himself rather than assigning less experienced officers to handle the legwork for him.

Again, he turned up nothing.

But there *had* to be something. Something right there in front of him, if Greg could only see it. No matter how many nights he spent poring over the reports, the figures, the graphs, the measurements and the photos, he couldn't piece it all together. Or even figure out which piece was missing.

Rubbing the back of his neck, Greg straightened and grabbed a cola from the fridge, hoping the caffeine would be the jump-start he needed. His whole life seemed to consist of looking for missing puzzle pieces. Professionally and personally.

Beth was hiding more pieces from him than she was giving him. Leaning against the counter, Greg drank the soda from the can, staring out the big window above his sink to the resortlike backyard he and Beth had spent those few short hours in.

She'd almost made love to him that night. He'd almost died when she hadn't.

He had to stop thinking about that night.

He couldn't believe Burt hadn't come up with anything substantial at all. He was the best. Which meant there was nothing to find.

Then, why did Greg feel so certain there was?

Can in hand, he moved back to the table, and stood there studying all the bits and pieces. If he viewed them from a different angle, would they reveal something new?

They didn't. Even sideways he saw the same words, the same pencil sketches, same figures, same images…

From Greg's vantage point, that dented front end

looked like a rabbit. The largest rabbit Greg had ever seen in his life.

He froze. Stared. Then, every movement deliberate, he slowly rounded the table, his gaze never leaving that rabbit-shaped dent. Only when he was facing the photograph did his eyes stray to the other pictures.

They were all of the same car. His dad's Thunderbird. Taken from different angles, different perspectives of the crime scene, the photos didn't all show the front of the car. But in every one that did—of the few left since the lab disaster—that dent looked like a rabbit.

One he recognized. "I'll be damned." There were rabbits and then there were rabbits. This one was missing its head; the front end hadn't reached that high. It was missing its bottom and feet, too. They would've been below the level of the bumper. But that middle, with the "paw" raised at a jaunty angle, was unmistakable. If he hadn't just been horseback riding with Beth, noticing shapes in the rock formations of the mountains that he usually overlooked, he might not have recognized the rabbit now.

But Greg remembered that particular formation. It was an infamous landmark to him, as it marked the spot of one of the worst nights of his life. He'd once been invited to a party at Rabbit Rock—he'd been sixteen, feeling privileged to be let in on the whereabouts of the secret gathering place. About thirty miles from Shelter Valley, in the heart of the most undeveloped, unpopulated portion of Kachina County, there was a clearing that abutted the south side of the mountains. The clearing was surrounded by an unusually thick grouping of palo verde trees, enclosing it, hiding it from the rest of the world. Making it the perfect place for teenagers to engage in illicit activities.

He'd been a fool then. A reckless teenage kid who'd thought he was invincible, and worse, strong enough to take on anything. He'd only seen the rock that one time, but he'd seen it in many different forms. When the hallucinations had been at their worst, he and that rabbit were the only two things in the world.

Tossing his can in the trash, Greg paced his kitchen. Went to the phone. Picked it up. Put it back down. What was he thinking here? Every one of the cars that had been stolen ten years ago, as well as every one that had been taken this summer, had been rammed into the side of a mountain out in a clearing no one but a group of rowdy boys had known about. It sounded even more implausible when he spelled it out.

He'd taken some long shots in his life, but he'd never reached quite this far. Greg rubbed his face. Rinsed it with cold water.

He reached for the phone again. He had to call Burt. This couldn't wait until morning.

Unless he really was losing perspective. How insane was he going to sound when he laid this on his deputy? How much credibility was he going to lose?

And how sure was he that he wasn't dreaming up the whole thing? Making something happen because he was crazy with determination to avenge his father's attack?

Phone in hand, he walked back to the table. Looked at the photos. The rabbit was still there.

He couldn't let this go. Greg knew what he had to do. He dialed.

"Hello?"

"Beth?" he asked, trying to stay calm. He wasn't too eager to have her thinking he was a mental case.

"Greg? What's wrong?"

"Nothing," he said quickly, hating the instant alarm he heard in her voice. She was so easily made nervous, and that bothered him. "I need to run something by an impartial party. Someone I can trust to be honest with me," he added, to reassure her, but also to make sure that he didn't talk himself out of asking for her help.

"Of course," she said, her voice completely different. Soft. Beckoning. "What's up?"

He glanced out at the pool. It would be light for at least another hour, maybe an hour and a half. "Have you eaten yet?"

"No, Ryan and I just got home. Today was my day to clean the Willises'. You want me to throw something in the microwave for him and then call you back?"

"How about if I come get you, we pick up something for dinner and take a drive?"

"Why do I get the feeling this is more than just an impromptu invitation to a picnic?"

Greg stared at the photos. "There's something I want you to see," he said slowly. And then he amended that. "Something I *need* you to see."

"What?"

"That's just it, I don't want to say." He knew he sounded way too mysterious. "I'm doing a sanity check," he finally admitted. "I've come up with this crazy hypothesis, and before I go any further with it, I'd like to show you the evidence and see if you think I'm off base."

"Of course," she said, her instant capitulation filling Greg with a sense of a righted world.

One way or another, he was going to have some answers.

"But if I'm going to have to look at something gross, I'd better not have dinner."

He chuckled. "I wouldn't ask you to look at anything gross," he said. "Usually when the evidence is graphic, wrongdoing is relatively easy to prove. Labs are wonderful things."

"Does this have to do with your father's case?"

Sobering, Greg carefully picked up the photos and slid them back into their envelope. "Yes."

"Give me ten minutes."

GREG CALLED THE Valley Diner and placed a take-out order. Chicken nuggets and fries for Ryan. Grilled chicken sandwiches for him and Beth. He didn't take time to change out of his uniform. He wanted to get to the rabbit before dark. At the last minute, he grabbed the spotlight from the trunk of his squad car, just in case.

The drive wasn't nearly as tense as it might've been if he'd been making it alone, dwelling on his obsession. With Ryan in his car seat between them, a sweet little guy in blue jeans and a tiny plain white sweatshirt, he and Beth had their dinner and spoke about superficial things. She mentioned someone she'd met in town that day—a woman he'd gone to school with. He talked about a tentative plan to turn his third bedroom into a weight room. She told him a couple of "toilet lady" jokes she'd made up while working that week.

Ryan, a soggy French fry in each hand, looked up at Greg when he laughed out loud at the last one.

"At least he likes the fries," he said, running a hand

across the top of the little boy's head. The toddler hadn't touched his chicken.

"Sha sha," Ryan said.

"What, sweetie?" Voice eager, Beth leaned toward him, her shiny auburn hair falling forward over her shoulders. "What did you say?"

Ryan held up both hands, showing her his fries. "Sha sha," he said again.

"French fries?" Beth asked. She was wearing jeans, too, and an off-white sweater that hugged those perfect breasts and tapered at her waist.

Ryan nodded. "Sha sha." He then attempted to put both fries in his mouth at once.

"One at a time, Ry," Beth said, pulling her son's left hand away from his mouth. It struck Greg that they were painting a family picture right there. He'd had no idea so much pleasure could be taken from such a simple thing.

It was still light when he pulled off the road, onto a dirt path, and then, putting the truck into four-wheel drive when the path came to an abrupt end, continued on. The adrenaline he'd managed to contain during the past hour came rushing to the forefront again when he noticed the tire tracks just off to his left. They weren't fresh. But they weren't twenty years old, either.

Judging by the lack of regrowth, they were less than a year old.

His excitement grew when he wound his way into the clearing and his gaze alighted immediately on the rabbit. It was almost exactly as he'd remembered. A little smaller, maybe. More weathered. There'd been more growth on the mountain back when he was a teenager.

He stopped the truck, although he didn't get out. Ryan's legs were bouncing a little in his seat, but with a

French fry in one hand and a plastic truck in the other, he was amazingly content.

Beth's son did not act like any other two-year-old he'd ever met.

"This is what we came to see?" Beth asked, glancing around the clearing.

Greg pointed. "That's what we came to see."

She looked toward the rocky side of the mountain. Ryan looked, too, dropping his French fry as he leaned forward.

"Sha sha," he said. Greg automatically reached for another one and handed it to the boy. Ryan took it without hesitation.

Greg didn't think anything of the act until he glanced up from the toddler to see Beth staring at him. "What?"

She shook her head. Greg was fairly certain he'd seen moisture in her eyes. "It's just nice, seeing him interact with you...."

So she was sensing it, too. This family feeling. Greg was glad that—at least on this—he wasn't alone.

"What is it about this rock that has you concerned?" she asked, turning to look out the window again.

"Look at it for a minute," Greg said, not all that eager to test his hypothesis. Now that he was there, he was more certain than ever that he was on to something. But if Beth didn't see any connection between that rock and the photos, he might have to concede that he was so desperate to get someplace, he was inventing a reason to continue the search.

Greg gave Ryan another French fry. "Do you see any shapes in that rock?" he asked.

"Looks kind of like something waving, doesn't it?" she said, her brows drawn together in concentration.

"Like there's an arm going from the round part up there, off to the side."

"An arm—or a paw?"

"Yeah!" she said, grinning at him. "It's definitely a paw."

Greg nodded.

She glanced from him to the rock and back. "So, are we playing a game, or is this leading somewhere?"

"Look again." Greg nodded toward the mountain. "Can you see the rabbit attached to that paw?"

"Sha sha," Ryan said, his plastic truck falling to the floor as he reached for the bag that contained his dinner.

Greg picked up the truck and the bag, letting Ryan poke his hand in for a fry. The child used one hand and then the other, coming out with double the bounty.

"Smart guy," Greg said approvingly.

He sobered, though, as he looked once again at the mountain in front of them. The sun was going down. It would be dark soon.

"Is that its head?" Beth asked. "That round thing? And his ears go up from there to the right? It's a jack-rabbit."

Bingo.

Carjackings. Jackrabbit. It was a long stretch.

Too long.

And yet…maybe this was part of his answer. The missing piece.

"We used to call this Rabbit Rock when I was kid," he said gravely.

"Way out here? How'd kids ever find this spot?"

"I'm not sure," Greg said. It wasn't anything he'd ever thought about. "I just know that certain kids talked about the parties they'd have out here. Only the coolest kids were invited."

"Then, you were invited for sure."

"Not right away," he said. "Not until my junior year in high school."

"Were the parties as good as you'd heard?"

Greg couldn't meet her eyes. Ryan was starting to droop, his head resting against the car seat as he chewed on a French fry.

"I only came to one," Greg said, staring at the rock. "It was one of the most horrible nights of my life."

Even in the growing dusk, he could see that her blue eyes had filled with compassion.

"What happened?" she asked.

"I was an idiot," he said. "Like a lot of sixteen-year-old boys, I was certain that the need to be careful didn't apply to me. I was young. Strong. Succeeded at most everything I set my mind to. Popular. Nothing was going to happen to me."

"I take it something did."

Ryan's eyes were slowly closing.

Greg nodded. "Drinking a few beers wasn't new to me," Greg related softly. "Didn't faze me at all. So, of course, I was certain that little mushroom thing wouldn't, either.

"The worst part was, I didn't even want the damn thing," he continued. "What I'd wanted was to preserve my reputation. I put a lot of stock in being one of the cool guys."

"Don't most people?"

He was tempted to ask if she had. But didn't.

"Probably. In a small place like Shelter Valley, word gets around quickly. If a guy chickened out or acted like a wimp, he might as well empty his locker in the training room and move in with the nerds."

"So what happened?"

He loved that voice. The one that wrapped him in warmth.

"I had a bad mescaline trip. Thought I was dying. The other guys were in another world, playing some version of football I couldn't figure out. I couldn't run. I couldn't breathe. They told me afterward that I stood in front of that rock for more than an hour. What I remember was knowing that some freak thing had happened to the world and only that rabbit and I were left. If I took my eyes off it, it might be gone, too, and then there'd only be me."

"My God, that must have been horrible. You were just a kid!"

"Yeah, well, that wasn't the worst part. That came when one of the guys dropped me off at my house and I had to face Bonnie and my dad. She took one look at my face and was terrified that I was going to die. My father knew better. He checked me out and then sent me to my room.

"I'll never forget the disappointment on his face as I walked away. I lost my father's unconditional trust that night."

"I'll bet you never did drugs again."

"Never."

"And you regained his trust."

"Eventually," Greg sighed. "But trust is a funny thing. Once you lose it, you never regain it in its original form."

THE SOLEMNITY IN Greg's words, and in the mood between them, touched Beth deeply. She had no memory of personal trust. And yet her heart understood exactly what Greg was saying.

"I thought we were on an outing to solve a case," she said softly, hoping to bring him out of a reverie that couldn't be pleasant.

"We are."

"Here?"

He nodded, and slowly pulled an envelope out of his pocket. Handing it to her, he flipped on the overhead light in the truck. But not before draping Ryan's blanket over the top and sides of his car seat, shielding the sleeping child from the harsh light.

Such a simple gesture. One that brought tears to Beth's eyes for the second time in less than an hour.

"Look at these and tell me what you think," he said.

Baffled by the lack of explanation, Beth took the envelope. There were pictures inside. She slid them out, curious. There were several pictures of the same car, taken from different angles. It appeared that the only real damage had been to the front end.

Until she exposed the image of the car's interior. It was little more than a black frame, burned-out.

Beth swallowed, aching inside. "Your father's car."

"Yes." He glanced at the photos. "Do you see anything at all that reminds you of something else?"

Frowning, Beth looked again, trying to help him. To find what he needed her to find. But he was being so vague, and—

"The paw waving," she said suddenly. She could feel the blood drain from her face as she raised her eyes from the photo to the rock outside, still recognizable as it gleamed in the headlights Greg had flipped on. "You think someone ran this car into that mountain."

The look Greg gave her was piercing. Demanding total honesty.

"Do you?"

"I think it's definitely possible. That paw is so distinctive."

"That's what I thought."

She couldn't bear to see any more. Slipping the photos back into their envelope, she passed the envelope to Greg. "Was your father found near here?"

"Not really."

"So his injuries were from a car accident?"

Greg shook his head. "He'd been beaten with some kind of blunt object, possibly fists."

"Why would someone beat him up and then ram his car into a rock?"

"Good question. And it wasn't just his car." Greg was tapping the envelope against his steering wheel. "All of the cars that were involved in carjackings that summer, and then again this summer, bore similar dents in their front ends."

Shivering, Beth gazed around at the dark desert night. They were all alone out there. Miles from civilization. "It's the connection you've been looking for," she said slowly.

"More than that, it's a place to look for the reason. There can't be too many people who know about this place."

"Where do you even start looking?"

"First thing I'm going to do is talk to Burt. He was the one who combed this area in August. And then there's an old hermit who lives about ten miles from here. The guys I partied with that night used to talk about him."

"That was twenty years ago. You think he'll still be around?"

"Maybe. He wasn't all that old back then. Story was, his wife had been raped and murdered in their home someplace in Tucson while he was at work. Had a life insurance policy that made him wealthy. He bought some land out here and wouldn't let anyone near the place. He was pretty warped from the whole thing. Unless he's dead, chances are he's still here."

Beth shivered again. Greg told the story as if it were an everyday occurrence. To him, the sheriff of an entire county, that probably wasn't far from the truth. She didn't want to live in a world where violence was commonplace. Where you had to fear the evil that lurked in unexpected places, at unexpected times.

She wasn't even aware that panic was starting to descend until she automatically initiated relaxation techniques. Why did she have such a strong premonition that evil could not be escaped?

CHAPTER TWELVE

RYAN WAS SLEEPING SOUNDLY, his head resting against the padded side of his car seat. "I'd like to check one more thing before we head back, if you don't mind," Greg said to Beth.

"Of course I don't mind."

Grabbing his spotlight, he climbed out of the truck, careful to shut the door softly behind him. His gun was a welcome weight against his thigh.

Approaching the mountain's rock face, Greg shone the light all over the ground, looking for tire tracks. While he couldn't make out one distinct and single set of tracks that led to the rabbit-shaped rock, it was obvious that the clearing had been used recently. And often. There were many sets of tire tracks, ranging in size from mountain bikes to four-wheel-drive trucks like Greg's, all crisscrossing each other.

"Looks like there's been some kind of racing going on through here."

He hadn't known Beth was with him. She'd left the truck door slightly open, obviously so they could hear if Ryan woke up.

"Or maybe just kids spinning their wheels, doing fishtails, practicing mountain bike tricks, that sort of thing. I feel like such a fool, with all this going on right under my nose."

"How could you have known?"

"I knew this place was here. I just thought everyone else had forgotten about it."

With her toe Beth smoothed a clump of dirt in the middle of one of the tracks. "I guess if you were looking for tracks that would prove your theory, this spoils that, huh?"

"Not necessarily," Greg said. He shone the light up to the edge of the mountain. "Look."

"No tracks," Beth said, sounding almost as though she felt sorry for him.

"Yeah," Greg said, walking more quickly. "No tracks, and an unnatural pattern in the dirt. Someone did this deliberately."

"To wipe out tracks?"

"That would be my guess." With the mountain now in the spotlight, Greg studied every inch of the rabbit formation. "But that's not what I was looking for," he said.

A moment later, heart pounding, he added, "*This* was."

Seething with mixed emotions, Greg stood there and stared at the paint mark in the middle of the rabbit's paw. Anger was in the forefront, but some elation and a curious kind of relief were there, as well. The paint wasn't from his father's car, of course; that would've long since worn away.

"It's the exact color of the car stolen from a young U of A dancer back in August," he said. "I'm surprised Burt missed it."

"Unless he didn't know about the clearing."

That had to be it. Though if anybody could find this little-known gathering place, it would be his star deputy.

Feeling an urgent need for connection, Greg slid his arm around Beth. Her long hair covered the sleeve of his uniform. Motioning back to the truck with his head, he asked, "Does he usually sleep this soundly?"

She nodded, her hair brushing his shoulder. "Unless he has a nightmare. He should be out for the night."

"He won't wake up when you get him home? Change him?"

"Maybe, but he'll go right back to sleep."

"He's a great kid."

"Yeah." Greg was curious about the sound of worry, not pride, in her voice.

He could no longer deny his suspicion that Beth was dealing with much more than the death of her husband. She was immediately nervous anytime he surprised her, which was definitely a giveaway. Although *what* it revealed he didn't know. When he'd called her that night, she'd been instantly defensive. Or that time he'd surprised her at the Mathers' when she'd been cleaning. And the time he'd shown up unannounced on her doorstep. She was afraid, that much was obvious—but why? Of what—or whom?

The darkness, the solitude, the idea that they were all alone out here, miles from anywhere, the fact that she hadn't moved away from him, gave Greg an unusual sense of security where she was concerned. "Can I ask you something?" he said.

She stiffened. "Yes."

"And you'll give me an honest answer?"

"If I can."

He almost changed his mind. But if what he suspected was true, she might need help—protection even. And he couldn't provide it until he knew where the enemy lived. Inside her? That was a possibility; it could certainly be part of the answer. Or was the enemy some-place else? Perhaps wherever she'd come from...

"Was your husband murdered?"

"What?" Beth turned to face him. "Why do you ask that?" Her arms were wrapped around herself, and she was as defensive as he'd ever seen her. He'd hit a raw nerve.

"I'm wondering, actually, if you might somehow have witnessed the murder," he said, determining to at least get it all out. "It would explain so much." He wanted to reach for her, pull her against him. And yet he understood that it would be the worst thing he could do. "Your complete inability to talk about your life before you came to Shelter Valley, your nervousness, which surfaces at unexpected times. Maybe even the reaction you had that night at the casino. Was he killed at one of your concerts? And is that why playing the piano seems almost painful for you?"

"Can we go home now?"

Without waiting for a reply, Beth hurried back to the truck. She strapped herself in and waited.

Resigned, disappointed, Greg followed her. But he didn't immediately start the truck. "Beth, I want to help."

"I know." She sat stiffly, facing front.

"I can't do that if I don't know what I'm helping with."

"I need to go home."

Had there been any feeling at all in her voice, he might have pressured her a little more, tried harder. As it was, there didn't seem to be much point. It didn't matter whether he kept Beth there with him or not. She'd already left.

Because he'd hit too close to the truth? And if so, would she come to him, talk to him about it when she got over the shock of his having guessed?

Or maybe he was conjuring this up, too, to help him accept the fact that the woman he was falling in love with wasn't nearly as willing to open her heart—and her life—to him.

In the duplex's only bedroom late that night, Beth sat on the floor in the dark by her son's crib and shook. The glow from the cheap shell-shaped night-light plugged into the wall was her focus. She kept her vision trained there.

Had she witnessed her husband's murder? Was that the horrible truth awaiting her if she ever fought her way out of her mental prison?

Was her lie about being a widow not a lie at all?

Cold, light-headed, she tried to find her way in the darkness of her mind, searched for anything familiar, any bit of recognition. A picture. A single memory.

Even a name.

Her son moved and her eyes were drawn toward the crib. Had Ryan witnessed the murder, too? Was that the trauma that had brought about his silence? From the very beginning of this nightmare, her baby boy had said his name. And hers. But never once had she heard him say "da da." One of the first words most babies seemed to say.

Pulling her knees up to her chest, she hugged them tightly, her hands clutching her upper arms. The shivers were uncontrollable. She couldn't get up to retrieve the quilt from her bed. Didn't want to be trapped beneath it, anyway.

What if she'd killed her husband? What if that was why she'd witnessed the murder?

Maybe it was why she'd run away with her son, only a gym bag, two thousand dollars cash and a couple of diapers in her possession.

"Oh God, Ry," she whispered brokenly. "What have I done? What am I doing to you?"

There were no answers, not from the sleeping little boy, not from inside her. Only debilitating fear.

Beth sat there long into the night, trying to find a way to go on.

"I KNOW NOTHING about any such clearing," Burt told Greg early the next morning. The two men, dressed in full uniform, were in Burt's office in the county sheriff's building, nearly twenty miles from Shelter Valley. Greg's own office was two floors down.

"What about the hermit who lives out near the foot of the mountains?" Greg asked. "Did you talk to him?"

Burt shook his head. "Far as I could tell, he's long gone. That shack of his looked deserted. I checked back a couple times and there was no sign of life."

Damn. The old guy had been his best lead. Or at least the easiest one.

Greg went over every detail of the case with Burt again, knocking ideas around, seeking his deputy's invaluable reasoning ability. In the end, they'd come up with nothing more than an agreement to continue searching.

"How soon can you and I take a trip out to Rabbit Rock?" Greg asked as he stood to leave.

Burt looked at his watch. "This afternoon?" he asked. "Around three?"

Greg was disappointed that Culver couldn't make it before then. But he smiled, shook Burt's hand, made plans to meet him back at the office later that afternoon.

Taking the elevator down to the first floor where his own suite of offices was, Greg tried to shake an uneasy feeling. Burt hadn't been brushing him off. The deputy was as eager as Greg to get to work on this latest development. Which was most likely why he'd picked up the phone and started dialing before Greg had shut the office door behind him.

Greg didn't turn right as he'd intended when he got off the elevator. He strode straight through the front doors of the county building and headed to his car, his other "office."

Keeping busy had always been a cure for the restlessness that sometimes nagged at him. That was the only reason he was going to drive out to visit that hermit's cabin for himself.

It was something to pass the time until he and Burt took their little field trip that afternoon. He was very eager to hear what kind of evidence his deputy would turn up before then.

If anyone could find the missing pieces that would make some sense out of a bunch of senseless crimes, Burt Culver could.

He was the best damn cop Greg had ever known.

THE HERMIT, JOE FRANCIS—although Greg had never heard anyone use his name—was still around. Greg smelled old cooking grease when he got out of his car on the old man's property. Calling it a front yard would be too generous. The weathered gray logs and boarded-up windows made the shack appear deserted. But that smell. Someone had been cooking there recently.

"Joe?" Greg called, with no idea if the old guy even considered the name his own anymore. Looking cautiously around, he stood still, hoping for a chance to explain before he got shot at.

Not that the hermit had ever been considered dangerous. As far as Greg had ever heard, Francis wasn't violent or out to hurt anyone. He just wanted to be left alone.

"Joe Francis?" he called again. "You here?"

As impatient as he'd been with Burt that morning, he was patient now. He hoped Joe would show himself eventually; Greg wasn't going to be able to leave without checking out that cabin. And he was loath to trespass on the man's private sanctuary without an invitation.

"Joe, you there?" he called again, taking a step away from the car. "I'm just here to introduce myself," he said. "I'm the new sheriff in this county. My name's Greg Richards."

He almost missed the set of eyes peering at him from a tall clump of desert brush off to the right of the shack. "Is that you, Joe?" he asked the clump.

It moved. And the eyes were gone.

"I mean you no harm," Greg said in the direction of the clump. Joe—or someone—had to be back there. The clump, surrounded by low-lying desert brush, was the only coverage for several yards. "I'm on official business, as you've probably figured out," he added. "But it has nothing to do with you. There's a slight chance you might be able to help me, though."

The earth was completely still. Hotter than most October days, that Tuesday wasn't providing even a bit of a breeze.

Moving around to the front of his car, Greg leaned against the hood, one hand on either side of him, ready to grab his weapon if he had to. That and his bullet-proof vest were all he had to protect himself, but he was prepared to take whatever risk was necessary. This mattered too much not to do everything he could. "There's no real reason you should want to," Greg continued. "But the way I see it, you and I have something in common. I'm guessing we both feel a need to have justice done. To know that at least one crime has been avenged, the perpetrator behind bars where he belongs, not out walking the streets. Free. Laughing. Having a good time. Capable of hurting more innocent people."

No movement.

"I'm not speaking as a cop here," Greg said. If nothing else came of this, maybe it would be cathartic to just say these things to someone who'd been there. "My father, an economics professor at Montford, was beaten and left for dead not too far from here about ten years ago. He lived the rest of his life paralyzed until he died last year." He stopped. Crossed his legs. Peered at that clump of brown scrub, willing it to move. "Last night I found some pretty substantial evidence at the base of this mountain. There's a good chance you're the only one who could help me out with it."

If that didn't work, Greg was going to have to give up. At least for now. Between Beth and this old hermit, he was beginning to feel like he'd lost all his talent for interrogation.

Or maybe he'd just forgotten how to talk to people outside of work and Bonnie's house.

"Okay, well, I'll leave you alone, then," Greg said, backing up to the driver's door of his car.

He pulled out a business card and tossed it in front of him. "If you know anything about the clearing on the south side of the mountain and you ever want to contact me about it, there's my card."

Frustrated beyond trusting himself to be compassionate Greg knew it was time to go.

"I told the other sheriff."

The voice was gravelly. Old and cracked. And not very loud.

But it was loud enough for Greg to hear.

Slowly, carefully, he turned back toward the bush. "Sheriff Foltz?"

No answer.

"What did you tell him?"

"Ten years ago. When the kids were banging their cars into the side of the mountain."

Greg had no idea if he was talking to a bent and gray, skinny old man, maybe with a long beard, or a sturdy muscled woodsman in the prime of his later years. He gave the brush an intent stare.

"You told Sheriff Foltz there were kids ramming cars into the mountain."

"Ten years ago. I couldn't stand to have them violating nature that way. They stopped right after."

There'd been no report....

Greg was sweating. Yet his mind felt clear and sharp. "You keep an eye on the place since then?" he asked.

"This mountain's good to me, I'm good to it. I hike over there every now and then."

"Still?"

"Yes. I spend a lot of nights on top of that mountain."

Which could explain why Culver hadn't found the old man. Then, too, Francis was pretty adept at not being seen.

"Have you noticed any activity in the clearing in the past few years?" Greg continued to address the clump of desert brush.

"The kids came back with their loud parties this summer. And they're running their cars into the side of the mountain again. I hiked all the way up the mountain to find some peace, and instead, heard that partying going on below. Went on all night long."

Considering the huge expanse of open ground around the shack, Greg found it a little odd that the old man regularly put himself through a rigorous mountain hike. He supposed most people thought they had to leave the life they had in order to find peace.

That was something he'd like to discuss with Beth sometime. He'd bet she had a theory on it.

"If you hear them again and have a way to get in touch with me, I'd sure appreciate a phone call," Greg said. "And in the meantime, if you ever need anything, let me know."

"Groceries," the old man said.

Greg frowned at the tree. "You need groceries?" He didn't know how mountain men provided for themselves, but he'd always assumed they hunted or grew whatever sustenance they needed.

"The walk into town's not bad, but I'm getting a little old for the walk back with all the groceries."

Hochie, the closest town, was a good fifteen miles away.

"Once every two weeks enough?"

"It's more than I go myself."

"Then, I'll be here tomorrow. And I'm going to bring the pre-paid phone with me."

He was eager to see what the old man looked like.

BETH SPENT ALL TUESDAY afternoon at the library, looking up death notices. And searching for articles on murder in a several-hundred-mile radius of Snowflake.

She got about as much from the computer files, microfiche and Internet sites she visited as she did from her own memory. It felt like the whole world was in collusion against her.

To celebrate that they hadn't been murdered, she took Ryan out for ice cream. And ran into Katie and Greg at the ice-cream parlor. He was still in his uniform, while Beth was in her "toilet lady" clothes. Sweats, with her hair up in a ponytail.

"Ryan!" Katie squealed. Ry walked over to his friend and stood there, watching her eat her ice-cream cone.

Greg walked over to Beth, too, but he wasn't as silent. "I tried to call you."

"I was at the library. My phone was on silent." Her pre-paid cell phone. The only kind she could get without a social security number.

He seemed a little curious, but mostly preoccupied.

"How about we take the kids to the park and let them drip ice cream over everything there?" he suggested.

She laughed and nodded, ordering quickly, and then the four of them strolled to the park adjacent to Shelter Valley's town square.

It didn't take Greg long to fill Beth in on the events of his day. The progress of the case. She'd been wondering about him, hoping she'd hear from him.

"So what happened when you met with Burt at three?"

Sitting on a bench beside her, but far enough away that they weren't touching, Greg shrugged. He was watching Katie and Ryan, who were attempting to sit on a miniature merry-go-round while they ate. The thing kept moving and the result was a combination of comedy and frustration. Depending, he supposed, on whether you were observer or participant.

"We drove out. He'd never seen the place before, and he saw that as a failure. Took it personally. He felt he'd let me down. Foltz told him nothing about the Francis complaint ten years ago."

Never having met Burt, Beth had no grounds on which to judge, but something didn't quite add up. The best cop in the entire county and he'd failed in so many areas. The clearing. The hermit. Evidence from the past.

"Are you sure Burt's telling the truth?"

Greg's look of surprise was answer enough. "I don't doubt it for a second. I trust the man with my life every single day I go to work. And he trusts me with his. Burt's a good cop. And that's all he is. He's married to the job. Ten years older than me with no wife, no kids. Just those horses."

"So what now? Do you talk to Foltz?"

"Burt's going to."

"This case is important to you. Maybe you should do that."

"Technically, it's Burt's case. And he's kicking himself enough as it is. I don't want my top deputy losing confidence in himself."

He knew better than she. He knew Burt. And at the moment she was viewing the whole world with suspicion.

"That old hermit said something today that struck me, and I wondered what you'd think about it," Greg said a couple of seconds later. The kids had finished their ice cream and, with sticky hands and faces, were crawling around in their jeans and sweatshirts on the merry-go-round.

"What did he say?" She wished he were sitting closer.

"You know how people always say grass is greener on the other side?"

"Yeah." She grinned at him. "But they obviously haven't seen the grass in Shelter Valley."

"Cultured," Greg said. He gave her a grin and quickly sobered. "Francis lives out there in the middle of God's country, with nothing but nature for company, and puts himself through miles of rigorous climbing to find peace."

"And you're thinking that peace is as elusive as the greener grass?"

"I'm wondering."

Peace was something Beth thought about a lot. "I guess for some it is that way. I prefer to think that if we try hard enough, we can quit thinking we have to run away from our lives and instead, find contentment in the little things that bring us pleasure or serenity."

Sounded kind of lofty when she put it into words. But the idea had kept her sane and functioning for more than seven months.

"Is that what you're doing?" he asked, giving her a sideways glance. "Trying not to run away anymore?"

"I'm trying to find peace in the little things," Beth said. The running wasn't something she could help.

She couldn't expect him to understand that.

CHAPTER THIRTEEN

"GRADY'S WORKING OUT very well." James Silverman was sitting with Peter Sterling in the state-of-the-art kitchen of the doctor's three-hundred-thousand-dollar condo.

"We're very blessed to have found him," Sterling said, sipping his early-morning herbal tea with care. James had made it too hot, but Peter didn't complain.

"He's on fire for the cause." Silverman smiled. "Almost reminds me of myself when I first met you."

Sterling eyed him carefully over the top of his cup. "You aren't still on fire?"

"More so than ever." There was no hesitation in James's reply. Or his heart. "It's just good to know there are others to help with the work. Gives me hope for the difference we'll be able to make someday."

The doctor nodded, smiled, but the smile wasn't as enthusiastic as it might have been. As it once had been. Lately, the doctor had been looking more tired than usual. His face more lined.

Something had to be done about the Beth situation. Now. Too much time had passed. It was taking its toll. They couldn't do this work without Dr. Sterling. He was a prophet—their prophet. His energy must be preserved at all cost.

"Still no news?" Peter asked, his brows creased, his eyes sad.

James bit back his own pain. His own feelings of betrayal, of loss, were nothing compared to the damage that had been done to Sterling Silver. "None," he said, not at all surprised that Peter had been thinking along the same lines.

And every day, the danger grew.

"I'm afraid I'm starting to obsess," Peter said, his head low as he shook it slowly. "I'm losing my positive outlook. I don't know how much longer I can go on."

Neither of them knew if someone might come to the door someday and try to shut them down. Someone from the police or the government. Someone who didn't understand.

"We're on the cusp of doing great work. We have so many dedicated people ready and willing to spread the good news. People like Grady, relying on us for a better life. Willing to make that happen. Not just for themselves, but for the rest of the world."

James's heart swelled with a sense of certainty that their work was right and good. True. That certainty drove him every second of every day.

"I don't understand why we didn't sense the negative forces," Peter said.

James sipped his tea, not even having to hold back a grimace anymore. He detested the taste, but after years of the morning ritual, he'd grown so used to it that he was no longer fazed.

"We're still men." James finally spoke aloud the conclusion he'd had to accept. "Which means we can be blinded by lustful desires."

"Sex twice a week probably fed that."

"I'm sure it did. As important a purpose as it serves, it appears to have led me into dangerous territory."

Peter glanced up. "So what's the answer?" he asked. "No more women for the two of us?"

James had been giving the idea much consideration. "I can't speak for you, but that's probably my answer."

Peter nodded, his eyes weary. "For me, too." He sighed. "I'm trying to hold on, but I don't know how much longer I've got."

Alarm raced through James. "Don't say that, Peter," he said. "We'll take care of this."

"I don't know what to do."

"Of course not—you're a doctor. Tracking criminals isn't your job. Your job is here. Full-time. But I'm still a prosecuting attorney. I have the means."

"And you've been using them."

"I've been using aboveboard means." James set down his cup, leaned toward his mentor. "And now I'll use ones that are more…creative and equally accessible."

"Illegal activities often bring about negative energies," Peter warned, his eyes serious.

"I've weighed the consequences and know in my heart that this is the right thing to do. Which in itself brings positive energies."

Silently Peter watched him. "So this will be done soon?" he asked, sounding like a needy child.

That need, the fact that Peter placed it in him, sealed James's decision. "It will be done."

"Will there be violence involved?"

"If the need arises, I will not hesitate to give that decree."

"You're a good man, James Silverman," Peter said, his face relaxing. "And you're doing the right thing."

"We both are," James said, smiling. Reaching over, he grasped Peter's shoulder. "We both are, Peter."

They were as angels, Peter and he, doing a work far greater than most mortals ever attempted.

Everything else paled in comparison.

Including the cost.

WHILE BURT FOLLOWED up with Foltz on Wednesday morning, Greg delivered groceries and a pre-paid cell phone—with clearly written instructions—to a deserted shack. If Joe was around he wasn't showing himself. Debating whether or not to try again later, Greg left the packages by the door. He didn't want to push the hermit.

Back at the office, he dealt with a staff issue, approved some budgets and signed off a completed community service order being served by Thelma Hopkins for attempting to lure a man from the Valley Diner to her apartment for a one-hundred-dollar hour of entertainment. By mid-morning, with all immediate business out of the way, he called Burt's office, only to find that the deputy was still out.

Greg was a little surprised at the relief washing over him as he hung up the phone. Had he really had doubts that his deputy would give the matter as much attention as Greg knew it deserved?

"Unit 1 to dispatch," Greg said, forty-five minutes later as he drove through downtown Shelter Valley.

"Dispatch, go ahead."

"I'm going to be off radio." He raised his voice enough for it to travel clearly. "If I'm needed, use my cell."

"Roger, Unit 1."

Greg turned off Main Street toward the mountain, thankful once again for everything Shelter Valley had to offer—small-town life, yet cultural and educational opportunities, too. Enough to keep enough of its young people from moving on. Made his job a hell of a lot easier sometimes—like now.

True, not everyone Greg had gone to high school with was still in town. Few of the teenaged party gang had hung around. Shelter Valley's small-town restrictions—as they'd seen them—had been responsible for the parties to begin with.

But Len Wagner was there. He'd played football at Montford and then for the Phoenix Cardinals—maintaining a decent five-year career in spite of the losing team. And then, when a big offer came that would take him to the East Coast, he'd surprised the world by retiring to marry a Shelter Valley High School teacher, three years older than himself, settling down and starting a family. Len had kids at the elementary school and at Little Spirits, as well. He also had interests in several lucrative business ventures and was one of Shelter Valley's most generous contributors. In his spare time he traveled all over the world fulfilling various philanthropic duties for the many boards he sat on.

Len Wagner was a changed man from the rebellious, daredevil teenager Greg had known.

On this Wednesday morning, he was at home in Shelter Valley with a sick first-grader.

"Kaylee's had a sore throat for over a week," Len told Greg, inviting him in for a cup of coffee. The Wagners' home was just down the mountain, a quarter of a mile from Will and Becca Parsons' place. Greg had never been to either home, but had heard from his sister that he'd be receiving an invitation to a holiday party at the Parsons. If he did, he was hoping to talk Beth into going with him.

Wagner's kitchen was as big as all three bedrooms in Greg's house combined. And the ex-football player seemed quite at home in the kitchen as he ground coffee beans and turned on the espresso machine—in spite of the huge hands that dwarfed the little measuring utensils he was using.

"You cook, too, Len?" Greg asked with a grin. Who would've thought, twenty years before, that the most hard-ass, irresponsible partier of them all would turn out to be a Mr. Mom.

It had been rumored during their junior and senior years that Len spent more time out at Rabbit Rock than he did at home. Greg was hoping the rumors were true.

"I can cook if I have to," Len said. "But Peggy loves to do it and I don't. Match made in heaven." He smiled with complete contentment.

Because of that smile, Greg had to ask, "You really mean that, don't you?"

"Yep." His once-rebellious acquaintance didn't even pretend to be manly in that tough-guy way he used to affect. These days he wasn't ashamed to let the world know about his softer side.

For a second there, listening to Len openly confess his love, Greg envied the guy.

"So, what'd you need to see me about?" Len asked moments later as the two men sat at a huge butcher-block table in Len's kitchen. "The county need some money, Sheriff? You know you didn't need to make a trip all the way out here for that. A phone call would've done it."

Greg sat forward, his gun a familiar weight against his thigh. He had to go carefully here. He couldn't be sure of what Len knew—or even if what he *did* know could implicate him or someone else who wouldn't take kindly to the involvement. He figured, too, that Len wasn't going to mess up everything he had going here.

"I need some help, Len," he said.

The blond man shrugged his broad shoulders. "Sure," he said. "I'll do what I can." And then, setting down the mug he'd been about to sip from, he murmured, "Official help?"

Hands around his own mug on the table, Greg nodded. "Tell me what you know about Rabbit Rock."

Len frowned. "You want to talk about Rabbit Rock?"

Greg nodded again.

"That's not exactly the kind of help I expected you to need."

Rolling up the sleeves of his uniform, Greg sat back, one forearm resting on the table. "It's important, Len."

"I figured as much," the ex-linebacker said. "Or else you wouldn't be coming to me."

"So what can you tell me?"

"I wasted two years there, made the biggest mistakes of my life, and am damn lucky I didn't die there, too."

Tensing, Greg forced himself to maintain his casual position. "From the partying?" Or was there more? Things he didn't want to know about Len? He needed information. But seeing Len such a changed man, in his beautiful home, caring for his sick kid, Greg sure as hell didn't want to be the one who sent it all crashing down around him.

"I suppose you could blame all the times I took my life in my hands on the partying."

Eyes narrowed, Greg asked, "How did you risk your life? What did you do?"

"Jumping off cliffs because I thought I could fly.

Fishtailing my rig so close to the edge of the cliff it should have flown. Filling my body with so many chemicals I didn't know who or what I was. Having sex with so many people I couldn't even begin to tell you who they were." Len paused, his somber expression the antithesis of his earlier smiles. "You can stop me anytime."

Greg tapped the side of his thumb against the table. "Was there anything else going on up there, besides the partying?"

Len glanced away. "Maybe. Why?"

"I have some pretty conclusive evidence that says someone's been driving cars into Rabbit Rock."

Len paled. "Again?"

Buzzing with adrenaline, Greg sat forward as he held the other man's gaze. "What do you mean *again?*"

Shrugging, Len looked directly into his eyes. "Years ago Culver came asking if I knew of any Phoenix kids who were hanging around out in Kachina County," he said. "I guess maybe you didn't hear about the whole mess, since it was just about the time your dad got hurt."

"You told Culver." Greg's entire body froze.

"Yeah." Len nodded. "I wasn't partying up at the Rock anymore, but I knew some of the punks who were, kid brothers of old friends."

Greg was going to forget about Culver for the moment. "And they were driving cars into Rabbit Rock?"

"Hell, no. They were damn pissed about the whole thing. Some street gang from Phoenix had taken over the place and pretty much told them that if they showed their faces there again, they were as good as dead."

A street gang.

"What gang?"

"The Bloodhounds. I told Culver about them. And I was told they disbanded not too long after that."

Which might explain why Greg had never heard of them.

Mind spinning, he asked, "So, if your friends stayed away, how do you know about the car thing?"

"Come on, Greg, think back. Do you think any of the stupid punks who went up to Rabbit Rock would walk away just because these bastards told them to?"

Of course he didn't. He knew what they would've done. "They went up the mountain and spied on them."

"Bingo."

"And watched them drive cars into the Rock?"

"Only once. I heard that after they saw what was going on, they decided the gang members were crazy enough to follow through on their death threats, and they found themselves a new place to party."

A street gang. Greg didn't like the sound of it. Any of it.

"You said Deputy Culver knew about the Bloodhounds?" It just didn't fit.

"I told him myself."

"You're sure it was Burt Culver?"

"Positive, man," Len's voice was dry. "He'd just picked me up for DUI a couple of months before."

Greg stood to excuse himself almost immediately. He had to get out, to think.

To make sense of this chaos, this confusion.

"I hear you're still living in that house of yours all alone, buddy," Len said, walking him to the door.

Preoccupied, Greg nodded.

"I've still got some connections," the big man said, grinning, as he patted Greg on the shoulder. "More beautiful women than you'd know what to do with. Just one phone call is all it'd take…."

"Thanks," Greg said. Any other time he'd have left it at that. Today, though, because the world had apparently spun off its axis and nothing was predictable anymore, he added, "But I've already found the woman who's going to move in." He clung to that thought. Something to hold on to. To believe in.

"Do I know her?" Len's grin had widened.

"Nope," Greg said, already regretting the words. "And she doesn't know she's marrying me yet, so keep this one to yourself…."

IT WAS A TOSS-UP—who should he see first? Greg drove around town, inventing reasons for Culver to keep Len's information from him—and passing by the houses of various people he knew were clients of Beth's, looking for her car parked outside.

He found it outside the Sheffields' three-bedroom bungalow.

"Greg?" The toilet brush in her hand didn't make the expression on her face seem any less frightened, any less hunted.

"Nothing's wrong," he said, used to the drill by now, even if he wasn't really any closer to understanding the reason for it.

"You don't *look* like nothing's wrong."

The alarm in her eyes gave way to compassion. And he knew why he'd come.

"How long till you're finished here?"

"Another half hour. I still have to finish the master bath and vacuum the bedrooms."

"I'll vacuum."

"Absolutely not," she said, but stepped back as he came in the door.

She looked adorable in her black sweats and white sweatshirt, her auburn hair up in the usual ponytail.

"You aren't going to vacuum this house!"

"Sure I am. You'll be finished sooner." And he really needed that.

"You're in uniform!"

"It's seen a whole lot worse than lint on carpet."

Beth shook her head. "Greg—"

"Beth," he interrupted, slowing himself down with effort. "I really need to talk to you and I don't have a lot of time. Please, may I help you finish here so we can have a few minutes?"

After one long searching look, she nodded and silently led him to the back of the house.

That was when Greg knew for sure he'd met the woman he wanted to have living in his house.

"I'VE KNOWN CULVER most of my life," Greg told Beth half an hour later as they sat together in his squad car parked just outside town. "I know there's got to be an explanation. I just can't figure out what it is. And I can't go to see him with my head full of doubts."

Her eyes were serious. "Maybe the doubts need to be there."

He couldn't accept that. "After all my years in law enforcement, I know there are very few things you can believe in, very few things you can count on. But loyalty to and from those closest to you is one of those things."

This was a tough one for him, something he struggled with. Trusting. Having faith in people. Shelby's defection—the way she'd just left without any warning after a lifetime of building trust, of loving—had robbed him of so many years, had rendered him incapable of developing a close relationship with anyone else. He wasn't going to let it taint him for the rest of his life.

"Just look at the facts, Greg. Burt missed Rabbit Rock. He missed the hermit. He's the only one talking with Sheriff Foltz, and there's nothing to say that he's giving you all the information he's getting. And now this…"

"Burt Culver knew my father. Hell, he was one of our most frequent visitors during those last years. He used to come over and talk with my dad for hours. Never gave the old man a hint that the conversation wasn't perfectly normal. Never lost patience with the repetition." Greg's mind was made up. "This is not a man who would've hidden evidence from me. Especially evidence involving my father."

"Unless they were guilt visits."

Fighting back a surge of anger, Greg tried to listen with an open mind. After all, he'd asked Beth to help him sort this out. He was too close to the situation; he knew that. And then he shook his head.

"He and my dad were golf buddies from way back. Culver's visits didn't just start when my dad got hurt."

"Okay," Beth said, hands crossed demurely in her lap. "Maybe something was driving him to act completely out of character when he withheld that information. You have no idea what circumstances prompted any of this. Maybe there's something here that involves a member of Burt's family. A person acting out of character normally does so to protect what matters most to him."

"Burt doesn't have any family."

"Then, what really matters to him?"

"His job." And there was no way Burt would jeopardize that. Not ever.

He couldn't even guess why Burt would've kept Len's information from him, but talking with Beth had allowed him to straighten out his own thoughts. One thing had become very clear. Knowing Burt's reason wasn't even important; Greg already felt sure it would be an acceptable one. Because he knew Burt Culver. Had faith in his deputy. Trusted him. And what, after all, was faith if a man didn't keep it in the face of difficulties? If he only believed when belief was easy?

It was nothing.

And without faith, life was nothing.

Greg had faith in Burt Culver.

And that was that.

CHAPTER FOURTEEN

"HE LOOKED ME straight in the eye and lied to me," Greg said, his expression hard as he stood, still in his uniform, by her front door later that same night. The look on his face, the acute effect Culver's dishonesty was having on him, struck Beth with fear. There was none of the compassion she'd come to associate with him. She realized something about Greg Richards: he did not tolerate liars.

Heart heavy with dread, Beth tried to maintain her equilibrium. Tried not to panic over something that had nothing to do with her.

"Please come in and sit down," she said. She'd already said it once, when he'd first arrived. He was intimidating in his uniform, so tall—and justifiably indignant.

He led the way over to the sofa. He even sat down. But then he stood up again, his hands shoved deep in his pockets as he paced.

Beth felt at a definite disadvantage, still wearing sweats she'd worn earlier in the afternoon. Ryan had been unusually difficult that night, and he'd kept her running from the time they got home until he'd dropped off to sleep just half an hour ago.

She'd thought longingly of a shower. But she'd known she should do her bookkeeping before she was too exhausted to keep the numbers straight. Paperwork was spread all over the small desk at one end of the living room.

Should she stand there, toe to toe with Greg? Or sit down and pretend she wasn't affected by his imposing stature? She sat. In the rocking chair that gave her a sense of security.

"What did Burt say?" she asked, because she wanted to help Greg. She didn't want to hear about Burt. She'd been ready to see the man exposed only hours before, and now was filled with this odd need to defend him.

As though his fate and hers were somehow tied together.

Greg was staring at her, but his gaze was vacant. She had a feeling he was replaying, word for word, his afternoon meeting with Burt Culver.

She wished this wasn't happening. Wished she didn't have so much at stake.

That she didn't care so much for Greg.

Or hate herself so much for deceiving him.

Beth lost her mental battle—she feared that the anger he was now directing toward Burt Culver would one day be directed at her. She and Burt were both liars.

And Greg's reaction to one could apply equally to the other.

She'd been furious when she'd thought of Burt double-crossing Greg. Because she'd been thinking only of Greg. Her vision had changed since that afternoon. To include Burt. And herself.

Shaking his head suddenly, Greg shrugged. "What did you just ask me?"

"What Burt said." Even if she wasn't sure she wanted to know…

"Not much. It didn't really get that far."

She frowned. "What do you mean?"

"I asked him if he remembered Len Wagner." Greg's expression was steely. Had there been any sign of emotion—even disillusionment—she'd have taken hope.

Greg started to pace, over to the window, around her paper-covered desk.

That paperwork made her nervous. There was no way Greg could know what she'd been doing—that every month she figured how much she'd owe in taxes and put that money away at the bottom of her towel drawer.

No way for him to tell, just by looking at the stuff on her desk, that she paid all her bills in cash—that she had no bank accounts.

But Greg was the sheriff. And a damn good cop. He could see things no one else even knew were there.

Like rabbit shapes in the front ends of smashed cars.

"I wasn't asking any leading questions," Greg said. Clearly the day's events were hard for him to accept.

"There was no thought in my mind of testing him or trapping him. I asked the question casually, as a way to open the conversation."

Her neck stiff from looking up at him, Beth guessed what had happened. "Burt said he'd never met Len."

Greg nodded.

"So maybe he forgot. It was ten years ago. Do you remember the name and face of every single person you've questioned over the past ten years?"

"Of course not."

"Well, there you go, then," she said, feeling a little more in control.

"Len Wagner holds an NFL record for yards run in a

single season," Greg said, his voice devoid of emotion. "Culver's second love, next to police work, is football. He'd remember if he was ever in the same room with Len, let alone questioned him."

"But Len wasn't famous then, was he?"

"He hadn't set the record yet, but he'd been signed by the Cardinals."

Okay, Culver had secrets. But sometimes good people did, for any number of reasons. Beth hated how quick she'd been to condemn Burt Culver only hours before. What kind of person did that make her? She'd been so heartless—so unforgiving—until she'd pictured herself in the same place.

She felt a little sick.

"What explanation did he give when you told him you knew he'd questioned Wagner?"

"He didn't."

"He just said nothing?" Beth couldn't imagine being able to stand up to Greg that way. Not unless something was life-or-death important.

Greg dropped to the edge of the couch, running a hand wearily through his dark curls. "I didn't tell him I'd talked to Len," he said, the first note of uncertainty creeping into his voice. "Since I have no idea why he's lying, I can't trust him with my progress on this case. I have a better chance of finding the missing pieces if he isn't going around hiding them from me."

"Wouldn't he already have hidden whatever evidence he could?"

"Not until he has to," Greg said. When he glanced over at her, Beth felt the prickling of tears. The steely look was gone. She almost wished it back. The disillusionment in Greg's eyes, the draining away of all the strength and confidence that made him Greg, was heartbreaking.

She could hate Culver for doing this to him.

But then she'd have to hate herself, as well.

"The more Culver tampers with things, the greater the likelihood that I'll catch him at it. Those photos that were mysteriously damaged, for instance. It was a risky move, but one I now suspect he was behind. I was getting too close."

"What do you think is going on?"

"I can't even guess," he said, his head leaning against the back of the couch.

She'd never seen him so exhausted.

"But you can rest assured I'll find out."

Beth did not doubt it for a second.

Which made him a dangerous companion for some-one with secrets… Someone like her.

"Come here," he said softly.

Heart pounding, Beth stared at him. He held out his arms to her. "Please?"

It was the undisguised need in his voice that she couldn't resist. Beth had no idea if she gave her heart lightly. Frequently. Or if she'd never fully given it be-fore. She knew only the here and now, and that she'd rather hurt herself than Greg.

She felt an overwhelming helplessness at the knowl-edge that hurting him was something she might not be able to avoid. Some things were completely out of her control.

And Ryan came first. That was the one constant in her life.

"Please?" he asked again.

There were some things within her control, too.

Trembling, Beth stood and went to him. If sex had been all he was asking for, she could have refused—for his sake as well as her own. But tonight Greg needed comforting.

Without a word he closed his arms around her, pulling her so tight against him she could hardly breathe.

"I'm sorry," she whispered, her lips against his throat. Sorry for whatever Burt Culver was up to. And sorrier still for the things she couldn't tell him.

She felt terrible guilt about that. But worse, she felt terrible fear of what she didn't know. Of whatever Greg might find out if she told him the truth, of what he might have to do with that knowledge. To her. And to Ryan.

His arms tightened briefly. Then his touch changed, lightened. He was cradling her, holding her, not hugging her. She could feel his heart beating beneath the palm she had on his chest. Felt the beat grow heavier. Faster.

She knew what that meant.

It was no surprise when his lips came down over hers, possessing hers. His kiss was not tentative. Or searching. It was the kiss of a man who desired the woman he held. Desired her deeply.

Beth desired him, too. Just as deeply.

Opening her mouth, Beth not only gave Greg everything he asked, she participated in the exploration. She'd been starving herself, denying every single personal need she'd had for so long, she just couldn't do it anymore. Not when allowing herself to need Greg was helping him, too.

She ran her hands over his shoulders, the cool cotton of his uniform shirt like a soft sheet beneath her fingers. She knew that whatever life asked of her from here on out, she'd always be thankful she'd known these moments. A perfect merging of body and mind. No, not mind so much as *feeling*.

Her unrestrained fingers wove themselves through his hair, satisfaction shooting through her as the strands curled around her fingers, almost as though they were holding her there, a part of him.

"Do you have any idea how good that feels?" he groaned, burying his face in her neck.

Beth didn't say anything. She couldn't. She just felt. And allowed those feelings to carry her...

He needed her touch. Needed reassurance in a world gone crazy with broken promises and broken rules. She knew he wanted to lose himself in the flames that had been smoldering between them for months.

God help her, Beth needed that, too. She was living on the edge. Her time could be up any day. She was fighting for the strength to endure, to shoulder her burdens and make the right decisions.

She needed him as badly as he needed her.

His hands skimmed her sides, touching her breasts, moving over her ribs, her waist, down to her hips, pulling her against the rock-hard length beneath the zipper of his slacks.

Still fully clothed, Beth unfastened the top button of his uniform shirt. Driven by an almost panicked urgency, she didn't listen to the voice of reason, or of caution. She didn't listen to any voices at all. She just kept unbuttoning as quickly as her trembling fingers could manage, revealing his muscular chest, and when she'd unfastened enough buttons, she pulled the shirt open, discovering his tight little nipples, dipping her head to run her tongue over them.

Greg groaned, tightening his hold on her hips, increasing her desperation. And then he relaxed his hands.

"If you don't stop that, I'm not going to be able to stop at all."

His voice was so husky she hardly recognized it. Beth wanted to pretend she hadn't heard him. To just kiss her way down his body and not be accountable at all. But no matter how intense her passion, she wasn't made that way. Couldn't be so irresponsible.

She also couldn't bear the thought of his leaving there tonight without making love to her first. As life in Shelter Valley continued and nothing happened—she wasn't finding herself or being found—she felt more and more uncertain, as though each day was a gift and she couldn't count on the next. She was consumed by the fear that if she didn't take this chance, she'd never have the opportunity again.

She lifted her head from his chest, then slid down between his legs until her knees touched the floor. She met his gaze directly. The desire she read there, the fact that he wasn't even attempting to bank it, had her belly spiraling with heat even as she attempted to calm herself, to think straight.

"I want to make love to you."

His words made it hard for her to think at all. "Nothing's changed." She wasn't even sure what the words meant. Only that she had to say them. "I can't make any promises beyond this moment."

He surveyed her silently for longer than she thought she could stand. Yet, because of her hope that the night might not be ending, she withstood the scrutiny.

"Can't make promises because you *can't?* Or because you don't want to?"

"Because I can't." It was painful to look at him. The thought of looking away was unbearable.

"But you want to."

"I want to be able to."

He nodded, looking like the sheriff hero of some western film, as he lay there sprawled on her cheap used couch with his shirt undone and that holster still hanging by his side.

"It's more than just sex," he said.

"Far more." Beth couldn't believe how great it felt to have something about which she could be totally honest.

"I'm a fool to let you do this to me," he said, his voice seductive. He pulled her up. Kissed her gently. "To accept your secrets…"

Beth kissed him back. Shivered when he ran his tongue along her lips. "There are so many things I don't understand," she said, acutely feeling the pain—and the ecstasy—of loving him. "But I can promise you that as soon as I do, you'll be the first to know." It was a promise she meant to keep. No matter what.

"Why—" he kissed her "—can't you—" he kissed her again "—let me help you understand them?" He asked the question, but prevented her from answering with a kiss that took away any chance she had of regaining control.

Beth Allen, or whoever she was, was about to have sex for the first time since she'd come into being.

GREG KNEW DAMN well he shouldn't do this. Even as he kissed Beth, kissed her and made himself senseless, he couldn't escape the foreboding sense of wrong. Wrong timing. Wrong circumstances.

But not wrong woman.

That was what drove him. Beth *was* the right woman
for him. He had control over so little where she was
concerned. Certainly not her and—as he'd just begun
to realize—not himself, either. His heart had given itself away in spite of his repeated warnings.

If he could at least have this, the most intimate communication there was between two people, if he could
feel they'd shared something that was for the two of
them alone, he would have one certainty to hold on to.

He stripped her slowly, reaching beneath her shirt
to undo her bra, pulling it off through the sleeve of her
sweatshirt. As their eyes met and held, his hands cupped
her breasts through the shirt.

"You have the most perfectly shaped breasts," he
whispered, and welcomed the ache in his groin when
her eyes darkened.

Lifting her shirt, he exposed her womanliness. His
entire body was heavy with desire as he gazed at the
white skin contrasted with the dark nipples that tightened while he watched.

"You don't have a bedroom where we can shut the
door." That had just occurred to him when he'd realized that what he wanted to do next was pull that shirt
right off her. "Ryan's way too young to get this kind
of education."

"It's okay." She cleared her throat but her next words
were just as husky. "He can't climb out of his crib yet.
If he wakes up, he'll call out to me."

Greg did not even recognize the man who stripped
off Beth's clothes and his own, then donned a condom
without any finesse at all. He was taken off guard by
the energy that coursed through him so strongly. Despite that, he could slow down, caress her gently, bring

her to the same point as he. Lying back on the couch, he lifted her up.

Then he lowered her immediately, sheathing his aching penis inside her. He had to stop for a second, not just because she was so tight and he didn't want to hurt her, not even because she was so tight and he didn't want to come immediately, but because she felt so incredibly *good*. He needed to savor that moment. To remember it always. To know how glorious it felt to be part of her, and she of him.

Beth groaned, fell forward until she was lying on his chest, planting her breasts against him, and began to rock. She loved him confidently, sliding along him with exquisite slowness, then knowing just when to move harder, faster, and when to use slow, seductive strokes.

I love you. The words repeated themselves over and over in his mind. She raised her upper body, and Greg suckled her nipple, briefly afraid that he'd said them aloud.

She was seductress and nurturer all at once, and he couldn't get enough. Couldn't possess enough of her or give enough of himself. He felt the orgasm coming and tried desperately to hang on. He didn't want this experience to end. Didn't want to return to the real world—a place where he didn't share her life.

And then he felt her tightening around him, her body pulsating with the power of release, and he spilled himself inside her, the spasms coming over and over again. In his mind there were shouts of incredible bliss, a brilliance beyond anything he could imagine, an awareness that he was someplace he'd never been before.

The end was different, too. Instead of deflation settling in, leaving him tired and ready for sleep, a serene joy spread through him. It gave him a sense of great peace. *I love you,* his mind said. Over and over. *I love you, Beth.*

And in that moment of grand awareness, he was almost able to pretend that she loved him back.

BETH CRAWLED INTO bed sometime in the small hours of the morning. Her body was sore in places she'd hardly noticed before, and that made her feel fully alive for the first time since Beth Allen had come into existence. Her skin, her nerves, were tingling with an awareness of what she'd just done. She felt healthier. Stronger. Calmer. And strangely, like she'd just done something she'd been commanded to do.

Suddenly shaking, cold sweat breaking out while the skin of her face burned so hot it was scaring her, Beth sat straight up.

Commanded to do?

What an odd thought to have. An incredibly frightening thought, somehow. Where had it come from?

Why did it feel so real? As though having sex because she'd been *told* to was a natural part of her life?

Who would have commanded her to have sex? And why?

God forbid, had she been a prostitute? Had it been her pimp who'd beaten her up? Was he the person she'd been running from? Trying to save her son from being part of such a sordid life?

Squeezing her eyes shut, she tried to return to the state of mind she'd been in seconds before, when the commandment thought had slipped out. She tried to recapture anything at all that might have been there. To get even a single clue to the truth.

And found nothing.

Great big damn nothing.

"I hate you," she whispered to the woman she'd once been, as tears dripped from her eyelids. "I hate you so much."

But whoever was hiding inside her didn't respond. That person remained numb and uncaring.

She eventually lay back down, automatically using relaxation techniques, and eventually drifted off to sleep.

If she had any dreams, she didn't remember them in the morning.

CHAPTER FIFTEEN

PUTTING PUZZLES TOGETHER might be a pastime for some. For Greg it was, in every sense, a vocation. Standing over the card table in his office, he studied the thousand pieces of a jigsaw rendition of cops' badges Katie had given him for his birthday a couple of months before. Bonnie had special-ordered it from a puzzle club she'd joined just for the purpose of keeping Greg challenged. Shaped like a badge, with no clearly defined edge pieces, it'd been a hell of a thing to get started.

The going was faster now that he was three-quarters of the way done.

Greg found the piece he'd spent at least an hour searching for—if he added up all the moments like this one, when he wandered over from his desk. A small piece, it had a rounded top and two interlocking notches. Its bottom left corner had the distinct darker silver that indicated it belonged to a badge on the right side of the puzzle.

Sliding the piece into place brought him great satisfaction.

With a few phone calls first thing that morning, he'd found it surprisingly easy to learn most of what he'd wanted to know about the Bloodhounds, the gang that, according to Len Wagner, had taken over Rabbit Rock ten years before. They'd been based out of Hohokom

High School, and while no charges had ever officially been brought against them, they'd had the reputation of being one of the roughest gangs in Phoenix. They'd been accused of drug dealing, robbery, even rape, although no decisive proof had ever materialized. Obviously their leader had been a professional. Knew what he was doing. And how to get away with it.

Then, ten years before, the gang had indeed disbanded, just as Len had reported. There'd been no record of any connection to car crimes in the gang's history. No police intervention, period, which made the whole disbanding appear odd.

As far as Greg was concerned, too odd.

He was looking for a piece with a pear-shaped prong. A light-silver tip. He picked one up.

Piece in hand, he strode across the tile floor to his desk. He had an old buddy from the Phoenix police department on the phone in ten seconds.

"Cliff, check something for me," he said without introduction or other social preamble.

"Sure, what've you got?"

"I need a list of possible members of a gang called the Bloodhounds. They reportedly disbanded about ten years ago."

"Ten-four."

Back at the puzzle, Greg put in his second piece of the morning. A good sign; his luck was changing.

Third piece in hand, he stopped to stare out the window. He knew he'd make headway on his father's case. The sky was more blue, the sun more vibrant.

Greg's heart was lighter than it had ever been.

He'd made love with Beth. She'd let him see her

naked. Touch her. Love her. She'd given herself to him in the most ultimate sense.

Life was good.

His phone rang. "I think I have what you're looking for." It had taken Cliff an hour.

"What?" He hadn't known for sure that he was looking for anything.

"Don't know how any of this connects, but one of my sources from Hohokom High tells me Colby Foltz was a member of the Bloodhounds at the time they disbanded."

Dropping the puzzle piece, Greg frowned. "Foltz?" he asked. "Any relation to Hugh?"

"Kid brother."

"Foltz never mentioned him."

"Didn't know him well," Cliff said. "Story goes that after her divorce, Mrs. Foltz moved to Phoenix with her youngest son. Hugh didn't see him much."

I'll be damned. Greg kept his breathing steady. "Thanks, man, I owe you one."

"Yeah, right," Cliff said. "In a million years maybe..."

Ignoring the puzzle piece on his desk, Greg hung up the phone and sat down.

A powerful street gang disbands for no apparent reason. A sheriff's younger brother is a member. There's a carjacking involving the father of one of that sheriff's deputies.

The sheriff's younger brother. A powerful street gang disbands.

Burt Culver, a man with no family, a man married to his job, a man whose superior was his closest friend.

A hermit who'd talked to the sheriff. An ex-football player who'd talked to Culver.

Dazed, Greg continued to sit at his desk. There were still some missing pieces. Like why a gang as professional and able as the Bloodhounds had resorted to carjacking. There were easier ways to make money. A lot more money...

And what kind of connection could there be between the current string of carjackings and a gang that had been disbanded for ten years?

How deep into this was Culver?

All were questions that needed answers. But at this point they were merely inconveniences, not problems.

Greg had the important answers. Before this day was out, he was going to be well on his way to avenging the senseless waste of his father's life.

He had to call Beth. And Bonnie. To let out a victory cheer.

Except that following too closely on its heels was a howl of anger. The pain of betrayal made a far greater impact than the satisfaction of victory.

He had to get Burt Culver off the streets.

And pay a visit to his mentor and predecessor, Hugh Foltz—a man he'd spent most of life admiring. A man who'd covered up the crime that had killed Greg's father.

And Culver—all those times he'd come to see Dad. Sat in his house, ate at his table...

Insides shaking with dangerous emotion, Greg made himself stay at his desk, weighing the facts, formulating a logical plan of action. The weight of the holster on his hip was a reminder of who he was. What he could and could not—would and would not—do.

Perhaps another puzzle piece or two was his best choice for a first move. Picking up the piece he'd dropped, Greg still didn't get up. His heart wasn't in the completion of a jigsaw puzzle. His mind raged too fast to allow for the quiet contemplation that accompanied puzzle building.

Instead of adding another piece to the badge puzzle, Greg stared sightlessly at the small stack of mail lying on his desk. A missing person postcard was on top; he recognized the familiar layout.

He got them all the time. They were part of a national program and had nothing to do with him or his job. They were sent biweekly to all Arizona mailing addresses in the hope that someone, somewhere, might recognize the person in the picture. Nine times out of ten they depicted children, and most often the disappearances involved known abductions, frequently due to custody disputes.

Out of habit, and because he was still too filled with energy to make his next move, Greg picked up the card and looked at it. Chances were slim that he'd ever be instrumental in finding any of these poor children, or in the arrest of someone vile enough to steal a child from home, but he looked diligently. Every two weeks. Every time the card came.

Just in case.

Leaning back in his chair, he studied the statistics first. *Brian Silverman.* There was a birth date and the date he'd disappeared. The boy was not quite two years old. Had been gone for more than eight months. He had curly blond hair. Blue eyes. Was missing from Houston, Texas.

He'd last been seen with Beth Silverman. His mother, presumably.

Beth. God, Greg needed to talk to his Beth.

This woman was thirty-four years old. Had blond hair and blue eyes. Was last seen in Houston, Texas.

As he always did, Greg looked at the pictures last. His mind suddenly numb, he looked again. The hair color was different.

He should never have had breakfast. The pancake syrup was not sitting well in his stomach.

Greg put the card down. His hands weren't shaking, he decided. He'd probably just thought they were because he was a little disoriented from the news about his father. And Culver. And Foltz.

Really, he was fine.

Just to prove it, Greg picked up the postcard again. Gave it a glance.

It fell to the floor as he made a run for the bathroom.

His breakfast was horrible the second time around.

"MERRILY WE ROLL ALONG, roll along, roll along," Beth sang under her breath as she pushed the vacuum cleaner back and forth across the floor of the Mathers' master bedroom. In deference to the unusually warm day, she was wearing a T-shirt with her cutoff navy sweatpants. The navy-and-white designer emblem across the front of the shirt made the ensemble a toss-up between a cleaning uniform and a fashion statement. What Beth liked most was the five dollars the duo had cost her at a close-out sale.

Close-out sales. And clean toilets. Ryan to pick up in half an hour. Greg naked. Beth's thoughts, running along only pleasant lines as she finished her last job of the day, entertained her. She hummed more of the song she'd been singing, since she couldn't recall any more words.

She thought she heard the doorbell.

Turning off the vacuum cleaner, she listened.

Yes. The doorbell rang again.

Hurrying to answer it, hoping—rather pointlessly, she knew—that it was Greg, she pulled open the heavy wooden front door with more energy than usual. She'd done everything with more energy than usual that day.

"Greg!" she said, thrilled that her wayward wish had been answered. She could get used to this very quickly.

"How long until you're finished?" he asked.

"A few minutes," Beth reported, feeling pleased. And then she really looked at him. Past the smiling lips and cordial eyes, to the man she knew.

Something was wrong.

Of course. *Burt.* Greg had found out something.

"I'll just be another five minutes and then I'll need time to load up my gear."

"I'll be in my truck."

He was still dressed in his uniform, but driving his personal vehicle. In the middle of the afternoon. That was odd. Greg always drove his squad car when he was on duty. The truck didn't have a radio.

Even odder, he didn't meet her eyes when she glanced back up at him.

Rushing, her need to get to Greg, to help him, comfort him, far greater than her usual need to pack everything in the order she'd determined was most efficient, Beth threw things together. She gathered everything and made her way to the car, toilet brush and broom sticking out from under one arm, a bucket overflowing with supplies suspended from that hand, her vacuum clutched in the other.

She slammed her trunk on the tools of her trade and locked the car, knowing it would be just fine parked out on the street, then hurried over to Greg's truck.

Staring straight ahead, shoulders stiff, jaw implacable, he didn't notice her coming. The passenger door was locked. He hit the button on his side, letting her in. He didn't come around to open her door. Didn't look at her as she climbed in.

"What's up?" she asked, hoping it wasn't as bad as it appeared. Her earlier good mood hadn't been strong to begin with, and the usual dread that was always so close at hand was already beginning to seep in.

Just once she wanted to be whole and able for Greg. Wanted to be there for him one-hundred percent, not busy dealing with her own problems. He'd done so much for her. Given her back so much of herself, if only in the form of the confidence she was gaining since he'd started to care so much about her.

Still without a word, without a look, he reached for a postcard on the seat beside him. Handed it to her.

Confused, Beth looked at it.

And couldn't move.

Couldn't breathe. Arrows were stabbing inside her skull. She had no idea where she was. What she was doing. She sat, head bent, simply reacting. Letting the unreality wash over her. Her heart beat far too fast, and she did nothing. Her skin was cold, clammy, yet her face burned. She didn't move, allowing the red haze to consume her vision.

"That's some secret you've been keeping."

The words were bitingly harsh. She wasn't sure what

they meant. Didn't recognize the voice saying them. Wasn't even sure they were directed at her.

"I don't know what part of this you found so hard to explain." The same bitter tone.

The words made little sense. Other than that, they were like little pellets, pummeling her at a time she wasn't equipped to handle them.

"Take me home," she said. Nothing mattered but that she get someplace safe.

On some level she was coherent enough to know that Ryan was safer where he was for the moment. And yet, she desperately needed to hold her son in her arms, needed him close.

This was an emergency. They might not have much time.

The engine started, the rumble a strange kind of comfort beneath her. At least she was going somewhere.

She didn't see the houses they passed, didn't notice the streets or the turns, didn't see a single person or sign. She saw nothing but that crumpled card in her fingers.

Fear escalated almost to the point of madness when the rumbling beneath her stopped. She waited for whatever was going to happen next.

Nothing did.

Beth looked up to see that she was parked outside her own duplex. For some reason she felt extremely relieved to be there. As though she'd been prepared to find herself somewhere else entirely.

"Thanks for the ride," she said very politely, inanely, and opened the truck door. Her exit might have been made cleanly if her knees hadn't given out on her as she attempted to jump down from the big truck. She caught herself with both hands on the seat, hitting her knuckles on the doorjamb.

The pain brought tears to her eyes. She welcomed the pain as something she recognized. Something she could concentrate on.

It gave her the strength to get herself to her door, find her key, put it in the lock. She saw no one, heard nothing. Just the key. In the lock. Open the door. Get inside.

The door didn't close behind her. It hit something big and solid.

The man who'd followed her in.

She might have screamed then. Might have broken into hysterical tears if she hadn't glanced up and seen the pain shining from eyes she'd grown to love. Eyes that had made such promises of love and safety the night before.

"I need some answers," Greg said. His voice was still that of a stranger.

A frightening, intimidating stranger. He was wearing a uniform. A gun. If he chose to detain her, take her away, she wouldn't be able to stop him.

Her eyes fell. Recognized the shape and width of those hands. This was the man who'd been naked in her arms.

She nodded. Turning unsteadily, Beth made her way into the living room. She wanted to sit in her rocker, but was afraid of the unsteady movement. She dropped to the old couch instead, bracing herself in a corner.

Afraid of Greg's reaction, she didn't look at that card again, although she wanted to. She desperately wanted to know what it said.

What it could tell her.

She was unsure what he was going to do to her.

Would he just arrest her and never speak to her again? Turn her over to some other authorities and never speak to her again? Take her son away and never speak to—

"I'm listening."

He was also standing. Too close. Telling her quite plainly who was in charge.

Beth opened her mouth, intending to say something. She realized he deserved answers. She wanted to give them to him.

She had nothing to say. She had to look at that card.

"Beth, now's not a good time to play me for a fool." The warning in his voice was more powerful than the words.

She was scared to death of him, yet she didn't fear he'd hurt her. Not physically. The danger he threatened was far worse than that.

"I've never played you for anything," she said. She tried to hold his gaze, but couldn't. She couldn't stand to see the stranger staring back at her.

"And you've never given me one damn answer, either," he said, jamming his hands in his pockets as he started to pace in front of her. "I'm giving you an opportunity to do so now. If you still refuse, you leave me with no choice but to take you in."

Did that mean there was a chance, even the slimmest of chances, that he might not?

She glanced at the card. Her name was still Beth. Odd, considering the circumstances, but she found a small bit of joy in that fact.

Beth Silverman. Fighting down panic, Beth found she still had no idea who that was.

"I woke up in a motel room a week before I came to Shelter Valley," she said.

She was thirty-four years old. That felt odd. A couple of years younger than she'd thought.

And her gaze landed on her son's precious face. *Brian Silverman*. Not Ryan at all. Tears pooled in her eyes, blinding her to the rest of his information for the second it took her to blink them away. And then, just before her eyes filled again, she saw his birth date.

"He's not even two yet," she whispered. Her baby boy had been barely a year old when she'd brought him here. Big for his age and much younger than she'd assumed. No wonder he couldn't talk! And potty-training him before he was two; it was ludicrous. Not fair at all to a little body that couldn't possibly be experiencing all the sensations he needed to, in order to be successful at that important venture.

"I'm running out of patience."

Stronger now, as though finally having possession of her son's birth date made all the difference, Beth looked up at Greg. Even through her tears she could see his jaw twitching with the effort it was taking him to be civil.

She held out the card to him. "This is what I know," she said. "It's all I know."

She was from Houston. She didn't feel any affiliation with the place at all.

"What do you mean it's all you know?" His tone was not getting any friendlier.

"Almost eight months ago, I woke up in a motel room in Snowflake, Arizona, with a splitting headache, a bad gash on my forehead and another one on the back of my skull. I had a bag that said 'Beth' on it, with some diaper essentials and a change of clothes for Ryan…." She couldn't think of him as anyone else. "An exercise outfit for myself and two thousand dollars in cash."

"Go on." He was still standing but had, at least, stopped pacing.

She shrugged, then met his gaze. "I had a baby with me who called me Mama. When I asked him what his name was, he just kept saying Ryan."

"From Brian?"

"I guess." She had a feeling he was always going to be Ryan to her.

"Then later, when I bathed him, I noticed a funny little V-shaped freckle mark on his knee. I have one, too."

Greg sat down, not next to her, but not on the other end of the couch, either. "So why were you there?"

The world was getting smaller again. Her vision was tinged with red.

"How did you get hurt?"

"I don't know." The words were a whisper.

Not only was she frightened to death at her lack of ability to help herself, her powerlessness, but she was also ashamed to admit the truth to him. What kind of a basket case ran away from herself?

"What do you mean you don't know?"

"I don't know," she said again, staring down at her hands. The gig was up. Unless...

Could she talk him into not turning her in? Could she get even one more night? Long enough to collect Ryan and run away?

Did she actually think she could hide from a lawman like Greg Richards?

"I don't remember anything." Finally, because she knew she had to, Beth looked over at him, saw the card in his hand. "Until you brought that, I didn't even know my own name, my son's age, where we were from. Nothing."

His eyes narrowed. "You're telling me you have amnesia."

Beth nodded, humiliated, scared, placing her life in hands she wasn't sure were ever going to be gentle with her again.

"I can't buy that."

"What?"

"You expect me to believe you don't remember anything about yourself?"

She nodded.

"Come on, Beth. It's not that I doubt amnesia happens, but I've been around you for months, and there hasn't been one sign of mental confusion. And it's not just me. It's Bonnie and her family, the people you clean for, everyone you've known in the more than eight months you've lived here. You'd have to be a pretty good actress to fool an entire town."

"It's the truth." And then, when the doubt in his eyes only grew more severe, Beth became desperate. It hadn't dawned on her that he wouldn't believe her. She'd expected him to be angry, yes. Do what he had to do, yes. But… "You *have* to believe me, Greg."

"You've done nothing but keep secrets from me since the beginning. And now, when I find out why, you come up with a story that's utterly fantastic. How can you possibly expect me to believe you?" he asked, his voice devoid of any of the warmth she'd come to depend on.

Because last night you made the most incredible love to me. Because I think I actually trust you. I need you. Because I love… "Because I'm telling the truth."

CHAPTER SIXTEEN

YEAH.

Sure she was telling the truth.

Another day, he might have believed her. Greg slumped back against the couch cushion, thankful in a highly ironic sense that he'd just found unquestionable proof that his deputy and his superior had betrayed him. That experience was going to save his butt now. He'd been such a lovesick kid with Beth, so willing to have faith and believe in something that he couldn't see or prove, that she'd probably be able to string him along even now, if not for his deputy's timely lesson.

And unlike Culver and Foltz, Beth had struck at the very foundation of his life. For one thing, harboring a criminal could've cost him his job. For another, she'd undermined his newfound ability to trust.

That auburn hair wasn't natural. He couldn't get over it.

A cover. Just like the amnesia was a cover. Smart, really, the way she'd kept her secrets. Made the whole thing almost plausible. And that much more damning. She'd obviously been planning this all along. She had her cover all ready in case she got caught before she got out.

He was sure he should be feeling something—anger

at the very least—but for now, he was going to go with the numbness that was all he seemed able to dredge up.

Surely she'd figured that she would be found out eventually. It was one of the first rules of conduct for people on the run. Always be ready, with no notice, to run again. To keep running.

He was lounging on her couch as though he had all day. Nothing to do. No crises to sort out. "It would've meant a lot if you'd been honest with me from the start."

"I was as honest as I knew how to be."

The intimacy in those warm blue eyes seared him. Just the night before, it had been as if God's angel had reached right down and touched him. His gaze roamed to the rocker behind her left shoulder. What was true and what was false?

"You aren't trying to tell me you didn't know you were betraying me?" he muttered.

He glanced over—and saw the bitter truth in her eyes before she closed them.

"I didn't think so."

"Greg."

There was such pleading in her voice that he could've been forgiven for feeling a twinge of caring. Of hope. Thankfully it wasn't a forgiveness he'd need to seek. Braced, he waited for her to continue.

"I know this is hard for you."

"It's not hard at all." He wasn't lying. He couldn't feel a thing. And he damn sure wasn't going to have her feeling sorry for him on top of everything else. He might have been taken for a fool, but he could handle it.

And recover.

With all parts still working fine.

"Please listen," she whispered.

"I heard every word you said," he told her in his best cop's voice. "And a lot you haven't."

"I know—" She bowed her head.

He could barely see her in his peripheral vision.

"—but I need you not just to hear but to really *listen* to what I have to tell you."

That was rich. Now that she was in trouble, she suddenly had things to tell him. Because the only difference between that moment and twelve hours before, when she'd lain naked beneath him right there on that couch, was the crumpled white card with the incriminating pictures.

He wanted to tell her that, but didn't see any point in dragging himself through the series of quickly fabricated lies that would follow.

"I'm scared to death, Greg," she said.

For a split second her raw emotion started to work on him. But only for a second. His armor had grown thicker than that. It would sustain him through this.

"For eight months now, that fear has been the only constant in my life."

No. He wasn't going to be sucked in. She was an expert at it.

If he wasn't so sickened by his own part in the whole thing, he'd probably admire her for those abilities.

"I have no idea who I am—why I was in that motel room—how I got hurt—who might be after me. Or worse, Ryan."

Greg studied his gun. He'd polished it early that morning, while he was waiting for people to get to work.

Of course, then, much of his extra energy had been a result of the incredible night he'd spent. The excitement he'd still been feeling. Yeah. Well...

"It was pretty obvious that I'd been in danger, enough so that I took my son in such a hurry that I didn't even grab my identification. I got cash from someplace and ran. But because I have no idea what that danger is, I can't fight it. I can't even be prepared for what I might have to run from, or what might be coming at me."

"Maybe you weren't running at all," Greg said, pretty sure his intent was to poke holes in her story. "Perhaps you'd just had your purse snatched, got roughed up in the process, but got away."

"I've considered that," Beth said slowly. "But then, why did I check into that motel under the name of Beth Allen if my name is really—" she paused, glancing down at the card lying between them "—Silverman," she finished. "And why would I have been carrying two thousand dollars in cash?"

Okay, so the purse-snatcher idea wasn't his best. He couldn't even imagine how horrifying it would've been for a young mother to wake up to the reality Beth said she'd found in that Snowflake motel. Or how strong that woman would have to be to cope all alone....

No. Greg shook his head. He wasn't going to let anyone make a fool of him again. He'd just come off a ten-year term. He wasn't doing it again.

Ever.

"Have you seen a doctor?"

"Of course not." She shook her head. "I'm in hiding."

That was convenient. "Like I said, Beth, amnesia happens, but not without symptoms and signs. I saw my father through years of therapy and I encountered more head-injury patients than I can count, so I have personal experience with these things. I just don't see how I can possibly believe you."

"By listening to your heart?"

He could tell she didn't really expect that to fly.

"You made one critical mistake," he told her now, in control of his faculties again. Fully numb once more.

"What?" she asked, turning, one leg on the couch as she faced him.

Her puzzled frown would have sold him on her innocence just a day earlier.

"I've gone over and over this so many times," she whispered, "it's all one big foggy mess to me. What did I miss?"

He wasn't going to play her game. Wasn't going to be a participant—a pawn—in whatever ugly scheme she might be creating.

Out of the blue, a mental picture of Beth up at Rabbit Rock flashed through his mind. The way she'd given everything she had to him that night, to comfort him, to help him fight his own demons. The way she'd understood...

No. He couldn't let himself go soft.

"Today," he said, a little less complacent. "You made the mistake today. Now. When I confronted you with the truth and you knew you'd been caught. If you'd just come clean, told me what this is really all about, I'd have done everything I could to help you."

Greg was barely aware that his voice had trailed off. That *was* all it would've taken. A plausible story. Hell, he'd been going along with her all these months, having faith in spite of her silence, understanding that she'd needed time. But he had to draw the line somewhere. There was a point when a man's belief wasn't a matter of faith but of *wanting* to have faith. It could make a fool of him.

With Culver and Foltz, he'd drawn the line in the wrong place. He couldn't do that again.

Not if he was ever going to trust his own judgment again.

"Even now you can't trust me with the truth," he said, regretting the words when he heard the emotion he hadn't meant to express.

He needed a drink. If this anesthetic ever wore off, he was going to hurt like hell. He should've taken time that morning to polish the leather of his holster, as well. Its scuffed surface wasn't doing much for the gun.

"That's just it, Greg," she said. He heard the tears in her voice but didn't look up to see if she was crying. "I *am* trusting you. For the first time in eight months, I'm able to trust my life, Ryan's life, to someone else."

God, that hurt. If only she'd said those words the night before... "Funny how that trust magically coincides with the very moment I discovered the truth on my own."

"It's not the truth."

She could've played it better if she'd injected a note of defensiveness into her voice rather than sounding like she was giving up so easily.

Greg picked up the postcard. Made himself study it. To remember the facts. "You're saying that this woman is not you? That the boy who's been missing for eight months isn't Ryan? That's not true?"

"No."

He was disappointed in her answer. As though, after all this, he'd still been holding on to some nebulous hope.

"Of course it's us," she said, leaning over to glance at the photos.

The expression on her face surprised him. She looked more hurt than anything else.

Yet *he* was the one who'd been lied to. Betrayed. Wasn't he?

"What's *not* true is that I knew who we were before today," she said quietly, sliding back to the corner of the couch, her arms wrapped around her chest. "I see now that I should have told you," she said. Again, her voice was resigned, not Beth-like. "And yet, what would've happened if I had? You'd have had to go looking for me and you'd have found out that I'd kidnapped my son and it would all be over."

She'd been fighting him since the first day they'd met, but suddenly there was no fight left.

And she should still be fighting him if she hoped to convince him not to turn her over to the FBI without so much as a goodbye to the baby boy she loved.

And she did love her son. There was no doubting that.

A mother didn't exist who loved her son more than Beth loved Ryan. Nor was there a mother who looked out for her baby's welfare more than Beth.

"Maybe I made a mistake, but I was doing the best I knew how," she said. "The best I was capable of doing. I have no idea why I'm running. And until I do, how can I possibly know how to proceed in any direction at all? How can I predict what kind of hell you might create?"

He wasn't used to going around creating hell for people, but okay.

"Think about it," she said. "I tell you—a cop, no less—and you start to investigate. You find out I've done something against the law and you're bound by your office to turn me in. Because I don't remember what happened, I can't even defend myself. I lose Ryan. I go to jail. And there's not a damn thing I can do about any of it."

He thought about that.

"Or what if I am in danger? What if whoever beat me up is itching to finish the job? To hurt Ryan? Your digging into things might alert someone. And before we even know *who* we're alerting, he's here. And it's too late."

That wouldn't have happened. He'd have protected her.

"I also went through a lot of times when I didn't want to know. Whatever I'm running from—not physically, but mentally, emotionally, inside me—must be pretty horrific if my mind's gone to such lengths to protect me against it. I spend a lot of time scared to death to find out what it is. What if, when I do, I still can't face it? What if I don't deal with it any better the second time around? What if I lose my mind and they lock me up in some nuthouse? How am I going to take care of Ryan?"

He remembered that night at the casino. The way she'd reacted to whatever had set her off.

If Greg's chest got any tighter, he was going to have go outside for some fresh air. Might not be a bad idea in any event.

She sure has a career in storytelling if cleaning toilets ever ceases to satisfy her.

That last thought was beneath him.

But how in the hell could he possibly know what was the truth? And how much of his reaction was simply a matter of Greg Richards, Mr. Nice Guy, being taken in again?

When would he learn? If the heartbreak with Shelby

had been like kindergarten in this life lesson, Culver
and Foltz were surely on the college level. So what was
he doing now? Going for a doctorate in how to have his
trust abused?

"Besides, how did I know I could trust you?" Beth
asked, startling him with a question too closely related
to his own thoughts. "I couldn't even trust myself."

In the past twenty-four hours he'd certainly learned
how *that* felt. "You might've thought of that before you
slept with me."

"I did." The simple words, emitted without hesitation, held a depth of emotion. "A lot. In the end, making
love with you was between you and me. It was personal. I could trust in that. But this is far bigger. This
is my son's life."

A pretty damn good reason to spin this incredible
tale.

She'd almost had him.

"So what was your plan?" he asked, more out of curiosity than anything else. And maybe to find out if she
could produce one.

Beth shrugged. "Nothing too fancy," she said. "Nothing really even too logical. For a lot of the time, I've
focused on just surviving."

Basic. But a good answer.

"I've been searching everywhere I could think of,
trying to find out whatever I could on my own."

He was impressed when she listed all the work she'd
done in the library, on the Internet. The hundreds of
hours she'd spent searching.

He could verify that she'd spent a lot of time at the
library.

Of course, she knew he knew that, so she could be

using this to convince him, when, in reality, she'd been doing something incriminating that entire time. Like working on whatever criminal activity she was involved with. Making contact with coconspirators. Perpetrating some kind of scam. Or creating permanent new identities for her and her son. Researching other places to run. Other jobs.

"I've also done a lot of studying on amnesia," she said softly. "My best guess is that this is hysterical retrograde amnesia. That means I could regain my memory at any time. And then I'd have my answers. I'd have the ammunition necessary to fight whatever battle awaits. I'd have a clue as to where and how to proceed."

Like he'd told himself many times in the past hour, it was a fantastic, incredible story. One he might even believe, if only...

"Why didn't you tell me this last night, Beth? You had the perfect opportunity."

"I had no idea what to say, no control over what you'd do with the information."

Her words were deadening his heart again. She'd been manipulating him, just as he'd feared.

"You're a cop, Greg. In some ways, the obligation that goes with the territory limits your choices."

"It also makes my ability to help you that much greater."

"Maybe."

He waited for her to say more. Needed her to say more, to offer him assurance, some kind of entrance into her most private thoughts. When she didn't, the armor surrounding him grew another degree heavier.

"Would you have told me today, now, anytime soon, if I hadn't found out?" Damn, it was almost as though he were begging her to give him enough rope… Inventing reasons he could still believe. Still justify this insane idea that faith wasn't faith unless it endured to the end.

"Probably not."

She'd cut the rope. He didn't fall nearly as far this time—it hardly hurt at all.

"So, the bottom line is, you didn't trust me enough to tell me."

Her eyes brimmed with sorrow as she held his gaze. "I guess—" She choked on the words.

"Then, how can you expect me to trust you?"

"I can't."

BETH WAS COLD. Her skin had goose bumps. Her fingers and toes and nose were freezing, as though she'd been outside in Maine during the dead of winter. But this chill was coming from inside.

She'd lost.

Maybe everything: A mysterious and frightening game for which she still had no definition or rules. Her one chance to know what real love could be. *Her son.*

Oh God. Ry. *What have I done to you, my precious baby?* Shivering, Beth sat up, forcing her mind to concentrate, considering only the next few moments. She couldn't think about Ryan and stay coherent. Not when losing him, losing the right even to see him, was so real—possibly imminent.

Over her dead body.

A strength of will she did not recognize passed through her, held her in its grasp. "I will give up my life before I let them have him," she said. And then frowned. As she sat there, she had no doubt whatsoever of the conviction in her words. She just had no idea where they'd come from.

"We're talking about Ryan?"

When she looked at Greg, it was almost as though he'd left and come back. She was seeing him differently.

The adversary? Or the negotiator? Was saying anything saying too much? She wasn't sure; she knew only that she had to tell him. "Yes."

"Who's them?" He sounded like a cop.

But a good one. A cop who cared about seeing the right thing done. Or was that just her own bias? Was she projecting upon Greg the things she needed to find in him?

She had to make a decision. Work with him. Or find a way to make things work in spite of him. Her time was up.

Beth took a long breath. Let it out slowly. Forced her mind to focus on only one thing. "I don't know," she said, taking the plunge. She wished she hadn't, when the shuttered expression darkened his face.

"I'm telling you the honest-to-God truth, Greg. Just now, I had a very deep and certain feeling that there's someone out there who's a danger to me and my son. Someone I'm protecting Ryan from. I don't know who. I'm assuming the 'where' is Houston, but I don't know that, either. I don't know why. I just know with complete conviction that I will die before I see him go back to *them*."

"There's more than one of them, then?"

"Yes," she said, surprised to be able to answer without hesitation. "I have no rational basis for knowing this, but I've never been more certain of anything."

"This isn't just a custody battle gone bad? It's not just Ryan's father you're running from?"

He still didn't believe her. He thought she knew more than she'd told him. But he'd called her son Ryan. That meant something.

"Maybe it is a custody battle," she said. "Perhaps one involving a powerful family or something."

The idea wasn't completely foreign to her. And yet, it didn't seem quite right, either.

His glance brooding, he sat there, an imposing figure in full uniform. He was the same man who'd made her feel so incredibly safe and secure—and loved—the night before. And yet...

Did he believe her, even a little? She couldn't tell. But she could only take his silence for so long.

She needed to get Ryan. To get out.

And how could she do that with the sheriff of Shelter Valley sitting in her living room?

She switched to the rocking chair. Dizzy now, as well as freezing, she was afraid she was going to be sick.

The red haze continued to come and go, a companion so frequent she almost didn't notice. Except for the horrible sense of helplessness that accompanied it.

If not for her son, she'd give in and let it just take her—and be done with it.

"What happens next?" she finally asked, when it appeared he might sit there forever. He'd shut himself off from her, leaving her no idea what he was thinking. What he was waiting for.

Or what he had planned for her.

She was so damn tired of being afraid. And yet, every corner of her mind was filled with terror. There was nothing else.

"I'm trying to decide that."

Her legs were shaking visibly. She couldn't stop them. "Are you going to call the FBI?" She had no idea how all that worked. Would she be spending the night in jail? What would they do with Ryan?

Light-headed, Beth began to rock, to concentrate on her breathing. To try to think. She had so damn little experience to draw on, to guide her.

Had she ever been in jail? Would she survive even one night there? Would she survive having Greg turn her in?

What would they do with Ryan?

Greg sat forward, elbows on spread knees, his hands lightly clasped between them. "Because there are some possible extenuating circumstances and because, as the sheriff of this town, it is my sworn duty to protect its citizens and because you are currently one of those citizens, I would like to do some more investigating before making any irrevocable decisions."

It was a mouthful. Spoken in a monotone. They could have been discussing a baseball game.

Beth continued to rock. To shake. "Okay."

She didn't know if she'd just been given a reprieve. Or a jail sentence. She just knew that, for the moment, she was out of choices.

CHAPTER SEVENTEEN

"I CAN'T LEAVE you here alone." Greg might have sounded embarrassed or apologetic. He didn't.

"Why not?" The question was out, and then the obvious answer hit her. "You don't trust me not to run."

"Can you assure me you won't?"

"No."

He nodded. "Wouldn't matter, anyway. You've already run once, which proves you're capable of doing it again. I would be remiss in my duties if I gave you the opportunity."

"So you're arresting me?" Where was the strength that had rescued her moments earlier?

Head slightly bent, he looked at her. "No. But I will if I have to."

This from the man who'd held her so tenderly less than twenty-four hours before.

Rock. Back, forth, back, forth. That was all she could do. Just rock.

"I don't suppose it would do any good to ask for a little more time?" He couldn't, in all conscience, give it to her; she understood that. She wasn't even sure what she'd do with it if she had it. What could she do that she hadn't already done? All of which had led her nowhere.

He didn't bother with an answer other than a long, serious stare. Heart pounding, she held her own, eyes focused on his. He was telling her something. She just wasn't sure what.

"I have a proposal to put to you," he said finally, breaking another lengthy silence. "Before I present it, I'd like you to bear in mind that this is not your only option."

Beth's throat was dry. She wasn't sure she was going to make it through the explanation without losing the contents of her stomach. The nausea had been steadily rising. If only she could wrap herself in the blanket that was folded neatly at the bottom of Ry's crib. Right where she'd left it when she'd made their beds that morning. Then she'd be okay. Maybe…

"This suggestion is based partially on the fact that I have no knowledge of what kind of enemy we might be fighting. As the possibility exists that you or your son could be in danger, I feel it would be best, initially at least, to conduct a quiet, unofficial investigation of Beth Silverman."

"Can you do that? Unofficially, I mean?"

He nodded. "I have connections. Favors to call in. I should be able to get information without alerting anyone that we're looking. That way, I can also get the background facts without giving any reason for needing them."

She liked that a lot. If only…

"But when you get the answers, you'll have to act on them." A sharp pain shot through her middle as she considered what that might entail.

"One way or another, yes." He nodded again.

He was doing a lot of that. Nodding. And very little looking at her. She was close to believing that she'd imagined the warm and wonderful feeling he'd so recently brought into her home—her heart.

She could believe she'd imagined one night. But she couldn't have concocted the past couple of months, could she?

Beth didn't think so. But then, her mind had a history of playing tricks on her.

HE WAS AN IDIOT. A complete and total fool.

But if he was going to fall, at least he'd go down true to himself. He would endure to the end. No matter how many times he listed the reasons he should have his finger on the dial that very moment, calling the FBI, he couldn't turn his back on Beth.

The thought of what could happen to her son—months in foster care, to start with—were also wreaking havoc on his repeated admonitions to wise up.

"Pack a bag for yourself and the boy." If he was going to get through this, he had to be businesslike.

The rocking stopped. She didn't get up. "Where are we going?"

"To my place." He'd already figured out it was the only way. "You and Ryan are moving in with me."

He'd never actually seen someone's jaw drop before.

"What will people think?" she asked while he stood there, waiting.

"That we're shacking up, of course." It was the only way.

Beth stood straight, met him eye to eye. "We can't do that," she said with more gumption than he thought he'd ever seen her show. "It's not like this is Houston, Greg. You know as well as I do that if we did something like that, everyone in Shelter Valley would know by nightfall."

"I'm counting on that."

"What?"

He took a strange satisfaction in seeing *her* with all the questions for once. And didn't feel a twinge of guilt, either.

Of course, he was trying hard not to feel much of anything.

"Look," he said, as coolly as he could, considering that he was doing exactly what he'd dreamed about— bringing the woman who belonged in his house home to live with him. "I cannot take you to jail, and I have to keep you someplace where I can be certain you won't run out on me. All the windows in my home have an alarm system that alerts me immediately if there's any tampering, and the doors have dead bolts that lock from the outside with a key."

She wasn't going anywhere.

And no one else would be getting in, either.

He wondered how often she had to color her hair— and Ryan's—to conceal the blond.

"Why can't you take me to jail?"

Why in hell couldn't she concentrate on the key-from-the-outside part? Dammit, he'd just told the woman he'd slept with, that she was now in essence his prisoner. Couldn't she at least yell at him about that?

Something had to make this job easier to execute.

"Because." He gave her question the succinct answer it deserved. The fact that it was also the only answer he had didn't matter.

"I still don't get why you'd do this to yourself, have the entire town talking about you. About us."

She was good. Playing the "concerned about him" card.

Or...she was the Beth he'd grown to love.

Either way, his answer was the same.

"Everyone knows we've been seeing each other," he told her, treading in dangerous waters. Dangerous to his determination not to feel. He was strangely reluctant, as well, to point out something that she apparently had not yet considered. "Because we have no idea of the enemy we might be up against, you're going to need all the protection I can muster," he said. "When everyone else in town sees their mail today, there are bound to be some questions. Sadly, most people don't pay attention to those cards, but the ones who do are going to be suspicious."

She paled, sank back to the rocker as the truth dawned on her. Clearly she'd given no thought to the seriousness of her current situation.

"They might not know you well, Beth, but they've known me all my life. They trust me. If I show them that you deserve our protection, not our condemnation, they will protect you without question. At least for a while. They would no more let anything happen to their sheriff, or anyone he loved, than they would to one of their own children."

"That's expecting an awful lot from people who don't even know me. To harbor me and Ryan with such...such conclusive evidence against me."

He wondered if she'd intended part of that comment for him.

"Anywhere else, and I'd agree with you," he said. "But not here. If I put out the word that there are extenuating circumstances and that people should hold tight, they will. They're bound to speculate among themselves, but they won't talk to strangers." And once he had her safely ensconced in his home, he wouldn't have to worry about the townspeople or what they thought.

He and Beth had other, more critical matters facing them.

Like the criminal charges he should probably be filing against her.

Ryan's future.

And the fact that if he was wrong about Beth, the people of Shelter Valley would not trust him a second time.

He wasn't even going to consider the state of his heart. That was no longer relevant.

BETH COULDN'T BELIEVE the speed with which Greg upended—and then resettled—her entire life. A call to the Willises had Ryan safely out of the way for an extra couple of hours. A second call to her landlord, and she was out of her lease. A run for boxes, a trip or two with his truck, calls to her clients canceling jobs. Five minutes to shower and change into the jeans and sweater she'd left unpacked. Finally, for the last time, she walked out of the dingy little apartment she'd grown to love.

During the whole time they packed and cleaned, she was never alone. Even when she showered, he'd insisted she not lock the bathroom door, and had been right outside when she came out.

Greg didn't trust her.

She wasn't even sure he particularly liked her anymore. His conversation was civil, bordering on kind—but distant. He was working.

Last night, she'd been his lover. Now she was a job.

And when he had to go into the office—a meeting with Burt Culver he'd told her nothing about—he dropped her at the day care with his sister. He could have locked her and Ryan in his home, and Beth didn't doubt that was coming, but he'd wanted to announce their liaison to the town as soon as possible.

Bonnie's day care would take care of that.

He'd told his sister not to let Beth close to Ryan; he insisted that Beth was exhausted and needed a rest. In effect, he'd put her under house arrest at Bonnie's. Bonnie loved him and trusted him so she'd gone along with it.

Beth didn't think she'd have run, anyway. Where could she go? And why? Greg might be her best chance at finding the answers she had to have. She'd decided to let him try. Life without him was unpalatable. As unpalatable as subjecting Ryan to a life on the run.

"You really love my brother," Bonnie said, her cheery smile cheerier than usual as she sat behind the closed door of her office on the main floor of the day care. Through the window, they could see the children playing. Ryan and Katie were off in a corner, Katie giving Ryan a tea party. The few other children left that late in the day were coloring at a table with one of the college students who came in after school when the day care teachers went home.

"I do," Beth said, barely managing to look Bonnie in the eye. Greg had told her how she had to play this.

But she didn't want to be playing. Not with his sister. Bonnie was the only "family" she had.

"I know he loves you," the other woman said, her gaze intelligent but happy, as well.

It amazed Beth how Bonnie, with her plump cheerfulness, her short body and lively dark curls, could still emanate such authority.

"I knew months ago that you two were meant for each other. I just wasn't sure either of you would figure it out."

Beth smiled, but her lips were trembling. If Bonnie only realized how impossible it was for Beth to figure *anything* out.

"Hold on to that thought," she said, pulling the crumpled card from the canvas bag monogrammed with her first name. "You might not be so happy in another second or two."

Bonnie leaned forward across her desk, grabbing Beth's hand. "Of course I will be," she said. "You're an answer to many years of prayer. I knew it when I first saw you with Ryan. You're strong yet sensitive, not afraid to nurture. You're intelligent. Independent when you need to be. Capable. When something bad happens, you land on your feet. You're exactly the type of woman Greg needs. Has needed for a long, long time. You would never have been scared off by Greg's responsibilities with my dad. If you'd been with him then, you'd have settled in and helped. Because you care, you know what's right and it's important to you to *do* what's right."

She wasn't going to cry; she couldn't afford to. But Beth had never been so close to just laying down her head and letting everything go, releasing all the emotion inside her. Tears in her eyes, she looked at Bonnie. "Thank you," she whispered.

Bonnie couldn't possibly realize how much harder she'd just made the next few minutes.

Silently, she handed Bonnie the postcard. It wasn't

part of Greg's plan. He'd determined that they should downplay the whole thing in an effort not to bring it to the attention of those who weren't going to notice it, anyway. According to him, that was most of Shelter Valley.

Bonnie's face paled visibly. Dropping Beth's hand, she sat up straight, every bit the intimidating administrator in spite of the brightly colored balloons painted across her shirt.

"Has Greg seen this?"

Beth met and held her gaze. Bonnie deserved that much. "Yes."

"He has?" Bonnie scrutinized her.

"Yes."

Taken aback, Beth watched as the other woman visibly relaxed. Her posture, as she sank down again. The expression on her face, from formal back to friend. And her eyes, changing from careful to compassionate. All in the space of a second.

"Then, we don't have anything to worry about."

"Bonnie…"

Bonnie forestalled her with a raised hand. "It's okay," she said. "It's not that I'm not dying of curiosity, and of course as your friend I want to know what's going on, but you don't owe me anything, Beth. I trust you. There's a damn good explanation for this. Whatever it is, you were left with no other choice."

"You didn't think that a minute ago, before I told you that Greg knew," she said bleakly. "Your reaction was pretty obvious." Not that Beth blamed her. She had doubts about herself, too. As far as the law was concerned, she was a criminal. The distribution of that card meant kidnapping charges had been pressed. And who knew what else she might have done?

"Of course I thought that!" Bonnie's brows drew together. "My reaction was panic, pure and simple. If he didn't know, he had to be told immediately, so he could get to work."

"So he could find out if I was worth trusting?"

Because she was looking down, Beth didn't see Bonnie's hand slide back across the desk. Was startled when she felt the other woman's comforting touch.

"So he could protect you," Bonnie said softly.

"What about protecting *him?*" Beth asked. "Until we get this straightened out, he is, in fact, harboring a criminal."

Bonnie shook her head emphatically. "I don't know what's going on and I suspect, since Greg didn't tell me, it's best that I not know—much as I might want to," she added with a grin that disappeared quickly. "But I have complete faith in my brother. He'll do the right thing."

The right thing. The words were a comfort to her, speaking to something elemental inside Beth. She had a very real sense that was all she'd ever wanted: to do the right thing.

"I'M NOT LYING," Burt Culver told his superior for the fourth time. His gut was one hard rock as he stood before Greg Richards's desk, watching his entire life turn to dust. "I've told you everything I know."

The sheriff tilted back in his chair, but Burt wasn't fooled by the seemingly nonchalant pose. Greg Richards was doing battle. And he was going to win.

He always did.

Because he chose his battles carefully and fought

only for what he believed in. It was probably the quality Burt admired most about Greg.

He'd just never figured he'd be on the other side during one of those fights.

But somehow Burt had to win, too. The job was everything to him. Always had been. His only motive had been to protect his right to be a cop.

Greg perused him silently. Waiting for him to crack, to say more. Burt had witnessed the tactic more times than he could count.

He was immune to it.

But not to the desperation driving him. If Greg Richards thought he was going to take his job away from him...

"I swear, Sheriff," he said, using Greg's title although he didn't often do so. "I was only on an information-gathering mission when Len Wagner told me about the Bloodhounds taking up residence in some clearing about thirty miles from Shelter Valley. I had no idea what the significance of the information was or why we should care. I reported back to Foltz and that was that."

"And the hermit?" Greg said, his tone implacable.

"I tried three times to find him, just like I told you. The place was boarded up. Looked deserted."

He was relieved when Richards nodded. But not really surprised. The sheriff had told him he'd been out to the place himself. And he'd be fair in his assessment of the truth.

"And the photographs?" Greg asked.

Eyes focused on the freshly painted ceiling, Burt gritted his teeth. He thought about lying to his superior. He *had* to lie. Just like that day he'd damaged the photos, he had no choice.

Sweating, Culver stood there. Time stretched before him. Empty. Pointless.

He wasn't at fault here. He'd done nothing but follow orders. He wasn't going to lose everything, when he'd done exactly what he'd sworn to do. He couldn't.

And then his gaze met Richards's.

It was over. He'd done his job. He'd had no idea there was a connection between the two series of crimes. Foltz had sworn to him... And then, when Greg had shown him the photos, he'd known. Damn! He'd only done what he was told, done his best. And it was all over, anyway.

Foltz, you son of a bitch, I have a new boss now. Until he crucifies me.

"I distracted the technician, put all the photos and discs together, loosened the cap on some kind of fluid..."

"Why?"

Humiliation was hell. A lesson he could have done without.

"Because if I don't have my job, I've got nothing."

Greg's feet landed on the tile floor with a *snap*. He stood, fists on his desk, as he leaned forward. "And where did you ever get the idea that tampering with evidence would preserve your job?" The words were no less deadly for their softness.

His coffin was lying before him. There was no longer any reason to follow orders. Or to care what happened if he didn't.

"Unless I destroyed those pictures, I was going to be implicated in the series of carjackings that killed your father."

If it was possible to hate himself any further, Burt

would have when Greg dropped back into his chair, the aura of unshakable authority falling away for an instant.

"You?" Greg asked, hardly able to look at Burt. "*You* were behind the carjackings?"

"Hell, no!" He hadn't meant to be so loud, glanced around to see if anyone was coming into the room to see what was going on.

No one did.

He stepped forward, careful to keep his hands folded in front of him and nowhere near the revolver Greg had asked him to place on his desk at the beginning of the interview.

The beginning of the end.

"I knew nothing about them," Burt said, consciously lowering his voice. "Back then, I didn't even know that the questions I'd been asking had anything to do with the carjackings. I'd picked Len up on a DUI a few months before. It wasn't the first time—he was a heavy-duty partier. Foltz sent me to question him, trying to find a link to a…problem he was having out in the desert."

Greg was listening intently, one fist at his lips.

"Then, out of the blue, I get this call from Foltz. He tells me that I worked on the case ten years ago. That I turned up incriminating evidence—evidence I didn't act on—and that he had enough witnesses who'd incriminate me. We could both go down, he said. He had some reports I'd signed. Investigations I'd done for him—always under the guise of something else. He had me neatly framed. I was the officer in charge and it looked like I'd closed a case in spite of hard evidence. He was taking care of things on his end and just needed me to watch things here."

"And to hell with protecting the safety of this year's innocent victims?"

Burt shook his head, surprised to find how badly it ached. "He told me about the Bloodhounds. But they'd disbanded. There was no way the two sets of crimes were related."

"He told you the Bloodhounds killed my father."

Shame was worse than humiliation. Burt would prefer death. "He told me they were responsible for the carjackings."

"Before or after you told me that my interest in the case was bordering on unprofessional because of my personal involvement?"

"Before."

"So what was it, some kind of game to them? A pastime? See whose car you can bump on the highway, get them to pull over, and then—like deciding on a flavor of ice cream—choose what you're going to do to the victim?"

Head bowed, Burt prayed the interview would end soon. Damn Richards for not seeing that he'd only done what he had to do. He was the best damn cop Richards had. He might have damaged some old pictures, but he'd been told no one would get hurt. That there couldn't possibly be a connection between the crimes ten years ago and these new ones. If he'd had any idea, he never would have listened to Foltz. He'd never have knowingly endangered the people he was sworn to protect.

"I don't know," he said.

"Did you know that Foltz's younger brother was a Bloodhound?"

"Colby?" Burt asked. "No way. Foltz was just telling me about him. Kid graduated with honors, went to Harvard. He's some hotshot law professor at one of them Ivy League schools."

"I'll just bet he is—" Greg said.

Burt had never heard such bitterness in his superior's voice.

"After sending my father straight to hell."

Culver felt the first nail seal that coffin shut.

BETH COULDN'T SLEEP. The night was too dark. The room was too dark. Her life was too dark. Nothing but black holes and shadows. Everywhere she looked.

The night-light was across the hall in Ryan's room. She'd wanted to keep the baby with her, but Greg hadn't budged. The boy needed his own space, he'd said. It wasn't natural or fair to have him so used to sleeping with his mother.

And it would be harder for Beth to steal away into the night if she had to cross the hall and pass Greg's open door first.

All their doors were open. Something else he'd insisted upon. Not that he ever crossed the threshold of her room. Or invited her to cross his.

Turning over, she tried to find in the hallway a brief glimmer from Ry's night-light. It was on a far wall, near the corner. Lighting his crib area but not the hall.

Beth sat up, bunched the pillows on the double bed in Greg's guest room, lay back down and waited impatiently for her relaxation techniques to kick in. This was her third night at Greg's house, her third night since she'd learned her own name, and those techniques had been cruelly absent the entire time.

She'd been able to play the piano to her heart's content, though. Had spent hours letting her soul speak to her without her mind's intervention.

Greg had never mentioned that he had a piano, too. One that wasn't as new as Bonnie's.

Sitting up again in the dark, she wondered what she could do without disturbing her reluctant keeper. She'd spent the past hour, the past three days, trying to remember. Poring over Internet information about Houston on Greg's computer, hoping to find something familiar.

Her mind was as vacant as the blackness surrounding her.

When it started to close in on her rather than merely surround her, Beth flew out of bed. Quietly she tiptoed down the hall to the kitchen at the back of the house. A place where she could safely turn on a light without waking Greg from his much-needed sleep. She'd known he was a busy man, but now that she was living with him—staying in his house, she quickly amended—she saw what an impossible schedule he kept.

Sliding the kitchen drawer slowly out so she could get the pad of paper she knew was inside, she wondered if the citizens of Kachina County had any idea how lucky they were to have Greg serving them—

"What are you doing?"

She dropped the pencil she'd been lifting from a tray in the front of the drawer.

"Getting ready to take notes," she said, hating how shaky her voice was. Shaky because it was Greg, not because he was a lawman.

Afraid to turn around, to see what he was or wasn't wearing, she stared at the contents of a junk drawer she'd just cleaned out the day before. She was in sweats and a T-shirt. Looked like she wasn't going to be needing them as uniforms anymore. Her business had quietly closed when she'd moved in with the sheriff.

"Notes for what?"

He came far enough into the room that she could see him out of the corner of her eye. He was wearing sweats, too. Black ones. And a white ribbed tank T-shirt. The kind muscle men wore in ads.

It looked better on him.

Beth turned. "Sometimes I write things down, free associating, hoping that when I read it over, something will make sense."

He frowned, his big frame dwarfing the small but elegantly modern kitchen. "That's something you can't do during the day?"

"I couldn't sleep."

She'd thought it was hard going from being strangers to lovers. That was nothing compared to the journey back. She looked at his hands, reaching for the refrigerator door, pulling out a bottle of water, taking off the lid, bringing it to his lips—and remembered how intimately she'd known those hands, those lips.

She watched him and wanted to cry. She'd already lost her past. Losing him meant giving up all the fragile new hope she'd had for the future.

Bottle in hand, he faced her. "You often have trouble sleeping?"

"Not often." She held the notepad in front of her, providing a shield between them—between her and the pain of being this close to him with everything falling apart.

"Is there something wrong with your room? The bed's too hard? Too soft?"

"No." And then, because she'd decided three days ago that she was going to trust him, tell him everything in case there was some important detail that she might miss, and to prove to him that she was never going to keep anything from him again, she admitted the embarrassing truth. "Since the…accident…I haven't slept without a light on."

"Oh." The answer seemed to shake him. Pulling out a chair, he sat at the table he hadn't shared with her since she'd been there. He'd eaten all his meals out. She'd had hers alone with Ryan.

She wondered if she'd be around to see Ryan graduate from a baby spoon to the real thing.

Greg didn't say anything. Just sat there. Beth sat down, too.

He seemed different, suddenly. As though she'd caught a glimpse of the man she'd known…

"I know you said it would be a few days before we hear anything, since your police contact is camping with his family for the weekend, but is there anything we can find out on our own?"

"You've done the people search on the Internet."

"It just gave me an address and phone number."

"Even if Gary wasn't on R and R, we probably still wouldn't know much. The clandestine kind of checking we'll be doing takes time. At this point I don't want anyone to be able to trace anything, not even a phone call."

"So nothing can be traced back to you." She understood and fully supported that decision.

"So nothing can be traced to *you*," he said, his eyes soft as he looked at her—really looked at her—for the first time in three days. "Until we figure out what you were running from, I have no way of knowing what kind of danger you might be in."

Beth was so glad to be able to talk to her friend that she almost cried. "What if you find something terrible?" She was trusting him when she didn't trust her own judgment.

He shrugged, seemed to be considering something, and then said, "I don't know."

Her stomach churned. She looked away. "After we made love the other night, I had this strange sensation that I'd…done well because I did what I'd been commanded to do. I seemed to accept quite naturally that that was something I did. Had sex on command."

When she glanced over, he was watching her broodingly, his expression somber. "Maybe you're running from an abusive husband."

Instantly, Beth shook her head. "I can't be married."

"If you don't remember anything, how can you be so sure?"

"I wasn't wearing a wedding ring."

"A point, but not a conclusive one."

"I don't *feel* married."

"Did you feel like a mother when you woke up in that motel room?"

She didn't want to answer him. "No." And when he remained silent, leaving her case full of holes, she said, "I can't be married, Greg. Not after what we—" Beth broke off. Embarrassed. And far too sad when she thought about what might have been.

He left her words hanging there, too, and she had no idea what he was feeling.

CHAPTER EIGHTEEN

"I'M AFRAID I might have been a prostitute."

Greg just couldn't remain immune. For better or worse—fearing it was only going to get worse—he was connected to this woman.

"You were not a prostitute," he said. Criminal she might be; a whore she was not.

"It would fit," she said, her beautiful blue eyes huge with anguish. "Sex on command is a way of life. Maybe my pimp was beating me. Maybe he was threatening to do something to Ryan and I had to escape to save him. Or maybe he refused to let me stop and I had to run to get Ryan away from that life. Makes sense about the money, too. Clients would pay in cash, wouldn't they?"

Greg sat there calmly while his mind raged. She'd obviously given this a lot of thought. Seemed truly distressed by the ludicrous idea. Surely, if she were faking the amnesia...

"Sex is instinctive," he said, trying to convince himself that he could talk to her about her nakedness and not feel the burning of desire. "An animal drive. The way you respond is also instinctive."

And oh, she'd been so sweet. And hot. And... "You did not respond like a woman to whom sex was a job."

Her eyes were fixed on the pad of paper she'd set in front of her.

"Maybe I forgot that, too. That sex was a job."

In spite of himself, he thought of all the months they'd spent together, getting to know each other—not the things they'd done, necessarily, but the spirit he'd come to know. He remembered the time he'd kissed her right there, out by his pool, and the way she'd stopped him. Because she couldn't make love lightly. And he thought of their one incredible night together.

"Beth, take my word for it, you didn't have anything to forget." And then he tried to concentrate on business because, contrary to his admonitions, his blood was running hot. "This 'on command' feeling you had—were there other feelings that accompanied it? Fear, maybe? Or disgust?"

She thought for a moment, still concentrating on that blank pad of paper and the little pieces she was ripping off the top page. "No." She peeked up at him and went back to the business of making confetti. "It was odd. Just a sense of having done what I was supposed to. But in a positive sense. Like what I'd done was right and good."

Greg was so focused on trying to analyze every clue, he didn't immediately notice that something was wrong. Beth had stopped talking, but she'd finished her previous sentence, so that wasn't particularly striking. She didn't fall out of her chair. Didn't make any sound at all.

She just stopped. Her hands froze, a dime-size piece of paper pressed between her thumb and index finger. Her entire body was stiff, unmoving. Her eyes alerted him first. They were focused on him, but it was as though she were blind, staring sightlessly through him.

"Beth?"

Greg leaned forward, tension gathering as he tried to assess her condition.

She didn't even seem to hear him.

He tried to remember everything he'd said. Everything she'd said. And drew a blank. An uncomfortable occurrence in itself for a man who depended on close observation to do his job.

"Beth," he said again, more firmly.

Oh God. Horror descended as the thought struck him. She'd taken something. Pills. Liquor. Both. Gulped them down when she'd come to the kitchen, and they were only now having their effect. He grabbed her hand, started to haul her out to the pool if that was what it took to rouse her from that catatonic state.

"No!" The shriek that filled his house was a sound he'd never heard before. "No!" The cry was terrifying, high and shrill and animalistic.

Pulling her hand away, Beth jumped up. The crashing of her chair went unnoticed. "No!" she shrieked a third time.

"Okay!" Greg spoke loudly enough for her to hear, but also as soothingly as he could. "It's okay, Beth," he said over and over, moving as she moved so that he stayed in front of her, trying to catch her gaze with his own. "It's okay, honey. It's okay."

It was a wonder Ryan wasn't awake and calling out to them. Greg hoped the little guy managed to sleep through whatever the next moments were going to bring.

Beth was turning in circles on the tile floor, not particularly fast but not slowly, either, as though she were looking for something.

"No, no, no, no, no..."

It seemed to be the only thing she could say. But she'd quieted down considerably. Was speaking more than shrieking.

"Okay, we won't," Greg said. He needed a doctor. Wondered who he could call in Shelter Valley in the middle of the night. It wasn't like they had a twenty-four-hour emergency clinic downtown.

Phyllis Sheffield. Greg landed on the name.

Phyllis would know what to do. He reached for the phone. Beth stopped turning and stared at him, the look in those blue eyes hard, determined.

And then, in one blink, as she really saw him, they softened.

"No."

What he suspected had begun as a shriek came out more as a wail.

"No," she said again, tears in her voice, as her shoulders fell, defeated.

"Sweetie?" Dropping the phone, Greg grabbed her, gently but quickly, under the arms, afraid she might collapse onto the floor. Like a rag doll, she sagged against him, her limbs uncoordinated. She was far too skinny, and yet became dead weight in his hands.

Thinking of the wireless handset in the living room—from which he could call Phyllis—Greg lifted Beth, one arm under her knees, one behind her back, and carried her out of the kitchen. He'd meant to lay her down on the couch, but unable to let her go, sat with her instead.

Cradling her like a baby, her head against his shoulder, he pushed the hair from her face. "Beth?"

She was crying. Silently. Tears dripped slowly down her face. Her eyes, when she opened them, were dull but no longer vacant. She looked ill. Exhausted. Shadows seemed to form under her eyes even as he watched.

"Beth?" he said again, battling an unfamiliar panic.

"Oh, Greg, it's bad."

That was when tears choked the back of his throat.

SHE WAS SHAKING so hard her teeth were chattering. Phyllis Sheffield had told her that was normal under the circumstances. Beth wasn't in physical shock. Her vital signs were okay. Phyllis had had Greg check them when he'd first called her, and she'd checked them herself when she arrived and again right before she left.

There were rough times ahead. But nothing she couldn't handle, the compassionate psychologist had assured her. Her memory wouldn't be returning if she wasn't ready to face whatever her mind had been hiding.

Beth still didn't know much, only vague recollections of feelings, but disconnected thoughts and flash visions were attacking her from every angle.

"Phyllis told you to relax and let them come, sweetie," Greg said softly, holding her. She hadn't left his couch since he'd first brought her in from the kitchen almost two hours before. It would be dawn in another few hours.

"I know," she said, her jaws vibrating. The way it had some winter, when she'd been locked out of her house. She was in New York. She'd forgotten her key....

Beth tried to grasp the memory. To see more. She was young. Junior high, probably.

And...

It was gone.

She was tired. So damn tired.

Phyllis had also said that if they could get through

this without medication, it would make things easier. She'd said that, then told Greg to call a doctor in the morning to get a prescription, just in case.

"Whenever you're ready to tell me, I'm here to listen," Greg said.

Phyllis had suggested he say that. Beth had heard them talking quietly by the door.

So far she hadn't told either of them anything. Except that she was having flashes. Of severe pain. And of pictures she recognized but that didn't go together.

She didn't know how to make sense of anything. Not really. But…

She was going to trust Greg. She couldn't trust herself, so she'd decided to trust him. She'd made a promise to herself three days ago. Couldn't let herself down. She had to trust him.

Trust him.

Don't keep secrets.

"I'm afraid."

"I know. But we'll get through this, Beth."

"It's bad." Worse than an abusive husband. She had a feeling it was even worse than being a prostitute.

"We'll handle it."

Phyllis had told him not to pressure her. She wondered if it was hard for him not to ask questions. She'd had her eyes closed when he and Phyllis were talking by the door. They'd probably thought she'd fallen asleep.

As if she could. She'd been trapped in a haze of pain and fear.

Talk. That was what she had to do. But to do that, she had to think.

Her heart pounding as panic sliced through her, Beth wished the red haze would carry her away.

"We had to say *right and good* at least four times during a session." She barely opened her mouth as she spoke.

Not missing a beat, Greg continued to stroke the hair away from her face. She loved him so much.

A picture of a padded table flashed before her eyes. A room, mostly in darkness, music playing, strong scents.

"They were massage sessions. I was a masseuse."

She thought about it. Knew it to be true. Yet rejected the idea at the same time. She didn't *feel* like a masseuse. Was more comfortable with the idea of cleaning toilets.

Greg still said nothing, just continued to stroke her, to give her something to concentrate on so she could stay in touch with reality. Beth wondered what he was thinking and turned to look up at him.

He smiled down at her, his eyes filled with such warmth, such strength, she wanted to die right then and there. During a perfect moment. And escape all the horrible things to come.

"I had to say *right and good* at least once every quarter of an hour. More often when the subject appeared amenable."

"Subject's a funny word to use," Greg said, his tone nonjudgmental. "Aren't people who have massages usually referred to as clients?"

"I suppose so." Beth tried to get back to that room, but another pain shot through her skull. "I don't know why I said that."

"I have to ask you something," Greg said slowly, "but please understand that I'm not trying to pressure you, nor will the answer change how I feel about you."

She looked up at him again, and a sense of fresh air

penetrated the suffocating darkness. "How do you feel about me?"

His eyes grew brighter, giving her the distinct impression that he'd had something very definite to say and then changed his mind. "I believe in you."

It was enough.

Probably as much as she was ready to hear.

"What were you going to ask me?"

"Were you being forced to do what you were doing? Was it against your will?"

Her chest constricted. The red haze circled her vision. "Yes." And then, just as clearly, "No." She stopped. Begged herself for answers, for anything that would make sense of the debilitating emotions consuming her. "I believed strongly in what I was doing. It was right and good."

She didn't even hear the words she'd said until she felt Greg stiffen, and thought back over them.

"What does it mean?" she whispered, a tiny child huddled in a corner. "Why do I keep saying that? And why do those words scare me so much?"

"I don't know, sweetie." His voice came from far off. "But I can promise you we're going to find out."

"Greg?"

It was very late. Or very early. He'd carried her to his bed and, still dressed in their sweats, they were lying together on top of the sheet. She'd been too hot for covers.

"Yeah?"

He'd told her to try to sleep. With her head on his chest, she thought she felt secure enough to do so. Ryan would be up in another couple of hours.

"What's going to happen if whatever we find out means we can't be together?"

He didn't say anything, just pulled her closer.

"I know you might not even want a future with me, but what if we don't have that option?"

"We'll have it."

"I'm scared to death I did something horrible. That I'm in trouble."

He didn't say anything.

"Tell me what you're thinking. Please." She was starting to cry. She didn't want to. She just couldn't seem to help it.

His sigh was more telling than any words. "I'm scared, too."

GREG WAS HOME all day Sunday. Word had spread around town that Beth was living with him, and that she'd been "set up" with the postcard thing—he wasn't sure where that had come from, but suspected his sister—and his cell phone rang on and off all day. When it woke Beth for the second time, he unput it on silent.

He spent a good part of the day playing quietly with Ryan. The little guy was an amazing kid, perceptive far beyond his age. Whenever he glanced over at his sleeping mother, his wide-eyed look seemed to tell Greg that he understood and that everything would be all right.

The toddler was probably seeking reassurance, not giving it, but Greg felt better, anyway.

He napped when Ryan napped, ate when the little boy seemed hungry, and at seven-thirty that night, when Ryan lay down in his crib, Greg climbed into his own bed across the hall, took Beth into his arms and willed himself to sleep.

His gut twisted at the thought of the next day, the answers he was going to get, one way or another. Burt. Foltz. His father.

And Beth.

He had to know.

And then he had to have the strength to endure whatever came next.

Beth sighed, her body pressing a little more closely against him, as though, even in her sleep, she needed the assurance that he was there.

He was. And he would be in the days to come. Somehow.

With that decision made, an evanescent peace passed through him, calming him enough to let him sleep.

GREG HAD HUGH FOLTZ and Burt Culver in his office by nine o'clock Monday morning. His buddy, Gary Miller, an old partner from the Phoenix police department who'd gone undercover when Greg went over to the sheriff's department, was moving mountains in Houston. And while Greg waited impatiently to find out what kind of challenges awaited him there, he tackled his own mountainous problem in Kachina County.

"I'm sorry." Hugh Foltz sat in the chair in front of Greg's desk. There wasn't even a hint of the bravado Greg had never, until that moment, seen him without. Just the slumped shoulders of a man who knew he'd come up wanting.

"Sorry's not good enough." Greg was seething, ready to tear somebody's throat out. Ready to howl with pain and trying to pretend he wasn't.

"He was just a kid, Greg. A sweet kid who got suckered by some punks, at a school he never should've been attending, with promises of protection and friendship. And by the time he figured out that he wanted no part of what was going on, he knew too much. They had their hooks in him and wouldn't let go. Threatened to kill his mother. My mother." Foltz wasn't crying on Greg's shoulder. Wasn't whining or courting sympathy. He was stating the facts. Unemotionally. Honestly. Just like Greg would have done.

Culver sat in the chair next to his ex-boss, facing his current one, his expression that of a man who'd lived too long, seen too much. He was pulling at his ear.

"When our mother left our dad," Foltz continued, "she took the kid—he was only a baby then—and moved to Phoenix with the first of many boyfriends. I finished college, had a life, paid far too little attention to this kid who needed a father figure. That should've been me." He shrugged. "I started investigating those carjackings, found out what was happening with the Bloodhounds and went in to bust them all. That's when I learned Colby was involved. It was up to me whether or not I sent him to jail. What kind of cop would I be if I couldn't protect my own kid brother?"

"An honest one?" Greg suggested harshly, threatened by the compassion he felt for the older man—a man he'd once admired above all others. Including his own father.

"My position was going to allow me to do something I needed to do. It was going to let me make something right. I was going to save my brother's life. Holding the incident over his head, I was able to force him to run all his decisions by me from then on and to make the right ones."

Culver looked at Greg.

"What about that little matter of justice?" Greg

asked. "What about the citizens you'd sworn to protect?"

"I did protect them," Foltz said. "Not in the way you would have." His right hand gestured in Greg's direction. "Not in the way the law would have me do, but they were nonetheless protected."

Culver shook his head.

"There was nothing I could do about the victims," Foltz went on, "but I could make damn certain the carjackings stopped for good. Which was more than any judge would've been able to do. The courts would never have gotten a conviction."

Len had intimated the Bloodhounds were that good.

"I went in with death threats that weren't empty, and I got the kid out. By the end of that month, the driving force behind the Bloodhounds was out of the country."

"Then, tell me why I've spent the summer cleaning up after a series of crimes that resemble those carjackings of ten years ago—right down to the indentations on their front ends."

"Rabbit Rock," Foltz said.

Greg nodded.

"The carjackings weren't a joyride," Foltz said, his eyes deadly serious. "They were an initiation process."

Greg sat forward, giving his full attention to the retired sheriff.

"Each pair of *applicants*—" the older man practically spat when he said the word "—had to steal a car. They could do whatever they wished with the victims, but it was understood that if they went easy, they weren't right for the Bloodhounds. In that case, they should count themselves or their loved ones as good as dead. Once the victim was disposed of in some fashion, they were to drive the car to Rabbit Rock, where the rest of the gang would be waiting. In order to prove they had no fear and that they'd do whatever they were told, the potential Bloodhounds had to drive that car full speed into Rabbit Rock. If they survived, then they were in."

"How many kids died in the process?" Greg asked quietly.

"Only one that I know of." Foltz's mouth was turned down at the corners. "Most of them were so strung out by the time they got to that point, they rolled like rubber with the blow."

"We've got another gang on our hands." Culver sat forward, speaking for the first time. "It's the only explanation. And I'm guessing either the drug traffickers Hugh scared out of the country crossed back over the border, or some punk who was once a Bloodhound decided to go into business for himself."

"God, I'm sorry," Foltz said, looking at Greg. "I'd rather be dead myself than know I'm the cause of the hell that's been happening on the highway this summer. I swear to God I was sure they were unconnected."

Greg stood. "Yeah, well, we don't have time for sorry. Right now, this county needs you. You're the only one who has the full story from ten years ago. Names, dates, all of it."

Foltz stood, too, hiking up a pair of jeans over the belly that had started to expand since his retirement. "How do you know I still have any of that?"

"Because I know you," Greg said. "Your brain has a record filed away for every single case you ever supervised."

Hugh nodded. Stepped up to Greg's desk. "About the Bloodhound deal, I'll put it all in writing—"

"Not now, Hugh," Greg said, forestalling any more of the contrition he wasn't in the mood to stomach. "What's past might be better just left there. For now, let's concentrate on the bastards messing up my present."

ONCE HE HAD the information he needed, it took Culver a little under six hours to track down the thirty-year-old loser who'd been terrorizing high school drug addicts into joining forces with him. Greg's discovery of the Rabbit Rock connection made an impossible task almost easy. The carjackings were indeed—and once again—an initiation process. They served one purpose: to prove loyalty to the point of death to Steel Crane, an ex-Bloodhound who'd been in and out of prison since his late teens. These crimes also ensured future loyalty, as they gave Crane something to hold over his members' heads. Him or jail. That would be the only choice left to them. And Crane knew guys in jail. Guys who'd make anyone who'd been "disloyal" wish he were dead.

Just after six o'clock that night, with Steel Crane in custody, Foltz and Culver left Greg's office. Greg had requested that they give him some time to consider any future action against either or both of them.

He was tired. Ready to go home. To have dinner with Ryan. And to cuddle up to Ryan's mother for as many hours as he could get away with. Sometime soon, he'd want to do more than cuddle. Sometime soon, he'd want to make love with her again.

He shouldn't, but he'd worry about that when he had to.

His cell phone rang as he was leaving the office. Greg picked it up on his way downstairs. Gary had handled his inquiries carefully—until he'd discovered there was a hit man after Beth Silverman. Then caution be damned; he'd called everyone he knew. The rest of what Greg's old partner had to say turned Greg's blood cold. With the bubble on top of his car, he made the twenty-mile trip to Shelter Valley in a record twelve minutes.

BETH HEARD THE garage door open when Greg got home. She'd fed Ryan, who'd gone to bed an hour and a half early, exhausted from the upheaval of the past couple of days. Her son was already a creature of routine, a little boy who liked his life organized and predictable. Taking after his mother.

She knew it all now. Like a motion picture with scrambled frames, her entire life had scrolled before her throughout that long day—until she'd fallen into a state of numbed acceptance, too weak to be afraid anymore.

It was Beth's own mental weakness that had started the whole thing. Or at least, her part in it. She'd been so culpable. So easy to brainwash.

And the things she'd done...

Feeling dead inside, she got up to open the door from the garage into the house. She'd been waiting for Greg. Waiting to tell him it was all over.

Unlocking the dead bolt, Beth was fully prepared to get through the conversation ahead without crying. Without asking anything for herself. Prepared to beg for Ryan, though. To somehow make Greg promise that he would not abandon her son, that Ryan would never be in the custody of his father or anyone else from Sterling Silver.

She was not prepared for the black-sheathed arm that came around the door, or the leather-clad hand that grasped her wrist and bent it back until she heard it snap.

Maybe that was why she didn't feel a thing. She opened her mouth to scream but no sound came out.

"Got you, bitch." The muffled growl struck the first chord of fear in her. And once feeling started, it didn't stop. The pain in her wrist was now so sharp she was afraid she might pass out. Or throw up.

Before she could do either, she was outside the house. In the dark, gassy smelling garage, another leathered hand came over her mouth. She couldn't breathe. Couldn't think. She was completely gripped by cold, dead fear.

"We do this easy, or we do it my way," the voice said.

He was enjoying this.

Beth knew then that she was going to die. Somehow that made all the difference. Freed her. She didn't even care all that much about dying if she could get the bastard away from Greg's house. Away from her son.

Greg would be home soon. He'd save Ryan.

"James sent you." She was surprised how easily she found the strength to talk, as he dragged her toward the running car. It was parked under a tree across the street. She wondered how the guy had managed to open the garage door, and then noticed glass from the window on the ground.

He was holding her hand, making it appear as though she were friendly with him, a willing companion. All he had to do was give her fingers the lightest tug and searing pain shot through her wrist, up her arm and into her shoulder. Ensuring her cooperation.

As long as he left her son alone, he didn't have anything to worry about. Her life wasn't worth the struggle. Not after what she'd remembered that day.

She stumbled and he pulled down on her hand. Slowly.

"It's already broken," she muttered. Were her words starting to slur?

The guy grunted.

"So how many years did he get you out of?" she thought about asking, but wasn't sure she'd actually said it aloud.

"Shut up." The words were accompanied by another tug on her wrist.

Oh. The pain was so sharp, spearing through her in white-hot agony. Death was even more painful than she'd imagined it would be. He tugged one more time.

Losing all sense of reality, Beth jerked forward and retched. She vomited all over the driveway, herself and the shoes of the man who appeared to be holding her head, but was in the process of breaking her neck.

He had to let her finish vomiting first. He couldn't get a good enough grip when she kept convulsing away from him. In a semi-delirious state, she wondered if that was supposed to be funny.

Mostly, Beth was just glad she was going to die before she was raped.

If James had sent him, the man gradually adding pressure to her neck was a rapist. A prominent Texas prosecuting attorney, James Silverman had one of the best conviction records in the state—except when it came to rape. During those trials, he often seemed to have commitments elsewhere. Beth hadn't known, until years after she'd married him, that James was not as right and good as she'd thought.

James had purposely thrown more than one case. But only cases of rape… Despite his "spiritual" beliefs, he'd begun to reveal his misogyny, his deep-down contempt for women. And over the years he'd gradually begun to develop sympathy for men who were, as he explained it, so tormented by women that they couldn't help being driven to punish them, to put them in their place. He didn't see it as an act of aggression but one of desperation. He got many of them off and then brought them into Sterling Silver. There, they received protection, sex twice a week and, occasionally, undercover jobs to do.

Lost in the story of her past, as she had been on and off for most of the day, she was hardly aware of the pressure, the nausea, the night.

Thoughts flashed through her mind, obliterating her awareness of the ground below her face, the unbearable pain in her wrist, the fact that she was never going to hold her baby boy again.

Her entire body convulsed with another spasm.

Beth's last thought, as the pressure on her neck increased, was that she'd never be able to tell Greg how much she loved him.

GREG DROVE FAR too fast, taking corners precariously, all the while telling himself that he was overreacting. There was no reason to assume, just because those postcards had gone out, that the man who'd been hired to track and kill Beth would be tipped off to where she was.

Beth had been smart these past months, kept a low profile. Very few people outside Shelter Valley had seen her.

Except… His blood ran cold. That jerk at the casino. He'd had a good long look at Beth while they'd waited around for the Reservation police. And while Greg had been giving his report, as well. The guy had been in the back seat of the cop car, probably staring out the window at Beth.

Greg had heard he was out on bail—awaiting trial. With information like this and an underground network that was more trustworthy than the CIA, he could've made some good money....

As he came through town, Greg laid on his horn, an accompaniment to the siren already blaring. The way cleared miraculously, images of people he'd known all his life passing by him as if in slow motion.

By the time he reached his street he could hear the rhythm of his heart in his ears. As soon as he knew that Beth was okay he'd calm right down. Consider the things Gary had told him.

For now, he couldn't even think about them.

Greg's heart pounded harder. And then practically stopped altogether when he saw the circle of people crowding around something on his driveway. His practiced eye registered the strange dark sedan parked with its engine running, across the street from his house.

The blood drained from his face. He felt it. Just as he felt the tears fill his eyes.

No.

He took everything in quickly. The neighbors he knew and loved, some crouched, some standing, peering over others' backs.

And then something struck him. That car was still there. Which meant the driver hadn't gotten away.

Could it mean that—

"Greg!" Carl Bush, a retired foreman from the Cactus Jelly plant, pulled open Greg's door as the cruiser screeched to a halt and Greg jumped out. "Thank God, you're here!"

"Where's Beth?"

"There," Carl said, out of breath as he ran beside Greg, pointing to the crowd on the drive. "She's conscious again and I think going to be just fine, but she won't let anybody look at her or touch her. She's holding that baby boy of hers and just keeps crying for you."

"Get out of the way!" someone shouted.

"The sheriff's here!"

"Greg's here!"

"Greg, thank God…"

Greg barely heard the loud chorus of voices that greeted him as the crowd around Beth melted back, making room for him.

"Deputy Culver already took the guy away." Greg recognized that voice. It belonged to his sister. "Sue called from next door. Said Beth wouldn't get up off the driveway. I came right over. She won't move, Greg. She…"

He didn't hear another word as he stared at the woman he loved and the baby she was rocking against her. She was a mess. Ryan looked petrified.

"Beth? Sweetie? Let's go inside."

She smelled so bad his eyes watered. Careful to make sure he had a firm grip on Ryan, as well, he lifted Beth to his chest.

"Greg?" Her gaze wasn't quite focused when she looked at him. "I couldn't trust anyone but you." Her eyes closed, scaring him. And then they opened again. "Take care of Ryan," she whispered before her head fell limply back against his arm.

"Somebody call an ambulance," he bellowed.

"It's already been here once." Bonnie was still beside him. "Culver called them. She refused treatment. I'll get them back."

"Geg?" the little boy said, staring solemnly up at him.

"It's okay, buddy, your mama's going to be just fine," Greg said.

And prayed that he wasn't lying.

WITH HER BROKEN WRIST in a cast, Beth sat at the kitchen table, carefully sipping the hot chocolate Greg had just made for her. It was hard to believe it had only been hours, instead of days, since he'd come home to find her incoherent on the driveway.

She didn't remember much about the time she'd spent out there—and figured, from what she did recall, that it was probably a good thing. It was enough to know that the people of Shelter Valley had more than lived up to the faith their sheriff had placed in them when he'd moved her into his home and told her she'd be safe there.

Even before she'd started retching in the driveway, they'd gathered together and formulated a plan—that included flattening all four tires on the sedan. Deputy Culver had been called immediately, when Carl Bush first noticed the strange car parked in front of his house. But the neighborhood men had already had James Silverman's hired thug under control before the deputy arrived.

"How you doing?" Greg asked softly, sitting down on the chair closest to her as he studied every inch of her face.

"Fine. Better," she amended.

"You should take some of those pills and get some sleep."

She was sure he was right. Still, she shook her head. "I'd rather talk."

He frowned. "The doctor said—"

"That other than an aching wrist and bruised neck, I'm just fine."

"You will be—after a good night's rest."

"Greg, please. I can go to bed, but I won't be able to sleep."

"Thank goodness Ryan went right down. It was way past his bedtime."

Beth smiled. Greg was a natural when it came to the daddy thing. She hoped that meant he'd be willing to grant her her promise.

"Once he saw that you were awake and smiling," Greg continued, "he seemed to take the whole situation in stride."

"I think Ry learned quite a while ago that as long as I was okay, he was okay."

"I imagine—"

"Greg," Beth interrupted, covering his hand with the one she could move. "I remembered everything today."

She saw the concern flicker in his eyes before he quickly doused it, and resumed the mild expression he was using to convince her everything would be fine.

"I'm one of the founding members of a cult," she said. "It's called Sterling Silver and it's located just outside Houston in a little community we built. Last I knew, we had almost four hundred members, most of whom live in our community."

"Correction," Greg said, his tone serious. "You're married to one of the founding members."

She blinked. "You know?"

Greg nodded. "Gary called just as I was leaving the office."

"I was a willing participant, Greg. We used the spa as a front to find prospective members. I scouted them out from massage clients and administered the first few levels of mind manipulation. Relaxation exercises, accompanied by subtle thought-reformation techniques. Any people who responded positively, I turned over to Peter Sterling."

"This happened only after you'd been brainwashed yourself."

"He'd been sued for malpractice." She summarized what she'd remembered that day. "He met James during the court proceedings, and over drinks the two of them commiserated about the terrible state of the world, the negativism, the destruction. James had been suffering from depression. Being a prosecuting attorney, spending your days face-to-face with the scum of the world, watching some of them walk away, is not an easy thing. Peter understood that. Just as James understood why Peter had allowed a woman to die when she'd begged him to do so. The two of them created a bond that could not be broken. They became inseparable."

"That must have been hard for you."

"Not really." Beth shook her head, thinking back—relieved that when she looked, there was something there. "James's depression disappeared. It was as though Peter had given him a new lease on life, a new purpose. The two of them were always talking about saving the world. They'd come up with one scheme after another, volunteer for any service project that sounded worthwhile. They were actually quite fun and invigorating to be around. James was a happier man. A better man. A better husband."

"So what happened?"

Beth shivered as darkness descended. On her mind. And her heart. "I don't know," she said slowly. "Eventually it wasn't enough. James's depression started to return. There was always something wrong, in their view, with the projects they were doing, something wrong with the people in charge. They always figured they could do better, think bigger. That was when Peter suggested taking things to a new level. He wanted to really change the world. James had been taking some positive thinking seminars. The two of them were convinced that with them in charge, they could create a new world without negative energy...." Beth's voice faded as she stared vacantly ahead.

Greg waited patiently for her to continue.

"I was skeptical at first," she said, "but their motivations seemed so good..." She sighed. "One minute we were all on fire, risking everything on a huge shot at making a real difference in the world. And the next..." She didn't want to have to face the rest. "They were going to put Ryan through two days of starvation in a dark room all by himself." She skipped through the memories. Reached the breaking point.

"While they gave him dialysis to clean any impurities from his system?"

He talked about the atrocities so calmly. Beth nodded, shocked. "I can't believe you don't find this appalling."

Greg's chin dropped to his chest for a moment before he peered up at her. "I find it so goddamn hideous, I want to murder those two men with my bare hands."

The barely leashed anger might have been frightening; instead, Beth found it reassuring.

"Boys didn't go through cleansing until they were two, but every time Ryan cried, Peter would tell James he—my baby—was filled with aggression. And Ry always seemed so much more aware, following us with his eyes, looking at us as though he understood things. Peter didn't like that, either."

"Sounds to me like maybe your husband's friend was jealous of your son."

No. It hadn't been like that.

Or had it?

Beth just didn't know. Couldn't be sure which thoughts were her own and which had been planted....

"For a long time I had no idea what was going on, but by then I knew things were bad. James was a powerful man with an army of loyal followers." She gave a convulsive shudder. "I'd had problems with them doing it to other boys, even when their parents approved, but I couldn't let them take Ryan, couldn't let them hurt my son."

She was seeing through red again, her mind cottony, her thoughts unclear. Greg's hand, rubbing her shoulder, brought her at least partway back.

"Of course you couldn't."

"Peter must have guessed..."

"What happened, Beth?"

"I was in a session, but had come out to give my subject a chance to disrobe. I overheard Peter telling James that now was the time. And then they were talking about me, about manipulating me, and James assured Peter he was willing to do whatever it took. He'd do to me whatever was necessary so he could 'save' his son from the aggression threatening to control him."

Tears in her eyes, she peered at Greg. "He was only a baby!"

"But nothing happened to him."

Greg was right. It was okay. She could breathe. "I left my client lying naked on the table. Never went back. All I had in the room was my canvas bag. My purse was in my locker in the women's dressing room. I grabbed the bag, emptied the cash register, took Ryan from the nursery and ran."

"Something tells me it wasn't that easy."

Beth shook her head, every muscle in her upper body aching. "I hitchhiked for three days, but they found me. Peter caught up with me in New Mexico. I think maybe he didn't trust James to bring me back. I don't know. He tried what he called *thought reformation* first. And it worked. At least some. After all, he was my prophet. But when I wouldn't give him Ryan, he got ugly. He touched me—" She stopped, hot with shame. Couldn't look at Greg. "Reminded me of my commandments. Reminded me that every man in Sterling Silver had to have sex twice a week. That I had a duty. But I fought him. That's when he started hitting me—"

"I'll kill the bastard."

Beth came up out of her own personal darkness to find herself still in Greg's kitchen, her knight there, ready to fight her battles. It was an odd sensation. To realize that she really and truly was not alone. It wasn't just her against the world.

"I'd taken some self-defense classes," she said, "and somehow managed to knock Peter out. I ran. This time I didn't hitchhike. I wasn't going to give them another chance to find me. I dyed my hair and Ry's, paid cash for that car from a sweet old country man who had it for sale on the side of the road, and drove all night."

"To Snowflake."

Beth nodded. She'd checked into the motel under an assumed last name, fallen asleep for the first time in almost twenty-four hours and woken up empty.

"The second day I was there, I found this old magazine with a story about Tory Evans. It told about her sister's accident in New Mexico. About the identity switch at the hospital. About Tory's abusive husband. And something struck a chord in me. Her story had a happy ending. Because of Shelter Valley. So I knew this was where I had to come."

Only, her story wasn't going to end as happily as Tory's. Beth was a criminal. In love with a lawman. He was going to have to turn her in.

He wouldn't be who he was, the man she loved, if he didn't.

There was only one thing that mattered now. "Peter and James are dangerous men, Greg."

"They'll be put out of commission. For good."

"You'll make sure that they don't get control of Ryan when I'm gone?" she asked. She couldn't think beyond saving Ryan.

Frowning, Greg looked confused. "Where are you going?"

"I'm not sure how these things work, but eventually to jail."

"You aren't going to jail."

"I kidnapped my son."

"You saved his life."

"I brainwashed innocent people."

"You were brainwashed yourself."

Beth's pulse sped up. She started to feel light-headed again. Couldn't even hope to keep up with all the places her mind had been that day. "Greg, are you telling me you honestly think I have a chance of being found innocent?"

"I'm telling you I know for certain there will be no charges pressed against you. My last call, while we were still at the hospital, verified that Sterling and Silverman are already in custody. James's thug talked."

She couldn't believe it. Couldn't believe it might actually be over.

"I think I'm going to pass out." Her voice sounded far off to her own ears.

"I'm here to catch you if you do."

The stars receded, and Beth looked him full in the face. He was there. Warm. Welcoming.

And still in uniform.

"Am I going to have to testify?"

"Yes."

She nodded, her mind returning to the early days of Sterling Silver. They'd all started out with such good intentions. "You know, they only wanted to make the world a better place," she murmured.

"I know you believed that. And perhaps Sterling and Silverman did, too. At first. In their own twisted ways."

Overwhelmed and exhausted, Beth sat staring into the hot chocolate she'd barely touched. "It's odd to think I'm beginning my life all over again. I'm not Beth Allen, but I'm not Beth Silverman, either." She had been nothing more than a puppet on a string. Even her career had been the result of their manipulation.

"You weren't a masseuse before you met James?"

Beth shook her head. "I was a pianist, playing with the Houston Symphony. It was when my agent got me an international tour that James convinced me I was wasting my talent on something as frivolous as music. Told me I could do so much more, that I could be the catalyst that helped save the world from destruction and despair. That I should use my strong hands to create good in the world."

Beth started to panic again when she thought about how easily she'd been duped. And wondered how she'd ever be able to trust her own mind again.

"What about your parents? What did they have to say about it?"

"My parents are both dead," Beth said. She'd grieved a second time when she'd remembered the car accident that had claimed their lives when she was seventeen. That memory, too, had come back earlier in the day. "I'd been living at Juilliard. The money was there for me to continue, so that's what I did. I graduated. And then I went on to college as my parents had always wanted me to. They wanted me to have something to fall back on, in case I didn't make it as a musician. I majored in business, graduated with honors, got the job in Houston and eventually met James."

Drained beyond capacity, Beth gazed sightlessly into the darkness outside Greg's kitchen window. She'd lived, almost literally, two lifetimes in that day. She had no idea how she'd survived.

"It's all over now," Greg said, almost as though he could read her mind.

He could probably read some of it on her face. He'd been studying her so intently all night, reacting immediately to every change in expression, making sure she had everything she needed. God, how she wished she was free to love this man.

Beth shook her head. "I don't think it'll ever be over for me," she said. "I don't know how anyone recovers completely from brainwashing. I mean, sure, thought reformation can be reversed—some of it's been reversed without my even realizing—but now I know how easily my mind can be persuaded to accept alternative realities. I'm such a weak person, I'll never be able to trust my own judgment."

"Stop it, Beth," Greg said, his voice firm. "What happened to you can happen to anyone, weak or strong. That's what makes brainwashing—what Peter Sterling described as thought reformation—such a frightening threat. But the important thing, the only thing that matters, is that you got yourself out. Even when you thought your mind had let you down, you trusted yourself, relied on yourself, made the most of what you had left, and managed to fool an entire town into thinking you were a perfectly normal grieving widow. You carved a whole new life for yourself out of nothing at all. That's strength in its truest sense."

She needed so badly to believe him. But...

"My mind did let me down. I was fighting the biggest battle of my life and it checked out. How can I ever trust myself now? How do I know that every time I'm facing a difficult challenge, it won't just check out again? I have no control whatsoever."

"Uh-uh." Greg shook his head. "You've got it all wrong." The passion in his voice was compelling. "Think about it. Sterling and Silverman had taken control of your thoughts. The only way to be free of those two, to let the so-called reformation wear off, was for you to be separated from those thoughts. Your mind had to go numb, not because you couldn't handle the facts, but so you could free yourself from the brainwashing."

He sounded so sure. Absolutely and completely certain.

"Are you just saying that because I'm at a low point and you know I need to hear it?"

"What good would that do in the long run?"

"None."

"Have you ever known me to lie to you? Or anyone else?"

"No."

"I don't say things unless they're true, Beth. You have every reason to trust your mind. Because it found a way to free you from a state that's considered impossible to escape from without medical help or counseling. Yet you beat all the odds. I'd say that's pretty impressive. I'd say no one else is likely to get away with telling you how to think again."

Tears filled Beth's eyes. Rolled down her cheeks. And kept rolling. Until she was a sobbing mass huddled against Greg's chest.

Lifting her, he carried her, crying so hard she couldn't see, to the living room.

Beth cried until she thought she'd never stop. Years of pent-up tension and confusion and hurt spilled onto Greg's uniform. And then, the tears were gone. Spent.

No longer necessary.

"Thank you." They were the first words either of them had spoken in almost an hour.

"You're welcome, Beth."

"I can't believe what a good friend you are to me."

"I love you."

Beth's head fell back, her heart pounding quickly. Scrutinizing Greg, she tried to convince herself that the moment was real. That *she* was real. That it was okay to be feeling what she was feeling.

"I love you, too." What a relief to say those words.

He lifted her face gently, giving her a soft kiss.

Beth answered him as completely as she could with her weary, aching body, finding new energy in his kiss. His mouth opened against hers and she responded instinctively, until she remembered. And pulled away.

"I'm married."

His eyes serious, he held her gaze. "I know."

They'd committed adultery.

Beth got up from the couch, surprised by how shaky she was. She didn't go far. Just to the other end of the couch.

"I have a business degree," she said, looking for something positive. She had no life. Maybe her education was someplace to start.

"You can get a divorce, Beth." Greg moved over, urging her close once again.

She shouldn't let herself walk back into his arms. But he felt so good. And she was tired of being alone—of being strong all by herself.

"I imagine we can get a quick one, considering the circumstances."

"We?"

"I figure I have as much of a stake in this as you do."

She stared at him, hardly daring to hope. "Why?"

He raised one eyebrow. "I can't very well get married until you can."

Beth might have started to cry again if she'd had any tears left. Greg had an uncanny way of making the confused seem clear, the impossible quite manageable. She began to chuckle. And then to laugh out loud.

"What's so funny?" Greg asked. He was trying to sound offended, but the grin on his face ruined the effect.

"Nothing's funny," she said, laughing even as she tried to explain. "I just feel so good after so much bad, I can't keep it in."

"I take it that's a yes?"

Beth didn't need to be asked twice. She wasn't really sure she'd been asked once, but she didn't care. Sobering, she placed her lips on Greg's, kissing him reverently.

"Of course it's a yes," she whispered.

Greg's arms wrapped around her, and Beth wanted nothing more than to spend the rest of the night, the rest of her life, loving him.

"Greg?"

"Mmm?" he murmured against her lips.

"Can we go to bed now?"

She thought he nodded, knew he lifted her into his arms, but was asleep before they left the living room.

She had all the nights of her life for making love. That night, she just needed to be welcomed home. By Shelter Valley. By the house that had been waiting for her. By the man who'd rescued her, and made her life complete.

She and Ryan had finally found something that was truly right and good.

* * * * *

We hope you enjoyed reading

SUSPICIOUS

by *New York Times* bestselling author

HEATHER GRAHAM and

THE SHERIFF OF SHELTER VALLEY

by *USA TODAY* bestselling author

TARA TAYLOR QUINN

Both were originally Harlequin® series stories!

Heart-racing romance set against the backdrop of suspense. Discover these stories of true-to-life women in extraordinary circumstances who are rescued by the powerful heroes of their dreams.

ROMANTIC suspense

Heart-racing romance, high-stakes suspense!

Look for four *new* romances every month from **Harlequin Romantic Suspense!**

Available wherever books are sold.

"You, Brett Colton, are as slippery as a snake-oil salesman."

"I prefer to think of myself as stubborn and single-minded. Not so different from you."

The suspicion on Hannah's face melted away a little bit more and she closed her lips around the fork in a way that gave Brett some ideas too filthy for his own good.

He cleared his throat, snapping his focus back to the task at hand. "When my parents remodeled the big house, they designed separate wings for each of their six children, but I'm the only one of the six who lives there full-time. You would have your own wing, your own bathroom with a big old tub and plenty of privacy."

For the first time, she seemed to be seriously considering his offer. Time to go for broke. He handed her another slice of bacon, which she accepted without a word.

"Where are you living now?" he said. "Can you look me in the eye and tell me it's a good, long-term situation for you and the baby?"

She snapped a tiny bit of bacon off and popped it into her mouth. "It's not like I'm living in some abandoned building. I'm staying with my best friend, Lori, and her boyfriend, Drew. It's not ideal, but with the money from this job, I'll be able to afford my own place."

"And until that first paycheck, you'll live at the ranch." He pressed his lips together. That had come out a smidge more demanding than he'd wanted it to.

Their gazes met and held. "Are you mandating that? Will the job offer depend on me accepting the temporary housing?"

Oh, how he wanted to say yes to that. "No. But you should agree to it anyway. Your own bed, regular meals made by a top-rated personal chef, and your commute would be five minutes to the ranch office. The only traffic would be some overly excitable ranch dogs."

"I know why you're doing all this, but I really am grateful for all you're offering—the job and the accommodations. In all honesty, this went a lot better than I thought it would."

"The job interview?"

"No, telling you about the baby. I thought you'd either hate me or propose to me."

Brett didn't miss a beat. "I still might."

Don't miss COLTON'S COWBOY CODE
by Melissa Cutler, part of
THE COLTONS OF OKLAHOMA *series:*

COLTON COWBOY PROTECTOR *by Beth Cornelison*
COLTON'S COWBOY CODE *by Melissa Cutler*
THE TEMPTATION OF DR. COLTON *by Karen Whiddon*
PROTECTING THE COLTON BRIDE *by Elle James*
SECOND CHANCE COLTON *by Marie Ferrarella*
THE COLTON BODYGUARD *by Carla Cassidy*

Available wherever Harlequin® Romantic Suspense
books and ebooks are sold.
www.Harlequin.com

HARLEQUIN®

ROMANTIC suspense

Heart-racing romance, high-stakes suspense!

Save $1.00

on the purchase of
COLTON'S COWBOY CODE
by Melissa Cutler, available
July 7, 2015, or on any other
Harlequin® Romantic Suspense book.

Available wherever books are sold, including most bookstores, supermarkets, drugstores and discount stores.

--- ✂ ---

Save $1.00

on the purchase of any Harlequin Romantic Suspense book.

Coupon valid until September 2, 2015. Redeemable at participating outlets in the U.S. and Canada only. Not redeemable at Barnes and Nobles stores.
Limit one coupon per customer.

52612581

Canadian Retailers: Harlequin Enterprises Limited will pay the face value of this coupon plus 10.25¢ if submitted by customer for this product only. Any other use constitutes fraud. Coupon is nonassignable. Void if taxed, prohibited or restricted by law. Consumer must pay any government taxes. Void if copied. Millennium1 Promotional Services ("M1P") customers submit coupons and proof of sales to Harlequin Enterprises Limited, P.O. Box 3000, Saint John, NB E2L 4L3, Canada. Non-M1P retailer—for reimbursement submit coupons and proof of sales directly to Harlequin Enterprises Limited, Retail Marketing Department, 225 Duncan Mill Rd., Don Mills, Ontario M3B 3K9, Canada.

5 65373 00076 2 (8100)0 12051

U.S. Retailers: Harlequin Enterprises Limited will pay the face value of this coupon plus 8¢ if submitted by customer for this product only. Any other use constitutes fraud. Coupon is nonassignable. Void if taxed, prohibited or restricted by law. Consumer must pay any government taxes. Void if copied. For reimbursement submit coupons and proof of sales directly to Harlequin Enterprises Limited, P.O. Box 880478, El Paso, TX 88588-0478, U.S.A. Cash value 1/100 cents.

® and ™ are trademarks owned and used by the trademark owner and/or its licensee.

© 2015 Harlequin Enterprises Limited

NYTCOUP0615

New York Times bestselling author
and queen of paranormal suspense

HEATHER GRAHAM

presents three chilling new tales in the
Krewe of Hunters series

On sale June 30   On sale July 28   On sale September 29

Available wherever
books are sold!

THE WORLD IS BETTER WITH

Romance

Harlequin has everything from contemporary, passionate and heartwarming to suspenseful and inspirational stories.

Whatever your mood, we have a romance just for you!

Connect with us to find your next great read, special offers and more.

HARLEQUIN®

A *Romance* FOR EVERY MOOD™

www.Harlequin.com